The Sins *of* Soldiers

The Sins *of* Soldiers

S. J. HARDMAN LEA

Matador
9 Priory Business Park,
Wistow Road, Kibworth Beauchamp,
Leicestershire. LE8 0RX
Tel: 0116 279 2299
Email: books@troubador.co.uk
Web: www.troubador.co.uk/matador
Twitter: @matadorbooks

ISBN 978 1785890 185

British Library Cataloguing in Publication Data.
A catalogue record for this book is available from the British Library.

Typeset in 11 pt Aldine401 BT by Troubador Publishing Ltd, Leicester, UK

Matador is an imprint of Troubador Publishing Ltd

For those who were there

Prologue

Inauguration Ceremony of The Memorial to the Missing, Thiepval, France
July 1932

Anson Scott has come here early, in the peaceful hour before the rest of the crowds. Now they are arriving in numbers and the soldiers and regimental bands are drawn up in front of the vast brick and stone monument. He has his own place at the back of a canvas marquee, on one of the rows set aside for relatives, war veterans and news reporters. Opposite him, two white-haired British generals climb towards their seats on the other side of the broad stair leading into the memorial. He sees the rainbow of their medal ribbons and marvels that there can be so many as they push their way into their stand, past a group of men and women, forcing them to step back. Suddenly, Scott's muscles tense. There is something too familiar about one of those figures behind the soldiers, some half-remembered quirk of stance or posture that has grabbed at his attention. What is it? The seats there are hidden in the shade of the flags while he is looking into the sun. He can't make out anything clearly but all his long-practised instincts are screaming silently at him:

Run.

He stares hard into the shadows, trying to distinguish details. Who is it? Then the banners flutter on the wind and the clouds shift and he sees her. She is sitting half turned so that her face is in profile as she looks up into the towering arches of the memorial. She is more than fifty feet away and he has not laid eyes on her for sixteen years, but there can be no mistake. It's Beatrice Tempest.

She was bound to come. She'd no choice. Not today.

He shifts in his seat, trying to duck down lower so that he is hidden behind the tall hat of the man in front. He had almost forgotten the peculiar lightness in his stomach that he used to feel whenever she was near.

Damned fool! After everything; all the years, the tricks and lies. Still it comes back to here and now.

Is it possible to get away before she sees him? No – the wide gravel path leading back to the entrance has been cleared ready for the arrival of the royal party. He will be horribly exposed if he tries to cross that. It is a gamble he can't take. He is stranded here until it is finished.

If she turns this way, she'll be looking straight at me.

The air seems to have grown hot in the last two minutes. It is hard to breathe. He rises to his feet and makes his way down the stand, trying to keep his face turned away from her until he can duck around the canvas side wall. There is a uniformed guard there who looks puzzled, but Scott mimes a pain in his stomach and pushes past him. The back of the stand is quiet. Everyone else has gathered along the main path, awaiting the arrival of the President and the Prince of Wales. He doubles over, gasping to catch his breath. Could she have spotted him? There is no way of knowing. For the moment, at least, he is safely out of sight. He'll have to wait through the ceremony and then make sure he is the last man to leave. Trying to push her from his mind, he looks away from the monument and out over the rows and rows of identical white crosses. Each marks the burial place of a soldier who died, anonymous, in the four years of fighting on the surrounding battlefield of the Somme.

How many of these men have I known? Did we sit together for a smoke, waiting for the order to advance? Talking about love and life, sharing the last of the whisky while the signal flares burst in the night? Have we laughed at the same jokes; smiled at the same comic turn in a concert party?

He is not aware that he has moved but finds that he is walking between the graves, brushing his hand over each cross in turn, trying to picture the man who might be lying beneath.

One thing is for sure. None of these is David. He's not here.

There is a commotion behind him and the bands start to play 'God Save the King'. Anson Scott does not even glance around to check that he is still hidden: he has lost himself to the past.

I guess there was always going to be trouble, right from the start. Looking back on that first night in France there was already a scent of tragedy, likes ashes blowing down the wind. But still I don't know if any of us could have done anything different. Maybe we were all just acting according to our natures. Me, her, Tollman, even David. Especially David.

1
31ˢᵗ December 1915
Picardy, France

It was New Year's Eve. My transport ship had been held up by a storm out in the Channel and I'd had to endure five hours of nausea before we could get in to dock in Boulogne. By that time, I'd missed my planned train connections so I reached the battalion a while after nightfall and I'd tramped the last four miles alone along cold, dark lanes. At first, I didn't believe I could have come to the right place. It was a chateau; a real French country house with turrets on the corners, a moat all round and a bridge leading to a gravel courtyard in front of the main doors. It seemed quiet; deserted apart from a bored sentry standing under a lamp by the barrier on the bridge. He looked over my papers, then gave me directions that took me through the doorway and along an unlit corridor leading to the heart of the place.

I don't know what I was expecting to find when I pushed open the double doors at the end of the passageway. I suppose I'd anticipated rigid military discipline and stiff upper lips, the whole British military myth. I couldn't have been more wrong. If the noise hadn't warned me, the chunk of bread that flew through the air past my head would have confirmed it. Inside, there was a rousing party in full swing, going headlong toward the end of the old year. It was so loud and bright I

1

was temporarily dazed by the glare of the electric chandeliers and the babble of voices and was glad to lean back against the door and gather my senses. It was also a pause that gave me the opportunity to make some mental notes about the scene. I knew I'd be needing them later.

The refectory was a big, light-panelled room filled by a U-shaped table that was littered with glasses, china and silverware. Seated around the table a couple of dozen soldiers were enjoying the last stages of what looked to have been a pretty opulent dinner. Facing me, at the centre of the table, a group of grey-haired men were caught up in sober discussion; it was obvious that they must be the senior officers of the battalion. To my right, lining one limb of the table, a gang of pink-faced boys glowed and giggled. I'd been well briefed before I set off and I knew that the British Army was recruiting its subalterns kind of young, but these lads looked barely out of kindergarten. Opposite them, on the other side the room, a handful of older guys were hunkered down behind a stockade of bottles. Before I could get a closer look at them, I was interrupted:

'I was sure I'd spotted a fresh face. You must be Scott, our new man. What a relief. We've been expecting you for days. No matter, at least you're here now.'

A slight man had appeared at my side. He'd an affable face framed by thinning sandy whiskers and the type of round, steel-rimmed spectacles that put me in mind of pictures of Teddy Roosevelt. In one hand, he was carrying a clipboard, complete with a thick wad of notes.

'Welcome to the Royal Pennine Regiment. I'm Clarridge, the adjutant.' With an air of satisfaction he took a pencil, licked the tip and made a deliberate tick against what I assumed must be my own name. 'Shall we get on and introduce you to Colonel Ireland straight off, before we get caught up in the toasts?'

He took my arm and led me around the table to the group of older officers I'd first noticed. Sitting in the centre, the Colonel was a stiff-spined fellow with a long nose and short white moustache.

'Where're you from, Scott?' he asked.

'From the United States, sir. I'm American.'

'Good God!' He'd had to bend forward as if his hearing was defective and I realised that he was even older than I'd first thought. 'What th'Dickens were you doing there?'

'Surveying for the railroads, sir. In Alaska.' It was the truth and nothing but, even if it was some way from the whole truth.

'Ah. I see.'

But from the puzzled expression on his face, it was obvious that Alaska was a location way beyond his experience. 'Done any soldiering?'

'Three years at West Point, sir. I passed out in the year of '06.' The date was accurate, at least.

'Not Sandhurst, then. Pity. But not bad, all the same,' he said, clearly relieved to have moved back to familiar ground. 'I like to have fellows who know what they're doing.'

There was a crash of breaking glass and a bread roll shot through the air from one end of the table to the other. The Colonel's eyes followed it in flight. He grunted a comment at the adjutant, then turned again to me.

'Pal of mine's got a cousin just moved up to Haig's staff at GHQ. Says we'll see real action soon. Fine time to join us. Meet the fellows. Everyone present tonight, Clarry?'

'Everyone bar two, Colonel. Alexander is on leave, I believe.' Clarridge thumbed through pages on his clipboard and gave a grunt of satisfaction. 'Yes, as I thought, although he's due back today. And Captain Tollman's away on a course,' he added, with rather less enthusiasm. 'Come along, Scott. I'll perform introductions.'

I was glad to move on before Colonel Ireland had the chance to ask any more awkward questions. I'd been correct about the sober quartet seated immediately around him: they were the transport officer, quartermaster, intelligence officer and a faded major with yellow-grey skin who turned out to be second in command of the battalion. All of them were polite enough but were obviously keen to return to their military arguments as soon as possible.

'Now come and meet *les gars*,' Clarridge said. His pronunciation was atrocious but later I'd get to learn how proud he was of the French vocabulary that he sprayed around like buckshot. He took me off to the group of youngsters sitting down one side of the table.

'These are the chaps who actually live with their platoons in the trenches. Gentlemen, this is Mr Scott, just joined us from the United States. I'm sure you'll make him welcome. And orders from the Old Man: cease fire with the food, please.'

The pack of youngsters greeted me like a long-lost cousin, confident in their well-scrubbed high spirits which I guessed were partly due to the number of empty bottles littering the table around them. The most vociferous were twins, pink-faced with white-blond hair, and identical except that one was sporting the faintest wisp of moustache.

'Are you really from America?' That was the clean-shaven boy. Without waiting for a reply, he rushed ahead: 'Absolutely top hole. Just like *Riders of the Purple Sage*.'

'Don't take any notice of him, Scott,' said the moustachioed twin, with the superior tones of the first born. 'He always talks rot. He's been obsessed with cowboy stories all his life.'

'That's a bit thick.' His brother took an indignant swig from his wine glass, managing to get most of it into his mouth. 'I only meant that it'd be good for us to have someone who can ride and shoot straight.'

I had to disappoint him. 'I'd be no great shakes as a ranch hand, I'm afraid. I get a kind of rash when I'm around horses.'

'You mean to say that you don't ride to hounds?' Another fresh-faced kid, sporting a moustache clipped to match his colonel, sounded appalled.

I realised my mistake a bit too late. How could I pass myself off as a typical backwoods American if I had to explain that recently my riding had been restricted to bicycles and tramway cars? I was saved by the younger twin cutting in.

'Never mind about your blessed hunting, Moore. I'll tell you what, Scott. You've arrived at exactly the right time. There's going to be a big push this next year, everybody says so. And we always get sent into the thick of it so you're going to see some really hot stuff in the next few months. Won't that be fantastic?'

Clarridge returned to rescue me from trying to answer and escorted me across the room. Out of earshot he peered at me over the top of his spectacles.

'I can see exactly what you're thinking, Mr Scott, and you'd be correct. They do act like a crowd of schoolboys, although that isn't very surprising really. Those Cooper twins are only fifteen months out of Rugby – Tom's the older one with the whiskers and the younger one is Tim, by the way. Still, they're good chaps and keen *comme la moutarde*, as the locals here would say. They've done pretty well up in the front line so far.'

On the opposite side of the table, we approached the more sombre group I'd noticed. Clarridge made a show of consulting his clipboard and murmured behind it to me.

'A word to the wise. These fellows are a completely different *tasse de thé*. They can seem a bit difficult at first, but they aren't all that bad really. Not once they get to know you.'

The men hunched over their port glasses had none of the

sozzled bonhomie of the youngsters we'd just left. Far from it. They reminded me of nothing so much as a gang of street hoodlums plotting who they should mug next.

'May I introduce Second Lieutenant Scott? He's been with the American Army previously.'

There was a silence before one of them drawled, 'Gosh. Lucky old us.'

The whole group was staring at me with blank hostility. Not one of them stood or offered a handshake. Finally, another voice spoke up.

'What do we need a bloody Yankee for?' It was a slight man with prominent teeth. He was glaring at me. 'Why the hell can't they find us one of our own, a proper gentleman?'

'Manners, please, Mr Wesley. There's no call to be offensive. This is an evening of celebration, after all,' Clarridge said with weary tolerance. 'Anyway, Mr Scott will already have given up his American citizenship before he was allowed to join us.'

It was certainly true that my only official identity now was as part of the British Army.

'On the other hand, old Weasel here has a fair point.' An officer with sleek dark hair, oiled flat against his scalp, was watching me carefully. It'd been him who had been so sarcastic at first. He gave me a tight, insincere smile, holding his head on one side.

'I mean, why on earth would anyone join a foreign army?' he asked. 'Are you just such a fire-eater that you can't pass up on someone else's fight? Is that it?'

I wondered whether he had put on that melodramatic voice for effect, all exaggerated consonants and nasal vowels. The adjutant blinked nervously.

'This is Lieutenant Henry Howerd, Scott. He's with C Company.' Clarridge said it as if he was apologising for something.

'So which is it, Scott?' Howerd went on, ignoring him. 'Couldn't you bear to be left out of our little scrap, or are you just here to spy on us?'

Even if he was only trying to be annoying, that was a bit too damned close for comfort. I shrugged my shoulders, looked him straight in the eye and stuck to my line.

'Fair enough question, I guess. Well, my mother was a Limey and I've still got a few kinfolk in Britain. I reckon it's as much my war as yours.'

'Well said, Mr Scott. That's the sort of fighting talk we like to hear.'

Clarridge sounded relieved as he steered me to a vacant seat a safe distance away, next to a burly man who was slumped forward onto the tablecloth with his head pillowed on his arms, snoring noisily. My new friend the adjutant was starting to show me a parcel of official forms and dockets that I needed to complete for him but before I'd had a chance even to look at them, we were interrupted.

'Bloody hell, will you put your little board away, Clarry? No business at the dinner table. It's just not polite.' Our slumbering neighbour had woken. He hadn't stirred himself to lift his head off the table, so he was squinting up at us through the one single eye that was visible. 'Do the man a favour and give him a break until morning,' he muttered. Then the effort of concentration was evidently too great and he closed his eye and fell asleep again.

'That's Vaughan, our medical officer,' Clarridge whispered. He saw me cock an understanding eye at the half-empty wine glass on the table and nodded in agreement. 'Can't handle his drink at all. He's actually a first-rate doctor, but...' He shrugged.

It almost sounded like the battalion would have preferred an incompetent surgeon, providing he could booze all night.

I was turning that over in my mind when a file of orderlies entered the room and cleared the last of the plates, leaving decanters of port and whisky behind.

'The Colonel's about to open the speeches. Are you going to stay for post-prandial refreshment?' Clarridge must have seen my expression, and quickly added, 'But if you're feeling all done in, I'm sure you could leave without causing offence. The duty sergeant will show you where to get your head down tonight and we can sort everything else out in the morning.'

It had been a heck of a long journey and I wanted to think through what I'd seen, so I made my excuses and slipped out the door, trying not to draw any more attention to myself. The day wasn't done, however. There was one more person I'd yet to meet.

I followed directions through the chateau to find the bed I'd been allocated, which they'd told me was up some stairs at the back of the place. The hallway was unlit and I was feeling my way along in the half dark when somebody hurried around a corner and barged right into me, nearly knocking me off my feet.

'I do beg your pardon. How clumsy of me.' I could only make out a tall figure in a great coat and muffler. 'Are you all right? I suppose I was expecting everyone to be at dinner.'

I couldn't see his face. Although he spoke quietly, his voice was very distinct, the sort that gets heard through a crowd without having to shout. My first thought was, *How bloody typically British – always contrite even when they aren't at fault.* I was probably a bit too sharp when I answered.

'I'm fine. I was just leaving. I'm new. I haven't found my way around yet.'

'You're sure I can't persuade you to stay and join us?' He was so sincere that it sounded as if I'd be doing him a great personal favour.

'I'm not much of a man for parties. Too much time in my own company, I guess.'

'I am sorry.' The way he said it, it wasn't clear whether he was apologising for assuming I'd want to be included, or commiserating at my lack of sociability. 'By the way, I'm David Alexander.'

I could see him holding out his hand and shook it. He'd a good strong grip.

'Anson Scott. I've just joined up.'

'Good for you. Always interesting to get some new blood into the battalion.' He stopped for a moment, as if something had just occurred to him. 'Now that is interesting. An American, by the sound of things, but named after a British naval hero. A curious combination – I wonder how that came about. You'll have to tell me more later, if you can stand my infernal curiosity. We'll meet again in the morning, no doubt. Goodnight.'

He strode off, leaving me staring after him. He might have sounded like some college professor but he moved fast and real soft on his feet, which explained why I'd not heard him coming. A couple of moments later, the dining room doors creaked open and I saw a wedge of electric light spill into the corridor. As he disappeared inside, there was a great roar of approval from the party, like he was a conquering hero being welcomed home. When I'd got over his smart observations about my name, I thought how good it must make a man feel to have that sort of effect by simply walking into a room.

2

The electric wiring hadn't been extended to the old servants' quarters up in the attics and the poky room where I slung my bag down was dingy and cold. Three floors below, the party was still buzzing while I spread my bed roll out on an ancient iron bed frame, lay back on the blanket and smoked a cigarette in the dark, sorting through my impressions.

I should have been satisfied because I'd managed to get through my first pack of lies without giving anything away. But I knew I'd got a problem. Fact was, the Royal Pennines were a whole lot sharper than I'd expected. Given my aims, I'd been keen to get into a traditional regiment, an outfit I could rely on to provide what I was looking for without stirring up too much curiosity, so I'd made use of the connections I'd been given to get me posted to a battalion that was renowned for its history, wild parties and military follies. And sure, the Colonel was indeed like some relic from Waterloo and I was convinced he'd swallowed all my guff. But Alexander, the fellow I'd just met in the corridor? He'd come over like a regular, friendly sort of guy, yet he'd also sounded way too clever, and inquisitive to boot. Then there was that slimy Lieutenant Howerd:

Just here to spy on us…

That's what he'd said. I suspected he was only trying to rile me, which hadn't worked, because I'd spent a lot of time preparing for that eventuality. However, he was still too close to the truth for comfort. I wasn't a spy. I was something at least as dangerous as that. I was an American newspaper reporter.

'I want to get a man on the inside. In the British Army.'

That's how it had started, ten months before on a dark afternoon in New York. I was back in town and out of assignments when MacManus, my editor on the *National Proclaimer*, dragged me off to the dusty old bar that served as an extension to his office; the place he always used when he didn't want to be overheard. He got us both a drink and started in on his pitch.

'This war,' he said. 'It's too good an opportunity to miss. We should be doing something.'

'Doing something?' I couldn't think what he was driving at. 'Like what – an editorial on the virtues of neutrality?'

At the time, there was a great deal of discussion in the air about whether the USA should choose to get involved in the war in Europe: MacManus himself had an Irish father and a German mother, so I wasn't sure where his loyalties lay. Perhaps he was considering using the *Proclaimer's* influence to sway opinion in Washington, to persuade the government to stay out of the fighting. I should have known better. Mac was a born newspaperman and always knew where the best story lay.

'All that's a done deal,' he said, waving his hand dismissively. 'We'll go in with the Brits and French, of course. Partly principle and partly a hard-nosed estimate of what makes the best sense politically and financially. It's only a question of when. No – that's not the big deal. What I'm looking at is a real story to entertain our readers here. Something that'll make a proper splash. And you remember what I always told you? What's the first rule?'

When I first started on the *Proclaimer*, Mac had instructed me in the art of newspaper writing. He had a real simple set of instructions.

'Rule number one: real news stories are always about people, not places or events,' I said.

11

'Glad to see you remember it.' He nodded fiercely at me, as if he shouldn't need to explain anything more, then grabbed both our glasses and took them to the bar to refill. When he came back, he picked up where he'd left off.

'So here's my big idea. The British Army – what's it really like now for a man stuck out in France? How does it feel for soldiers in the front line in a modern war? Do they care about the French, or do they just want to get home? Do they hate the Germans? Really? That's the stuff that'll sell papers, if we tell it properly.'

'But surely there must be reams written about that – what about all the London papers?' I was very fresh back in the country and hadn't caught up with what was happening in Europe.

'That is exactly my point. There's no proper stories coming out, not the sort of thing you and I would call a proper story. Everything is censored to hell, and the only stuff that makes it to print is predictable garbage about heroism and sacrifice and nobility and all that sort of horse manure. Nobody's getting any real, detailed information about the British Army any more. What with their intelligence services, and them censoring any letters from serving soldiers, we just can't get hold of any reliable facts. And what's the second rule for a good newshound?'

'Rule number two: no facts, no story,' I recited. According to Mac, that was the only other principle I'd ever needed to know.

'No facts, no story,' he repeated, banging his hand four times on the table edge, once with each word. I couldn't decide whether it was the whisky or the frustration that was getting to him.

'So? What's any of this to do with me?' I'd got an idea where he was heading but I wasn't going to make it any easier for him, or any cheaper.

'So what do we really know now? Only what the Brits let us, only what they want us to hear, and you can bet that it's all been bent and twisted to suit their purposes.'

I could see what he meant. The year before, there'd been a big splash about the alleged atrocities inflicted on civilians when the Germans invaded Belgium and now we had piles of government releases about the gallant British soldiers fighting on the Western Front.

'I want to get a man into the front lines with the British Army,' he said. 'Find out what's actually going on. Real detail, you know? Not what units are stationed where and how far they've advanced and how many Germans have been captured – the usual junk that's in all the London papers. What we need is…' he hunted around for the best description of what he'd got in mind, 'human interest stories. That's it. Human interest.'

It wasn't a phrase that I'd ever heard before, although it would become common later, but I understood exactly as he went on.

'How officers beat up on the ordinary soldiers. How they're sent out to get killed pointlessly. How there's stuffed shirts in charge of decent men. How there's idiots making decisions. How the soldiers just want to go home. You get it: proper eyewitness material that'll show folk all over the world what this war is really like. Not just here in the US, but everywhere – even in England.'

He was talking faster now, carried away with his own vision. He looked at me and pointed his finger my way. 'Only problem is, we'd have to get somebody right up and into the fighting and the only way we could do that is to get somebody to volunteer to join the British Army. Maybe someone with a British mother? Someone like that could dig up all sorts of useful information that we could work up into a proper report back here.'

That was his style, insinuating what might be possible without actually asking me whether I'd consider doing it. Still, he was right. It was a bright idea, although with one obvious drawback.

'What'd happen to that poor sap if he gets caught?' I said. 'Wouldn't he be facing a court martial? He'd get shot, most likely.'

'Sure, sure.' He dismissed that with a wave of his hand. 'We'll have to put together a watertight cover story, of course. But just think about it, though. For someone with enough guts, it's a unique chance to make history. What d'you reckon?'

I didn't say anything. I was thinking. He was right, and if it could be done, it'd need someone with some military experience, someone with no family ties, someone who'd got enough know-how to survive. In short, me.

Mac could see I was interested. He finished his drink and started to talk again. 'I figure you'll have to join up as an officer, so you'll have enough freedom to send stuff out. And I'd not be expecting anything for a while. You collect details, you write the bones of an article and you keep it all secret and coded until you get a chance to send everything back.'

I was about to ask how he thought that would be possible, but he beat me to it, leaning forward as if we were already sharing a secret, talking fast and quiet. 'From what we know, the officers out there censor the soldiers' letters, while their own can be put through a superior, or they can pass them themselves, on a basis of trust. That obviously wouldn't be smart for you – too obvious if anyone started to get suspicious. Instead, I've been asking around, all discreet, and I've uncovered one or two pick-up points in France you can use so you can avoid battalion censorship completely. From there, they'll send anything on to the USA via Switzerland, or Holland – somewhere neutral, so it isn't easy to track it either way. If you use your usual shorthand, there's nobody else but me can read it anyway. That's how you get it to me. From this end, seems like there's a regular mail service out to the trenches from London, which means I'd be able to keep in touch with anything important. All sent out through our contacts in England and carefully worded, naturally. Reckon that'd work?'

I did. Although he sometimes sounded like he was pitching a line, underneath that half-Irish bluster, he was very canny.

'We just need an agreed code word so you'll know a message is from me.' He looked around for inspiration, then down at his glass. 'How about... Jack Daniels?' He tested the sound of it like he was tasting the bourbon. 'A bit too obvious – so maybe, John Daniels?'

'OK , that'd work. If I agree to do it.' I wasn't going to roll over just yet, but that didn't make any difference to Mac.

'We'll publish it anonymously, you'd obviously not be able to use your own byline. I'd got in mind something along the lines of "True Scenes at the Front: Letters from a Modern William Russell." Something real classy like that.'

I knew that he was crazy about Russell's war reports from the Crimea, so that was his highest compliment.

'If anybody guessed it might be you, we'd just flat deny it, say you were back in Panama, or wherever. When it's over, you can take the plaudits.' He lit himself a thin, pungent cigar. 'So all you have to do is get yourself to England, volunteer to serve for King and Empire, and then keep your head down. Hell! If you manage to keep enough notes, you'll be able to write a book about it someday. What'd you say?'

'Maybe it could be done,' I said, real slow. I didn't want him to see how excited I was at the prospect.

'You bet. And if there's one man who can do it, it's you.' He leaned forward and slapped me on the shoulder. He knew he'd got me hooked. 'OK, it'll be a bit more dangerous than anything we've sent you into before. But hey… nothing ventured, nothing gained. And I'll be behind you all the way. So you're good to go?'

I nodded once. What else was I supposed to do? Not many men get offered the chance to do something that really matters. And it sounded straightforward enough. How could I turn it down?

That had been then. Now I'd made it to France, it looked a bit different. As I crushed out the stub of my smoke the noise from below swelled into loud cheers and I reckoned that the speechifying must have ended. A raucous yell echoed up the stairway.

'Happy New Year. Here's to 1916!'

They all sounded cheerful enough down there, but on my own in the darkness, it seemed like the new year was coming with more hazards than I'd anticipated. Still, I told myself I was used to taking calculated risks. And even if my new comrades were a lot sharper than I'd expected, I was sure that I'd get through in one piece somehow.

Poor bloody fool.

3

Next morning, breakfast was a quiet affair, with only a few weary individuals picking at the food on their plates. The only exception was a yellow-haired man in subaltern's uniform who was reading a broadsheet when I arrived.

'What a load of drivel!' he muttered from behind the newspaper. 'Why can't they ever write something worth reading?'

I smiled to myself as I sat down and poured a cup of coffee. He put his paper to one side.

'Morning. Scott, isn't it? Good to meet properly.'

I recognised his voice easily: it was David Alexander again. I'd been expecting him to look like something special, judging by the cheers he'd raised the night before, but he'd an ordinary, clean-shaven, square face that was attractive mainly because of his manner of speaking. If he'd stayed all through the party, he wasn't showing the effects like the others. He was turned out real neat and tidy, immaculate in white shirt and buff breeches and a fancy pearl tie pin that must have been worth a month's pay.

'Have you heard? We're being moved straight back to the front. We were supposed to be here for another few days but something's come up and it seems we're needed. I'll be a few hours behind the rest of you because I've got to take a working party out to collect some supplies that aren't due to come through until this afternoon. Sorry to miss your baptism, it looks as if you're going to be thrown straight in at the deep end.'

'Suits me. I've got to start sometime, so it may as well be today.' I drank my coffee down.

He peered at me, looking vaguely surprised and then laughed. 'That's the great thing about you fellows from the wild frontiers. No fuss, just ready for action.' He folded his paper and stood up. 'See you later.'

Of course, he couldn't know that I was thinking the sooner I got acquainted with the trenches, the better. It was what I'd come for, after all.

Everyone I'd seen the night before was assembled for morning briefing by the time the Colonel and adjutant spoke to us with details of our destination and transport. I'd chosen an inconspicuous spot at the back of the old stable block that served as the assembly room so that I could examine the faces around me, making some mental notes for future use. Then I heard my own name.

'Mr Scott will join C Company, to fill the vacancy with them.'

Clarridge was nodding in my direction. C? I remembered that was Lieutenant Howerd's company. It might have been my imagination, but I thought I detected a twitch of anticipation in the room.

The adjutant was continuing: 'I'm sure you'll see plenty of action there, Scott, especially when Captain Tollman gets back.' He darted a rapid look around, as if he was warning everyone to keep quiet. 'The other subalterns can show you the ropes and there's always Sergeant Fox to make sure the men don't give you any trouble.' He moved on to the orders for the day, leaving me to consider what it was about this Tollman that seemed to make everybody uneasy.

We weren't due to move out until the afternoon, which gave me a chance to cast an eye over my new platoon during morning parade. The soldiers were a fit, tough bunch who drilled and handled their weapons with casual expertise, which suited me just fine and dandy. I might have volunteered for a stupidly dangerous job but I figured my chances of living to tell the tale were much better than if I'd been with a bunch of amateurs.

If that was encouraging, better news yet was my platoon sergeant, although it didn't seem that way at first glance. All good regiments rely on their senior NCOs and I'd made a point of going to introduce myself after drill, but when I walked towards him I had my work cut out not to turn tail and run. From a distance, Sergeant Fox was nothing remarkable; a man of about my own height and build. Close up, he was terrifying. Over the years I'd worked with some rough types – track layers, lumberjacks, leathernecks, crooks and thugs – but when it came to scary, none of them came anywhere near Fox. Under the peak of his uniform cap, he looked like something that had been dug up in a graveyard. He'd no lashes or brows or moustache or whiskers and his skin was stretched white over his skull, except for dark shadows around his eye sockets.

'Something I can do for you… sir?'

His voice was like someone sawing through timber and there was no doubt that the pause before the last word was deliberate, to let me know that he only used it as a matter of necessity. When he swept his cap off, I saw that his white scalp was completely bald, matching his face, so that it was like looking at a living skull. By now I was ready for him, however, and didn't flinch while I told him I'd been attached to the company. I made a point of shaking his hand, which wasn't military etiquette by a long shot, and did feel a bit like gripping onto a skeleton, but I had a feeling right off that I'd need Fox's support if I was going to run the platoon. I was correct. In the following months he was one of the men I got to depend on for keeping us all alive.

At noon, the entire battalion lined up on the road in a human caterpillar a mile long and retraced the route I'd come by the night before back to the rail depot. We were loaded onto a train made up of two dozen cattle trucks for the troops and an ancient dilapidated passenger car for us officers. Within a couple of minutes, the rest of the subalterns had dozed off, catching up with the excesses of the night before, which relieved me from having to field any more tricky questions about my previous life. I was content to sit quiet and watch northern France pass by the window while we lurched and rattled our way eastwards, stopping and starting at pointless junctions before eventually being tipped out in a one-horse town in the middle of nowhere. It was dusk by the time we'd formed up into column and marched out across a main square that was lined with piles of smashed masonry. The leading companies started to sing:

The Sergeant-Major's having a time, Parley-vous.
The Sergeant-Major's having a time, Parley-vous.
The Sergeant-Major's having a time,
Swinging the lead behind the line, Inky-pinky Parley-vous.

I'd get to know all the verses of that one, and a hundred more like it, before I was quit of the war. Back then, I was only pleased to be with a bunch of men in such high spirits. As we swung off towards the front I looked around, expecting to see signs of military activity, but these were the quiet times at the beginning of the year and the night was only broken by the occasional rumble and band and flare on the skyline. If it hadn't been for the loudness of the explosions and the unfamiliar marching songs I could've almost felt like I was watching a Fourth of July celebration in the USA.

For the first part of the night a bright moon shone on the

paved road that took us through the wreckage of shelled-out farm buildings. There we diverted onto a muddy path that snaked between broken walls before it sloped down into the ground to become a deep ditch that twisted its way onward towards the front. The Colonel and most of the battalion turned off from the main route but Howerd led me, Tom Cooper, Moore, and the rest of C Company straight on. It looked like I was heading straight into the front line.

I'd knocked around all over the world and I thought I'd seen most of what it could offer: good, bad and terrible. In spite of my experience, however, I wasn't prepared for the trenches of the Western Front. Probably nobody ever could be. It was the weird combination of smells that hit you first. Wet earth, sewage, chloride of lime, fried bacon and explosive cordite, all combined with the scent of rotting meat, like someone had cooked breakfast in a druggist's laboratory in the back of a slaughter house. And then everything felt too narrow and closed in. It was an underground maze of twists and turns and dead ends, all filled with the echo of muffled voices, the sound of boots clumping on the duckboards, and glimpses of the shadowy figures of working parties. Our maps were useless and there was no one to guide us so we kept getting lost and having to turn back, all one hundred and fifty men in the company reversing and retracing footsteps, cursing in whispers.

A freezing mist came down at dawn, by which time we'd about got ourselves found again. Suddenly we were surprised by a rush of soldiers coming the other way. It was the outgoing company, from a Territorial Army battalion by the look of their shoulder badges, all falling over their own feet in their hurry to get back to their billets. They earned themselves a chorus of insults from our men and a growl from skull-faced

Fox as they jostled past, which only made them run quicker yet. I was still too raw to realise that we were dangerously late. We should have relieved them before dawn, which would've allowed them to get clear before first light. As it was, we were all mighty lucky that the fog covered our movements and cloaked us from the enemy field guns.

Finally we came to the end. At a T-junction, our path divided left and right, forming a single deep trench with walls higher than a man is tall and topped off with sandbags to create a parapet on either side. There was a ledge or step built onto the front wall about three feet up to allow soldiers to perch and see over the sandbags, and every few yards it kinked around a buttress to create a series of separate fire bays. I knew the anatomy of the trenches well enough to realise that we'd arrived. This was the front line.

The men spread themselves out along the bays, leaving Tom Cooper and me to carry on until we located Lieutenant Howerd in the company headquarters dugout – a pretty grandiose name for the cramped cavern we found at the bottom of some rough steps hacked out of the chalk in a dead end branch off the main trench.

Three officers from the Territorials had waited down there to hand over to us. They were fidgeting and nervy, obviously anxious to escape as soon as they could. Even to my newcomer's ear, what they had to say about that stretch of the line sounded sketchy and Howerd made himself comfortable on an upturned wooden crate to put them through a long list of trivial questions. It was clear that he was enjoying their discomfort.

'Look here, surely we don't need to go over absolutely everything? I've written it up in the notes,' the Territorial Captain said. He was a man with all the vigour of an aging hound-dog. 'We've had every sort of mayhem: mortars, rifle grenades, artillery. If you ask me, Jerry's got this stretch absolutely taped. Do you know how many chaps we've had killed these last two days? Five! Five good lads, all shot by the same sniper. You're welcome to it. Good luck to you.'

He grabbed his revolver from a flimsy table, probably something pilfered from one of the nearby villages, flung his knapsack onto his shoulder and before even Howerd could come up with a sarcastic crack, he and his subalterns had scurried up the steps and away.

I looked around in the dim light filtering down from the entrance. The dugout was about the size of the loggers' shacks I'd bunked in years back, barely large enough for the table and makeshift seats, with beds constructed of chicken wire nailed over wooden frames standing along the sides. A row of coat pegs had been hammered in by the steps, the walls were smeared with soot, wax dripped from the stub ends of candles stuck on nails and the atmosphere was thick with the smell of old fat, cigarettes and sweat.

'Pretty fair, as dugouts go,' Tom Cooper said. 'We've had much worse. It's dry, there's room for everybody and for once it's meant for someone bigger than a pygmy.' He prodded at the ceiling. 'That's good too. Thick enough to stop most things except a direct hit. As soon as we've unpacked our stuff and Moore has pinned up his Kirchner girls, we'll be snug as a bug.' He threw himself on one of the cots and bounced up and down, casting his dignity to the wind.

'No time for playing the schoolboy when we've work to do,' Howerd said and turned to me with his usual sneer. 'You're not going to be much use, Scott. Why don't you stay down here and read through whatever drivel they've written up in the trench notes while the rest of us start to sort out this mess?'

Two hours later, my head was swimming with details of bomb stores, gas gongs, drainage sumps, barbed wire pathways, observation posts, listening saps and the rest of the paraphernalia of modern warfare. There was no sign of any of the others returning, so I climbed up the dugout steps and out into an eye-wateringly bright January day. The last of the morning fog had cleared away and a smart breeze was blowing straight down the line of the trench. Suddenly, there was a kind of fluttering sound directly overhead. I ducked behind the sandbags and looked up, thinking it must be new military technology I'd not heard about yet, a prototype airplane or barrage balloon or some such. When I saw what it was I had to laugh.

Soaring on the wind in the sky above there was a kite, the sort of toy that children make, with a long tail of paper bows that streamed behind as it swooped from one turn to another. It was painted with red, white and blue Union Jack colours that showed up bright against the dirty chalk of our parapet.

A soldier I recognised as one of my own platoon was sitting on an empty cartridge crate nearby, pulling an oiled cleaning rag on a string through the barrel of his rifle. He stood up as I came his way.

'What's the game over there?' I nodded toward the kite.

'Not sure, sir.' It looked as if he was trying to make up his mind whether I could be trusted. Then he added, 'If it's who I think, it'll be worth going to watch, sir. You'll likely find some fun.'

There was another narrow communication ditch nearby that led me down a twisting path and into the fire trench that faced out into No Man's Land. Coming out of the shadows, I stopped short. In front of me, two men were crouching up on the fire step thirty feet apart, each of them holding a ramshackle arrangement of mirrors and rods –

periscopes that allowed a safe view over the sandbags. In between the pair of them, David Alexander was standing in the middle of the trench. He'd not changed out of the smart uniform he'd been wearing at the chateau and looked bizarrely pristine in his cord breeches and yellow leather gloves. In one hand he was holding a ball of twine, while with the other he was tweaking the string that stretched to the kite above. He was talking out loud as he watched it pirouette in the air.

'Come on, come on. You know you want to do it... you can't stop yourself. Come on.'

What the hell was going on? Alexander hadn't seemed like a half-wit before, far from it, which made his antics even harder to understand now. Next instant, a single rifle bullet cracked overhead. The string broke with a twang like a banjo and the kite crumpled in the air and fluttered down into the trench.

'Did you spot him?' Alexander called out.

'Aye,' replied the soldier nearest me. 'Right about where you said he'd be.' He was a corporal – a grizzled man who had a short clay pipe gripped upside down between his teeth.

'What about you, Stephen? You've the best sight of the lot of us.'

'He's dug in below that iron plate, Mr David, in a heap of old wire.'

The young private at the other end of the trench was still staring through his periscope. Alexander bent down to pick up the wreckage of his toy and then caught sight of me watching.

'Scott! Excellent. They said that you'd been posted to us. Welcome to the joys of C Company.' He seemed to treat it as completely normal that I'd seen him playing around with kids' toys. 'We're just doing a bit of tidying up.'

He held up the string and paper wreckage. I had no idea

what he was talking about or what he was up to, and it must have been written clear across my face.

'So sorry, should have explained. My fault. It's just that Old Bill here – that's Corporal Keeble, officially,' he said, waving a hand towards the pipe smoker, 'found out that the Territorials who've just left had lost a few of their chaps to some sharp fellow with a sniping rifle.'

I knew that already. It was a recurring entry in the notes I'd been reading, one of several sections that had given me food for thought.

'I worked out a few likely spots and decided we'd try and tempt him into showing his hand, hence the kite. Give the devil his due, he's a fair shot.'

Alexander nodded his head as if considering a philosophical problem in a classroom, not a lethal marksman who would blow the brains out of any one of us given the opportunity.

'Aye, he can shoot a bit,' the corporal butted in, 'but if he was really good, he'd have rumbled us and then we wouldn't know about his hidey hole, would we?'

That surprised me. Surely he wasn't supposed to answer back like that. And wasn't he supposed to say *sir*? This was getting more interesting by the minute. I'd understood there was a big divide between officers and men in the British Army. Maybe it was something I should report back on. Alexander didn't seem bothered by the informality at all.

'That's true, Bill, very true. And it's a mistake that will lead him to a sticky end, I regret to say.'

Right then, I really didn't know what to make of David Alexander. How could someone with his drawing room manners survive in a war zone? It sounded like he was genuinely sorry for the German sniper's error of judgement. On the other hand there was something about the way he said it that gave me a bit of a shiver. I'd never met anyone like him before.

While I was considering that, Alexander had taken off his gloves and folded them into a pocket. Then he unstrapped his wristwatch and handed it to the corporal.

'Here you are, Bill. About three minutes, if you wouldn't mind.'

He vaulted over the parados at the back wall of the trench, very nimble for a tall man, and disappeared behind the cover of the sandbags, leaving the corporal gazing at the watch and counting down the seconds. He didn't feel the need to explain anything to me, so I sat back and waited to see what would happen when Alexander's allotted time expired. At the end of three minutes Corporal Bill handed the watch to me, then unslung his rifle, took off his uniform cap and stuck it over the muzzle. He held the cap just above the level of the sand bags and jigged it up and down slowly, pacing a foot or two along each time. From any distance away in the enemy lines, it would look just like some raw recruit bobbing his head up and down for a glance across No Man's Land – a fine juicy target for that sniper. Sure enough, the third time he raised the cap, I heard the crack of a shot and it spun away as if the wearer had been hit in the head. A second later, however, two deep reports boomed out from behind our position, one after the other in quick succession.

'Got him!' the young private shouted. 'That's fixed the bugger.'

Corporal Bill picked up his cap and wiggled his finger through the bullet hole that perforated the crown, shaking his head.

'Good effort, Jerry, but not good enough,' he said. He looked at me as if he was trying to take my measure. 'Not bad

27

with a pistol, is Mr David. When it comes to rifles, though, he's the best I ever taught, even when he was a lad. Different class to anybody else.'

I could hear the possessive pride in his voice and considered how long he must have known David Alexander, who had just come into view, strolling back along the trench. Under one arm he was carrying a large bore rifle with two massive barrels side by side, the sort of weapon I'd once seen a big game hunter use. He propped the gun against the wooden revetting that lined the trench and started to brush the mud off his tunic. He was looking thoughtful.

'I suppose that might not have been absolutely fair play,' he said. He must have seen the expression on my face and went on. 'It's just that it doesn't seem quite right to use an express rifle for anything smaller than a rhinoceros. Ah, well, I suppose we have to make use of the best weapons for the job. May I take a look, Stephen?'

He took the trench scope and examined the outcome of his marksmanship. 'Well, it might not have been sporting, but it was certainly effective. Pity I've had to muck up a clean uniform.'

That gave me a bit of a start. I'd been taken in by his quiet, amiable manner. Now he was making no bones about having just stalked and shot a man. OK, it was war, but it was darn cold-blooded all the same, and the only qualms he'd got were that he'd used the wrong sort of gun and got a tad dirty.

'No need to worry about your jacket, Mr David. I'll sort it out for you later,' the young private muttered.

'Good man, Stephen. I wouldn't trust anyone else to look after me. Well now, I suppose that's the end of fun for the day. We'd better get back to more mundane labours.'

He turned to me and gave me a great beaming grin. It lit

up his face, changing his serious, academic expression into something utterly different, something much more reckless and restless.

'Come along then, Anson Scott. Let's see what state they've left the trenches in for us. This way to the war.'

That's how he is still fixed in my recollection, face angled up into the sun, smiling. There was nothing I could do except give in with good grace and follow him.

4

In those months of the war, the pattern was to spend four days in the front lines at a stretch and then four at rest. I'd already decided it'd be best not to try to send anything out to MacManus too soon, to give me the chance to get settled in and concentrate on learning the ropes of life in the trenches. As it happened, for most of that first tour, life wasn't too bad. The men were well set up and knew exactly what they were about and as I'd suspected, Sergeant Fox was superb. Sure, there was Howerd, who I'd marked down as a first rate snitch, but he was more than off-set by David Alexander.

Alexander seemed to have adopted me into his gang. It turned out that the corporal and private he often rattled around with weren't just part of his platoon: they'd worked on his family's land back in England, which is how they knew one another so well. Why did he decide I'd fit in with them? I don't know. Maybe the novelty of an American in the Royal Pennines fitted with his inclination towards the unconventional. Maybe he was smart enough to know that his restless nature needed reining in by someone more cynical, which I was well qualified for. Whichever, he looked after me while I found my feet, even when he was rostered to be at rest, and wherever he went his entourage, Corporal Bill and Private Stephen Oliver, went with him.

That first afternoon, following the kite trick, I was given a lecture every ten yards:

'I know that trench warfare may sound like a random business – mind that hole in the boards – but if you keep your wits about you, you can tip the scales in your favour.'

That was how Alexander started, in his best professorial style. 'Now here, you see, these sandbags are really too low. Don't you agree, Bill? Especially for tall fellows like me. Watch out for yourself, Scott. Heads down. There are bound to be more snipers around.'

He bent over to stay under cover as we came to a stretch where the trench was much shallower. Sure enough, a bullet whipped just above his head and thudded into the sandbags behind.

'There! See what I mean. Everybody all right? Good. We'll need to dig out this section tonight.'

So it went on. I learned more about the intricacies of modern warfare in those few days than in all the next two years and didn't know how lucky I was. David Alexander knew the trench business backwards and wasn't afraid to pass his knowledge on. The way he read the subtle signs and sounds of the front put me in mind of scouts I'd met out West, except that I never saw a frontiersman as neat and tidy as him. Anywhere else, I'd have been wary of someone who looked so buttoned up. With him, it was clear that I couldn't judge him by any of my normal standards. For a start he seemed to know the name of every soldier we passed, and his nickname, and his wife's name. Even more interesting for me, they all looked delighted to see him. It wasn't what I'd been expecting when I'd agreed to MacManus' proposal, and I was starting to think that maybe I'd need to change my planned approach to my articles. When I got back to my own platoon, Sergeant Fox gave his own stamp of approval:

'Mr Alexander showing you the ropes, sir? Aye well, you'll be all right then. Stick tight to him and you'll not go far wrong. He looks a right toff, but he'll do.'

I'd worked out already that Fox was not a man to mince his few words, or stand on ceremony, and I figured that was a glowing recommendation.

'If every officer is as smart as him,' I said, 'seems to me that we shouldn't have any big trouble winning the war. Only I guess he's not exactly typical.'

Fox's pale lips gave a bit of a twitch, which was as close to a smile as I expected to see from him. 'There ain't many officers as good at soldiering as Mr Alexander, that's true.'

'And he seems to be on real friendly terms with everyone, which is a help, I guess…' I was pushing my luck, leaving that one dangling, I knew, but I was curious to see whether there was anything else I should know about the perfect David Alexander.

He was about to say something, then stopped and settled for: 'Couldn't comment on that. Not my part to say, sir.'

Fox knew he was being pumped for information and had clammed up on me. It didn't make any difference, however. Collecting opinions had been my business for years and I understood that his refusal to tell me anything else was significant, as was the way he said it.

So who was it in the battalion that didn't care for Alexander?

From my point of view, it was hard to think who would have taken against Alexander or why. Except for those occasional flashes of mischief when he was with people he trusted, he was generally quiet and it wasn't like he shirked work. That professorial exterior hid an inexhaustible energy. I considered myself pretty tough, but he was like human whipcord. He could get by on less sleep than anyone I'd ever met and I'd often find him sitting up way into the night to finish off the interminable paperwork, breaking off every now and then to read from one of the volumes of poetry he kept in his pockets. Sometimes he'd even read aloud and I figured he was trying to provide some education for his batman, Private Oliver. I had half a mind to make that the basis for a short scene in one of my reports at some point, something like 'Teaching in the Trenches'. He did have a few other little quirks. Apart from his neatness, he used his own cut glass tumbler for whisky instead of the tin mugs the rest of us made do with, and he always washed his hands before eating, but those were only minor eccentricities which bothered nobody.

For myself, Alexander was the ideal companion, a fascinating mix of professional assassin and gentleman of leisure. Every day, I got to like him more. And yet I still couldn't get rid of the vague sense of unease that was lingering at the back of my mind. It wasn't the trenches, or the bullets or shells or mortar bombs. They were all the physical manifestations of the perils of war and I'd come expecting those, as well as the particular dangers of my own situation. No – there was another current in the waters out there, something dark and dangerous and menacing. I just couldn't figure out what it was. That was dumb of me. All I needed to do was tick off the list of the old sins – lust, greed, anger, laziness, gluttony and pride. At least three of those were going to cause trouble. And then, of course, there was the seventh, the most destructive of them all. Envy.

We'd get to that one before the end.

The truth started to get clearer the first night Alexander decided it'd be safe for me to go on duty alone.

'It's nice and quiet and there's only the one patrol out in No Man's Land so it's the perfect opportunity for you to take a stroll around. You can relieve Moore and it would be worth popping up to the listening post. The fellows out there can feel a bit isolated.' He made it sound as mundane as a horse doctor visiting an outlying farm back home. 'I'm going to sit up with a dram to finish these reports and then I have to take them back to the Colonel.'

I shovelled my compass, notebook and electric torch into my coat pockets and went up the stairs. When I glanced down from the top step, he was sitting in a dull pool of candlelight with his papers and whisky glass. Then the heavy curtains sagged closed behind me.

In the daytime, the front lines were miserable ditches full of dirt and curses, alternating short spells of fear with long periods of boredom because we had to avoid any activity that would be spotted and bring down a storm of explosives. After sundown, they were transformed into something different. I might have been a hard-boiled reporter, but even I could appreciate the moonlit labyrinth that bustled with bunches of men loaded with every sort of burden. You'd see spades, rubber boots, coils of wire, crates of ammunition or grenades or sandbags full of grub, and then where two carrying parties met at a junction there was chaos and a deal of gesturing and jostling, but without any of the usual shouting and swearing. Because whatever we did, ferrying supplies or wiring or digging out collapsed trenches, it had to be done in complete quiet. Life after dark was like an old silent movie, but there was always a weird beauty about it.

That night I stood for quite a while, soaking up the atmosphere until I had to move aside for a party carrying water in old gasoline cans. That broke the spell and I figured I'd better get a move on up to the front line. After a few minutes' search I found Moore sitting out on the sandbags watching over a handful of men who were repairing the gaps in our barbed wire.

'Come and take a look at the view,' he said. He was wrapping a dressing around one hand and I could see that the bandage was stained dark.

'Are you OK?' I asked.

'Bloody wire. Springs back when you're least expecting it. Just as well it doesn't hurt too much.'

34

I climbed up and sat with him on the parapet. For some moments all I could see was made up of shadows of grey and black until the night was lit up by a stream of coloured signals shooting up from the German line. They were maybe a couple of hundred yards to one side of our position but our wiring party had to freeze like statues until the flares had all floated to the ground and gone out.

'What was all that about?' I asked Moore.

'Might have been a raid of ours, I suppose, but it was probably only some windy Jerry getting trigger happy.' He listened carefully. 'That seems to be it. All quiet now, so I'll be off to get Vaughan to stitch this up and stop it bleeding. The patrol's not in yet. You'd better make sure our sentries keep a good watch and don't plug them by accident. G'night.'

He hopped down into the trench and disappeared into the darkness, leaving me on my own, right at the sharp end of the war, with my pulse beating a bit faster than normal. But taking the lumps of an infantry officer was part of the deal for getting the information I needed, and anyway, I'd been out and about with Alexander plenty enough to be familiar with the scenery. I set off on my rounds.

By the time I reached the far end of our patch, I'd persuaded myself that everything was fine. The sentries were all awake and alert and the night was quiet enough, apart from the usual thud of the big guns up north and the occasional crack of a rifle shot. As I turned back, however, I couldn't get rid of the nagging sense that something was about to happen. I dismissed the thought and found my way to an opening a couple of feet wide in the front wall of the trench. It led into a narrow gully heading directly away from our lines and above it someone had chalked a drawing of a man holding one hand to his ear. I switched off my torch, ducked under the sign-board and started out towards the listening post.

The way out to that post was skinny, like a tight tunnel with no roof. It was also as black as tar and within seconds I'd lost track of distance. I tried to keep a tally of steps as I crept forward – twenty, thirty, forty – and was beginning to think I must be halfway across No Man's Land by now. The way I was going, I'd be dropping into the German front lines before long. Next moment, there was a whoosh and bang and a magnesium flare exploded above me. I nearly leaped right out of the trench. Only a few feet away, a human skull was sticking out of the earth, the light shining white off its bare bones. Slowly, it turned so its black eye sockets were staring straight at me and I'll swear that every hair on my body stood up in terror.

'In here. Quick, sir.'

I could breathe again. It was only Sergeant Fox. I scurried forward to join him. He was crouching at the entrance to our listening post – a shallow circular pit where two other men were already lying prone against the sloping sides.

'Thought I heard something a minute ago. Not sure now.' Fox was whispering, his skeletal face pushed close to mine. 'Want to listen for yourself?'

My heart rate had about got back to normal and I pulled myself up toward the rim of the post, settled on my elbows and concentrated. There was a trick to this I remembered from years back. In one very hard Alaskan winter, game was scarce and my partner, an ancient Russian, was the only man that had been able to bring fresh meat into camp. After days of fruitless hunting, I'd swallowed my pride and asked him his secret.

'Stop your eyes, shut your nose and you hear better,' he told me, like it was obvious. So now I closed my eyes and breathed through my mouth.

This is what I heard. First, a low rumble like a cart crossing a wooden bridge, which was heavy artillery firing miles

36

away; then high above that was the faint whistle of the wind in thickets of barbed wire and finally, every so often, a tiny metallic clinking from in front of our own lines. That was rats foraging through all the old tins cans that had been tossed away over the parapet. I started to relax. There was nothing out of the ordinary. Then, just for a moment, and right at the edge of my hearing, I caught a new noise. A shuffling sound like something or someone was on the move over by the German front line. Was that a muffled grunt? In their trenches or coming towards us across No Man's Land? I stayed dead still and listened hard for a good five minutes but I couldn't make it out again and wasn't sure whether I'd really heard anything or just imagined it.

When I slid back into the middle of the post, Fox was staring at me, looking puzzled. He tapped one of the men on the shoulder to let him know that we were leaving and then started back to our own lines with me hard on his heels down the sap until we arrived in the main fire trench again.

'What's that stuff with closing your eyes, sir?'

'A long time back, a friend told me that was the best way to hear when you're out hunting.'

Fox grunted while he considered the suggestion, then nodded his approval. He unslung his rifle and propped it against the wall. 'I could do with a smoke and we're tucked down out of sight here.' He pulled a crumpled packet out of his uniform packet. 'Fancy one? They're only Woodbines.'

I reckoned that was as good as a gesture of acceptance and took one from him. He held his old soldier fashion, cupped back into his palm between thumb and index finger to hide the glow and we stood in neighbourly silence while the man on duty on the step above kept watch. I'd just stubbed out the remnant of my cigarette when the sentry leaned forward abruptly and pulled back the bolt on his rifle with a steel snick.

'There's someone out here, Sarge. I'm sure I just saw them. Over yon. Coming our way.'

Fox and I hopped up to join him, but a veil of cloud had drifted across the moon and it was difficult to see further than a few yards. I unbuttoned the flap of my holster and pulled out the revolver, silently cursing the standard-issue Webley – it was way too heavy and clumsy, even for me, who'd practised pistol shooting for hour after hour not so long ago.

'There, sir. Look.'

The sentry pointed his rifle at a gap in the belt of wire only fifty feet away. A shaft of moonlight had broken through the cloud, shining down on a handful of dark shadows that seemed to have risen from the earth. They were racing towards our fire trench, zigzagging across the broken ground. For a second, I couldn't believe what I was seeing, before my brain leapt into action:

It's a German raid. They'll be on us in a moment.

Fox was already on the move. He'd jumped down and was running to intercept them, trying to pull his bayonet free at the same time. I plunged after him and the two of us clattered along the trench, waking the off-duty men dozing under their ground sheets.

'Password?' I heard a sentry yell.

The only response was a scarlet flare that soared up from the German lines opposite and burst into flame high above us. Outlined against its red glow I saw the shape of a man already straddling our parapet. He was massive. Above his head, he held a sort of bundle; a long dark shape that was writhing and squirming in the glare. Before I could bring the Webley up and get off a shot he hurled his burden over the sandbags, then leaped down after it, clearing the seven foot drop with an ear-splitting crash as the boards splintered under him. I was still trying to gather my wits when I saw two other men slide quickly into the trench and then suddenly there was a volley of incoming machine gun bullets that whistled across the top of our sandbags, splattering sand and chalk everywhere.

I was on the point of taking a shot at the three attackers myself, when I heard the sentry release his rifle bolt and realised that Fox had relaxed and was unclipping his bayonet. As the cloud of dust settled, I finally worked out that this wasn't a German raid. It was only our own men returning from patrol. I let the pistol down and leaned back against the trench wall, my whole body limp as the tension started to subside. I thanked all the stars I'd not been able to shoot at them.

My sense of relief didn't last long. The bundle that had been thrown into our trench shook itself and uncurled reluctantly. In the fading light of the flare, I saw it was a man, a slight lad wearing a German soft cap and high boots. He started to whimper and clutch at his head but in a flash the giant who had thrown him had jumped up and aimed a running kick at him, catching him in the ribs. He rammed his boot into the boy's belly again, and then once again, rolling him into the mud in the bottom of the trench.

'Hey! You!' I was too outraged to keep my voice down. Without thinking, I started to raise my revolver again. 'Knock that off. Right now. That's an order.'

For a moment, I thought he hadn't heard as he delivered another sickening kick at the boy, but even while the lad doubled over he whipped around and turned on me with a speed that was almost supernatural for a man his size.

Everything went deadly quiet. I didn't need anyone to tell me I'd landed myself in deep trouble. In the silence I could hear every duckboard creak as he stalked up to me and stood toe to toe, so close that I could smell the stink of his breath. One side of his face was stained black and his eyes were rimmed with red, staring down at me with a mixture of contempt and disbelief. Slowly, he reached out an arm like a tree trunk and pushed my pistol aside like it was a plaything. In a growl like distant thunder he said:

'And what the fuck have we got here?'

5

The red flare had dulled to maroon while I stood looking up at the looming figure, unable to find my voice, the pistol dangling uselessly by my side. He continued to stare at me, eyeball to eyeball, without blinking. Eventually, I managed to clear my throat with a cough.

'I'm Second Lieutenant Scott, C Company, Royal Pennines.'

'Hellfire, damnation and buggery!' He stood back and jabbed me in the chest with a short straight stick he was carrying on a strap around his wrist. 'You've some fucking manners to learn. Trying to order me about in my own company? I'm not having that. Especially not from some one-pip bloody wonder who's only just arrived!'

I kept quiet. The big man went on at me, emphasising each point with a thrust from his stick so that eventually he had me pinned back against the sandbag wall.

'First…' Prod. 'I've got to get little Fritz here back to battalion HQ for questioning. Then…' Another prod. 'I'm going to catch up with some sleep. After that…' A real vicious poke. 'I'll deal with you. Whoever or whatever you are. Fucking idiot.'

He gazed fiercely at me again to make sure that his threat had sunk in and then marched off down the trench, half pushing, half lifting the prisoner along, shaking him every few yards like a dog with a rat. The men who had been with him on patrol brought up the rear at a safe, respectful distance.

The night felt even quieter once they had gone. I looked sideways at Sergeant Fox, who had made himself busy counting the cartridges in his ammunition pouch.

41

'And I guess that was…?' I didn't need to finish the question and I was almost sure I knew the answer already.

'Captain Tollman,' Fox replied. 'He must've got back from leave earlier tonight and taken the boys straight out. It's one of his favourite turns. He crawls through the wire right up to Jerry lines and looks for a sentry who's a bit separated from the rest of his mates. Then he just reaches over the parapet, grabs the poor bugger by the scruff of the neck, lifts him out and carries him back for our intelligence staff to interrogate.'

I couldn't be sure, because it was always difficult to make out any emotion in Fox's hoarse voice, but it sounded like he had some reservations about the whole business. It was impossible to tell whether that was with regard to the intelligence staff or the captain, or maybe both.

'I'd better get back to the listening post,' he said. 'The lads'll be wondering what the hell has been going on.'

I was sorry to see him go. I didn't scare that easily but that confrontation had done nothing for my nerves and I would have been glad of his company. As it was, for the rest of the watch I found I was stopping every few yards to listen, imagining the Prussian equivalents of Tollman lurking nearby. There were no more alarms, however, and at the end of my duty I set off back to the company headquarters.

The dugout was in a dead end off the main trench and the final stretch of my way was completely deserted. By now, a freezing dew had settled on our positions and gathered in all the low ground so I could hardly see where I was putting my feet. Every sound I made echoed back distorted, and I began to have the eerie sensation that I was being followed. I was mighty relieved when I came to the canvas curtains at the entrance to our headquarters and I was looking forward to a quick shot of whisky with Alexander before I turned in. To my surprise, however, there was no sound from the dugout below and only the faintest glimmer of light. All my fears came flooding back, magnified many times over. I tiptoed slowly down the chalk stairway, stealthy as I knew how, trying to get at my pistol once more. On the bottom step I came to an abrupt halt.

Only one candle was still lit. By its flickering light I saw a body sprawled across one of the bunks. Even before I saw the face, I knew from the size that it was Captain Tollman. He was lying back, head flopped limp and both eyes wide open, unblinking and fixed on the wall opposite. It looked as if he'd been dead for hours. I crouched on the step, fumbling with the catch on my revolver. Who the hell could have done this? Were they still here?

The swish of the curtain behind me made me jump round so quickly I nearly fired off a shot by accident. Just as well I didn't. Starting down the stairs was a familiar pair of highly polished boots and I let out a sigh of relief. David Alexander. Right then, I needed reinforcements and he was the best man for the job by far.

'Are you all right, Scott?' he said, unbuttoning his coat. 'I've not seen anyone look that pale since Father found the butler siphoning off his best port.'

I gestured at the corpse with the muzzle of my revolver. All Alexander did was laugh. He dropped his greatcoat onto one of the pegs and flipped his cap up over it.

'Don't worry about Tollman It's just his way. He always sleeps like that.'

As if the mere mention of his name had roused him, there was a grunt from the bunk. My feelings were flipping between relief and dread while I watched Tollman straighten his head with an audible crunch of vertebral bones. Then he lifted his great shoulders slowly off the bed.

'That's twice you've pointed a gun at me, you fucking imbecile. If there's a third time I'll knock your brains out, I swear.' He got up, massaging his neck, while he peered out at me under lowering brows. The sight of his little red-rimmed eyes triggered a sudden vivid memory.

I'd told the Colonel some of the truth about my life that first night. I really had worked on the railroads in Alaska for a spell after I quit West Point, and in the spring of '08 I'd been part of a team checking the track up on the Arctic border. When the weather closed in, we found shelter in a dry cave under a rocky butte and got settled in for the night. The cave went back a way so we lit a fire up near the entrance and started to dry off. Next thing we knew, a big old bear was towering up in front of us. It must have been hibernating and it was feeling pretty mean at being woken unexpectedly. For a moment it stood, blinking at us with angry little eyes that glinted through its thick winter fur. Then it shook its head, snarled and started to lash out. We just abandoned our stuff and took to our heels.

In the close quarters of the dugout, Tollman was every bit as overwhelming as that bear. His head brushed the roof and his bulk eclipsed the puny candle flame. When I'd met him in the trench I'd assumed his face had been made up with camouflage for the night raid, but now I saw that he was marked with a strange pattern of pigmented circles that scarred all the right side of his face, from his cheek into his drooping black moustache.

'Morning, Tollman. Patrol went off well?' David Alexander's quiet voice cut across my memories.

'Well enough. I got a prisoner for the intelligence boys to grill. Only then there was this stupid bastard trying to interfere when we came back in,' Tollman said, gesturing in my direction. 'Sod all use to man or beast, he's going to be.'

There was a moment's silence before Alexander cut in smoothly to rescue me. 'I was just about to take him to inspect a fascinating new stretch of Jerry's wire, so we'll leave you in peace.' He shot me a warning glance. 'Come along, Scott, we've work to do. The Captain here will probably feel more comfortable in his own company.'

Tollman raised his head and squinted suspiciously at Alexander. His eyes were smaller and meaner than ever as he tried to work out whether he had just been insulted, but by the time he might have figured it out we were up the steps and gone.

For the rest of the night, I was glad to keep Alexander company during his session as duty officer, even though it should have been my chance to catch up on sleep. I figured I was a whole sight better off in the open air rather than cooped up with Tollman in a confined space underground. The down side was that by breakfast time, after morning stand-to – the twice daily ritual where we and the Germans both climbed onto our parapets and fired off a few volleys of meaningless shots towards each other – I was yawning over my mug of coffee. In the afternoon, Howerd, Moore and I were smoking the air blue in the dugout while we filled in a whole bunch of forms. I'd almost forgotten that armies spent more time on paperwork than actual fighting and I could barely keep my eyes open until help came from a direction I'd not expected at all.

'I say, Scott, you look done in. Why not stay down here and catch some shut-eye, while I cover for you up top?'

It was Howerd. I looked up from the forms to see whether he was being sarcastic, but for once his face was sincere.

'I suppose we've been coming a bit high-handed with you over the last couple of days. Think of this as a small gesture of apology. It'll be all right. No one will disturb you for a while, and you may as well catch up while you can.'

I should have been more suspicious, but I guess my instincts had been blunted by the scares of the night, so I accepted his offer gratefully. When the others left I was glad to lie down on one of the bunks under the promising smiles of a collection of Parisian show girls whose pictures Moore had pinned up. I closed my eyes and, despite the syncopated thud of outgoing shellfire not far off, was asleep within minutes.

'What on earth do you think you're doing, man?' A furious voice roared at my ear, shattering my dreams in an instant. 'Skulking down here! Sleeping through the day. For God's sake, everyone else is out in the line, working. Intolerable! Utterly intolerable.'

I shook myself awake and sat up to find the irate face of Colonel Ireland hanging above me. Over the Colonel's shoulder, Clarridge looked worried. I shot to my feet and tried to get out an explanation at the same time as pulling on my boots.

'Sorry, sir. Howerd said he would—'

The Colonel's exasperation cut like a lash. 'Don't make it worse. Dereliction of duty. No one else to blame. Absolutely unacceptable. Nothing more to say to you now. Report tomorrow when we're back in billets. Deal with it then.' He spun on his heel and limped stiffly up and out of the dugout. The adjutant hung back long enough to give me a consoling pat on the shoulder and then scurried after him.

I sank back onto the bunk, hardly able to believe what had just happened. Tollman and Howerd apart, I felt like I'd been starting to settle into the Royal Pennines, and without making myself too conspicuous. Now it looked like I'd stirred up the ire of the commanding officer himself. I didn't notice the blanket across the doorway move until there was a barely suppressed chuckle from the entrance. Tollman was standing on the top step blocking out the light from up above.

'Sleeping on duty, Mr American?' His eyes glistened

maliciously. 'Not a very good start to your career. What will they think of you back home when the Colonel gets you thrown out and sent away with your tail between your legs?'

His scarred face twitched up in a one-sided grin. I pushed past him into the afternoon light, thinking to find Howerd and demand an explanation but the devious little devil had made himself scarce and I couldn't see hide or hair of him. Instead, I found Alexander in the fire trench laughing at the sign to the listening post, where one of the company jokers had changed the drawing into a cartoon face of Lord Kitchener.

'What's up, Scott? Where've you been all afternoon? It looks as if you've lost a pound, or even a dollar, and found a penny!'

I filled him in on events, trying not to sound too concerned. '... so now I've got to see to Colonel Ireland as soon as we're back in reserve.'

'Up to that again, are they?' Alexander nodded, looking sympathetic. 'It's a trick they've used before on other new men. Usually they work it so Tollman arrives to bawl out their unsuspecting victim. It's incredibly unfortunate for you that the Colonel turned up first today. In fact, he doesn't get up to the front line very often. Bad luck. It probably won't be as tricky as you think, because...' He stopped himself finishing the sentence. 'Anyway, I can try to smooth things over tomorrow, if you like.'

'No thanks. I'll sort it out for myself, one way or another.'

I knew he meant well but I was too angry for good manners. I hurried off to find my own platoon, cursing my stupidity and furious with Howerd and Tollman. So much for my mission. Now what was going to happen? I'd done my research before I set off from the US but in all the possible scenarios I'd rehearsed, I'd never anticipated being accused of dereliction of duty. I had to hope that I might get away with only a slap on the wrist from the Colonel. On the other hand, if he was really serious, I could be looking at a full-blown court martial.

6

I woke before daybreak. Alexander, Howerd and Cooper were still asleep as I crawled out from under my blanket and rubbed the dust clear from the single grimy window. There'd been no opportunity to look around before; we'd left the trenches in driving rain and marched out to these billets in a farmhouse a few miles behind the lines. By the time we arrived, it was late into the night and we'd no inclination to do more than find an unfurnished room up under the eaves and flop down to sleep. This morning, however, it looked like the rain had stopped finally, and the dim shapes of buildings were just about discernible in the grey of pre-dawn. I left the others snoring, pulled on my tunic as quiet as I knew how, and set off to take a look around. While I was aiming to produce a series of pieces about life and work at the front, it would do no harm to send some descriptive pieces about our surroundings as well.

The camp was beginning to stir with a sort of low grumble. Not far off, I could hear the company cooks making breakfast. Some wiseacre was clashing his pan lids together like steel cymbals and I guessed that he'd decided that if he was working, he didn't give a damn if he woke everybody else. The sky got lighter and in the distance there was a pattering noise like corn popping in a pan – it was still near enough to the trenches to hear the rifle fire. I got my first look at the farm that would be our home every time we came out of the front lines. It was a medium-sized spread that might not merit being termed a chateau but was still a fair property, all built in a square. A stone-faced house with long windows made up one side, facing across to a large barn. The row of cottages where we junior officers had been quartered filled in a third side, looking across to a gap opposite that gave onto a rutted lane. The middle of the farmyard was filled with a massive pile of manure, high and mottled, its lower slopes oozing into a shallow gutter. I was thinking about the stink and the bugs that would breed in there in warmer weather when there was a familiar scratchy voice by my ear.

'They always put their muck heaps right by the house.' Early it might be, but Sergeant Fox was up and about. 'Messy foreign buggers. You'd think they'd know it doesn't do to keep the shit by your kitchen.' He sniffed his disapproval, stepped carefully across a cess-stained puddle and strode off towards the cookhouse.

I decided to pass on food. I was trying to persuade myself that I didn't care what happened to me but my stomach had other ideas, fluttering and bouncing around, so I stayed outside to make notes. Whatever happened they could still be useful. After a short spell, the other officers sauntered out of the mess towards the men paraded for inspection. I was keeping a sharp lookout for Howerd, but it was David Alexander who came to talk.

'Are you all right, Scott? I didn't see you at breakfast.' He gave me a sympathetic look.

'Fine, thanks.' I still didn't know him well enough to admit to my fears. 'I don't suppose you've seen Howerd this morning?'

I badly wanted to catch up with that little snake in the grass so as I could force him to own up to the truth before I had to see the Colonel, and he'd managed to avoid me all the previous night.

'Sorry, no. If I do see him, I'll tell him you want to talk to him.'

He marched off, leaving me feeling a bit sore. I'd hoped

that Alexander would be smart enough to appreciate that I could be worried about what had happened the day before.

Goes to show that you can't trust anyone. So to hell with the lot of them.

I set off for the main house and the Colonel's office. It'd be pretty ignominious to be dismissed with a flea in my ear so soon, but there was no way of avoiding it so I squared my shoulders and walked across to face the music.

As I approached, the door to the farmhouse swung open and Clarridge's spectacles winked at me around the door frame.

'Come in, come in. We've set up the orderly room through here.'

He beckoned me in to a sort of antechamber to the main parlour of the house. In normal times it would probably have been crowded with polished furniture, but now it was bare except for the battalion's makeshift office equipment, a pair of tables made up of planks resting on wooden trestles. One was neatly arranged with two telephones, each with an exactly aligned notepad, an office typewriter and an equally precise corporal. The other table was invisible under stacks of military manuals and directives, maps and instructions, with volumes piled high at crazy angles in danger of toppling to the floor. Clarridge's cap was resting on top of the tallest and most unsteady of these towers.

'*Excusez-moi pour le désordre*, but we haven't had much chance to sort anything out yet. Now, you're not the orderly officer today, are you?' He consulted a list on his desk. 'No, I thought not. So what can we do for you?'

I was starting to get riled. Even Clarridge, who'd seemed decent enough, wasn't bothered by the fact that I could be in serious trouble.

'Colonel Ireland told me to report to him,' I said without mincing words. 'That business yesterday, you remember.'

'Yes, yes. Of course.' He combed through his whiskers in embarrassment. 'He's on the blower to brigade HQ at present, but he should be done in a few minutes if you'd care to wait.'

I stayed on my feet, making a show of examining the memoranda and timetables pinned onto the large notice board until one of the corporals told Clarridge that the telephone lines were clear, and I was waved through to the commander's office.

Colonel Ireland was sitting with his back to the door. It looked like he was busy adjusting something on the desk in front of him. He didn't turn around as I came in. I drew myself up to attention, stamped my heels on the floor and threw him my best salute. Still he didn't acknowledge my presence. For maybe half a minute the two of us remained like that before a mechanical stuttering noise outside broke the silence, making me jump before I realised that it was only a typist in the next room. Then I remembered that the Colonel had seemed hard of hearing and gave a loud cough.

The Colonel turned slowly. I repeated my salute, neat as I knew how.

'Oh. It's Mr... err, isn't it? Expecting Clarry. No matter. Just polishing m' sword. Won't trust anyone else. Magnificent, don't you think?'

On the desk, next to its leather scabbard, lay an old style infantry sword. The naked blade shone like mirrored glass as he stroked the shark-skin grip.

'It's beautiful, Colonel. Very impressive,' I managed to say, after a moment.

'Quite. Most effective weapon at close quarters. Now, what can I do for you?' His eyebrows shot up, like he was making a courteous enquiry.

That was a bit of a surprise. I had to gather my wits pretty smartly. 'You told me to report to you when we returned to billets, Colonel.' This wasn't at all what I'd been anticipating.

'Ah, yes. Now what about?' He looked up to the plaster mouldings of the ceiling as if he was hoping for divine inspiration.

'I think you were disappointed to find me in the dugout yesterday afternoon, sir.'

'Was I? Oh yes. Mustn't do that sort of thing. Wrong impression for the men. Know you're new but can't seem to be shirking and all that. Best be more careful.' He half turned away and then swivelled back. 'Anything else?'

'No, Colonel. Thank you, sir.' I saluted him again and backed out of the room, hard put not to shake my head in amazement.

'Everything all right then, Scott?' Clarridge looked up from behind his parapet of papers.

'I guess so. Maybe not quite what I'd anticipated.'

He just nodded and went back to his work as if I'd not said anything other than he'd expected. I was too confounded to ask anything, so I opened the door and walked out into the sunshine, feeling a bit like a man who'd just downed two large shots of whisky on an empty stomach.

All the rest of the day, through the exercises and drills, I was mulling over the events of the morning. How the heck did anyone think that Colonel Ireland was fit to lead a fighting battalion? It was beyond belief, but apart from having got me off the hook, it was also exactly the sort of information I'd been looking for. When we were free from duties in early evening I went looking for a quiet corner out of the way where I could get all my notes and observations down on paper. The farm itself was too busy, but out in the field beyond, past the lines where the horses and mules were tethered, the battalion forge was deserted. I figured nobody was likely to interrupt me there, so I sat and wrote everything down in my own coded shorthand. I was planning on keeping my notebook in my pocket – it wouldn't be smart to have something that damning in my kit bag where it could be discovered too easily – but I'd no intention of it being readable if anyone did find it. I was still writing when the bugle sounded and I had to hurry back to wash up before dinner.

The battalion mess had been set up in the dining room over at the main house. While I was rounding the dung heap, the farmhouse door opened and two officers came out. Although it was getting dark, I could easily recognise both Tollman's bulk and the smaller figure that clung to him like a shrunken shadow.

'How nice to see you survived your interview with the Colonel,' Howerd said as they passed by. He never was able to pass up on a cheap shot. 'I do hope that you weren't punished for an innocent mistake on your part. I mean, any of us can oversleep, can't we?'

Oozing hypocrisy he sloped off after Tollman, who was already striding out of the farmyard.

'Come on in, Scott,' one of the Cooper boys called from inside.

'We can't start to play until you stop spoiling the blackout,' his brother added.

I was late and a crowd of officers had already gathered in the mess before dinner. It reminded me of one of the smoke-filled bars I'd used to drink at back home – different country, different climate, different war, but the same bare boards and plain tables and the same weather-beaten men sprawling out on a mixture of armchairs and benches. Just inside the door, the twins were sitting side by side at a beat-up piano. Alexander was leaning up against it, cigarette in hand, talking to a short, brisk man – I remembered he was the intelligence officer, Foster.

'You look a touch more cheerful than this morning, Scott. All well then?'

'Yes and no, I guess. I went to see the Colonel about that business yesterday, but he hardly seemed to remember it. Is he always that vague?'

'Ah! One of those mornings, was it?' Alexander asked. He cleared his throat like a man who felt he had to make an embarrassing but necessary explanation. 'You have to remember that Colonel Ireland has commanded the Royal Pennines for twenty years now, and with considerable distinction in the main.'

'Sure, in the days of muskets and swordplay.' I wasn't being as cynical as my voice made out. After an hour or so thinking about what I'd already got noted down, I was keen to find out any more archaic practices.

'No, really. He used to have a reputation as a real fighting man. But of course, you're right. Soldiering has advanced from last century, what with machine guns, artillery, barbed wire, aircraft and all the rest of it and it's true the Colonel doesn't seem to have moved on. Recently he can get rather…' he drew in a deep lungful of smoke while he sought for the appropriate word, '… abstracted.'

Foster nodded his agreement. It could only be good news for me, in both senses. I decided I'd dig a bit further.

'Isn't that a bit risky? What happens if he turns a bit *abstracted* in the middle of an enemy attack? Do we have to push him around in a bath chair?' I was trying my best to sound concerned. Inside, I was crowing with satisfaction. This was exactly the sort of information I wanted to uncover. The folks back in the USA were going to love this one – "Ready for battle. Only one century too late".

55

'That's an amusing image, I must say. Actually, there's not much to worry about because Clarry is an exceptional adjutant – the only man I've ever met who actually enjoys administrative duties – and all our company commanders have knocked around a fair bit.'

'So it's all OK providing there's a decent captain in each company?' I quizzed him. This would make for another very interesting line to follow up. It was getting to the point where I almost had too many ideas rattling round in my head. This time, I might have been a bit too blunt, because Alexander paused before answering, as if he was considering how much it was wise to tell me.

'That's about it. And A, B and D have sensible chaps with fighting experience while… well, you know who we've got. I know he's not to everybody's taste, but if you need a fellow to hold a section of the line, he's just the man.'

'If you say so.' I couldn't make it sound convincing. Even that early on, I knew there was something very wrong with Tollman. 'He and Howerd were going out when I arrived – don't they stop in the mess for dinner with the rest of us?'

'The Colonel prefers us to eat together but there's no absolute rule that we have to stay in billets. Those two are a law unto themselves and they usually take themselves off drinking and womanising in town,' Alexander replied.

Better and better; another storyline: "Straight-laced officers and loose women". I'd have to be careful about that if I wasn't going to offend the delicacy of the reading public back home, although I was confident that Mac would tidy up anything I sent and pat it into shape before printing.

'I shouldn't expect to see either looking too rosy in the morning,' Alexander went on. It sounded like he might be going to say more but the clang of the dinner gong put an end to further conversation.

As predicted, both Tollman and Howerd were kind of subdued at breakfast the next day. Alexander persevered in asking them about their views of the trenches, getting only morose monosyllabic replies for his pains. He was as pleasantly polite as ever and I couldn't think why he was bothering to persist until he dropped me the merest flicker of a wink. Then I cottoned on to the fact that he was only doing it to stir them up. It worked pretty well and they left to see to their rounds as soon as possible.

For the rest of us, after a morning of training and supply exercises, Alexander proposed a visit to the nearest town. That was fine by me. I was keen to gather in as many impressions as I could but by then, the sky was grey and threatening rain and no one else was very eager.

'But it's only a couple of miles away,' Alexander pleaded, 'and the weather will probably hold off – anyway, we shouldn't get any wetter than if we were up at the front.'

In spite of his cajoling, it was just the two of us who set off at a smart pace down the paved road after lunch. To start with, conversation was impossible because of the noise of gunfire blowing down the wind from the front that drowned out even Alexander's attempts at whistling. Eventually, the sound of explosions grew fainter and he started to talk instead.

'Thanks for coming along. I do like to take a look around somewhere new and it makes a pleasant change to have a kindred spirit to hand – someone else who takes a keen interest in what's going on around him. It's not a common attribute, you know, although useful in many walks of life, as I'm sure you'll have discovered.'

The way he said it made it sound almost like a question. I glanced at him but he'd got his usual bland face on and I couldn't decide whether he was being clever. I had to hope that he wouldn't follow too far down that line.

He went on. 'Anyway, this may be the only opportunity for a while, because they'll have us back on normal carrying party duties from tonight.'

'Aren't we supposed to be at rest, back here in reserve?'

'Now there's a neat army euphemism for you – *at rest*. Doesn't it just conjure up a nice image? We officers lounging around drinking whisky and the men taking part in improving exercises or playing cards. What it really means is a minor respite from bullets and shellfire, with a chance to catch up on sleep if we're very lucky. But generally, at night, we have to lug stuff up to the front lines in the dark. Better yet, sometimes we're allowed to have fun putting up new barbed wire in front of the trenches.'

He sounded angry, swishing out with his stick at a clump of dead nettles at the side of the road. That made me think twice – his concern for his men didn't sit with the rest of the information I was collecting. Once again, I was reminded that David Alexander was difficult to fit into a conventional pigeon-hole. 'The men don't look too unhappy with it,' I said, trying to draw him out further, as we turned down a long straight road. Before the war, it must have been lined by tall plane trees. Now there were only short stumps that had been scarred and stripped by howitzer shells.

'True enough. What always amazes me is that they don't resent us officers having more chance to rest. I used to think that was a recipe for a communist uprising until Stephen – my servant, you know – said it was a fair exchange for the fact that we're more likely to get killed.'

He paused, lost in his own musings, which gave me the opportunity to consider the extent of his education. I'd not expected that sort of political insight. Then he turned to me and his face lit up with one of his rare, devil-may-care grins.

'Personally, I'll take danger over boredom every time. Life would be too dull otherwise.'

I was still trying to reconcile that with his quiet, matter-of-fact manner, when the road dipped into a shallow valley and we came into town. It was a place called Bray-sur-Somme, more of a large village really, with a grey stone church and a bunch of solid two-storey houses. One small hotel and a few shop doors were open, but most of the blue shutters were closed up, either against the war or the weather, because the sky was black with cloud.

As we entered the main square, spots of icy rain began to fall. Before we'd even had the chance to button up our greatcoats, the shower thickened into a full-on hail storm.

'Good grief! That's put the lid on exploring. Come on, Scott! Over here.'

We took to our heels, sprinted across the square and ducked into the open door of the Hotel de la Place. It was already crowded inside and while it was only early in the afternoon, the light was going fast under the storm clouds. A girl with flaming red hair and a bored face was putting a taper to the oil-lamps. She waved us towards vacant seats without a word. As we shed our wet coats, Alexander raised one eyebrow.

'Cheerful lassie, isn't she?'

'Maybe just tired of serving foreigners all the time. Someone must be making a fat profit out of us but I'll bet she doesn't get much of it.'

I took a look around the room. It was full of soldiers. Some were finishing a late lunch, smoking and arguing in the midst of bottles and plates, while others, like us, had sought shelter from the weather and were chatting over cups of tea. They were from a range of different battalions and I took the opportunity to study their colours and badges.

'Seen something interesting?' Alexander had been watching me. He was such an easy companion that I wasn't always as wary as I should have been. I scrambled for an explanation.

'Just curious, I guess.' I pondered for a moment. It might be worth trying to blur my tracks by admitting to a minor crime. 'It's a habit of mine. I've kept a journal for the last ten years or so. Not every day, but I like to keep it up to date.'

'You're not alone. Lots of men do write diaries out here, although we're not supposed to, for fear of giving away vital information if they fell into unfriendly hands, I suppose. In practice, nobody really bothers about it, not unless you get too nosey. That could make people uneasy.'

He gave me one of his steady looks that I was beginning to understand was his way of sounding a gentle warning.

Fortunately, at that moment the girl with the Titian hair reappeared. '*Messieurs*, what will you take?' Her English was quick but accented.

Alexander stumbled out his order in schoolroom French. Without thinking, I followed his lead and explained that we would not stay for long, it was just that we had to shelter from the appalling weather. I was rewarded for my efforts by a look of surprise that transformed her sulkiness as she called through to the rear of the hotel.

'A man of parts, indeed!' Alexander said. 'Not only a soldier, but bilingual to boot. How many other talents are hidden under that unruffled exterior? You interest me more and more, Anson Scott. How do you come to speak French like a native?'

I pondered on the answer before deciding on something close to the truth. 'There's no big mystery to that. When I was up in Alaska working on the railroads for a few years, I was teamed up with an old Russian guy. His English was a mite stretched, but I'd been taught some French at school, so in the bad weather, when we'd spend weeks on end snowed up in the woods shut away from the world and we'd only conversation to keep us sane, he took it on himself to educate me.'

I remembered old Viktor blowing smoke from an evil-looking briar pipe in the gloom of a long December afternoon while he pitched one yarn after another, switching back and forth between educated French and coarse English.

A different waitress, older and taller with dark hair, brought tea for Alexander and coffee for me. I suspected she must be the sister of the other girl because they had similar features.

After a polite pause while he allowed me to tackle my coffee, Alexander put down his teacup and fixed me with a look that suggested I'd better keep my wits about me. Much as I liked him, there was no doubt that anybody as smart as him was a real threat to my safety.

'Now, Scott, I did warn you about my inquisitiveness, so I make no apology for it.'

I took another gulp of coffee, buying myself time while I waited to hear what was coming next.

'What I want to know is this. You're clearly a well brought up fellow…' He held up his hand to stop me protesting. 'You may try to hide it, but it's obvious to anyone to see. How on earth did you succeed in getting away to the back of beyond to build railways? I really would like to hear. I've often imagined being able to escape from the norms of civilisation myself but I know I'd never be able to persuade my family that it was reasonable. Do tell me how you managed it.'

He looked at me earnestly, as if he actually wanted an answer. At that time, I was still deceived by his conventionally English exterior and it was hard for me to imagine him kicking against the traces of his upbringing. I thought he was just trying to find out how much of my cover story was true. Still, there was nothing in those bits of my past that was controversial.

'As well as normal drill and gunnery, West Point taught us the basics of army planning and administration, which included how to draw accurately so that we could make military surveys.'

'Lucky you,' Alexander said. 'It certainly sounds more thorough than anything in Britain. I'm ashamed to tell you that our military education is still founded on parade ground discipline and rifle practice.'

Leaving a pile of coins on the table, we shrugged back into our damp coats and I continued my story in the doorway.

'But it didn't take long to discover the army wasn't really for me. Not in peacetime at any rate. No action and too much routine, I guess.'

He nodded as if he understood exactly, while I went on.

'So I quit before boredom got me into trouble. At least with that training, I was able to earn a living of sorts. And that's how I ended up in Alaska. No big deal, really.'

I wasn't about to tell him how I'd only been three years on the railroad before I'd gone back to a very different occupation.

'I'll have to bring Beatrice up to date in my next letter,' he said. 'She's my fiancée, you know, and I think she's already quite intrigued by you.'

He'd taken me by surprise once again, because I was pretty sure that he hadn't mentioned anything about a girl before. In fact, if it wasn't for the letters he was always reading, I couldn't even have guessed that she existed.

'I have a picture of her here somewhere, I think,' Alexander said, rummaging through the depths of his pocketbook. 'Here – it's not a very good likeness, I must say, and it was taken a while ago.'

He handed me a small photograph. It showed a girl standing with her back to a window so that her face was thrown into shadow, making it hard to be sure what she might actually look like.

'Pretty girl,' I said, like you always did whenever someone showed you a photo of their wife or girlfriend.

'I suppose so. I've known her such a long time that I suppose I take her for granted.'

The way he said it, I couldn't decide whether he thought she was a looker or not. Born reporters are supposed to have natural intuition. If that's true, I never was a real newsman because at that moment I had no inkling about the impact the woman in the photo was going to have on the rest of my life. As I gave the picture back, my only thought was that she might be a fair bit younger than Alexander.

A few drops of rain were still splashing in the puddles as we stepped out into the square, but the sky had cleared. Alexander turned and gave me his grin again.

'You'd like Beatrice, I'm sure. We must meet her when we can arrange it. Did I mention that she's nursing out here in France?'

7

That evening started deceptively quiet and civilised. After dinner the mood in the mess was more restrained than the previous night. As Alexander had predicted, we'd been ordered to provide squads to take supplies up to the front line after dark and so most of us weren't drinking too much. I was glad of the calm and after the recent hullabaloo it was good to sit by the fire and read through the newspapers for the previous week. I liked to keep one eye on who was writing what about the war in the British press and we near always got the papers sent out from London in a couple of days. Opposite me Moore was leafing idly through a guide to fox hunting in the English shires. As I was folding back a sheet from *The Times* he put down his book and looked across at me.

'You're a clever cove, Scott. Do you think any of those reports are true? They only ever seem to print good news. Now I know we're always going to beat Jerry, but still…' He was a simple soul, but good-natured, and he looked puzzled by his own doubts.

'Well, I never heard of a war correspondent near the fighting, not out here anyway.' For once, I was telling the absolute truth. 'I guess most of their stuff is based on what they get fed officially, plus a slice of gossip they might overhear by hanging around in the safety of General Staff HQ.'

He thought about that, then nodded and went back to his reading. The company gramophone was playing a quiet piece of Mozart, one of David Alexander's own records, I was pretty sure. Alexander himself was preoccupied on the other side of the room, playing bridge with the Cooper boys and

Dr Vaughan, who was complaining about the unfairness of playing against twins. Close by, Tollman had a table to himself with a game of solitaire laid out in front of him and a bottle of whisky at his elbow. His scarred features were furrowed and it seemed to my surreptitious examination that he was still suffering from the effects of the previous night.

Howerd had returned to his normal obnoxious self more quickly. He was crouched by the window together with Wesley, watching the progress of a pair of cockroaches across the floor.

'There you are, I told you the little one would win,' said Howerd, settling himself into an armchair. 'That's another guinea you owe me, Weasel. You shouldn't bet when you're such a rotten judge of racing form.'

The music came to a close and Tollman gave up on his game, gathered his glass and playing cards and flopped heavily down in the chair next to Howerd.

'Bloody good evening, yesterday, Henry.' He was talking loudly and his voice carried through the mess. 'Wouldn't mind visiting there again soon. The booze could have been better but the food was OK.'

Howerd gave a twitch of his lips and ran the tip of his tongue along the bottom of his moustache, which put me in mind of a lizard catching flies.

'But think about the girls,' he said. 'The red-headed bint was definitely giving you the eye and that Juno of a sister...' He sucked his breath in and wriggled in his chair. 'Both of them looked on for a good gallop to me. We'd be doing them a service to oblige them, don't you think?'

Tollman grunted and emptied his glass while he considered it. 'Separately or together?' he growled.

'Whichever you prefer,' Howerd giggled, which was an unpleasant, high-pitched whinnying noise. He looked over my way with a leer.

'How about you, Scott? Feel like joining us for a few hours of physical jerks with the natives? I'm sure we could persuade the tarts at the hotel to take on all three of us.'

He cocked his head to one side and aimed his nasty stare at me. All of a sudden, it felt like everyone in the room was watching us. I didn't have to be too smart to understand that the entire exchange had been designed to come to this.

'No, thanks.'

I'd never considered myself any bit prudish. In my job, I'd got to spend a fair amount of time in both bars and brothels and I'd known my fair share of girls. But it was easy to see what he was trying to do so I kept it short and matter of fact.

Howerd wasn't going to let me off the hook that easy. 'Oh, I see,' he said, drawing out his vowels knowingly. 'Not quite your cup of tea? Scared your prowess might not match up to us?' He waited for the insult to sink in. 'Or maybe your tastes are – how shall I put it – a little more *classical*?'

I knew I needed to stay out of trouble but it was all I could do not to knock his teeth down his throat. Before I could say anything, a fresh voice intervened.

'I do think that's a bit much, Howerd. I don't know about Scott, but I for one have had enough of hearing the two of you brag about your conquests.'

My rescuer was George Moore, who had set aside his guide to hunting. His young face was stern. 'It's not the sort of behaviour that befits English officers. You should be ashamed, the pair of you.'

Howerd clapped his hands together with glee like a spoilt child. 'Oh dear! Mr Moore doesn't approve of us, Blackie. And I imagined he would be the first to appreciate the joys of female company, judging by the naked ladies he likes to stick up over his bunk. What on earth shall we do with him?'

Tollman didn't reply. He slopped more whisky into his glass

and rested his head back in his chair without saying a word. At that moment, the fire crackled and spat out a shower of glowing sparks. One of them landed on my shin and I leant forward to brush it off my breeches. As I did so, I happened to glance up and so I caught a glimpse of Tollman's face – it must have been hidden from everyone else in the room by the wing of his armchair. His eyes were fixed wide open to show the whites all round and he was staring at Moore, who had buried himself in his reading again, all unsuspecting. In that moment, I began to understand what sort of creature Tollman was, because I'd seen that look before.

A while back, before the war, the paper had sent me to cover the execution of a man who'd picked up a carving knife one morning and butchered the family living in the tenement next door, for no reason anyone had been able to detect. The scrawny runt they led out from the condemned cell shuffled along, head down like he was accepting his fate. But his remorse was a sham. There was just a second before they pulled the bag down over his face when he lifted his head and glared at the row of us witnesses standing there. There was no doubt that if he could have gotten free, he'd have slaughtered all of us in the room as bloodily as he could, before he considered making his escape.

I'd never thought to see that vicious malevolence again, but there it was, five years later and a couple of thousand miles away. The expression on Tollman's twisted face, as he surveyed George Moore that night, brought back such a vivid memory that I let out an involuntary yelp. I did my best to cover it up with a fit of coughing and sat upright again, kidding myself that nobody would have taken notice.

But, of course, he had. He pointed a thick finger at me. 'And there's something about you I don't trust, either, Mr Bloody Yankee Doodle. Nobody can be so damned worthy. What is it that you're trying to hide?'

Suddenly he leapt to his feet, and threw the pack of cards away from him, scattering them wide across the floor. He towered over me, where I was still sitting in my armchair, then bent down so that his mouth was by my ear.

'White as snow you might be, but your sins are a much deeper scarlet than ours.'

I'd no idea what the hell he was getting at, but it was obviously supposed to be significant. Although he'd dropped his voice, the mess had gone silent and his venomous whisper was plenty loud enough for everybody to hear him. He knew that none of them would dare to provoke him. The bridge players were studying their hands carefully, while the others had taken cover behind their news-sheets. He stood up, looked around him for any challenge and belched his contempt into the silence. I stayed silent, trying to work out how much I'd allow myself to tolerate before I hit him.

But right then, I heard a clear voice from behind me, innocently enquiring, 'That was First Isaiah, wasn't it?'

David Alexander.

Tollman spun around away from me, quick as ever. Alexander was smiling all bland and inoffensive as he leant back from the card table.

'I mean, *scarlet sins* and all that. I think I remember being set it as a text at school. But I wouldn't have had you cut out for a parson. It just goes to show that one should never judge by appearances.'

Tollman glowered at him but he couldn't outlast Alexander's wide and innocent gaze. Eventually he growled something undecipherable under his breath and lumbered out of the room, Howerd slithering along close behind him. The normal chatter of the mess returned, someone rewound the gramophone and the bridge players picked up their hands and restarted their game.

I sat for a minute, pretending to read the newspaper until Dr Vaughan left the card players and headed my way

'Unsavoury pairing, aren't they just?' He took the chair next to mine. 'It's a most unedifying habit, seeking your own pleasures in the weaknesses of others. You did well not to rise to the bait there, Mr Scott. There's a lot who would have flared up and found themselves in trouble. Discreet of you, very discreet.'

He gave a series of little nods, his eyelids drooping more and more with each one but just when I was sure he must have fallen asleep, he shook himself awake. 'I'd best be away. But mind yourself with those two. While Howerd's not really dangerous, Tollman's a different beast altogether. I'll tell you what, drop in and see me at the aid post some time. There's always coffee in the pot, and we can have a bit of a chat. Maybe it'll save you a good deal of bother in future.'

He yawned, then waved a limp hand and took himself off, leaving me to consider his warning. In spite of the events of the evening, I wasn't scared by Tollman, not then. I believed I'd met his sort before and their threats had always turned out to be empty bluster. But I was troubled by the evil in the glance I'd seen him throw at Moore. I should have let myself be guided by that instinct.

8

It was a while before I got to take Vaughan up on his invitation. The army had spun us a couple of times through spells in reserve and then stints back at the front, and I'd enough to worry about coping with the hazards of trench warfare, without bothering myself about Tollman or Howerd. That's what I thought, anyway.

My naivety lasted until one wet afternoon after we'd had a salvo of enemy trench mortar rounds land close to our stretch of the line. That early on in 1916 the front was still quiet and we viewed enemy fire as a kind of novelty act, so although I was officially off-duty I took myself off to the front line trenches to see what was going on. George Moore was officer of the day and he was already up on the fire step checking out the line opposite through the usual makeshift periscope. Close by, four men from his platoon had constructed a primitive shelter in the trench bottom, using two waterproof sheets and a length of angle iron. They were brewing up tea in a small brass kettle on top of a pocket spirit stove.

'It's no use – I can't make out where those damned bombs came from,' Moore complained, without looking away from his eyepieces.

There was a surly growl from behind him. 'Makes no bloody difference. One dead German is the same as any other to me.'

Tollman had barged into the trench, dangling a blue-painted crate in one massive hand like it weighed no more than a school dinner pail. He swiped out with his swagger stick at one of the privates, catching him across his shoulders.

70

'Here, you. Bring your weapon and look sharp. You too, Scott. I'll show you something useful.'

The scared look on the soldier's face suggested he'd have preferred an order to charge over the top single-handed, but he hefted his rifle and set off along the trench after the Captain. Once we'd rounded the corner, Tollman smashed open the lid of the crate with his boot and pulled out a grenade, much like one of our normal bombs, and a short steel rod he clipped onto the grenade.

'I'll bet they didn't tell you about these back in training, Mr American. They never bloody do. Here, you,' he tossed the bomb to the soldier. 'Show him how it's done.'

'Yes, sir. Captain Tollman, sir.'

The man looked terrified and his voice quavered. His hands were shaking as he demonstrated fitting the steel rod down his rifle barrel. Tollman stood over him, tapping his stick against the palm of one hand.

'Now give it here. Quickly, man. The whole bloody German Army could have invaded by the time you were ready.' Tollman shoved his stick into a gap in the boards, grabbed the rifle and turned to me.

'In the manual it says to kneel down and rest the butt on the ground because of the kick.'

He looked to see whether I was following him and I nodded. I could see there would be a heck of a recoil.

'But that's a load of tripe. See...'

He yanked it up to his shoulder with no more care than if he was standing at the normal rifle butts, aimed it above the parapet and pulled the trigger. There was a loud bang and the grenade flew up in an arc and out over No Man's Land and exploded on Jerry's lines.

'That's how it's done.' Tollman didn't even trouble to turn his head to me while he picked up another bomb. He loaded and fired that, and then another, before throwing the rifle back to its owner.

'Now bugger off back to your section,' he told the private, who threw a rapid salute and scuttled away. 'I'm off to write up last night's report. You stay here and tidy the rest of this lot away, Mr American.'

Almost before he'd finished speaking, he turned and strode quickly back down the trench like he was late for an appointment. At the time, I didn't think twice about that. I was just glad to see the back of him as I started to pile the remaining grenades back in the crate.

My relief didn't last for long. He'd been gone barely thirty seconds when I heard a succession of thuds in the distance, then a whistling noise overhead that got shriller and louder and louder. The next moment the sky above me was filled with German trench mortar bombs. There was no time to run. I dropped to my knees, hugging the front wall to offer as small a target as possible. Just as well. The heavens fell in with a great crash. The ground bucked and heaved and the trench disappeared in a thick cloud of dust.

When the world stopped moving, my ears were ringing and my sight was blurred by thick, choking smoke. I was undamaged, but just above my head the parapet had been blown away and there was a six foot hole in the back sandbag wall. I was thinking how lucky I'd been when I heard the shouts.

'Bearers! Stretcher-bearers! Quick, now.'

They came from close by. I ran back the way I'd come.

Around the traverse, the fire bay where I'd left Moore and the tea party had taken a direct hit. It had been smashed apart, devastated by a huge crater that was smoking with green fumes and smelled of roasting meat. My boot caught against something metallic. It was the soldiers' little kettle. I bent down and picked it up. It was still hot but amazingly the brass was only slightly dented. Its owners hadn't got off near so light. Curled around the rim of the bomb crater, one body lay like an island in a sea of blood, while the man who'd showed me the rifle grenade drill was alive, just about, with his chest staved in by a four foot pillar of chalky rock. The other two soldiers had plain vanished, atomised by the mortar blasts. All that was left of Moore was a greasy smear of rags plastered on the trench wall in a man-sized outline and a dismembered arm in khaki with a subaltern's shoulder stripe. I had to turn back around the traverse to throw up until my stomach was empty.

When I returned, the fumes had dispersed and I saw that Alexander and his team had arrived. Corporal Keeble was organising a stretcher party to carry the dying man back to the regimental aid post. The dead soldier was already covered over decently with a ground sheet and Alexander was scattering chloride of lime over Moore's pathetic remains. He picked up the severed arm and knelt bareheaded to set it down gently at the side of the dead soldier, murmuring so quiet that I could barely hear:

'Life is real. Life is earnest
And the grave is not its goal.
Dust thou art, to dust returnest...'

He broke off as I got near and turned to me. 'You look pretty ghastly, Scott. Why don't you cut along to the aid post with the bearers and see Vaughan? We'll sort things out up here. It's never nice, I'm afraid, when it's someone you know. You do get accustomed to it after a while, sadly.'

But under his air of calm and competence, it wasn't hard to spot that he was badly shaken up, same as me.

The medical station was located in a blind alley trench off the main communication line. When our sad little procession arrived, Vaughan only lifted the blanket covering the body, took a quick look and waved the stretcher away down the trench with a shake of his head. I was shaping to follow them, but he'd have none of it. Once he'd discovered that I wasn't back on duty for a couple of hours he insisted on showing me around his domain, a large, low-roofed dugout where the mixture of disinfectant and chloroform made a welcome change from the normal trench stink.

'I know it's a bit fragile, especially overhead, but I had to make the choice between space and solidity and I may well need the capacity sometime. I don't trust the butchers that operate at Advanced Dressing Stations. Barely trained, those lads are. Some of them aren't even out of medical school. Our boys'll get a better chance with me here if they need it.'

Looking around, I didn't doubt that. He'd always seemed half asleep whenever I'd encountered him before, but here at the front, he was bright-eyed and alert and the post was impressively kitted out with tidily arranged racks of surgical instruments and the shelves of drug bottles.

'Take a seat. Coffee?'

Without waiting for an answer he filled two mugs from a pot on a stove in one corner and pushed one across his operating table to me.

'Sorry not to offer you anything alcoholic. This'll be much better for you. Cheers.'

I took a gulp and was hard put not to gag. It was the strongest, bitterest stuff I'd ever drunk. When I peered at the mug, the liquid in it was black as tar and about as viscous.

'You'll get used to it, you know. We all do.'

I looked up, thinking that he was talking about his coffee but he was far more serious.

'Death, I mean,' he said. 'Sudden, violent, random death. Even the most sensitive souls get toughened up in the end. Not that

I'd have put you for a shrinking violet. Far from it indeed. You've settled in fast enough, for a man fresh from the wilds of… Alaska, was it?' And he watched me craftily over the rim of his mug.

I thought that maybe I preferred him half asleep like before, so I stayed quiet while I took as big a drink from my mug as I dared. After a moment, I did my best to change his line of thought with a question I had actually wanted to ask him anyway.

'Tell me, Doc, is it normal for someone to sleep with their eyes open?'

'You've seen Tollman's prize turn, have you then? That's why Howerd calls him Blackie, after Alexander told us about the pirate captain Blackbeard, who always slept with his eyes open.'

'And there I was thinking it was because of his sweet nature, or maybe his face. Is that pigment a birth mark of some sort?'

'Now there's a story attached to that, and one worth the telling.'

I tried not to wince as he emptied the other half of his coffee in one swig and then pulled up a folding canvas chair. 'It happened last year, when we hadn't long been out from England. The battalion was holding the line up by Ypres when we were attacked by a whole horde of Prussians. Big fierce devils they were and tough with it. They took the company by surprise just before dawn and for a while it was touch and go whether we'd be overrun but Tollman's platoon was in reserve and he's never been scared of a fight. Soon as he hears the commotion, he gathers together Jack Fox – Corporal Fox as he was then – and a handful of men and rushes them up to the front line. They wade into the scrap full lick and that turns the tide and drives the Prussians out. But just when we're thinking it's all over and done, Jerry lets rip out of the dark with one of his new flame-throwing machines. A horrible thing that poured jets of liquid fire over our boys, until they were screaming and burning and blazing like human torches. Bloody murder, it was.'

He shook his head at the memory. 'They shot the devil carrying the infernal device but not before the entire section had been fried up. I didn't see the fight myself, but I had to look at the boys that were carried back to the aid post, charred and shrivelled black stumps that they were. Only two of that platoon ever got back to service – Tollman and Fox – and you'd not say either of them were exactly unscathed. Fox got promoted for his pains, as well he might. He used to be a good-looking sort of lad, but within a few weeks his hair started falling out, then his eyelashes and eyebrows, and finally he lost all the pigment in his skin. When he was home on sick leave his wife took one look at him and slammed the door in his face. He'd only been back out here for a couple of weeks when a neighbour wrote to tell him that she'd left to set up house with a cousin and never wanted to set eyes on him again. The regiment is all he has left now.'

'And Tollman? What happened to him?' I reckoned I knew the answer.

'He's a different matter altogether. To begin with, we all thought he'd got away with only those scars on his face. Before long I knew his brain had been affected too, when he started sleeping with his eyes wide open, as if he needed to be sure that he'd never be caught unawares again. And then his behaviour changed.'

Vaughan went to pour himself another shot of his poisonous coffee. He gestured towards my mug but I shook my head quickly.

'Tollman had always been a hard man but after his immolation,' he pronounced the word as four separate

76

syllables, 'we're seeing the real bitterness at the heart of him. He strikes out at anyone who dares cross him, accidentally or not, especially if he thinks that they aren't likely to hit back. I think he's driven by reasons that wouldn't make sense to you or me. It's as if that one terrible experience has set off a lust for destruction he can't satisfy.'

He leant forward with his chin resting in his hands, as if he was thinking what to say next.

'Is that safe?' I asked. 'Can't the Colonel keep him in check?'

I waited, but there was no answer. When I looked across at Vaughan, I saw that he had gone to sleep, right there in mid-conversation.

'Doc? Are you all right?'

He opened his eyes and peered blearily at me. 'What? Oh, sorry – I'd gone again, hadn't I?'

He dragged himself to his feet, poured himself another mug of coffee and drank it down in one. Then he took out a silver snuff box and inhaled a pinch of dirty brown powder. When he looked up, his eyes were bright and alert again.

'That's better. Caffeine and nicotine,' he explained. 'Usually works. Now where were we?'

I was fascinated by his antics. A front line medical officer who fell asleep mid-conversation? It seemed like everyone in the Royal Pennines was worthy of some sort of comment in my reports. 'Do you always have trouble staying awake, Doc?'

'You've spotted it, then?' Vaughan sounded faintly surprised. 'I've got this wretched dyssomnia – narcolepsy, the French doctors call it. Damned inconvenient, especially when everyone thinks it's alcohol-induced. I can get by most of the time, with a little pharmacological stimulation every now and then.'

He took out an enormous pipe and filled it with dark

tobacco. Within seconds the post was filled with such dense brown smoke that it made my eyes water.

'You were just telling me about Tollman. Is there anyone who can keep him in hand? What about Alexander?' I asked. 'He seems like a decent enough fellow.'

Vaughan peered at me through the fumes. 'Aye, so he is, so he is. Decent, quiet, well-mannered, David Alexander. ' He drew noisily on his pipe. 'He's a good man, right enough, but don't be too taken in by appearances. In his own way he's at least as tough as Tollman; totally at home when it gets rough and dirty.'

He took another pinch of his snuff, without offering me any. It seemed to buck him up even more.

'But you're an interesting man too, Scott. A born survivor, I would have said, although you do ask a lot of questions for a newcomer. Maybe you should tread a little more careful.'

I was beginning to get used to members of the Royal Pennines being smarter than I'd expected, so I was prepared for him. 'Me? I'm just a straight-talking American who likes decent company, a drink, and a fair fight.'

'Hah! We'll see.'

He snorted his incredulity but I'd said all I was going to and I'd no intention of giving him anything more. I braced myself, gulped down the stuff in my mug and then left him fumigating the aid post. It was only when I was stooping in the doorway that I was struck by a thought that made me stop dead like I'd bashed my forehead on the timber lintel. I'd almost forgotten the evil stare that Tollman had aimed at poor George Moore that night after he'd intervened on my behalf. Now I remembered both that and the speed Tollman had left the front line after he'd fired off the rifle grenades. Was Vaughan right? Had he deliberately stirred the Germans into retaliating? A man of his experience was bound to have known that they wouldn't take his attack lying down. But if so, which of the two of us had he planned to do away with? Moore or me?

That night I added a new line to my notes.

Sometimes, not all our enemies are in the trenches opposite…

9

I thought that by now I'd got acquainted with most of the characters who would impact on my new life. I was wrong. I'd still to meet the last player, the final element in a mixture that would eventually prove lethal to more than one of us.

When we came out of the line again, I was getting more and more concerned about the notebook I was carrying in my pocket. I was very aware if it slipped out of my jacket and someone happened to get a close look at what I'd written – coded or not – I'd be up in front of a court martial pretty quick. Before I'd left to cross the Atlantic, Mac had given me details of three locations in France which could act as mail stations for my stuff, avoiding the military authorities. One of them was only a few miles away, a barbershop close by the station in Amiens. If I could come up with a plausible reason for going there, I could get this first batch of information safely away. Unwittingly, it was David Alexander who provided the perfect opportunity.

'How do you fancy a trip to the seaside, Scott? A civilised jaunt and lunch with a beautiful woman.'

We were in the mess at our farm billets after dinner. Alexander was as calm as usual but for a passing second I wondered exactly what he was proposing. He saw my expression and followed up quickly.

'No, no – nothing like Tollman and Howerd's squalid little adventures. It's just that I've scrounged the opportunity to meet up with my fiancée tomorrow and I thought you might care to come along. She's got a day off and managed to persuade the hospital matron that she can be trusted to her own devices for a few hours. '

'Great. Swell,' I said.

Any chance to explore new territory was fine by me. If I could gather more information about life away from the front, so much the better. Anyway, I was more than a tad curious to see what sort of woman had got herself hitched up to Alexander. Then I had another thought.

'Are you sure I won't be in the way? How long is it since you last met up? I don't want to mooch about playing gooseberry to two lovebirds.'

He smiled with amusement. 'No cause for concern there, I promise. You won't be intruding on any romantic tryst. Anyhow, Bea says she's dying to meet you, so you've got to come along, or I'll really get it in the neck.'

'But where are we going? And how are we supposed to get there?' I guessed the army wouldn't much appreciate it if we weren't back in time.

'I've persuaded Clarry to wangle us a couple of passes for the day. We're due to meet up with Beatrice for lunch. She's working in one of the big hospitals on the coast near to Paris-Plage. That's the seaside bit of Le Touquet and there's a decent restaurant there I used to go to when I was training. As for transport – if worst comes to worst, we can always pick up the train but I had in mind getting into Amiens first thing and then catching a lift in a truck or an ambulance heading north.'

That settled it. This was a heaven-sent opportunity. Ideally, it would have been better if I could have gone on my own, but at least I thought I could trust Alexander. Even if he did spot something, he'd probably not create a fuss. I didn't need any further persuasion.

'Sounds good.' I hesitated for a minute, just to make it sound more natural, although given his disposition to tidiness,

I was pretty sure he'd take the bait. 'Could we stop in town for a quick shave and trim on the way through? I'm getting to feel like a real roughneck and someone said there was a decent barber near the station.'

At sunrise next day we were on our way to Amiens in one of the battalion service wagons. I was all too aware of the thick envelope in the pocket of my greatcoat as we came towards the guard post by the gate. We slowed up and there was a nasty moment when I suspected we were going to be stopped. Then the sergeant on duty saw who was in the wagon. He just stepped back to let us through and saluted. Even so, I spent the rest of the short hop into town looking forward to getting rid of the damn stuff.

It didn't take long to find the barber's – a dim-lit, narrow-fronted place extending back from the street. David took first go in the chair and had his hair cropped by an elderly man who barely spoke more than two words together. Was this the fellow I had to rely on to send my articles safely away? The place was empty otherwise and he was certainly discreet enough. I waited until David was done and had wandered off outside to see if he could possibly find us a ride, at least for part of the road.

'I was recommended to come here by Mister Daniels,' I said as he was working his shaving soap into a lather. His face didn't give anything away, so I went on: 'Do you remember him?'

'That would be Monsieur John Daniels, yes?'

That was a relief. At least I was in the right place, talking to the right man. All I could do now was trust that Mac's confidence in the arrangements was well founded. I took the plunge. 'He said you have another job as a postman. Good for delivering mail.'

He stopped as he was about to lather my face, put down his bowl and brush and held out his hand. I took the packet of papers from my jacket, checked the seal and gave it to him. It disappeared into a pocket on the inside of his white apron, and that was the last I saw of it.

Maybe I should have thought harder about where it was heading and what the articles inside might do. At that stage, I was just relieved to see the back of it.

I hoped the man was as efficient a mailman as he was a barber, because I was all done – shaved and trimmed – in a matter of minutes. As I emerged from the shop, Alexander was heading back my way. He'd got his big smile on his face.

'We're all fixed up. I've found an ambulance chap who's heading for the coast and is happy to take us. He's just over there.'

He was pointing toward the other side of the street, which gave me another nasty turn, because the man waving to me was sitting at the wheel of a small, grey-coloured Ford with red crosses on the back and a painted cartoon badge on the door – it was one of the American Field Service cars that were attached to the French Army. The USA wasn't in the war at that time, but I knew that most of the AFS drivers were volunteers, students from the big colleges on the East Coast. The last thing I needed was to meet up with someone who could ask awkward questions about what I'd been doing before I joined up. I was starting to run through explanations in my mind as the car started towards us, but to my relief, the guy behind the wheel was a cheerful-looking fellow with a neat, short beard who certainly didn't look American. He didn't sound it either.

'*Beau Daurelle, a votre service*. Jump in, *mes amis*. I've got some folk to pick up at Boulogne so I can take you almost all the way to Paris-Plage.'

His English was fluent but accented, and I couldn't place where he might have come from originally. Wherever, I hoped he'd got his papers sorted out. I knew the military police were very hot on picking up on odd characters roaming around behind the front lines and it'd be a pity to be late because of that. As it turned out, whatever documentation he had was pretty effective, and we were waved through all the check points on the outskirts of Amiens. I needn't have worried about the time either; the man knew his bus all right and drove with real zip, using only two speeds – fast and faster. He wasn't disposed to chatter, but spent most of the time singing loudly so that between him and the wind rushing past, conversation with Alexander was impossible also and for the first time that morning, I felt I could relax. I'd thought I should make some mental notes about life in France away from the army – they'd be useful for filling in a spot of local colour as background for my articles. However, while the main road north was busy with trucks, cars and bikes, once we'd turned onto a small lane at a little place called Doullens, the fields stretched away fallow and empty on either side, the lane was quiet and the string of small villages we passed through quieter still. Apart from the crumbling wreck of an old castle, Auxi-le-Chateau looked pretty much the same as Douriez and then Maintenay, all low houses clustered either side of a crossroads. After a while, I found my thoughts drifting away from observations for my writing, while I started to wonder about what sort of girl we were about to meet up with.

More than seventy miles, but less than two hours later Daurelle set us down by a crossroads and stopped singing for long enough to point us in the right direction. He gunned his motor and shot off in a cloud of grit and a snatch of song.

'That's odd,' said Alexander, watching him speed away. 'I could have sworn he said he was going to Boulogne, but that's the road up to Montreuil. He didn't seem like the sort of man to get lost.'

I shrugged. 'At least he's got us here with time to spare.'

The scent of pine sap and ozone told me that we were near the sea and we only had a short walk across a bridge before we came to the coast and then to Paris-Plage. It was a well set up, handsome place, that had obviously been a thriving resort before the war and showed little sign of having gone out of fashion. There were fine brick buildings lining the promenade, the day was bright and clear and even the English Channel was shining an opal green. Early for our rendezvous, we sauntered through the town centre, taking in the sights. If I'd been a tad disappointed by the dullness of the countryside on our journey to the coast, this place more than made up for it. The streets bustled with gleaming motor cars and smartly dressed officers and I was struck by the number of women among the crowds. A few were British nurses but most were smartly turned-out French ladies who strolled in the morning sunshine as if the war was a delusion – if it hadn't been for the persistent grumbling of the guns carrying down the wind, that is. There was even a photographer's studio with a board outside offering special rates for officers, and before I'd had a chance to object Alexander had dragged me inside. He insisted the two of us pose in front of a painted landscape of Roman pillars while an old-time cameraman set up his apparatus and took half a dozen pictures that he promised would be sent on to David via the battalion.

After that, we wandered down the promenade and on along the beach. There were banked-up sand dunes that gave some shelter from the breeze and we sat down to smoke and watch the waves break out to sea. It was hard to believe that the war was going on less than fifty miles away.

'Pleased I bullied you into coming along now, Scott?'

Alexander was sitting cross-legged on the sand, blowing smoke rings up into the breeze. 'You couldn't have missed this, you know. It's such a fine day to be alive.'

He was right about that – it was one of those dazzling silver-blue winter mornings, where the low sun warmed our shoulders and glinted bright off the water. I lay back, crossed my hands behind my head and blew out a plume of smoke that flicked away on the gusting wind. Before I'd had a chance to send another chasing after it, I had to brush away a speck of dirt that had landed on my face. It was followed by another few grains of sand, and another, and then by a miniature avalanche that trickled down the dune and flowed round my shoulders.

'And how do you explain this, gentlemen? Lounging about by the seaside when the world is at war?'

I turned and squinted up against the light. There was a woman poised on top of the ridge, silhouetted against the sky. She was pushing at the sand with her foot so that it cascaded down onto the two of us below. It was impossible to make out details of her face but she was wearing a dark coat that was moulded tight against her body by the sea breeze. And it was quite a body. Even through layers of clothing, I got an instant impression of the curves of her breasts and hips. She launched herself into the air and jumped down the slope, landing at Alexander's side in a flurry of swishing skirts, and a throaty gurgle of amusement.

'Good morning, fair maiden. Well met by sunlight.' Alexander leapt to his feet and smoothed down his jacket, then bowed formally and kissed her on the cheek. He turned to me. 'Mr Anson Scott. As you may have gathered, this is my fiancée, Miss Beatrice Tempest.'

She stepped forward and held out her hand. I was almost too dazed to take it.

On the drive up I'd been wondering what sort of girl would

be a suitable match for Alexander. You came to know men fast in the confines of the trenches and I liked and trusted him as much as anyone I'd ever met. I'd also got to understand that for all he looked like a tall, quiet college professor, underneath that there was a well-concealed unconventional streak, bordering on the reckless at times. Even so, and maybe partly due to the misty picture he'd shown me in Bray, I reckoned that he would've got himself engaged to some mousy, academic girl, who was completely in awe of him.

But what had I encountered now, in the flesh, on a sunlit beach? She was incredible. From that first moment, it was impossible to ignore the fact that Beatrice Tempest was a truly beautiful woman. She had that rare combination of perfect bone structure, flawless complexion and generous physique, so perfect it was almost terrifying.

What was even more disconcerting was that she could easily have been Alexander's sister. She too was tall and the two of them had the same shape of face and the same colouring, although in her case her bone structure was much more classical, and her hair was darker and streaked through with a blue-black sheen. My surprise must have been obvious and she started to laugh. That was the moment it happened. In that tiny fraction of time, with that slant of her eyes and twitch of her lips, her face was transformed beyond mere beauty. Instantly, I was certain of two things.

First, Beatrice Tempest was the most desirable woman I'd ever seen. Second, that I was deep in trouble – worse than the dangers of trench warfare; even worse than the hazards of my real job.

She was still standing with her hand stretched out. 'He really should have warned you, Mr Scott,' she said. 'We're often mistaken for siblings, while actually we're only cousins once removed or something similar. Don't worry about it. The surprise will wear off.'

She was wrong. The surprise would never wear off. And even if I'd not recognised any attraction before, I would have known it the moment she opened her mouth. Her voice was as low pitched as Alexander's also and I defy any red-blooded man not to be stirred by a husky contralto, a sound like silk falling to the floor.

Somehow, I managed to mumble a few commonplace words before the three of us ambled back along the beach towards the promenade. Deliberately, I lagged a little behind Alexander and Beatrice who were chattering away, neat and carefree, while I was trying to work out what had just happened to me. I'd known my share of girls before, but they had always been short-lived affairs with both of us knowing that I'd be moving on soon enough. I had never come across a woman like Beatrice Tempest and she'd knocked me clean off my feet inside two minutes. For a man like me, that was kind of hard to understand, especially when I knew she was already engaged, and engaged to a man who was the closest I'd got to a real friend. I had plenty enough to consider as I kicked along the sand that bright morning.

I was so distracted that I didn't notice how far ahead they were until I had to run to catch up as they made for a narrow building sandwiched between two of the large hotels. Its brick wall was decorated with a mural of a seagull painted with gaudy blue feathers.

'This is La Mouette,' Alexander said. 'I know it's not much to look at but it's the best restaurant in these parts by a country mile. I used to take refuge here for a taste of civilization away from that ghastly training camp down the coast. Just as well we're here early. It's getting busy already.'

We went into an atmosphere of warm, tempting smells – cooking, alcohol and expensive tobacco. The dining room was more than half full but Alexander must have been a familiar face during his spell at Étaples, because he was greeted with enthusiasm by a waiter who looked ancient enough to have fought in the Franco-Prussian war forty years before. He beckoned us to a table by the window, brought drinks and took our orders. On top of my confusion about Beatrice, my sense of unreality was growing by the minute. Here we were, only a matter of hours away from the battalion, enjoying all the luxuries of a civilized and prosperous existence.

'See what I mean, Bea? When he just sits thinking like that, the dead spit of the chappie in the poem? Childe Roland, I mean.'

Beatrice turned and looked me over, her lips compressed together as if she was considering his suggestion seriously, an effect that was undermined by the twinkle in her eyes.

'Something of the questing knight, perhaps?' she said. 'All that dark brooding intensity.'

I was caught between surprise at her boldness and pleasure at the compliment. As she went on, I realised that she was pulling my leg.

'But didn't Roland go off searching the wilderness for his missing sister? Somehow I shouldn't think you came over the sea to track down mislaid relatives.' Her mouth twitched in mischief. I saw that she was much younger than my first impression. 'Anyway, I think that David is very lucky to have found you. If I can't watch over him in person, he needs someone sensible and reliable to contrast with his wilder side. You have realised that, I hope?'

I was downcast. *Sensible* – hardly the most encouraging adjective. Then I damned myself for a fool, because only a fool would be looking for encouragement from another man's fiancée. I scrambled for a reply.

'I'd say it's my good fortune to have found him, Miss Tempest, and the rest of the company too.'

That sounded awkward but it was the best I could come up with.

'Well said, sir, and elegantly too!' she exclaimed, clapping her hands together, before turning to Alexander. 'I do believe that you've found us a fellow Cavalier.'

That made no sense to me and David had to explain. 'Our families are near neighbours in England, so Bea and I were practically brought up together. When we were children, we had a game where we divided the world into either Cavaliers or Roundheads. We and anyone we liked were, naturally, Cavaliers.'

'So in the battalion I guess that would make Howerd a Roundhead?' I said.

'You have it, absolutely.'

'And Tollman is…?'

'The roundest of all Roundheads. The telltale sign being that he takes himself too seriously.'

It sounded like he was about to launch into more detail but before he could get too carried away, lunch arrived. It was a gastronomic extravaganza that gave the lie to wartime rationing and occupied all three of us for a spell. I was just grateful for something to take my mind off Beatrice.

By the time I'd got my nose up from my plate, the room had filled up with every sort of uniform, either British Army khaki, much of it with the red shoulder tabs of headquarters staff, or the horizon-blue jackets of the French Army. Most officers had come in twos and threes together and were obviously from the same units. I couldn't help noticing that some men – both British and French – were partnered by fashionably dressed and made-up women. In those cases, as soon as they arrived, they were quickly ushered away to a discreet area that had been partitioned off from the rest of us diners. Around the edges of the drapes, I could see a man's hand lingering on a silk dress, fingers cupped around the woman's shoulder, holding her close. Alexander noticed me watching.

'Just as well that you came with us, Scott, or Bea and I might have been mistaken for a little dalliance. We'd have been shunted off behind those curtains before you could say—'

Beatrice broke in mock indignation. 'Hardly, David. I can't imagine that anyone would seriously think that we might be interested in that sort of thing. Not your sort of behaviour at all, don't you agree, Mr Scott?'

Her lips curved up in a wicked smile and she gave me a lift of her eyebrows, inviting me to join in her teasing. I was having too much trouble trying to avoid thinking anything about being shut away with her.

'Anyway,' she said, 'I don't feel to have the necessary style to be a companion of convenience.'

It was a downright lie, and any sane man in the world could have told her so.

'You have more natural style than any other female in the room, as well you know, my dear,' Alexander said.

I could feel that he was trying his best but it came out stiff and avuncular, as if paying her compliments wasn't natural to him and somehow it only made me feel uncomfortable. Then he grinned at both of us, which was much truer to his real self.

'However, I promised Scott that we wouldn't cause him any embarrassment, so should you be nursing any salacious intentions, you'll have to curb your instincts and seek entertainment in our surroundings.' He wagged his finger discreetly at the tables around us.

The volume of conversation in the dining room was rising, fuelled by liquor and martial gusto. No one seemed to take any notice of the regulations about avoiding military matters and most of the talk was of the big push coming that was going to break through the German lines. I listened carefully, making mental notes of anything that might be useful.

'They all seem so confident that we're going to win the war this year,' Beatrice said. She too had been eavesdropping on the discussion between two artillery officers behind her. 'They're right, I suppose, although no one seems to think of the price that'll have to be paid. Whenever it happens our wards will be filled to overflowing. And every man killed has his family or friends, even that unlucky man you wrote about last month.' Her face had changed again. She was serious and sad now. I couldn't decide which mood suited her best – either was making my pulse jump.

'Poor old Moore. What a messy way to go.' Alexander sighed heavily. He emptied the wine bottle into our glasses and raised his own in a silent toast. 'At least we know it was quick and final, which is a blessing of some sort. I couldn't bear to be smashed up but not completely finished off – it would be so desperately undignified.'

His pleasant features were looking grim.

'But it's a job that has to be done,' I said. 'And we all volunteered, so I guess we can't cut up about the risks. Like I heard my sergeant say to one of the platoon, "if you can't take a joke you shouldn't have joined up".'

'There you are, Bea. You were absolutely spot on.' Alexander was restored instantly to his normal calm. 'Just when I'm in danger of getting morbid, Scott here drags me back to earth with good old-fashioned horse sense.'

In spite of being knocked over by Beatrice, I'd managed to recover enough of my senses for polite conversation by then. I was just hoping I hadn't been gawping at her too obviously.

'Alexander told me you're a nurse, Miss Tempest. Are you working somewhere nearby? I didn't know they let you ladies get this close to the fighting.'

'It's not as close as I'd like to be,' she said.

Normally I'd have reacted with a cynical laugh at that sort of bravado, but the effect of her deep voice was to make the hairs on my arms tingle and I sat quiet, just listening to her.

'I don't want to spend all my time sitting safely at the coast but I may have to go on attachment to one of the city hospitals before they'll allow me anywhere near a clearing station,' she explained. 'I'm only one of the VADs and the trained nurses still treat us as ignorant underlings.'

'What's a VAD?' There were a hundred and one sets of initials to get used to in the army, but that was a new one on me.

'Voluntary Aid Detachment,' she said. 'You see, there aren't enough qualified nurses to deal with the numbers of casualties out here, or at home come to that. They set up the VADs so that girls who are old enough can volunteer, mainly to do simple tasks in hospitals so that the real nurses are free for the more medical work. You start off in England with some basic training, but when you're old enough, and have enough experience, you can ask to be transferred abroad.'

'Sounds like a smart enough idea,' I said, doing my best to keep her talking.

'Perhaps. In practice, however, it means that all the menial tasks are handed down to us while the professional nurses do the work they consider to be the more important. I've had enough of scrubbing down floors and tables and instruments to last me a lifetime already.'

She held out her hands for inspection. I thought I'd seen less damage on a railroad navvy. Her fingers were red and blotchy with uneven torn nails and raw cuticles.

Alexander took one of her hands in his. 'The penalty of war service, I'm afraid,' he said. 'At home, Scott, she was the

93

belle of local society, famous for her smooth complexion and light touch, but now…' he let the sentence tail off into rueful affection.

'I'll bet you still brighten up the day for the boys on your ward, Miss Tempest.' It was as much as I dared say, and she shot me a look that mixed surprise with warmth.

Alexander topped us all up with wine yet again and lifted his glass to the both of us. 'Here's to the appreciation of beauty.'

He smiled at Beatrice and drank his toast down in one.

'Have you heard anything from home?' she asked him while coffee was brought by yet another antique waiter whose tremor threatened to overturn each cup before he had set it down.

'A couple of letters from Mother. Nothing remarkable.'

Beatrice turned her gaze my way. 'Do you have a large family, Mr Scott? Are they all in America or is there anyone in England?'

'No. I lost both parents a while back.' I'd have preferred to sound more interesting, but it was better if I didn't offer too much opportunity to delve into my background.

'I'm sorry.' It sounded like she meant it. 'We shall have to adopt you as an honorary member of our family then. If you get a few days' leave you could go and stay in Norfolk. Don't you think, David?' she appealed to him. 'After all, it's only a fair exchange for surrendering the comfort of your life back home to fight alongside us.'

I smiled at the pair of them, but inside I was angry with myself. All it took was the admiration of a beautiful woman to make me feel like the worst sort of crook. At that moment, I came close to packing the whole thing in and settling for being a simple soldier.

Alexander shook his finger at me in mock warning. 'You've

no chance now. Once Bea has got you in her sights there's no point in struggling. Better give in gracefully, as I did.'

'I was being serious. A man like Mr Scott should understand the spirit of old rural England. After all, that's what drives most of us to put up with this war.'

She sat back awkwardly, as if feeling that her sincerity had ruffled the social niceties of luncheon. Alexander swept into the conversational breach.

'You are quite right, as ever. We'll have to make sure that Scott sees enough of the real England when he gets the chance. Meanwhile, we need men of his calibre out here.'

'Honestly, David!' She gave him a severe stare. 'I honestly think you are happier playing at war with your band of chums than you ever were back home, and that is not a sensible way to behave.'

She sounded like a strict schoolmarm giving one of her favourite pupils a real dressing down. I was fascinated to watch as Alexander could only sit stammering and blushing, unable to produce a coherent reply. Beatrice's shoulders began to shake and she started to giggle.

'If you could only see yourself, David! It's so rare for me to catch you out,' she spluttered, clasping her hands in front of her face.

She was still chuckling as we left the restaurant and walked back through the fading winter afternoon along the coast road. It wasn't far to her hospital quarters. I'd got over the immediate effect of meeting her by then, so when we got there, I stood back a way, making out that I was admiring the sun setting over the sea, to allow the two of them space for goodbyes.

Their parting lasted only a couple of moments. I'd seen how unemotional he was over lunch, but I was still expecting Alexander to kiss her; give her a hug at least. Instead, he just stood close, placed his hand on her shoulder like she was a favourite niece and talked quietly for a minute or so. I thought that if I'd been engaged to a hot girl like that, it would have taken a crowbar to prise me off her.

Beatrice stepped forward. 'Goodbye, Mr Scott. It has been a great pleasure to meet you at last. I'm so relieved to find that David has a real friend out here.'

She held out her hand, and I couldn't stop myself holding on for a while longer than necessary. Even then, I didn't want to let her go.

10

The fine weather didn't last. Within a week of being sent back to the front line, we were hit with torrential rain so that before long the trenches were awash and floating with every manner of trash. In places, we were paddling waist-deep so that everybody was sodden, cold and bad tempered. I even heard Alexander grumble once, although in his case I reckoned that was mainly because he couldn't keep his uniform clean. Only the Cooper boys were happy, after Tim had joined us in C Company, transferred across to replace Moore. There were some advantages, however. The Germans must have been in the same state, because there wasn't much artillery or sniper fire and we didn't lose any more men.

The problem for me was that I'd got nowhere to write down my notes except under cover in the dugout. We'd kept it dry with sandbags at the top of the steps, so anyone who could think of an excuse crammed in there to take shelter, which meant that I'd never got any privacy. After a while I remembered what Alexander had said concerning diaries and figured that my best plan would be to be brazen. Some folks did keep their own journals, even when it was against army rules, so it'd create less suspicion if I just got on with it openly, rather than trying to hide it away. Actually, with the weather being so foul there was little enough to record, and I was beginning to doubt whether I'd have anything worth writing down. How dumb could I have been?

The first hint of danger came from a source I should have spotted already as a possible problem – the mail drop. Every morning, come rain or shine, whether we were in the trenches or out in billets, the boys could expect to get a message within a couple of days after their loving wife or mother or daughter had handed it in to the sorting office in Liverpool or London or Glasgow. It was an impressive feat of organisation, which I'd noted for future reference. When we were out in billets, the mail got dumped daily on the mess table and generally it had all been collected in a couple of minutes. I never bothered to look at it; there was nobody going to write to me.

One evening, however, I noticed there was a solitary letter still left over at dinner time. I might not have taken any note if it hadn't been for Henry Howerd hovering around looking as shifty as a cross-eyed dog. Something was obviously attracting his attention, which got me interested, so I wandered over to take a closer check.

'I think it's a letter for you, Scott. How unusual.'

Howerd shuffled closer so he could watch. He was correct. The square brown envelope was beat up and frayed at the edges but it was clearly addressed on a type-written label: ANSON SCOTT, ROYAL PENNINE REGIMENT. It had been mailed from England and there was no return address, but I was relieved to see that the line of communication we'd set up was working. When I picked it up, the envelope had a ragged tear across one corner – it might have been just possible for someone devious to have sneaked a look inside.

'Post forwarded on from home, old boy? Employers finally found out where you've run off to with the annual takings?' Hidden under the usual insults, Howerd was fishing for information and both of us knew it.

'No. Probably my aunt.' He couldn't know all my aunts had died in the nineteenth century.

'Unusual for a lady to use a typewriter. How quaint.'

Howerd was nobody's fool. I could feel his eyes on my back as I took myself off to a quiet corner of the mess where I could open the letter and read through it in peace. It was typed on plain paper and the text itself was innocent enough but hidden in a mass of platitudes were a couple of paragraphs that contained the real essence:

I hope you're keeping out of danger over there. Remember we are all thinking about you back here, although we're not worried about you. You are no doubt taking the opportunity to settle in well in the army and learn everything you can. How fascinating to hear that you can even get a haircut in Amiens; it's good to find out that your standards haven't dropped.

That was an obscure way of telling me that they were pleased with the stuff I'd sent out already. I took a glance at the pages of new material in my notebook – I'd need to get that on its way soon. As I put both the letter and notebook away in my inner tunic pocket, I thought I caught sight of a flicker of movement in the doorway but when I looked up there was nobody there.

Maybe I'd have been more wary if it hadn't been for an unexpected announcement from Colonel Ireland at battalion briefing the following morning.

'Gentlemen. As you know, this section of the front is normally fairly quiet. That is about to change. Need to shake things up. Yesterday, orders direct from headquarters. Been selected to plan and execute a major raid on the enemy trenches in company strength.'

While the room was still buzzing, he handed over to Foster, the battalion intelligence officer, who went on to explain the plan. The idea was that we'd cross No Man's Land under cover of a sharp artillery bombardment, break into Jerry's front line and take as many prisoners as possible, then destroy the dugouts and defences before retreating to safety.

'C Company will do it, of course.' Inevitably Tollman was first to speak, even before Foster had a chance to draw breath.

'We're up to full strength and we've got the best record for aggressive patrolling. It must be us.'

There were a few objections shouted out but Foster silenced everybody.

'The Colonel and his staff have already discussed this and made a decision. We agree with Captain Tollman – C Company, it shall be. I have all the details ready to hand.'

No one in the company made any objection. In later years, this sort of surprise attack was all too common and came to be little more than a game of Russian roulette for everyone involved. This first occasion however, we were all pretty excited by the prospect.

'Boot polish on everybody's face and no shiny badges. Weapons are clubs, knives and bombs only. No rifles.' Captain Tollman was giving out instructions in the mess to all of us company officers the afternoon before we were due to return to the front line to launch our raid. 'Officers can take their revolvers if they have to but I don't want to hear a single shot fired except as a last resort. Any damn fool who gets trigger happy and alerts Jerry answers directly to me.' He stared in my direction, making his feelings obvious. 'In fact, I think that we'll leave you out of this one, Mr American. We don't need someone wet behind the ears arsing about and buggering up the whole business.'

I wasn't prepared to take that sort of provocation lying down and was about to protest when a finger jabbed me sharply in the ribs and stopped me short before I could open my mouth.

'I quite understand the logic.' It was David Alexander, who had been standing behind me. 'But won't we need all the officers we have once we're out there in the dark?'

Tollman glared at him for daring to interfere but Alexander only looked him straight back, as helpful and courteous as ever.

'All right then.' He was grudging. 'He comes with us, but he stays up top out of harm's way, to keep guard over the way out. Even he can't bugger that up.'

The start of that first raid went off like clockwork. We would have done a war party of Apaches proud when we assembled in one of the reserve trenches, waiting for the covering artillery shoot to begin. Our faces were painted up with boot polish or burnt cork, everyone had swapped their hats for dark woollen caps and the variety of weapons we carried would have satisfied the most murderous savage. On my count, clubs studded with nails, jagged knives and sharpened spades were favourites, together with the Mills bombs that bulged in everybody's pockets. I wasn't surprised at all to see Tollman swishing his leather-coated stick around, but David Alexander's choice of weapon was more unexpected. At first sight, he seemed to be unarmed but then I realised that he was wearing a nasty-looking set of brass knuckles on either hand.

'No time for sporting gestures tonight,' he said. 'It'll be close-quarter work and messy with it, so if I do have to hit anyone, I don't want him getting up again in a hurry.'

I thought of Vaughan telling me that Alexander was tough – it was looking like the doctor was a good judge of character. As for me, I was the only man carrying a pistol, or rather two pistols, one on either side of my belt, because Alexander had handed me his to wear as well as my own. Much as I disliked those heavy Webleys, it seemed to me it might be useful to have some extra firepower to cover for unexpected eventualities. Tollman was studying his watch.

'Everybody ready. Get those ladders up,' he growled. I heard the word get passed along the trench. I slicked the safety catches of the revolvers to off.

There was a roar that split the night apart as the gunners

started their barrage bang on cue. Immediately, two of our lads rushed out into No Man's Land. Their job was to clear a pathway through the enemy wire for the rest of us while the artillery was building to a crescendo.

'Now,' Tollman yelled. 'Get going!'

The whole company – all hundred of us – lit out across into the open. It was messy going, with the rain having churned up the ground to mud, so we were slipping and slopping every which way, but for once, we'd got it timed dead on. The field guns stopped at the exact moment we threw our ladders down into the enemy front line and we caught the Germans cold, sheltering down in their dugouts.

The company split into two groups, with Tollman leading his platoons one way and Alexander taking his lot the other, leaving me on my own. I was feeling very vulnerable, out there in the open by the top of the ladders, and I crouched low on the sandbags, head down to keep the drizzle out of my eyes. I couldn't see much down in those trenches but it was easy to follow how they were getting on by the shouts of alarm and intermittent rifle shots, and then the thud of our Mills bombs exploding down in the dugouts. I kept a close eye on the luminous face of my wristwatch – ten minutes was all the time we had reckoned before the defence would get organised. After that, we'd have a hot time getting back safe to our own trenches.

There were still a couple of minutes in hand when I heard the drumming of boots down in the trench and Alexander's men rushed back and threw themselves up the ladders, pushing and shoving a handful of dazed-looking prisoners along with them.

Alexander himself was the last man out. He paused at my side, breathing hard. 'That's all of us. Only one lad down. Dead. Head shot. Any sign of Tollman yet?'

I shook my head. He looked at his own watch.

'Right. We're away. Don't linger too long.' And he clapped me on the shoulder and vanished into the darkness.

He was correct. It was more than time we got clear. Still, there was no sign of Tollman and the rest of the company. The intensity of rifle fire was increasing and I could hear more and more of the deep explosions of German bombs. Big trouble was brewing down there. Which also meant that I'd no choice but to stay put. I might have been left behind as the rearguard, but I was resolved to be a damn good rearguard. The luminous minute hand on my watch clicked on again – we were cutting it fine. At last, a crowd of our boys rushed up to the ladders, scrambled up them and took to their heels into the night. Quick as I could, I started to throw the ladders down into the trench so as the Germans couldn't chase us out, but even as I started on the last one, I stopped short. There was still one man missing. Where was Tollman?

I couldn't possibly have missed him, of all people. That meant he was still down there somewhere. I couldn't make my own getaway. I had to be sure either that he'd got clear or that he wasn't going to make it. The trench was way too deep for him to climb out on his own and I had to give him a chance. I let the final ladder drop back into position, took out both revolvers and laid them out on the parapet next to me, one on either hand. Then I knelt on the top sandbags and peered down into the gloom. Suddenly it had gone awful quiet.

I was beginning to get seriously worried when I heard a volley of shots close by. Next moment, I caught sight of the Captain, hurtling along the trench towards the ladder as if the hounds of hell were after him, and with good cause. Round a corner came a pack of German soldiers with rifles and bayonets, pounding along and baying for blood. I watched one of them stop and hurl a hand grenade, throwing it overarm like a baseball outfielder. It flew over Tollman's head and exploded just far enough in front to miss him, but it slowed him up a touch. They were gaining fast. I didn't like shooting unsuspecting men at close range but there was no choice. I grabbed hold of the two Webleys, jumped up on top of the parapet with a revolver in each hand and gave them all twelve bullets at close range. They hadn't been looking for anyone else and the last thing they were expecting was a rain of heavy bullets from above. Half of them dropped before they knew I was even there, and the rest dived into the shelter of a dugout. I figured that should have given Tollman the few precious seconds he needed to climb the ladder and get clear so I threw down the empty revolvers and turned away, expecting to see him high-tailing it across No Man's Land. But he wasn't there. There was no sign of him anywhere.

'Here, you stupid bastard. Quick!'

I ran back to the trench. Tollman was still down there but the remaining ladder had gone. It must have been blown apart by the last grenade. He was trapped by the eight-foot sheer side of the trench like a bear in a pit. There was no time to think. I flung myself flat across the sand bags, and reached down towards him.

'Take my hand. Jump for it.'

A man with his instincts didn't need any encouragement to snatch at the one chance for survival. He shoved his stick into his belt and leapt up to grab hold of my wrist. All of his bulk was swinging from my right arm while his boots scrabbled for purchase on the boards and I knew straight off that I was in trouble. He was too heavy for me. It was all I could do just to hold him with my rain-slicked hand – there was no way that I'd be able to haul him up. What was I supposed to do?

Another stick grenade came spinning up through the air. It exploded just beyond us, showering me with bits of metal and stone. The Germans had got wise to the fact that there was only the one of me up there and they were back in full cry. I gritted my teeth and held on. I'd been posted as rearguard and that was my job – come hellfire or damnation, there was no way I was going to let go of him now. But the strain was too great. Slowly I was being pulled down over the edge of the trench. In another second both of us would fall back into the German front line, where we'd be slaughtered.

Suddenly, someone threw themselves down next to me and another pair of hands grabbed a hold of Tollman's wrist. I glanced sideways. Even under layers of black cork, Fox was unmistakeable. I should have known that he'd never have abandoned anyone from his company. Between the two of us, we started to pull Tollman up. We weren't clear yet. A bullet cracked past my ear. The Germans were closing in fast. With one final back-breaking heave we hauled him out, the three of us sprawling in a heap in the mud. At that vital moment, a handful of men rushed up out of the darkness and pulled us to our feet while they hurled their Mills bombs into the German trench.

'Well done, Scott. Let's go.'

It was David Alexander. He'd spotted the imminent disaster and led some of his own platoon back to cover our escape. They were only just in time. Those few bombs kept Jerry heads down for long enough for us to sprint back across No Man's Land, yelling the password for the night as we leapt over our own parapet bags. Multi-coloured flares burst into the sky from the German side and their machine guns opened up all along the line but they were too late. We'd got home clear.

Back in the shelter of the reserve trenches, I leaned against the wall to catch my breath. Even Sergeant Fox was panting but he gave me a small nod of approval, which I figured was worth more than any medal I'd ever be awarded. Alexander was doubled over, hands on knees, wheezing loudly. He must have covered twice as much ground as the rest of us but he'd got his huge buccaneer's smile on his face, even while he gasped.

'Hell's teeth, Scott... thought you must've got a Lewis gun there... Never heard anyone shoot that fast. Got you out of a tight spot there, Tollman.'

But the Captain, who had been sitting on the fire step while he wiped a mess of blood and hair from his swagger stick, stood and lumbered off without a word. Alexander straightened up and made a wry face at his departing back.

'Sorry, Scott. Graciousness has never been one of his more obvious virtues. You weren't seriously expecting thanks, I hope. No matter. Here. I've a present for you – something I lifted off a peg in one of the dugouts over there.'

I'd not noticed it before but he was holding out a German webbing belt with a wooden holster attached to it. Inside it was a Mauser automatic, a real beauty that held a twelve-shot magazine and was supposed to be the best handgun anyone had ever made. It was a generous gift and timely given that I'd left both the Webleys out in No Man's Land. I carried that pistol through the rest of the war and a fair few of the years since, but I never fired it or even cleaned it without being reminded of him.

That was the end of the raid, which we judged to have been a striking success all round and a good excuse for a party when we were back in billets. We'd shown Jerry he wasn't going to get things all his own way and the Colonel was very happy with us, not only because of the prisoners we'd brought back, but because David had also had the presence of mind to grab hold of a bunch of German maps in one of the dugouts. From my own standpoint, I felt I'd proved a point to Tollman. Not that I expected any gratitude for saving his hide. But because he always picked on soft targets, once he saw I could take care of myself, maybe he would go looking for easier prey. I ought to have had more sense. Tollman would never let up on anyone he considered to have crossed him. I should have left him for dead. God knows, it might have saved us all a heap of misery.

11

We were piggyback racing in the darkness.

'Come on, Tom. Faster!' Tim Cooper was screaming. 'They're catching us.'

It was a close-run thing, but he was right. The twins had been out yards in front, but the gap was closing.

'Go on, Blackie. We're going to win.' Howerd was beating at Tollman's shoulders like a real racehorse jockey as they lurched across the square in hot pursuit.

'No more, Anson. No more.'

David Alexander was chuckling too much to keep a grip round my shoulders. He slid off and slumped onto the cobbles and I came to a panting halt, hands resting on my knees, trying to catch my breath. David had been right; so far the evening had been a real hoot and I'd not had so much fun for many months. Toting David on my back in a mad piggyback race across town had made me laugh longer and louder than I could remember and although the designated winning post was in sight – the town horse trough – I was grateful to give in and watch the Cooper boys just get home in front of Tollman and Howerd by a whisker.

'Victory!' Tim shouted as Tom's knees buckled under him and the pair of them rolled to the ground, while Tollman dropped Howerd into the horse trough without a word. Sadly, it was empty, or I'd have laughed even harder.

To start with I'd had my reservations when this evening's outing was suggested. It was a reward for the success of our raid. Colonel Ireland had a relative working with the top brass up at HQ near the coast, who let us know that the maps we'd filched from the German lines had turned out to be particularly valuable. They were so pleased that the entire company was given a pass for the evening – the men to the estaminets in Bray, while we officers had commandeered the battalion transport truck and gone further afield into Amiens for a dinner at one of the hotels there. I wasn't sure how much I'd enjoy hours spent in the company of Tollman and Howerd, but I couldn't let the others go without me, so there were six of us who sat down to work our way through generous steaks and a skinful of red wine. By the time we'd finished, we were mostly half-cut and it'd seemed like a real fine idea when Tim Cooper suggested we pair up for a piggyback race from one side of town to the other and back.

Once we had all recovered from the race, we set off in search of a bar that might still be open. For the first time in weeks, the sky was clear and dry, and in the blackout the stars were clear as I'd ever seen. We weren't the only folk taking advantage of the fine night. In the gloom, it seemed like the place was teeming with small groups of British and French officers all hell-bent on having a good time for a few hours, and we weren't the least sober by a mile. And where there are soldiers with money to throw around, I guess you'll always find girls willing to collect some of that money. Within fifty yards of the main square, the first of them flitted out of a side alley, sidled up to Tim Cooper and linked her arm through his.

'Hello, sir. A good evening,' she said, in passable English. 'I can walk with you?'

He looked at her, very surprised for a moment. 'I suppose so, miss – I mean, mademoiselle.'

It seemed that Tom was about to say something to his brother, but before he could, he also had a girl by his side, giving him the eye. I dropped David a wink, and watched the

Cooper boys trying to decide whether they should be worried by these unexpected attachments, or be proud to bask in their newfound attraction to women. I just hoped that they weren't so naïve as to think this was the start of a great emotional story, rather than a one-night arrangement, but both their companions were young and pretty, at least as far as I could judge in the half light. We sauntered on a-ways and in a matter of moments, we were the centre of attention for half the female population of Amiens, or so it seemed. Even Tollman had a woman hanging off either arm, while I'd acquired the company of a black-eyed, dark-haired girl who stuck even closer when she found I could talk to her in French. The only one of us who wasn't similarly encumbered was David Alexander. I thought that in some well-practised way they must be able to sense that he was already spoken for.

I became aware that we weren't sauntering along aimlessly any more – the girls were steering us away from the main network of streets.

'Where are we going?' Tim asked.

'This way, sir. This way,' his girl said. 'To our house. We are very nice. We show you a *bon temps*. A very *bon temps*.'

Tim turned around to the rest of us. He was holding her hand, and I suspected he'd never been that close to a woman before, outside of his dreams. He looked eager and excited.

'Why shouldn't we?' he said. 'You never know what could happen to any of us tomorrow.'

'That's the spirit,' Howerd encouraged him. 'Get some experience in the ways of the world, lad. Why not, indeed?'

Tom Cooper looked much less keen. 'But don't you think these girls are...' He was reluctant to finish, but Tollman stepped in for him.

'Bloody well hope they are tarts,' he grunted. 'Bloody waste of time otherwise.'

110

'Is the place OK – clean and all that?' I asked my girl quietly, in French. 'It'll be important for the youngsters, for their first time, you understand?'

'Yes,' she said. 'And those are good girls. They will be careful with your young friends.'

We turned down a narrow alley and stopped at the front door of a tall house whose windows were all covered with blackout blinds. There was no red or blue light, and no sign of it being an officially regulated brothel, but there was no doubt in my mind about its function. Nor was there in Tom Cooper's either.

'I don't think this is such a good idea,' he said, detaching himself from the girl on his arm. 'Maybe we should get back.'

I don't think Tim even heard him. He'd got his arm around his girl and they were giggling together. Howerd pushed open the door.

'Come on. Let's get to it. Don't hang around out there.'

He and Tollman went in with the women in tow and Tim close behind. David Alexander, Tom and I were left in the street. I wasn't reluctant to get further acquainted with my girl – it had been a long while since I'd had a woman – but I could see they were troubled.

'This probably isn't for me, either,' David said. 'I'll go back with you, Tom, and then we can send the transport back to wait for the others.'

'But Tim's in there. There's only Tollman and Howerd. He could be...' Cooper started. His face was earnest and it was hard to know whether he was worried about his brother's safety or his loss of innocence.

'It's all right. I'll stick around in there and make sure he doesn't get into too much trouble,' I said.

They both looked relieved as they turned and made their way out of the alley. I turned the door handle and entered.

Inside, the place wasn't decked out like some of the establishments I'd seen in big cities. It looked more like a conventional front parlour than a gaudy brothel, and the old lady sitting in the armchair reminded me more of somebody's great-aunt than a Madame running a house of ill repute. There was no sign of the others, and I guessed that they had already been led away up the staircase to private rooms beyond.

'You are ready?' The girl I'd been talking to was waiting at the bottom of the stair. She came close and kissed me, once a chaste kiss on the cheek, and then a kiss on the lips that was anything other than innocent. She was wearing perfume, a scent of violets that was somehow familiar. It should have been erotic, the final touch to her allure. Instead it doused my lust completely. It was the same perfume as Beatrice Tempest used. At the memory, all my pent-up desire was gone in an instant.

I stepped back from her. 'I am truly very sorry, mademoiselle, but I shall have to decline for this evening.' I hoped it sounded less stilted in French than it would have in English, and hurried on to explain. 'It's not anything about you. Only a memory of a lady.'

Both she and the old lady were starting to look angry, but their expressions changed when I added:

'But you have already been most pleasant company, and I would, naturally, like to recognise the sacrifice of your time.' I produced some bills from my wallet and tucked them behind an ornate clock on the mantleshelf. 'I hope that will also cover my young friend's expenses.' It would be better for Tim if he didn't have to produce his money to pay for his first real experience. 'May I wait here for him?'

Madame nodded happily and I sat down on a settee opposite her, while my rejected consort gave me a wave of her hand and disappeared into a back room. We talked about the sadness of the war, and the needs of young men who are far from home, and whether the world would ever return to normal when it was all over.

I'd suspected I wouldn't have to wait too long for Tim, and sure enough, after half an hour, he came clattering down the stairs, a little dishevelled, but looking extremely pleased with himself. I was touched to see that he remembered to thank Madame before we left – in those situations good manners always help keep everyone smiling. Unfortunately, I was pretty sure that Tollman and Howerd wouldn't remember that, if they'd ever known.

Outside, Tim didn't say a word, but trotted along beside me, whistling snatches of songs to the night. He certainly didn't seem to have suffered any regrets from his evening, whatever his twin's reservations. As we made our way back to the main square, I was glad of his staying silent, so that I could mull over a couple of things that were bothering me. The first was that I was almost certain someone was following us. As soon as we'd left the brothel, there seemed to be an echo of our footsteps down the narrow streets that persisted for a beat too long, and when I looked around quickly, I caught a glimpse of a shadowy figure making a sudden turn into a doorway. I'd been very careful to cover my tracks, so who might be keeping a watch on me, and why?

The second, and equally as concerning, had been my reaction to Beatrice's perfume. If just the scent of her could turn me away from a romp with a handsome and willing French girl, I was in more trouble than I wanted to admit.

12

Should I have let Tollman die in the German trenches on the night of our raid?

That was the question I started to ask myself for real after we got our first real glimpse of his nature. It happened in March, when winter really came to the trenches. The rain had kept up following the raid, and we lived through days of continuous grey drizzle, slopping around in the dirt and rain and flooded trenches and losing more men to trench fever or foot rot than shellfire and mortar bombs. I continued to make my own notes and tried not to think about Beatrice Tempest.

The sole break from soggy monotony was our night patrols. Whatever the weather, we went out in pairs after dark to prowl around No Man's Land, checking our own wire or creeping close to the enemy to pick up any signs of unusual activity. It was dangerous but it was our only break from the misery and damp below ground, and soldiers hate boredom almost more than anything. So when we started off patrolling it was an almost welcome diversion, a game that wasn't too risky providing we were sensible.

Within a few weeks, however we had to face up at last to the certainty that Tollman was playing to different rules than the rest of us. And that the name of his game was murder.

The snow started one evening when Alexander and I were finishing off a pot of coffee in the fug of the company dugout. He'd just come in from checking the state of the front line, while I was about to go out on duty. The mail had been delivered that afternoon and I'd had another letter.

Your uncle says to tell you he got your latest letter. It was real informative, he opined, although he was disinclined to believe that everything could be just as straightforward as you make out.

It was always a relief to hear that another package had got through to MacManus. I'd had the occasional nightmare where my envelopes were still sitting at the barbershop, waiting to be found by some inquisitive busybody and handed over to the military police.

I'm going to show your letters to our neighbour Mr Daniels, who I'm sure will find them most enlightening, even if he'll likely find them a bit different to what he's been expecting. Do keep writing, though.

I'd been asking myself how Mac would take to my articles. I knew they weren't what he'd anticipated, maybe not what he wanted, but I could only write as I found, and I was painting an honest account of life in the Royal Pennines. It sounded as if that was still OK, and he was still planning on publishing them. Even so, and not for the first time, I hoped that he wasn't going to do something stupid. Even with all the names and locations altered, if he acted immediately, it'd be way too obvious that it had come from somebody right up in the front line, which meant that the British Army would spare no pains to dig me out.

'You're looking pensive, Scott,' Alexander said. 'Nothing too troublesome back home, I hope?'

'No. Nothing important.' *At least, I hope not*, I added mentally.

'By the way, I've been meaning to ask you something ever since our raid,' Alexander said. 'Where the devil did you learn to shoot like that? Something else they taught you at West Point?'

'No. That was Viktor, my old partner; the man who taught me French. He'd been with the army…' I added hastily, 'the Russian Army, that is, years back, until he had to leave town in a hurry. Some sort of political thing, I think. Anyway, he'd spent a while hiding out in a travelling circus, performing a trick shot act.'

'That's quite a tale. Like something from one of Tim Cooper's books, indeed.'

It was a good story, and also had the merit of being largely true. 'Anyway, in our quiet moments I got him to teach me some of his tricks. Seemed as if they might be useful sometime.'

I remembered Viktor nodding approval as he watched me blowing lumps off a dead tree stump with his pair of old Navy Colts.

'Good for you,' Alexander said. 'It certainly came in handy that night.'

He went back to his reading. He was occupied with a brochure he'd been sent by one of the swanky London stores that was doing a good sideline in peddling handy devices for the boys at the front. Suddenly, he looked up.

'Listen to this, Anson: "Whether on safari or in the front line, this is the indispensable luxury for you. Why compromise on comfort? With our full size, fully waterproofed, canvas folding bath, you can relax in the one of the great joys of civilised living, whatever the location."'

He threw down the mail order catalogue onto the table. 'What do you think of that? There'd be plenty enough space for a folding bath back at the farm.'

If it had been anyone else I'd have known they were joking but Alexander was the only real fighting man I'd ever met who took much care of his appearance. I reckon the only aspect of the war he ever groused about was the lack of soap and hot water. And he'd been lucky enough, or clever enough, to have been allocated a room to himself in one of the outlying cottages of our billets, so I could see that he might have the opportunity to indulge himself.

He was obviously giving the prospect some serious consideration. 'D'you suppose that we'd be able to get enough hot water?'

I couldn't think why he was asking me, but he wasn't, of course. I'd just got so used to the continual presence of Stephen Oliver – the young blond soldier who doubled as Alexander's servant – that I'd almost forgotten he was cooking supper on a spirit stove in a niche at one corner of the dugout.

'I'm sure I'd be able to manage it, Mr David,' Oliver said, 'if that's what you wanted. I could ask one of the cooks to siphon off from one of their boilers.'

'Brilliant. What would I do without you? All settled then. I'm going to order one of these contraptions right away.'

I was still grinning at his enthusiasm as I picked up my cap and buttoned my coat at the top of the dugout steps. Outside, the trench was steeped in a yellow-grey light, the wind had shifted around to blow straight down from the north and there was a bite in the air that was kind of familiar. I stuck my head back around the sacking curtain over the doorway and called down to Alexander.

'Looks like the weather's on the change again. If I was still up in Alaska, I'd wager there's snow on the way, and a whole pile of it too.'

'Excellent. Let's hope you're right. Anything would be preferable to this miserable rain.'

I hadn't lost my nose for climate and Alexander wasn't disappointed. By the middle of the evening flurries of white

117

flakes were falling over the trenches and blowing under the blackout curtain at the top of the steps. When I stamped around the line at midnight it was impossible to see more than three feet in front and I only found the dugout entrance again by groping along the trench wall until I fell through the doorway. The wind subsided before daybreak but by then the trenches were banked two feet deep and trampled into ice in parts so that climbing up onto the fire step called for real acrobatic skill.

When I looked out to the east just after dawn, however, the view was well worth the effort. The rising sun was glistening off clean folds of white in No Man's Land where the morning before there had been piles of trash and shell craters and thickets of barbed wire. It was an amazing transformation. But that wasn't the whole picture. While I stood and admired the scenery, I realised that something else strange had occurred. I was accustomed to a background of gunfire at all hours of day and night, either ours or the enemy's, but now there had been no sound at all for several minutes. The utter quiet over the gleaming snow made me suddenly feel as if I'd been swept back in time and I was up in the North again, on one of those crisp, sharp Arctic days.

Alexander forged his way along the trench, followed by Corporal Keeble and Oliver. He climbed up to join me.

'So even war can be beautiful,' he said, looking through his periscope. 'It almost reaffirms one's faith in nature.'

The peace was disturbed by a distant throbbing sound. Thousands of feet above us, three tiny bright shapes glinted in the rays of the rising sun and the drone of aircraft engines buzzed louder as they passed overhead and on into enemy territory.

'They won't spot much today, not unless the gunners are bloody stupid,' Corporal Keeble muttered from down in the trench. He was sitting on a groundsheet, filling his pipe.

'Why not?' I hadn't stopped to work out why the artillery had gone quiet.

'Stands to reason, sir. The guns never want to give their position away, neither ours nor theirs, because if they do, then they're asking to get plastered by counter-battery fire.'

Stephen Oliver joined in. 'But why would it give their position away if they open fire today, Corp?'

I'd been just about to ask the same question and was glad I hadn't needed to look dumb.

'If you ever get the chance to watch them gunners in action, you'll see that every time they fire there's a bloody great flash of light comes out the muzzle of the gun, and that flash is red hot gas that clears a nice dark patch in the snow for fifteen feet in front on a day like today. Sends a clear signal up yonder.' Keeble jabbed with the stem of his pipe. '"Look at me! Here I am, a nasty big bugger of a howitzer!" So then the airman signals down to the ground, and before you know what's happening, whizz, bang, crash. No more field gunners.'

'Quite right, Bill, quite right. We shan't have to worry about shellfire today, which makes for a pleasant change,' said Alexander. 'But I'm sure their snipers will still be at work, so we had best keep warm and watchful.'

The obvious task of the day consisted of clearing the trench and dugouts and it turned out to be a surprisingly tricky job. The drifts had raised the floor level so much that every time we tried to chuck snow over the parapet, our shovels must have showed clearly above the sandbags. The Germans weren't likely to miss that opportunity and pretty soon most of us were nursing stinging hands from the impact of machine gun bullets on the steel blades of our spades. However careful we were, it was almost impossible to avoid providing a tempting target. The first time my own platoon got caught out, I watched two men drop their tools like hot irons, while a third looked at the shattered shaft of his shovel with open-mouthed amazement and then started to pick splinters out of his face.

'You stupid sods. What did you bloody well expect?' Sergeant Fox was cursing them out, although I knew him well enough by then to be pretty sure he was finding the situation funny rather than dangerous. 'You know Jerry's always got a fix on this line but if you wanted to find out for sure, why not stick your useless fat heads up instead and stop wasting good spades.'

Suddenly, I heard shouts from the boys in the section and looked up to see a salvo of round projectiles already in the air, looping over the traverses to pitch around the corner in the next fire bay. The soldiers who had been sent there to shore up the sandbags yelled out. When I peered cautiously around the corner to size up the nature of the attack, I had to bob back quickly to avoid a missile which burst on the wooden revetting.

'It's only a snowball fight.' I was caught between being amused and relieved.

Fox crinkled the skin of his forehead, which I guess would have been raising his eyebrows if only he'd got any. He continued his snow shovelling while I went to join the fun.

It was the Cooper twins who were engaged in a mock hand grenade battle with men in the bay beyond them, bowling snowballs in slow lobs. A dozen soldiers from the platoon were leaning on their spades, egging them on.

'Go on, sir, give them a volley. You've got 'em on the run now.'

'Look out – incoming fire!'

Four large snowballs looped in a shallow arc and splattered against the trench wall.

'Cease firing.'

A voice shouted from the invisible opposition and a

moment later a trio of toughs out of my own platoon shuffled around the corner, grinning from ear to ear. Two of them had a frosting of white on their caps, while the third had a red welt under one eye so it looked like the Cooper boys had given as good as they'd got. For a second any differences in rank had evaporated, just leaving a bunch of young men enjoying a few minutes' sport. I made a mental note of the scene to write up later.

'Captain's on his way!' someone called down the trench, and then repeated it again, more urgently: 'Tollman's coming!'

It was near comical, the way there was a moment when everyone stood petrified, followed by chaos when they all tried to run off in different directions. The soldiers in our working party tripped over their own spades as they tried to dodge around each other and ended up in a heap of arms and legs, while the Cooper boys were still frozen with big wide eyes, like twin rabbits caught in a poacher's snares.

'Hold steady, men.' With his usual knack of being in the right place at the right time, David Alexander had come around the sandbags. 'Just stand to your spades and look busy. No cause for alarm.'

More than anything, it was his quiet voice that calmed them down and they went back to their shovelling smartly. I leaned myself back against the trench wall, watching to see what would happen next. Alexander scooped up a fistful of snow and chucked it over my jacket, smeared another handful over his own shoulder, then packed himself a snowball and stood, tossing it casually up in the air and catching it again.

'What the fuck's going on down here?'

The bellowing was getting close and the wooden duckboards were vibrating underfoot. Just as Tollman's angry face appeared around the twist in the trench, Alexander slung his snowball. It splattered hard off the sandbags, making

Tollman duck away. When he straightened up again, he was wiping the snow out of his eyes.

'Whoops! Terribly sorry.' Alexander got in with his apology before Tollman could explode. 'Missed by a mile – my mistake.'

I'd never truly seen what a novelist might call 'a picture of contrition' before but I reckoned Alexander's face was a perfect model for it. He was standing tall, square and innocent in the middle of the trench, which left Tollman fuming and swinging his swagger stick impotently. I half expected to see jets of steam coming out of his nostrils any moment. He glared around him but the soldiers were all heads down, industriously occupied with their shovels.

'Couldn't resist the temptation,' Alexander said. 'Scott here was such an inviting target. I know, all very schoolboyish. I'm surprised at myself, really. And such a rotten shot, to cap it off.'

He grinned apologetically. If Tollman had known him better, he'd have recognised that as a sign that he was being toyed with. One of the guys in my platoon was hardly able to choke back a laugh and broke into a fit of coughing. Tollman spun around to stare in his direction but the man was already swinging his spade busily once more.

'Fancy joining us in a proper snowball fight, then? I'd be delighted to have you on my side. I could do with some support.' Alexander waved his hand at his snow-marked uniform.

'Fucking idiots,' Tollman snorted. 'Grow up, the lot of you.'

He stamped off up the trench, slashing with his stick right and left, hitting men and sandbags indiscriminately. Before he turned the corner, he squinted back over his shoulder and gave Alexander a hard stare, as if he couldn't quite figure out what had happened. He was always good enough at dishing out the insults, but didn't know what to do when he thought someone might be poking fun at him.

For a few seconds after he disappeared, Alexander stood with one finger raised to his lips, holding everyone quiet. I could tell by his face that he was trying his best not to laugh out loud. A moment later, it was too late and everybody – including me – had cracked up into guffaws.

While I was laughing, I realised that this was why the boys in the company idolised Alexander. Behind his neat, mild-mannered exterior, he was the only man able to face Tollman down and treat the confrontation as a joke. I couldn't decide whether it would be better if the Captain had heard us or not – maybe it'd nudge him to mind his manners. Then I stopped chuckling. I was being dumb. What had Vaughan said? *There's a bitterness at the heart of him. He'll attack anyone who dares cross him.*

Suddenly, I was hit with an attack of the shivers, which wasn't due to the snow and ice. That moment, I was absolutely certain we hadn't begun to see the reality of Tollman.

I was right to be worried, even if I would never have been able to guess who he was going to pick as his next target. Clearing the snow kept all of us in C Company occupied and warm for a while but the novelty of being weather-bound wore off darned quick. For the next three days, we were pretty well cooped up in the frowstiness of the company dugout, writing reports and scribbling letters, playing whist and drinking whisky in the intervals between speedy tours around the line to check that all was quiet. Even the rats that shared our shelter were getting bold and familiar. I don't suppose it was too difficult for me or Alexander. I'd had plenty of practise at being snowed in and I'd my own observations to collect and notes to make, while he could always take refuge in one of his volumes of poetry, but it was tough on the youngsters. Fortunately, Tollman was called back on attachment to battalion headquarters leaving us with a good deal more breathing space, in both senses of the phrase. Even so, by the middle of the last evening of our stint, everyone was getting twitchy and maybe we'd all drunk a bit more than usual.

'I'm so bloody bored, caged up like this with nothing to do. I can't even get dealt a decent hand of cards.' Tim Cooper had been hitting the sauce throughout the evening and the liquor made his pink face even more flushed than normal. He threw down his last trump in disgust. 'If my luck doesn't improve, I swear I'll go up top and take pot shots at Jerry to stir things up a bit.'

Howerd had just made some sort of quip about the bravado of the young when the entrance curtain at the top of the steps was thrown back in a blast of icy air and a familiar bulk blocked the doorway. Tollman had returned.

'I'm glad you're getting bored, Cooper, because I've got the exact thing to perk you up.' He threw a bundle of white rags down the stair to land by Tim's feet. 'HQ wants to know whether the Hun keep their machine guns manned in weather as dirty as this, so I volunteered to take a patrol and find out.'

Nobody spoke for a couple of seconds until Tom – the older twin – blurted out, 'That's utter madness!' He was aghast. Then he recollected himself. 'I'm sorry. I didn't mean to be rude, but it's a clear night and the moon's up. If there are any German sentries awake over there, they'll shoot you down like sitting birds.'

'Not when we're wearing white camouflage, they won't.' Tollman gestured at the pile of cloth on the floor and set himself square in front of the younger Cooper. 'Come on then, boy. You wanted to stir things up a bit. Do you really feel lucky enough to go out tonight?'

The youngster couldn't get out any sort of reply. He'd frozen in position, his glass halfway up to his gaping mouth.

Tom Cooper butted in again. 'He can't go.'

Tollman lowered his head. He'd been grinning in his weird, lopsided sort of way, but now he was starting to look mean again. Fortunately Tom spotted his mistake and fell back to military formality.

'I only mean that he's off duty for hours yet, sir, and he's already had too much whisky.'

'Not to worry, big brother. I'll be all right. I'm not afraid of a few Germans.'

Tim drew himself up and picked up his revolver, but we could all see that his hands were shaking like he'd got a fever when he tried to tighten the buckle on his Sam Browne, and his face was a match for the bleached cloth by his boots. Tom took the pistol out of his hand and put it down.

'No, Tim. We know you're not scared, just not in a fit state.' He turned to Tollman. 'I'm volunteering to go in his place, Captain. Is that all right, sir?'

Tom had the good sense to stick with his formality, but I still thought he was riding his luck. Tollman pondered for a moment.

'All right. One of you will do just as well as the other. Might even be better with you.'

I couldn't work out what he meant by that last bit but there was no time to consider it. Tollman had started ripping holes in the sheets and Tom followed suit.

'Come on, Tim. Make yourself useful and lend me a hand with this pantomime outfit.'

Pretty soon, the two of them were wrapped in white sheeting like a couple of Eskimos and Alexander, Howerd, Tim and I went up into the trench with them to watch them go out on patrol. I still had a sick feeling about the whole stunt,

125

but at least Tollman was right about their camouflage. Clouds had drifted over the moon and they were near invisible in the snow, ghosting into the silent background of No Man's Land within a few yards. There was nothing else to do once they'd crept away, but Tim stayed shivering out on watch with the sentry while Alexander and I started our nightly rounds of the company posts. After midnight, we came back to the dugout and handed over to Howerd. Tim had already returned. He was sitting biting his nails and drinking yet more whisky.

'What the bloody hell's going on out there?' he asked. 'They should have been back hours ago. It can't take that long to slip over to Jerry's lines and back again, can it?'

Alexander had settled himself back on one of the bunks and answered without opening his eyes.

'Any number of things can hold you up on patrol, Tim – you know that. Sometimes all you can do is sit tight and wait until it's safe to move again. I shouldn't fret just yet.'

He turned his head away from the candlelight to sleep. I settled to filling in returns about the state of our supplies while Cooper sat opposite me, stretching and cracking the knuckles of one hand with the other. Finally, he came to the end of his patience. He reached over and pulled the pad of report forms right out from under my pencil.

'Come on, Scott. Let's go up and find out whether there's anything to see or even just hear. There must be something happening.'

I didn't need much persuading to quit my clerical chores and Cooper looked like he could do with the company, so we left Alexander asleep and went back up to the fire bay. It was still the same sentry on duty. He was peering out over the snow and stamping his feet quietly to keep his blood circulating.

'Nothing to report, sir,' he whispered. 'I thought I'd

spotted something a few minutes ago, just to the right there, but I can't be sure.'

The words were barely out of his mouth when a single shot cracked flat across the snow, ominous in the stillness. It was a pistol and sounded like one of ours. I guess we all held our breath then, waiting and hoping there'd be nothing more. But we knew there would be. Not five seconds later flares whooshed up from the German trenches and burst high up over the tangled wire. We leaped up to join the sentry on the fire step and squinted into the blinding magnesium light. Even with every dip and hollow in the snow standing out like purple bruises there was no sign of Tollman or Tom. The machine-gunners must have had a better view than us, however, and in an instant the night was ripped apart by a pair of Maxim guns. They were firing in long bursts one after the other and had threaded incendiary tracer bullets through their ammunition belts, so that lines of red fire stitched across the white glare of the flares. Tim Cooper grabbed my arm, gripping his fingers tight, until the lights floated slowly down to the ground and went out. The machine guns fell quiet and silence and darkness returned, all the blacker after the flares. Not daring to move a muscle, we could only stand and wait, frozen like ice statues ourselves.

For long minutes there was no movement in No Man's Land. Tim let go of my arm and punched at the parapet in frustration.

'We've got to go and find out what's happened to them.' He sounded desperate. At that instant a voice whispered out of the gloom, not twenty yards away.

'Patrol coming in.'

Before our sentry could respond a massive hunchback form struggled towards us through the banked snow and then slipped and collapsed on the parapet. It split into two shapes, one lying inert on the frozen ground while the other towered above. It was Tollman, come back from No Man's Land. He'd been carrying Tom Cooper across his shoulders.

'Give me a hand, you stupid bastards. They're bound to open up again. Lift him down.'

We scrambled out of the trench and grabbed hold of Tom. The German machine-gunners must have spotted the movement by our line and as we lifted him over the parapet, bullets were zipping around our ears. I felt a smart sting across my face, like being caught with the lash of a whip, but it was only a scratch and in a moment we were all under cover again.

When we lowered Tom onto the fire step, we could see straight off that he was badly shot up. The white camouflage sheeting was soaked through with patches of sticky darkness and it looked like he'd been run over by an express train – both his legs were swinging limp, with one foot facing backwards compared with the other, and fragments of thigh bone were sticking out through the bloody sheet. He was still conscious and let out a horrible groan when we set him down.

Alexander came running into the fire bay with two stretcher-bearers and the doctor close behind. Vaughan took one quick look and then closed his eyes for a moment as if he was in pain himself.

'Sweet Jesus, but you're a bloody mess, boy,' he muttered angrily, as if he was blaming Tom for his wounds. He opened his eyes again and snapped at his orderlies: 'Get him back to the aid post, quick. He'll not make it if we try and send him up to the clearing station like this.'

The bearers lifted him onto a stretcher and staggered off along the trench, poor Tom moaning with pain at every jolt.

'For the love of God, get a move on and get the morphia out.' I could see that Vaughan was shivering, and his pupils were huge in the moonlight.

'Will he be all right, Doctor?' Tim Cooper could barely speak.

'I don't know. It looks bad. I'll find out more when I've had a chance to...' The doctor didn't even finish his sentence before he set off at a run to catch up with the stretcher.

Tim started after him, then checked and turned back. 'Thanks for bringing him back, Blackie.' His voice had cracked into a strangled alto. 'He wouldn't have lasted the night out there if you hadn't risked yourself to carry him in.'

He picked up the Captain's massive hand, shook it twice and then tore off towards the aid post. Tollman stared after him, expressionless and silent, his shoulders still heaving with his exertions.

'Let's get back under cover. We all need a drink; you most of all, Tollman,' Alexander said and he led us back to the dugout.

The candlelight was dim and flickering but it was plenty enough to see that the Captain was crusted with streams of Cooper's blood, running down from his shoulders in rivulets like he'd been flogged. It didn't look to bother him and he made no move to clean himself up as he sat down on the edge of a bunk and poured more whisky into the dirty enamel mug that Tim had left on the table. His face had an odd expression, the scarred side twitching with muscular spasms in a mockery of a smile.

'Here's to successful patrols and happy returns.' He emptied the mug in one giant gulp and gave a grunt. Then he pointed at me.

'Looks like you've got your real souvenir of the war, Mr American. An honourable scar, and from a German as well. That's a good joke.'

I couldn't think what he meant for a moment and then realised that my cheek was still throbbing. When I felt it, there was a neat straight wound on my skin that was hardly even bleeding. I'd been lucky – it must have been a spent bullet or a ricochet otherwise I'd have been missing half my face.

'Anyway, I've proved my point.' Tollman picked up the bottle. This time he drank straight from it until it was empty. 'They're always on the alert over there. Even those stupid bastards at HQ can't deny the evidence of their own eyes when they see someone smashed up like Cooper.'

He threw the bottle down on the floor and seemed disappointed that it didn't smash. Then, still wrapped around in the blood-steeped sheets, he rested his head back against the wall and was asleep in seconds with his glazed eyes staring up at the boards of the roof above. Alexander and I looked at one another in mute agreement, grabbed a pack of cigarettes each and headed up to smoke outside for the rest of the night. However cold it was up top, it had to be better than breathing in the same air as Tollman.

That wasn't the end of it. Vaughan must have been a darned good surgeon, because he managed to patch Cooper up and keep him in one piece long enough to be carried along the trenches to the clearing station. When we got pulled out of the snow and back into billets, we heard that he was still alive and had been transferred across to the main divisional hospital on the outskirts of Amiens. I guess we'd have written off Cooper's injuries as a normal risk of patrolling if it hadn't been for Clarridge's good nature in organising an afternoon without formal duties for young Tim so that he could visit the hospital the afternoon after we got back from the front. When he returned, he brought news that finally showed us what Tollman was capable of.

It was late in the evening and David and I were sitting in the mess, wondering where Tim had disappeared to, when one of the medical orderlies came to the door to fetch us over to the medical post where we were needed to look over an emergency case. We were pretty puzzled by that, but it wasn't like Vaughan to waste anyone's time so we set off right away. The doctor met us himself at the door.

'It's young Cooper. He only got back into camp a few minutes ago and came straight over here. He was looking terribly shaken up and I was all set to dope him down with a sedative draught when he started to pitch me this yarn about his brother and Tollman. That's when I thought it would be better if the two of you were here as well. Three brains are better than one and it saves me having to repeat it to the both of you later. Anyway, it's best you hear it first-hand. Come along in, but go gentle with him. He's close to hysteria as it is.'

Tim was sitting on one edge of the table that did double duty as both operating couch and office desk for Vaughan. It was certainly true that he looked all done in, with his shoulders hunched up so that his uniform looked too big for him. His face was a mix of bewilderment and exhaustion and he didn't even look surprised at our arrival, only launched himself straight into his story.

'I saw Tom this afternoon. He was too bad to move on to a base hospital, so they've held on to him in Amiens. I managed to persuade them to let me in to see him.' He swayed back and then forward as if he was about to pitch face-first onto the floor, but caught himself and jolted upright.

'You don't know how horrible it is, sitting uselessly by the one person you're closest to in life, just watching them suffer. At least he didn't seem to be in much pain, but I'm sure he's no idea they'd had to take both his legs off.'

He swallowed hard, and I thought that he was about to break down then, but he managed to go on, massaging his temples with both hands like he was warding off a violent headache.

'I sat with him for about half an hour, prattling on to him about nothing in particular whenever he came round from the drugs. I was about to leave, it was nearly dark and I was risking being late already, when he woke up properly and looked at me as if he'd just realised I was there. Until then, he hadn't really said anything at all, but suddenly he started to talk. His voice was so weak that I had to put my head down to his pillow to hear him. It all came out in little short bursts but for a few minutes he was absolutely lucid. This is what he said:

'"You know that he did for me on that patrol. Tollman – he set it all up. We got lost to start off with and it took ages to find a lane through Jerry's wire. But I felt we were all right. We hadn't made a sound, and we must have been damn near invisible in the snow. Then I stood up to get a better look. That's when Tollman whipped out his pistol. Bastard. He fired off a shot above their trenches. Warning them. Just one shot. Their machine guns opened up. It was point blank. He was lying down. I wasn't. I got hammered. Damn that bastard to hell. He knew what he was up to. He did for me as if he'd shot me himself."

'He went quiet and I saw that he'd passed out again. After a couple of minutes, I realised that I really had to go but when I stood up he opened his eyes, grabbed my hand and said, "Watch out for yourself, little brother." He drifted off and I had to run. I couldn't even say goodbye and God only knows when we'll meet again, if he does…'

Cooper's voice tailed off into a sigh and he fished out a handkerchief and blew his nose. 'Why would Tollman do that? What was he playing at?'

'Morphia talk, young Tim, that's all it was. Morphia.' David Alexander was the first of us to find his wits and his voice was composed and certain. 'Don't you think, Scott?' He shot me a warning glance and I muttered something in agreement.

'Absolutely right, Mr Alexander. It's a recognised phenomenon in men who have been sedated with morphine derivatives, you know.' Vaughan was quicker on the uptake than me and leapt in to follow Alexander's lead, spouting facts about cerebral confusion and drug dosages and the different opiates that could be used and previous medical cases he had seen, and the well-known paranoia of severely wounded men. It was quite a performance and he'd almost convinced me, let alone Cooper, by the time he finally ran out of steam.

'Even so, I'd stay out of the Captain's way if I were you, young Tim,' Alexander said. 'He won't want to be reminded of having lost an officer out on patrol. Best lie low, if possible. And at least Tom's alive, that's the fact to hold on to for tonight.'

The doctor took his cue and led Cooper off towards his billet, still talking about delirium and its effects on memory. We watched them leave the aid post and set off across the cobbled yard before David Alexander sat himself down and produced his cigarettes.

'Good thing Vaughan's so quick witted.'

He tapped the tip of his cigarette repeatedly on his silver case, lost in contemplation, before putting a light to it.

'That was a pretty ugly story. I suspect it'll be impossible to establish the truth of it, so there's little that we can do.' He blew out a smoke ring and watched it drift to the floor. 'It is a bit of a worry to think that we might have a Royal Pennine officer sneaking around trying to get his chums killed, don't you think?'

That was close to being the greatest understatement of the entire war. He was as calm as if we'd been discussing the state of the weather and if I hadn't known him so well, I'd have marked him down as the iciest of cold fish.

'So you don't really think Tom was delirious?' I'd formed my own opinion all right, but I was interested in his view.

'It's just possible that it was all the drugs talking but knowing him as we do, I suspect that's exactly the sort of trick that Tollman would pull. He reminds me of a boy I knew at school whose favourite prank was to dare someone to climb up the tallest tree in the grounds and then stand at the bottom and rock the trunk, just to watch the look on the other lad's face. And in this instance, Tollman would have calculated on double the thrills, because he'll be waiting to see poor old Tim go to pieces now that he doesn't have Tom to take care of him.'

He stood up, ground out his half-smoked cigarette and flicked the glowing stub into a steel waste bucket.

'All we can do is to watch out for Tim, in case Tollman is minded to try anything similar on him. We'll have to keep all our wits about us. He's not likely to try anything with you or me because bullies like him like softer targets than tough old beasts like us, but even so, we should be wary.'

13

A couple of weeks later I got to visit the hospital myself. The snow had made it difficult to replace our supplies and Doc Vaughan was running low on some of his essential drugs. Now that the days had warmed up and the snow had cleared, he needed an officer to pick up a fresh batch of medications, including morphine. I thought that Tim would want to go and see his brother but Tom had already been moved out to the coast on one of the hospital trains. Nobody else was keen, so I volunteered. It'd give me an opportunity to send out a batch of paperwork I'd managed to put together. I was getting fed up with feeling anxious about carrying it around.

I got the battalion truck driver to take me into Amiens and drop me opposite the usual barbershop. For the first time, as I opened the door, there was someone else inside, although he was in the course of leaving, head down with a French uniform cap pulled low over his eyes so that his face was hidden. By the time I'd thought to look around, he was whisking around a corner further down the street. From his furtive manner, I suspected he might have something to do with the onward journey of my mail, but there was also something vaguely familiar about him, something I couldn't place. Could I have met him before? That might not have been very safe.

After that, the shop itself was empty, apart from the owner standing silently stropping his razors. 'Who was that man?' I asked. 'The one who's just gone out?'

But he only shrugged, as if he didn't know and didn't much care. Since there was nobody else in the place, I didn't need to go through the rigmarole of yet another haircut.

I just handed over my envelope and left, heading for the hospital. It was a fine spring morning out on the streets, the walk was enjoyable and it was easy to put my concerns about the strange man to one side. I dawdled along roads that were bustling with troops and locals and lined with shops and cafés. On one corner there was a lingering smell of fresh coffee. Together with the bright sunshine and the old buildings it suddenly put me in mind of the day at Paris-Plage. That reminded me of Beatrice Tempest. I'd managed not to think about her for days and I was quick to push the thought away this time. She was Alexander's girl and anyway, I'd most likely never see her again.

I stepped out smartly and came to the old convent that had been converted to look after casualties. It had a high wall and gates leading into a front courtyard, where there was a porter who showed me the way to the pharmacy. It was at the top of the building, past all the wards. I'd never been that comfortable around injury or illness, and that had got worse since the business with Tom Cooper, so I didn't hang around. Fortunately, they'd already parcelled up the drugs that Vaughan had requested and I only had to scribble a signature before making my way back down again. I couldn't hurry, loaded up with cartons that made it difficult to see where I was putting my feet. As I came to the bottom of the stairs, I heard the door to the ward there swing open and I stopped to let whoever it was go through to the front door.

'Thanks a lot. Very gallant of you, I'm sure.'

It was a female voice.

'My pleasure,' I said. When I peered around the boxes, I saw a blond girl in a nurse's uniform.

'Ooh!' she said, giving me the eye. 'You're a better bit of stuff than we normally get to see in here. Very nice. Foreign as well, by the sound of things.'

Judging by her accent, she came from somewhere in London, and not from the smart side either.

'Now really, Gladys. Behave yourself. The poor man's probably got a wife and children at home. You can't flirt with everybody.'

At that moment, I darn nearly dropped all the boxes. Someone else had come through the door, and I knew exactly who it was. Nobody else had a voice like that. Next moment, she'd spotted me.

'But it's Anson Scott. What on earth are you doing here? Surely you haven't been wounded?'

It was a long time since anyone had sounded so concerned about my health, let alone a girl who'd been occupying more of my thoughts than was safe or decent.

'Hi, Miss Tempest. No – I'm OK. Just picking up some drugs for our medical officer.'

The two of them went out into the courtyard, with me following.

'You go ahead, Gladys,' she said. 'I'll help Mr Scott carry his boxes. I'll catch up in a minute.'

That gave me a jolt, like a stimulating electric shock that ran up my spine. I told myself she was only trying to catch up with news about her fiancé.

The blond girl snorted. 'Don't do anything I wouldn't,' she called back. She waved cheerfully as she vanished onto the street.

Beatrice took one of the cartons from me. 'Do you have to go right now? It's such a pleasure to see you again.'

'I've got a few minutes before they come to pick me up.' I was wishing it was an hour, whilst knowing that was very dumb.

'This way, then.' She led the way around a buttress to a secluded corner of the courtyard. 'I'm off duty now but we're not supposed to be seen fraternising when we're in uniform, whatever that means. How ridiculous – you'd think we were complete innocents abroad. Anyway, at least here, I'll not get into trouble. Nobody can see us.'

I wasn't sure about the not getting into trouble part, but it was true that we couldn't be seen. It was a bright, sheltered niche with no overlooking windows, only a bench under the branches of a twisted tree that was bursting into leaf. I sat down next to her.

'I thought you said you hadn't been wounded. What happened to your face?' She reached out and put her fingers to the scar that had formed along my cheek.

'Just a scratch. Nothing really.'

'It's very dashing, I must say,' she smiled. 'And it stops you looking so stern.'

If she'd said it differently, I'd have suspected she was flirting with me. Right then, I was pretty sure she was just being friendly, in her own uncomplicated way. When she smiled, I wasn't quite so sure and as she took her hand away, I moved on to easier ground.

'I'm sorry I didn't know you were in Amiens. I'd have looked out for you. Have you been here very long?'

'Didn't David tell you my transfer had been approved? How absolutely typical. He's so caught up with this whole war and fighting and danger and excitement that he doesn't give me a moment's thought.' She made it sound like she was annoyed, but she was smiling a half smile, which suggested to me that she didn't really mind that much. 'Actually, we only arrived a week ago, so I can't really blame him.'

'But this is where you wanted to be, isn't it? Close to the action? I'm sure I remember you saying that at Paris-Plage, and I reckon in your shoes I'd feel exactly the same.'

She leant back on the bench. 'Why, thank you, Mr Scott.'

She sounded surprised. 'You have no idea what a relief it is to hear a man who thinks a woman can have a mind of her own. Even David doesn't really approve of my being in a situation that might be hazardous.'

'I'm sure he's only concerned for your safety. That's all. He's too smart not to appreciate having you near at hand.'

'Obviously then you aren't concerned for my health, Mr Scott, if you truly think I do have good reason to be here.' She was teasing now, which made me both smile and worry at the same time. What the hell was I playing at?

'How is he, anyway? I haven't heard anything for a few days. I suppose his letters won't catch up with me for a while.'

'He's fine – as ever. It's been a bit tricky out there, with the snow and all that, but we've been OK.' I considered telling her about Tom Cooper and Tollman, but it didn't seem right to trouble her with our concerns.

'And are you all right, Mr Scott?' She placed her hand on my arm. 'I've been thinking about you out here on your own, such a long way from anybody who knows you.'

I was caught unawares by her sudden switch of mood. Now she wasn't being flippant. It was so long since a woman had asked me anything like that I answered without thinking too much.

'I'm OK, thanks. I guess I'm used to knocking about on my own. There aren't that many folk I've ever been close to.'

It looked as though she was going to ask something else and I was relieved to hear a truck grind along the street and stop outside the hospital. It had to be the driver, come to collect me and the medicines.

'That's my ride, Miss Tempest. Got to go. It was good to see you.'

'Let's hope we meet again soon, then.' She smiled at me. She'd got the darkest blue eyes I'd ever seen. Hastily, I touched my cap to her, grabbed my stack of cartons and left.

She called after me: 'Tell David to write. And let me know when you're coming next time.'

I climbed aboard the truck whistling 'Yankee Doodle' out loud at the prospect of a next time. As we pulled away from the sidewalk and swerved around an ambulance parked there, I was reminded of David and me and our lift to Paris-Plage and was overtaken by a twinge of guilt. Then I told myself not to be so sensitive – it wasn't a crime to feel bucked up by talking to a beautiful woman. Life might be short, and it couldn't do any real harm, could it?

The driver was a silent type and didn't speak a word on the way back to our farmhouse billets, which I was glad of because it left me free to replay her voice in my mind. It was only as the farmhouse came in sight that I thought of something odd, something that I didn't comprehend at all. Beatrice had been sure that Alexander knew when she was being transferred to Amiens. If that was so, why hadn't he volunteered to come to the hospital himself?

14

That evening in the mess I told Alexander I'd seen Beatrice. There was a part of me that had wanted to keep our encounter a secret to myself, which bothered me somewhat. But she would most likely tell him anyway, so it'd seem very odd if I hadn't said anything first.

'Of course,' he said, slapping at his forehead like a man who'd overlooked some irritating minor detail. 'She did tell me she'd persuaded them to let her move. How very slow of me not to think that she would have got there by now. And I forgot to tell you. I'm sorry. I hope it didn't come as too much of a shock, bumping into her like that.'

'No. It was a pleasure to see her.' That was definitely true, but I managed to say it like it was a conversational nicety. 'If you'd told me, I'd have changed places. She'd have preferred to see you, I'll bet.'

I probably would have swapped too. If I'd thought there was a chance that I might bump into her again on my own, I'd have had the sense to avoid it. That's what I told myself afterwards, at least.

'It doesn't matter. I've had a useful afternoon going through uniforms with young Stephen. I'll drop Beatrice a line and let her know I'm behaving myself. In any event, we couldn't both have gone – one of us has to stay around to keep an eye on matters here.'

He was right, there. Whatever the truth of Tom Cooper's tragedy, Tollman hadn't moderated his behaviour. If anything, his brutality was even more blatant. Wherever we were for the next few weeks, in the front line or in reserve positions or out of the line back in the farmstead, you could follow his trail by the angry faces left behind him. It seemed like he couldn't be near anyone without lashing out in some way or other, so that by Easter most of the soldiers were looking a good deal more scared of him than the Germans. He never set foot in the trenches without whipping some poor devil with his stick and he always picked out the man who was least expecting it. Maybe it was surprising there wasn't any reaction from the men in the ranks, but what could they do? If they'd tried to fight back, he'd have accused them of striking an officer and we all knew where that would end – in the centre of a hollow square facing the firing squad at dawn. Actually, the soldiers didn't seem to resent the viciousness of their captain too much. I guess they just accepted him as part of the unavoidable hardships of army life and they knew he was a good man in a fight, which excused a lot in those days.

It wasn't just the men who suffered, however. Tollman picked on the officers too. He didn't actually beat up on them – he was way too smart for that – but he was learning other tricks. If he couldn't use physical violence, that left plenty of ways to make life miserable. His favourite time was after dinner in the mess back in billets, when he could pollute the atmosphere with his own particular brand of poison. It was petty stuff taken one incident at a time, but over the weeks it amounted to a pile of nastiness that put everyone on edge. The gramophone was quiet after a stack of records were knocked over and smashed; the usual games of bridge now seemed always to end with a barrage of accusations of sharp dealing, whether Howerd was playing or only watching; if anyone left a book or a newspaper half read, they would never see it again; one of the youngsters in A Company found that the rabbit's foot charm he believed would save his life had somehow been shredded up. Every day Tollman and Howerd hung around the mail drop that provided them with boundless opportunities for malice: a new photo sent from home would stir Howerd into action.

'Is that your wife? What a looker – she must have all the fellows back home buzzing around. Is she a little plump – or is it that we're expecting a new arrival? How long is it since your last leave? Last year, was it?'

It wasn't only that sort of cheap stuff. There seemed to be a spate of letters that went missing when they were expected. I was mighty glad that any instructions for me would be phrased in carefully disguised words that would have meant nothing to casual readers, even ones as devious as Tollman.

Oddly, one man who Tollman didn't pick on was Tim Cooper. I'd been expecting him to select Tim for special treatment now he was on his own, without the support of his brother, and anyone could see that Tim was having real trouble holding together. Up in the trenches, Alexander and I made sure he was always occupied, even if that meant he got a lot more of the daily subalterns' chores than his fair share. When we were out of the line, it was a different story. The Cooper boys had been at the heart of all the jokes and games and music in the mess after dinner. Now Tim would just pull a chair over to one corner and sit staring at the wall, silent and solitary, chain smoking and drinking one whisky after another until he could barely stand. He was even banned from playing the piano after an evening of slow, sad tunes that depressed the heck out of everyone. No one would tackle him straight on about it but the piano lid was discovered locked the next night and nobody admitted to seeing the key.

The only man who dared go near him was Tollman. While everyone else left Tim to his own misery, Tollman would draw up another seat to sit by his elbow and ask how Tom was getting on in the hospital back home, then growl commiserations about losing his brother. And the weirdest aspect of all? Even though I was pretty sure in my own mind what had happened to Tom Cooper, I reckoned that Tollman meant what he said – in his own warped way, he really did feel for Tim.

The only other officers immune from his spite were Alexander, the doctor and me, though I did still catch the occasional sideways glance in my direction when he thought I was looking the other way, which made me feel a mite wary. I guess maybe we should have stepped in to defuse his malice but in those days, in a traditional regiment like the Royal Pennines, any effort to help one of Tollman's victims would have been taken as an unacceptable slight on the man's ability to stand up for himself.

If Tollman had still been company captain we'd have found it too much of a strain when we were in the front line, where it was work enough to look out for your own skin. Fortunately, Vaughan had finally put his foot down and sent the Major home to convalesce, so Tollman was promoted to Major and second in command of the battalion, which meant that he spent most of his time up at headquarters. That kept him out of our hair, although it also made his appearances less predictable. More than once Alexander or I had to scramble along the trench half asleep to stand by and protect our men from the worst of his abuse. It made for exhausting work, but I'd plenty of experience at managing on only a couple of hours sleep and Alexander seemed to be made of different stuff from the rest of us – a type of elastic rubber maybe, that can stretch very thin without snapping and always rebounds into shape again. After a time, Tollman must have got bored with us hovering over his every move and his visits became less frequent, so we congratulated ourselves that we'd worked out how to keep him under control.

But with his increased power in the running of the battalion at headquarters level, he'd found other outlets for his malevolence. I discovered one of his new tricks one day back in billets when I was heading into the main farmhouse to file a report on the state of some stores I'd checked over. Before I could turn the handle, the door had flung open and Skully Fox stormed out, muttering angrily to himself and near knocking me over in the process.

'Fucking officers. Fucking menace.'

I stared after him, slack-jawed. I'd never heard Fox say anything that could be interpreted as a criticism of his beloved Pennines. Before he'd gone ten paces, he swivelled on his heel and glared back at me, which was still pretty scary however well I'd got to know him by then. He pointed a bony finger.

'You can't go around sentencing good men to hard labour for not finishing a job that was too bloody stupid in the first place.'

I was about to tell him that I hadn't been sentencing anyone to anything when he carried on: 'Somebody's got to stop that mad bugger. What are you going to do about it, Mr Scott?'

I was more mystified than ever now and seeing me looking flummoxed he spat into the manure heap in disgust and walked off, leaving me scratching my head. Then Clarridge threw open the window of his office and peered out, sunlight flashing off of his spectacles. He called after Fox's retreating figure but he was too late to catch him, so spotting me instead, he leant further out and beckoned me over.

'When you can, try to calm Sergeant Fox down, Scott, but keep it on the quiet.'

'What the hell's the matter? I've never seen him so worked up.'

Clarry looked right and left with all the subtlety of a bit-

145

part melodrama player. 'Best not discuss this here. *Pas devant les hommes.* I'll come outside.'

In a secluded angle of the barn he filled me in on the situation. 'Now that he's been promoted, Major Tollman has taken charge of the orderly room parade.'

He peered at me over the top of his spectacles as if that should mean something to me but I couldn't see where he was heading. The orderly room parade was where any of the men who'd committed minor misdemeanours were sent. Before I arrived in France, I'd been expecting it to be full of disgruntled and rebellious would-be mutineers. Whenever I'd been in charge of it, however, there had only been a familiar band of habitual culprits, who deserved no more than a dressing down for being drunk and disorderly and some minor punishment like extra chores fetching and carrying for the cooks.

Clarridge gave a sigh of resignation and explained. 'It's their latest tactic. When the company's up in the trenches on support, Howerd invents some ridiculous task, like rewiring the whole of our front, and orders some of the men to carry it out. When the job isn't completed, he puts the soldiers on a charge and as soon as we're back in reserve they come up before the Major for judgement. He's been having a delightful time inventing new sentences. Last week it was forced marches carrying full kit, which was bad enough, but this morning he really excelled himself. Three of the lads from Howerd's own platoon got sent to dig out a new latrine trench in a single night.'

If that had been my own men, I'd have been angry. It wasn't humanly possible.

Clarry shook his head, sadly. 'Give the chaps their due, they'd actually had a pretty fair stab at it, but they weren't quite done by dawn. That gave the perfect opportunity when they were hauled up for punishment this morning. Fox had come along to speak up for them but Tollman just cut him off short and sentenced all three to double-duty working parties. The poor devils will be labouring literally day and night for the next four days solid. It really isn't right – nobody should have to do that. It's not right at all.'

Clarry took his glasses off and started to polish them on his tie in tight little circles. I reckon he was as dismayed at Tollman's abuse of army procedure as Fox had been angry about the abuse of his men.

'You've got to have a manual of military law somewhere in that pile of stuff on your desk,' I said. 'Why not get the Colonel to send out a memorandum that all disciplinary issues must be dealt with according to the official rules? That should fix them, or at least give them food for thought.'

Clarry brightened up. '*Bonne idée*, Monsieur Scott. Brilliant, in fact. Why hadn't I thought of that myself? I shall get right onto it.'

He scuttled off, restored to his normal enthusiasm. I never found out how he engineered it but an order came round signed by Colonel Ireland reminding all officers that punishments could only be set according to the army regulations. In a matter of days the orderly room had returned to its normal routine. Fox must have worked out that I'd had some part to play in that, because he made a point of seeking me out to thank me for sorting things out.

'It's right that Captain Clarridge is back in charge of the defaulters. Much better. Good job, sir.'

He gave me a curt nod, which was his equivalent of effusive congratulations.

One way or another, those spring weeks gave me plenty of material for my reports. It still made me edgy, sitting out in the open in the mess to write, but I figured it was a lot less suspicious than hiding away. I'd asked MacManus not to contact me again because it was too dangerous. In return I was trying to send out any valuable details as regularly as possible. I'd managed to get myself elected president of the company mess, so I was licensed to make frequent visits into Amiens to order in supplies, which meant that I could visit the barbershop at the same time. At one stage, I was getting my hair cut so often that I started to be on the receiving end of mess banter about keeping a girlfriend in town. I was aware of the danger of coming and going from the same place all the time. Once, I did feel like I was being watched when I walked out after a letter drop, but when I looked around the road was just normally busy with motor cars and trucks and groups of men heading for the station: nothing out of the ordinary. I figured it was still safer than keeping all those papers in my jacket and anyway, I was only edgy because I was feeling guilty about something completely different: Beatrice Tempest.

I'd tried to push her to the back of my mind but I couldn't. I got into the habit of looking up and down the streets whenever I was in Amiens, hoping for a glimpse of a familiar VAD uniform. Once or twice, I even made a detour to go past the hospital again but I didn't see her, no matter how slow I dallied on the sidewalk. It was just as well that Alexander didn't mention her that much in conversation, because I'd have found it tough to act normal. Still, it wasn't clever in any way, hankering after her. For a start, she was somebody else's girl, and that somebody was the best friend I'd got in France. Beyond that, I knew I needed to keep all my wits about me just to stay safe, or as safe as was possible on the Western Front in 1916. I had to forget about Beatrice Tempest, and quick.

As the days got warmer and longer I thought I'd succeeded. I did still get unexpected flashes of recall – the line of her nose, the curve of her upper lip, the sway as she walked – but

I'd managed to remain concentrated on the job at hand. By the beginning of May, in spite of Tollman's efforts, and even with the repeated gut-wrenching tension of our days in the front line, I was giving myself a slap on the back that we were holding everything together OK.

The one place we hadn't looked for trouble was in Vaughan's own territory. After a quietish stretch up in the reserve lines we'd been pulled back to rest again. It was a bright afternoon on our second day and I was heading for the trodden-down field we used for parades and drill when I caught sight of David Alexander talking to the doctor. They were in the doorway to the cottage that served as the medical post and I was too far away to hear the conversation. I knew there was something out of kilter, however, because when Alexander came away he strode straight through one of the puddles of manure, kicking up such a cloud of mud and filth that it covered his boots and breeches.

I changed course and went to find out what had disturbed him so. Vaughan was leaning up against the door post, his eyes half closed in distant contemplation by the time I came up.

'I've never seen Alexander look so shook up before, Doc. Don't tell me, let me guess. It's got to be something to do with Tollman.'

He came awake again, lit his pipe and took a long drag on it. 'Aye, lad. Right on the button. His latest trick – a short arm parade this time. Ever seen one?'

I shook my head. 'Only heard about them.'

'Well, you'll know that the army takes a dim view of what we'll call social disease.'

I did know that. I'd already been collecting details about the amount of sickness due to venereal conditions, and while the brothel we'd visited in Amiens had been clean and well-run, I was pretty sure that many weren't, including some of the ones that were authorised by both the British and French armies.

Vaughan was packing his pipe down again. 'We medical officers, together with the senior battalion officers, are supposed to hold regular inspections to check for signs of disease. I have to say it's one of my stranger duties, looking over lines of men standing with their trousers and underpants down by their ankles. Degrading for them at the best of times.'

I could believe that. It was hard to think of anything less dignified.

'The CO used to hand the whole miserable business over to me so that at least there was a professional aspect to it. I managed to be fairly discreet. Not with Tollman. Humiliation is the order of the day. You can guess how it goes – a whole section of men lined up out in the open, with no pretence at privacy, bare-arsed to the world and the weather. Then Tollman walks along the line sneering and tapping that bloody stick of his while he casts an eye over their privates.'

I wasn't surprised, since it was typical of his behaviour. What I still couldn't see was why Alexander should have been so disturbed by it.

'Today, he'd picked out one of the sections from C Company, whether by chance or intent I'm not sure, but it gave him the chance to pick on young Oliver – the laddie that's Alexander's servant. "What's that miserable thing hiding out under your shirt there?" he growls at the boy. "Call that your manhood? It's pathetic. I've not got an eyeglass strong enough to check if there's any sign of infection. Lift it up, man. Lift it up so I can have a decent look. Too delicate to get your hands dirty, boy? How do you manage to take a piss, then?"'

I could easily imagine the scene and the look on Tollman's face.

'Oliver's a good, popular lad but he is a bit sensitive and by now, he's gone a dirty grey colour and he's rocking on his feet. There's a bit of muttering from the other men. You know how they resent it when one of their pals is getting picked on – but Tollman turns on them quick with one of his glares and that puts paid to any grumbling. I was about to move us all on and get matters finished off, when he started in on Oliver again.

'"I don't know why we're wasting army time on you, Private. We all know that there's no chance you'll have caught the clap, is there? Not a pretty boy like you. Not one for the ladies in any way, everyone can see that. We'll not waste any more time – parade dismissed."

'But before he stalks away, he takes his stick and fetches a swipe at Oliver, below the waist, if you take my meaning. The boy doubles over and drops to the ground with his chums gathered round him and I get them to carry him into the aid post to make sure he hasn't ruptured anything. That was an hour ago. I'd only just finished examining him when Alexander turned up at a run, white as Jack Fox and furious. I've never seen him so angry, even when I'd reassured him that his man was all right, just a wee bit bruised. If he runs into Tollman in his present mood, we'll maybe see some fireworks.'

Vaughan tapped his pipe out on the stonework of the barn and went back to his patients.

I'd no chance to catch up with Alexander that afternoon and didn't see him again until late evening when we were all loafing around in the mess after supper. He walked in and advanced directly on Tollman who was dug in to his usual chair with the inevitable pack of cards and whisky bottle. I held my breath, waiting for the explosion because his temper must have been simmering all afternoon, but fortunately by then his diplomatic nature had come to the fore.

'I gather you've taken over the medical inspections, Tollman. Don't you think that's rather overdoing the duties of second in command? Surely it would be better if the company officers oversee them. More tactful and all that, don't you know.'

Tollman said nothing for a moment, sloshing the whisky in circles in his tumbler until it started to spill over the rim. He lifted his hand to his mouth and licked the liquor from his fingers one at a time and then growled:

'All right. Have it your own way. I was getting bored with the clap parade anyway. You can do it if you want to spend your time looking at other men's tackle.'

It sounded like he'd backed down, but I was watching him closely and I saw the glint of calculation in his little eyes. Alexander nodded just the once and went to join the card school on the far side of the room. Within a minute or two, he was back to his normal calm self and I reckon he'd forgotten all about the confrontation. I stayed put pretending to read over my own notes, nursing an uneasy feeling in my guts. I could sense that he'd just made a serious mistake. Loyalty to his men was a great virtue – you could always rely on him to speak up for anyone in his platoon and they loved him for it – but this time he'd given away a weak spot in his armour. And although Tollman had showed no outward sign, I was pretty certain that he'd have taken note and stored up the knowledge, awaiting his moment.

15

'How are your circus tricks, Scott? The stuff you said your old Russian pal taught you?'

David Alexander accosted me in the mess one evening when we were back in reserve. I assumed he was joking at first, but he looked serious enough so I put down the newspaper I was reading.

'Some of them are easy enough, I guess. Either pistol shooting or knife throwing. With a spot of practice I could get them up to scratch, if I had to.'

'Good.' He pulled up a chair and lit a cigarette. I could sense his unconventional side coming to the fore. 'I think I'm going to need your talents, along with a few of the others. We're going to put on a show.'

'How do you mean? What sort of show?'

It was all the enquiry he needed and he settled himself back. 'At the end of this week, it's the two hundredth anniversary of the founding of the Royal Pennines. The Colonel wants to hold a celebration to mark the event.'

'Sure,' I said. 'There's a war raging across the world, a rebellion in Ireland and submarines attacking ships on the ocean. But we've got to have a party.'

'Don't be so miserable.' He gave me his grin and I knew whatever I said wouldn't make any difference. 'We've got a few days off duty now, and I agree with Colonel Ireland – we should do something. He's offered to host a mess dinner while the men will get extended leave passes to go into town. But in addition, however…'

He paused, and I finished his sentence for him: 'You came up with the idea of a concert party.'

'Absolutely right!' He blew out two smoke rings, quickly, one after the other. 'I've been enquiring around and there's a wealth of unexpected talent in the battalion. With a couple of days to rehearse, we should be able to produce a night to remember.'

A night to remember? It was certainly that, and more.

The evening began so well that I couldn't have suspected what lay in store. Concert parties were a feature of life behind the lines everyone enjoyed. Sometimes they were put on by a visiting music hall troupe, but most often they consisted of a series of acts drawn from the amateur talents in the battalion. In my time, I must have seen a dozen or more different performances but the foundation day celebration is the only one that's stuck clearly in my memory.

It started with all eight hundred men of the battalion packed into the massive open-sided barn out in the fields a hundred yards from the main farm. A makeshift platform had been built out of planks and trestles at one end, with a sort of orchestra pit made of straw bales and there was a line of wire strung from side to side that carried stage curtains made from canvas ground sheets. In the front row of the audience, the Colonel and his officers had the luxury of folding chairs. Behind them everyone else was crammed onto wooden benches. The NCOs and seasoned hands grabbed places in the middle with the new recruits jostling and shoving at each other for space at the sides. A few latecomers, or the guys who kept themselves apart like Fox, stood in the long grass outside. The atmosphere was hopping with a mixture of relief and celebration and the anticipation of a wild evening to come.

The performance was kicked off by our regimental drummer – a skinny boy with thin wrists and arms that looked too long for his tunic sleeves. As the last beat of his drum roll died away, the curtains parted and Alexander stepped forward onto centre stage with a speaking trumpet.

'Welcome, Colonel Ireland, and all of you Royal Pennines, to our evening's entertainment.'

For the last two days he'd been rushing about to cajole and persuade and rehearse, so that the evening would be a success. Now he was in his element, dressed in best uniform, except for the addition of a swanky silk opera hat he'd found from somewhere. He grinned – a true, raffish, pirate's grin.

'Tonight I give you the first and quite probably the last performance of the Very Lights – a unique group of acts by your own company officers. Volunteers, more or less. Just like every one of you.'

He knew the men well – that got him a massive laugh and he took off his hat and waved it around all four corners of the barn, milking the crowd. I was peering round the edge of the curtain. I'd seen a few successful showmen in my time but David Alexander would have held his own with the best of them.

The curtain parted to show Tim Cooper sitting alone at the piano and there was a faint groan from someone in the front row. I sympathised – judging by his recent moods, I figured we were in for a pretty dismal start to the concert. We'd got a surprise coming. I don't know how Alexander had worked on him but for the first time since his brother's injury Cooper gave us the sort of ragtime we'd been missing for weeks. When he started, it looked like he was only going through the motions, doing his best to give us a decent show, but by the time he'd worked his way into his first number and felt the applause, he was going at it full tilt, stamping his foot and rocking on his seat like he'd never had a care in the world. When he came to the end and stepped forward to take his bow, I saw Vaughan flash Alexander a quick thumbs up.

Cooper was followed by a demonstration of juggling by one of our transport officers, who tossed a set of Indian clubs around with unexpected skill, and then a series of musical acts, some more polished than others. In the second half of the programme two D Company subalterns fumbled their way through a comedy routine that was hopelessly under-rehearsed but still had us all rolling around in fits because of the number of smart and rude prompts from the audience. Howerd was on next and surprised me with a display of clever conjuring tricks – I should have worked out that he'd be good at anything involving deceit and sleight of hand. After him it was my turn. We'd decided that I would put on a display of knife throwing stunts that I'd not had much time to practice and it was a relief when I got through the routine, including opening a champagne bottle from twenty feet away.

Like all true showmen, Alexander had saved his best until last and ended the concert with the newest officer to join the battalion, a rosy-cheeked boy called Warren Walker who made Tim Cooper look like a grizzled veteran. The show had been a rip-roaring success so far but that boy couldn't have been more than seventeen and I asked myself what the hell David was doing letting him loose on the finale. I needn't have worried. The lad picked up a trumpet, stepped right up to the edge of the stage and started to play like I've never heard before or since. He started off with a medley of bugle calls, weaving his way through all the familiar sounds that framed up our army days, hitting every note fast and bright and true so they streamed out in an effortless ripple of noise. Then he went straight on into the old marching songs that kept us cheerful while we swung along a load of weary miles of French paved road and I realised that he'd been joined by young Tim accompanying him on the piano.

That scene is seared into my brain like it was yesterday

– the barn packed side to side with khaki, David Alexander standing at one side of the stage, turned out like a Piccadilly swell, and the last rays of evening sun that slanted in low under the roof and gleamed off the polished brass of the trumpet.

'What about one last song, something for us all to sing along to?' Alexander was bringing the show to a close and the men let rip a huge roar of approval when Tim started in on one of their traditional favourites. At the chorus, everybody joined in:

'There's a long, long trail a-winding
Into the land of my dreams,
Where the nightingales are singing
And a white moon beams.'

On the edge of the crowd even Sergeant Fox was singing. I got a sudden glimpse of the young man he'd hidden away behind his ghastly appearance. He saw me look at him and the corners of his mouth twitched up. Next to him, the soldiers were swaying in time with the music and I saw at least one of them have to mop a tear away.

Suddenly I was overwhelmed with an utterly new sensation, a conviction so strong I knew I'd never shake it.

This is where I belong. Right here, with these men. I've fought alongside them, I've lived with them, suffered and laughed with them. These are my people.

I sat down abruptly on the edge of the stage, feeling faint. The one thing that we'd never anticipated had happened. In spite of the importance of my mission, in spite of the lies I'd told, in spite of the antics of Tollman and Howerd, I had truly become an officer in the British Army. At that moment, I was committed heart and soul: I was in it with them to the end.

16

When the last of the applause died away, the barn emptied fast. The men set off with a purpose across the fields, heading towards the local estaminet and I guessed there'd be some sore heads come morning. We officers were a bit more sedate when we followed our own path back to the farm. I lagged behind the rest, still shocked at what had happened to me, trying to work through what the implications might be. Before very long, fortunately, nobody was in much of a state to notice my abstraction. Although conversation started soberly enough, with the Colonel asking Vaughan his opinion about the medical effect of the naval blockade on the German population, the whisky was being poured in even larger measures than usual and within minutes the talk had degenerated into ribald jokes and tall stories.

When we finally went in to dinner, it was an even more lavish affair than when I'd come out at New Year. Course followed course until I'd lost count. Even by Royal Pennine standards the booze was flowing like water, and not any common or garden water at that. I'd originally intended to hold back and stay sober but I was sitting in a bunch with the youngsters and Alexander and the doctor, and I was still rocking from the emotions of the concert party. By the time it got to the port and after-dinner speeches, I was half-cut like everyone else.

Colonel Ireland stood up to speak. For once all his faculties seemed to be working. He was fluent about the regiment's centuries of active service, the generations of men who had passed through, and the officers and men who had served and died for their country. As we sat down again after the toasts, I couldn't help but cast my mind back to the men who were missing from New Year's Eve. I was still sober enough to remember George Moore and Tom Cooper. I pondered on how many of us would be around to see in the next year.

There was a chink of steel on glass. It was the sort of signal that introduces a new speech and I looked up in surprise. This was not part of the planned celebration. Across the room, at the other side of the table from me, Tollman was tapping his knife on a wine glass. Next to him, Howerd was looking mighty pleased with himself, licking along his moustache in that sly way that was a sure-fire sign of mischief brewing. Gradually, the chatter dropped away. When the room was completely silent, Tollman rose to his feet. His scarred face was serious and completely sober.

'What's he up to?' Tim Cooper whispered to me. He wasn't the only one to be puzzled, judging by the expression on the faces around us.

Suddenly, I knew what was about to occur. It looked like it was destined to be my night for emotional revelations. I was right.

'Colonel Ireland; gentlemen,' Tollman said. 'I'm sorry to have to spoil the party, on this of all nights, but important information has only come into my hands today and I have to speak up now. The sad fact is that even while we sit here, on this celebration of our anniversary, our beloved regiment is being betrayed. Yes, I say, betrayed.'

If I hadn't been feeling sick at the knowledge of what was coming, I'd have been laughing into my whisky at his overblown style.

'What's the penalty for a soldier who sells out his comrades-in-arms?' he demanded. 'I ask you because there's a man among us, right here...' He swung an arm around to include the entire party, 'yes, here in this room, pretending to be one of us, while all the time he's been spying on us.'

'What the hell is he on about?' Vaughan was awake enough to be bemused.

I knew exactly. All that time, I'd been so confident I was safe, while that scheming devil had known just what I was up to. He'd simply been watching and plotting when to show his hand for maximum effect. Although he'd set his face stern and serious, I knew that he was enjoying himself. That's why he'd chosen this occasion to make the announcement in public, rather than inform the Colonel as soon as he'd found out. He was going to watch me squirm in front of the entire party. And there was absolutely nothing I could do about it.

'Are you all right, Scott?'

Alexander nudged my elbow. He was looking at me with an expression that was mixed between enquiry and concern. I spread my hands wide, helpless. This was part of the price I had to pay for being found out. I could only sit tight and take what was coming.

Tollman dropped his voice into a dramatic whispered growl. He reached into an inside pocket and pulled out a sheaf of paper, which he held up in the air, brandishing it like a trophy he'd won.

'This is what I'm talking about. An analysis of exactly what this battalion has been doing at the front.'

For a second, I was baffled – he couldn't possibly have laid hands on any of my original notes. Then I realised exactly what it was he was holding, even as he explained.

'News reporting, that's what this is about. But not in our own country. I doubt any of you will be aware of it, but over the last few months there's been a series of articles about the war printed in an American newspaper – some rag called...' he made a great show of peering at his paper clippings, '...

the *National Proclaimer*. Stories about the British Army on the Western Front. Tales about us at the front that have grabbed the sensation-seeking public over there.'

In spite of myself, I couldn't hold back a little smile of professional satisfaction. I hadn't known until then how much interest I'd stirred up back home. Tollman glared at me.

'The paper hasn't dared spell it out clearly, but it's obvious to anyone with a degree of intelligence that these articles must have been penned by someone who is actually serving in the army right now, someone with first-hand knowledge who isn't afraid to break all the rules of decency – and military laws – to make a name for himself. When I first heard about this, I wondered who could possibly sink so low.'

It was cunning of him, to make out that he'd known about the articles before he'd suspected anything about me. However bulky and bullying he might be, he was never stupid.

'Then I turned my thoughts to someone in our own ranks, someone who is forever scribbling down notes under the guise of writing a diary. I wrote to a private detective company in America and commissioned one of their men to poke around the offices of the newspaper concerned. His report arrived in this morning's post, together with all this rubbish – copies of the articles themselves.'

He threw down the newspapers on the table in disdain.

'Shall I tell you what that detective found out?'

He didn't need to wait for an answer. 'The editor of this paper is fond of his whisky and my man was able to trick him into admitting that the stories are true, first-hand accounts from one of their reporters who's managed to sneak into the front lines in the guise of an officer serving in the trenches. Unfortunately, in spite of being plied with drink, he wouldn't produce a name.'

I supposed I had to be grateful to MacManus for that small

discretion, although it would've been better if he'd denied everything. Tollman ploughed on:

'It only took a small bribe to one of the office boys to get around that. The *Proclaimer*'s special correspondent on the Western Front is better known as...' Tollman stopped and stared around him again, squeezing as much drama out of the moment as he could. By now it felt like I'd gotten to be a magnet for every eye in the room. 'Scott! Anson Scott.' He pointed at me. 'He's not a soldier. He's a sham, a bloody gutter journalist, spying on all of us so that he can scribble his miserable little stories to entertain the American public and make his reputation. How much did they pay you to betray your friends, you Judas?'

I couldn't do or say anything. I shook out a cigarette and lit it, pleased that my hands were steady.

Having broken his news, Tollman was getting to the point of his revelations. His voice was raw and spittle was starting to fly from the scarred corner of his mouth.

'You all know the army regulations on censorship. They're designed so that none of us can give away information that might help the enemy. We understand those rules and live by them. Not this impostor. Oh no – not him. He doesn't give a damn about censorship because he's no officer and gentleman – he's a second-rate bloody scribbler. If it was any of us writing articles for the newspapers in England we'd be court-martialled and broken down to the ranks at best. Thrown into prison, more likely. Why should he be treated any differently?'

He pointed his finger at me again and it was actually quivering with emotion.

'There he sits, condemned by his own words. Words printed clear in black and white. He deserves everything he'll get.'

He threw himself down onto his creaking chair, mopped

the spit off of his face with a corner of the tablecloth and folded his arms. He'd done his job pretty well. Howerd had known what was coming of course, and was watching me like a bug stuck on a pin. Around the table the others were caught in various stages of consternation. Tim Cooper had his mouth so wide open I could see his tonsils and the rest of the youngsters looked equally baffled. David Alexander was staring down at the tablecloth as if he was concentrating hard on what he'd just heard. The other company officers were muttering ominously between themselves and Clarridge looked even more worried than usual, pulling away at his whiskers. My main concern was with the group of senior men around the Colonel. The transport and intelligence officers looked unfriendly, while the padre's face suggested that he'd be jostling for a good place at the head of the lynching mob. I'd always known that if my cover was blown I could expect a tough time. However, I was damned if I'd give Tollman the pleasure of seeing just how much he'd shattered my life. I sat back and blew a cloud of smoke in his direction, making out that I didn't give a tinker's cuss about him.

All the accusing eyes tracked sideways from me and set on Colonel Ireland. He had stayed in his seat. His mouth kept opening and then shutting again, while his forehead was screwed up into laboured furrows. Eventually, he managed to find his voice.

'Don't really understand all this, but suppose I have to thank Tollman. Shall have to relieve Scott of all duties. Report to Provost Marshal tomorrow. Damn shame. Reflects badly on the regiment.' He stared at me, looking stern.

'Mr Scott. You will be held under guard until headquarters send the Provost Marshal down. Surrender your revolver to the duty sergeant.'

He gestured towards the sergeant at the entrance, but I

was blowed if I was going to be marched off like a common criminal. Before the man could move, I stood up and made my own way out. The room was completely quiet and the sound of my boots on the floorboards was like somebody knocking in coffin nails. The door closed behind me. I was back in the darkness of the corridor once again.

I'd almost got away with it. But we'd always known that I was working on borrowed time, and that time had just elapsed. The Royal Pennines had lost another officer, and the only front-line war correspondent on the Western Front was out of business.

17

The guardroom was a bare locked cell converted out of a store room behind the farm, with a single chair and a bunk with no blankets. It wasn't the hard bed that kept me awake that night, however. It wasn't even the fear of a court martial. I'd no great faith in the leniency of army justice but I didn't seriously believe that MacManus would sit idly by while his favourite reporter was locked away in a British jail, and I suspected that if he started to kick up a fuss, the British government would be keen to get an interfering busybody out of the way without too much argument.

No. What kept me pacing slowly up and down the room, lighting one cigarette from the butt of another, was the sense of failure that weighed me down like a pair of lead boots. Only that evening I'd allowed myself, finally, to think I'd found a place where I fitted in. A place where I was doing something worthwhile, not just labouring to earn my keep or sell newspapers or please the editor. For the first time, I'd felt like I belonged. Now all that had been swept away. Worse than that, nobody had spoken up on my behalf. I knew that most of them were scared of Tollman, but why hadn't David Alexander said something? If there was one man I'd grown to trust, it was him.

Now it looked to me like I'd been completely wrong. The Royal Pennines were a bunch of dyed-in-the-wool bigots, just like I'd been expecting when I left the USA, and they were only too happy to see a foreigner get his comeuppance. But that thought didn't give me any consolation. By dawn I was wallowing in my own misery and doubly bitter that nobody

165

had even taken the trouble to come and see me – not Alexander, not even Fox.

Not long after the bugle had sounded the call for morning parades, I heard voices approaching my cell.

Bloody hell. That was quick. They really must want to get me out of here. Probably don't want me to contaminate anybody else.

I was sure it'd be the Provost Marshal's men. They took care of all the criminal matters in the army. I hoped they weren't going to do anything undignified, like lead me away in handcuffs. Tollman would love that. I sat down on the bunk and got ready to face them.

To my surprise, when the door opened, it wasn't a pair of hard-faced military policemen standing there. It was someone I'd never seen before – a slight man, a major in the Guards judging by his badges, but who was also sporting the red and blue chequered armband of General Headquarters staff.

'Scott? I'm Menzies, from GHQ. Section 1b.'

Neither his name, nor his post, meant anything to me. It didn't make sense. What was a staff officer doing here?

'Colonel Ireland called me last night to ask for advice,' he went on.

That was odd. When I'd been arrested the night before, the Colonel was going straight to the military police. Menzies must have seen the surprise on my face.

'He's an old friend of a relative of mine, you see. And he knows that I'm currently involved with matters of...' he searched around for an appropriate explanation, then seemed to decide that plain speaking was easiest, 'matters of espionage and intelligence.'

Now I was worried. This man could have me thrown in jail with a snap of his fingers. There wouldn't even need to be any formal hearing or procedure. Nobody would know where I'd disappeared to.

'You'll appreciate that your position in all this business is very irregular. You've broken army regulations and are liable for court martial.' He looked at me, his eyebrows raised. 'That would be the usual course of action, as is being demanded by some of your colleagues in the battalion.'

It wasn't exactly hard to think who they might be.

'However,' he continued, 'that would seem rather unfair.'

Unfair? What the heck did he mean?

'You see, Mr Scott, we've been aware of your activities since you began. One of my men was keeping watch over the barber's in Amiens, which we have had our doubts about for some time. He saw you and another subaltern there and took steps to identify the pair of you. Then he saw you going in and out of the place frequently and kept a watch on your other movements. We've opened every letter you sent out of France.'

That explained why I'd had the feeling of being observed so often, although it immediately raised another question. 'I don't get it – if you were intercepting my mail out to my editor, how come those articles appeared in print back in the USA? Tollman had them – he was waving them at me last night.'

Menzies pulled out the chair and sat down. 'You have me to thank for that. My first inclination, when your letters were handed on to me, was to suppress them and to bring you in on a charge. Then I read through what you were actually writing, and realised that would be a missed opportunity. Your stories weren't actually critical of our cause, nor had you given away any military details, as such.'

'No,' I said. 'That's not why I'm here. I'm not a spy and I'm not a purple prose man. I wanted to write about real life in the trenches, not some sanitised and censored pap that could have been slung together by any old soak sitting in a café in Paris, or London or Boston.'

I leant back against the wall and folded my arms. I knew I'd maybe said more than I needed, but now that everything was out in the open, I decided I'd rather show my true colours.

'In my view, I think you achieved that rather well. In fact, better than you might have thought. Your "Missives from the Front Line", as they were headed, have created something of a stir in America, and a stir that is largely sympathetic to the British Army.'

Menzies looked at me, gauging my reaction.

'I reckon that's not what my editor was expecting when he sent me here. But he and I have worked together for years and he's a fair man – he trusts what I tell him.'

I thought I'd skip over MacManus' Irish-Boer ancestors. All that mattered was that he'd printed what I sent him without changing the tone.

'Whatever the reason, those articles started to appear at just the time when your government was on the brink of deciding whether to enter the war on our side. Under those circumstances, I and my superiors felt that it would be advantageous to let you continue.'

I let out a deep breath. I was starting to feel that I might not be in as much trouble as I'd imagined.

'Given that,' Menzies said, 'my advice to your colonel has been that you should not be charged with anything untoward in this matter and that you return to your normal duties without delay, with the proviso that you refrain from further newspaper reporting. We mustn't allow the other officers to believe that the censorship laws can continue to be flouted. It's only a pity that your major – Tollman – decided he'd prefer to unmask your activities in public himself rather than reporting to us and letting us deal with it, but neither Colonel Ireland nor I believe that should bar you from resuming service.'

I stayed sitting for a minute, taking in what he'd just

said. I wasn't getting thrown out. I was still part of the Royal Pennines. Better or worse, I was in the war for keeps. I wanted to jump up and down and holler for joy. Instead I matched his poker face and played it short and sweet.

'Thanks, Major. I'm grateful.'

'Not at all. If you'd been writing anything damaging to us, rest assured that we'd have tried you as a spy and shot you without a second thought.' He looked at me without any flicker of emotion. I thought that for all his unassuming demeanour, this would be a dangerous man to cross. Then he gave me a small smile. 'I should tell you that, personally, I rather enjoyed your articles. Glad to see someone tell the truth about soldiering for a change.'

It was good of him to tell me so, but I was distracted by a sudden inspiration. While he was speaking, I'd been racking my brains, trying to work out who could possibly have been watching me. 'It was that ambulance driver. The one who gave us a lift out of Amiens. He's your man, isn't he?'

Menzies wouldn't either confirm or deny it. He looked down at the floor for a moment, seemingly lost in thought and when he raised his head, he ignored my question altogether.

'Do try to stay alive, Mr Scott,' he said. 'You're the sort of fellow I might have a need for in future.'

I'd the distinct feeling that working for this man might be even more risky than what I'd been doing so far. Before I could say anything, however, he'd stood up and left, without a handshake or salute, or anything else.

I was still sitting on the bunk, collecting my thoughts, when Tim Cooper burst in a few minutes later.

'I'm the bearer of good news, Scott. You're a free man. Colonel's orders.' Cooper slapped me on the arm. 'Congratulations. Welcome back.'

'I know. Someone came to tell me. But I still don't completely understand what happened after Tollman's stunt last night.'

'I'll explain later. Right now what matters is that you're still a Royal Pennine, and still heading into this scrap with the rest of us.' It sounded like he was informing me that I'd been let off class detention so I could turn out for the school football side. 'And that means you've got work to do and parades to inspect. Come on.' He grabbed my arm and hauled me out of the guard house. 'I'll fill you in as we go.'

He told me the rest as we marched across to the parade ground.

'It was all very surprising, really. After you'd left, Tollman started up again about it being a disgrace a newspaperman was allowed anywhere near the regiment and that they'd got to get the Provost Marshals in immediately. And maybe that would have been curtains for you, except for Alexander. If it hadn't been for him...'

I was relieved to hear that. The idea that Alexander had abandoned me to my fate had been smarting all night.

'He'd been pretty quiet after you'd been ordered out, thinking about what to do I suppose, and he had a whispered chat with Clarry. Then he called over to Tollman and asked to have a look at those newspapers – your newspapers, I suppose I should say. The Captain – sorry, Major – didn't look too pleased about it, but he'd no choice and handed them over. Alexander took his time reading it but there was still a fair old buzz going on when he stood up in turn.

'"Colonel Ireland; gentlemen," he said. "I'd like to say a word about this affair. I should start by admitting that I don't like feeling my trust has been abused any more than the rest of you."

'I was a bit surprised by that because I'd been expecting

him to say something in your defence. Before I could get too upset, he continued: "But I've been reading the whole of these articles of Scott's. And I have to say I think they're rather good."

'He was just as quiet as usual, which was probably more effective than if he'd shouted, and everybody stopped to listen. "It seems to me that we're forever grousing about the rubbish that gets reported about the war. Almost everything we see is both facile and jingoistic and obviously written by people who've never been anywhere near a trench."

'The doc joined in then: "That's right. Very true." I didn't think he'd been either awake or sober enough to follow what was going on at all, but I was wrong.

'"Everything that Major Tollman said is correct," Alexander said. "I don't dispute that, but it seems to me that we've only heard the case for the prosecution so far. After reading Scott's article, I asked myself two questions. First, should we feel betrayed? Second, has he let down his comrades in the Royal Pennines? And the answer to both is – no. There's nothing in any of this that gives away military secrets or anything we would find an embarrassment."

'Just as well you hadn't written anything too sensitive, Scott, or else we might still be saying farewell,' Tim added, as we started across the field. 'Anyway, Alexander went on for a while about your reports being unique and valuable, and how that sort of thing should be encouraged, rather than condemned. I wish you could have seen Tollman's face by the time he'd finished. Talk about thunderous! It looked as if he was about to start up again, but Alexander held up a hand and silenced him.

'"While I think about the matter of avoiding the censor, I am just curious as to how you corresponded with the enquiry agent you hired in America. Did you ask your senior officer to inspect it?" Well, that left Tollman stumped. As soon as he stayed quiet, we knew he'd simply picked up his blue pencil and signed his own stuff through with all the rest of the men's letters he'd just censored, which meant that he was guilty of flouting military regulations too. Clever point, don't you think? Trust old Alexander to pick that out.'

Tim was obviously enjoying retelling the story.

'Alexander pushed on: "So I say, well done to Anson Scott. It's long past time that our story was told properly, instead of the tripe that usually gets printed. Speaking for myself, I don't see that he has anything to be ashamed of."

'"Bloody right, old boy. Absolutely bloody right." That was Vaughan, again, sounding as if he'd been on the bottle a bit too much.

'I threw in my own twopenny worth as well to back Alexander up, for whatever it was worth, but it was still nip and tuck at that point. There was a lot of muttering going on around the room and not all of it was friendly, I have to say. You can imagine who was keen to see the back of you.'

'Don't tell me,' I said. 'Howerd and all his horrible lot.'

Tim nodded. 'We all knew that it would be down to the Colonel to have the final say. I was a bit reassured to see that Clarry had gone over to him and was whispering in his ear, but when the old man shook his head slowly and the way he got to his feet again, I thought maybe you were still in for the high jump.

'"Can't have men flouting the rules. Ends in anarchy. Not acceptable. Grateful to Tollman there for bringing the matter up, even if he did also break the rules to investigate it."

'I have to say that my heart sank when he said that. Tollman was sitting back trying not to look pleased with himself. I should have had more faith in the Colonel, because he held up one hand and went on.

'"However, I also agree with Alexander. Well argued case. No great harm done by Scott's scribblings. So, difficult decision as to what to do next. Best course of action, consult with higher authority. I'll phone GHQ tonight. Talk to someone there – a sound man, know him well. See what he has to say."

'He made to sit down as if he'd finished. Tollman got to his feet. I tell you, he was actually frothing at the mouth, he was so angry. "I demand that Scott is punished according to regulations, Colonel," he said.

'Well, that got the old man back up again in a flash. I've never seen him look so fierce. "I remind you it's my battalion, Major. No demands. This is a delicate matter. Best wait to see what young Menzies thinks. He's got friends in high places. He'll know what's best."

'So that was that. Tollman walked out seething and all the rest of us got on with the bash. And a jolly good do it was, too. Pity you had to miss it. At least the Colonel's nephew, or godson, or whatever, had the good sense not to be swayed by Tollman and his lot.'

He looked at his watch. 'Oh Lord! I'm on guard duty in a minute. Better run.'

Later in the morning, I found Alexander working his way down a huge mug of coffee he'd just been brought by Stephen Oliver. Compared with the few other pasty-faced individuals I'd bumped into in the mess, he was looking indecently cheerful.

'Seems like I've got you to thank for my still being here,' I said. 'I admit I wasn't looking forward to getting thrown out, just when I was starting to enjoy myself.'

'Don't mention it. It was hardly a great act of heroism, only a few words to put a bully in his place. You'd do the same for me, should the need arise, I know. Isn't that what friends are for?' Then he grinned and said, 'Anyway, how on earth would I have explained it to Beatrice? She'd never have given me a moment's peace.'

At the mention of her name, my pulse jumped. I couldn't help it, even then. I did my best to keep my straightest face on and fortunately, he'd got something else on his mind. 'I must say, I'm impressed that you joined up just to get a good story – that is true dedication to the art. Are you going to give up writing now?'

'Yes and no.' It was a relief to be back on more solid ground. 'I can't stop noting down what I see because I've been at it so long, it's second nature to me. I guess it'll become more of a personal journal now. Maybe something to publish after the war.' I remembered that had been MacManus' suggestion before I left Boston.

Alexander took a sip of his coffee. 'In some ways, that is a pity. I held on to those articles of yours and looked through them properly over breakfast. You're pretty good at it, aren't you? Writing, I mean. How long have you been a newspaperman?'

'Since I left the railroads. Most of what I told everyone was true. Anson Scott is my real name, by the way – my grandfather was a real admirer of the British navy. And I did attend West Point and worked in Alaska, but after a while I went back east and signed up with the *Proclaimer*. For the last five years I've been a war reporter, usually following the Marines. Cuba, Nicaragua, Honduras, Veracruz – I sent back copy from everywhere. This stunt was my editor's idea – he's an Irishman with German kin, but he was anxious that the US public should see what the war is really about.'

'Now it all makes sense. I was always puzzled by the way you fitted in so well with us from the off. Anyway, I'm going to send those articles on to Beatrice for an impartial view. Did I tell you that she's finally managed to get her posting? Of course, you saw her there. I'll bet she enjoys reading your stuff as much as I did.'

'Thanks. And thanks again for last night. I only hope you haven't stirred up Tollman. He's not a guy to tangle with.'

I couldn't forget either George Moore or Tom Cooper.

'Oh, our beloved Major is just too accustomed to getting his own way.' Alexander waved away my fears with an airy hand. 'He'll have to take this one on the chin now, because it's his own fault. He overplayed his hand and lost the game. That's the end of it. We've nothing more to fear from that quarter.'

And I believed him, or at least, I wanted to.

18

I kept my word and wrote to MacManus to tell him I couldn't send him any more material, which we'd always known might occur. I guessed he would still be happy to have managed a run of articles that were world firsts. I had been concerned about how the rest of the battalion would take the discovery about my dissimulation in the light of a sober day, but I never had any further trouble. I guess there was a lot more to fret about than one stray American newsman dumb enough to join a fight he didn't need. Mostly, they took Alexander's lead. More than once in the mess and the trenches, I heard someone brag that while other battalions had to make do with fancy poets and artists, the Royal Pennines had its very own war correspondent. At any rate, after the foundation dinner, I seemed to have become the regimental authority on all world affairs. The men in C Company were always showing me British newspapers with underlined inaccuracies and scribbled corrections.

In short order, however, there wasn't much opportunity for reading for any of us. Things were beginning to heat up at the front, in every sense of the word. In army terms, the war was getting busy. The country was swarming with hundreds of the new Kitchener battalions made up of civilian volunteers, all getting ready for the big push that everyone knew was coming in the summer. Jerry was more lively too, with air raids on our camps and towns and barrages onto the front lines. Looking back, there isn't any great military episode that sticks in mind, so much as a series of small incidents.

With the beginning of May the weather bucked up, and

we got a spell of long, hot days. I never could decide which was worse – cold, wet and muddy winters, or dry, stinking and bug-ridden summers. The trenches were layered with stagnant gas that made you feel polluted from the inside. Then the insects got to breeding in their millions – there was plenty enough for them to feed off, I guess. Massive, shiny green and blue blowflies swarmed around the latrines and then crawled around our plates and mess tin. But worst of all was the lice.

Sure, lice get everywhere. But when there's a load of men living cheek by jowl with little chance of washing, they become a real nuisance. I remember the first time I saw how bad it could get. We were out in the reserve lines and a section of my platoon who were off duty were sitting out on the fire step naked to the waist. First off, I thought they were just sunning themselves, but then I saw they were all covered with bright red wheals, striped across their backs like they'd been flogged.

'What's going on here?' I asked the nearest man. He was running his fingers along the seam of his grey army shirt.

'Just chatting, sir. Got yer, yer little bastard!' He pinched something between his finger and thumb. 'That's the end of you, bloodsucking little bugger.'

'It's the trench version of fox hunting, except on a slightly smaller scale.' Alexander had come up on my shoulder. 'Show Mr Scott the quarry.'

The man passed me the bug he'd just squashed. It was a grey-pink insect half the size of my fingernail. I don't get queasy about much, but it made my flesh creep to think of all the thousands of them living on our bodies, feeding off our blood.

'Best get the doctor to see to that,' Alexander said to the nearest man. He'd taken his gloves off and was running a finger along one of the scarlet lines on the man's back. At one end of the scratches a blob of green pus bubbled up onto the surface of his skin.

'If we don't want to lose you to the sick parade, you're going to need some treatment.' Alexander turned to me. 'Ever had lice, Scott? You will out here, no matter how often you change your kit. When the little devils start crawling around they're so infernally itchy that it's impossible not to scratch and then there's a risk of infection.' He shuddered. 'So damned unclean. I'll have a word with Vaughan and see what we can do when we come out of the line.'

The next time we were back at rest we were given orders to march our men into town for a bath and change of uniform. Disused breweries were the army favourite for makeshift bathhouses because of the vats and pipework, but for us the baths were in a converted dye factory on the outskirts of Bray. Alexander and I led our men along the dusty road, through battered wooden gates and into an enclosed yard, where there were trestle tables set up along one wall. As soon as the gates had closed behind us, there was a loud blast on a whistle.

'Uniforms off, the lot of you. Quick now. You ain't got all bloody day,' a quartermaster's sergeant shouted. 'Everything off – tunics and trousers to the right, shirts, underpants and socks to the left. Into them baths.'

He didn't need to say anything more. There was a race for the door and a scrimmage of naked bodies trying to get through all at once with me and David – the only ones still fully dressed – bringing up the rear at a more dignified pace.

The works was a long shed with a row of big stone vats that I guessed had held chemicals for the dyeing business. Now they were chest-high full of clean hot water that steamed and smoked with a smell of disinfectant. The boys had already jumped in and the nearest vat was full of youngsters larking around like kids down at the swimming hole, splashing and ducking each other until the water splashed over the side. Further along, the older men had started on the serious job of getting cleaned up and were scrubbing at themselves with bars of brown soap, paired up so that one could clean the back of another.

'Not exactly Jermyn Street's finest concoction. That's probably guaranteed to take the surface right off your skin. It's hardly surprising it kills any lice.'

David Alexander handed me a fresh bar of dry soap. It was the rough carbolic stuff that they use for heavy laundry and now I knew what was making the smell. Still, it seemed to be doing the trick. The inlet pipes had stopped running, but the boys were still able to wallow around in the warmth for a minute or two before there was another whistle and the sergeant appeared at the entrance.

'That's your lot. We're draining off now. Everybody out. Grab a towel. Fresh kit at that far end.'

Outside, in a different yard, the boys collected clean uniforms from a bunch of bored corporals. The whole exercise, from turning in through the gate to marching out at the other side, took twenty minutes at most but it was a huge boost to morale. As we tramped back to billets, the men were singing the whole way.

'Amazing, the restorative effect of hot water and clean clothes,' Alexander said as we walked along. 'I'd have had to desert by now if officers weren't allowed into Amiens for a clean-up periodically. From today, however, I shan't even have to rely on that. The bath contraption I ordered came through this morning, brought up from the mail office. Do come and take a look at it. I'm planning on a good long soak before supper.'

I was intrigued by the prospect of a folding bath, so on

my way over to the mess that evening I made a detour to the cottage where he was quartered. The door was closed but when I knocked it swung open and I was enveloped in dense clouds of steam, swirling like the innards of a Chinese laundry. I could barely see my hand in front of my face.

'Scott? Is that you? Apologies, I'm not quite ready yet. Come in and close the door. There's the dickens of a draught.'

When I stepped into the room, the steam had thinned out a tad. There were puddles of dim light around candles stuck in empty wine bottles and the place was awash with the scent of violets mixed with Russian tobacco. Some of David's opera music was playing quietly from the horn of a gramophone.

'This is a bit more like civilisation, don't you think?'

Peering through the mist, I could see a large green canvas tub sitting on the boards in the middle of the room, surrounded by the jugs and bowls and basins that must have carried the hot water. The only sign of Alexander was a hand trailing over the bath side, holding on a glowing black cigarette. Then a tidal wave of water lapped over the rim and flowed down over the side and across the floor as he sat up, glowing with sweat and heat.

'Stephen. Pull up a seat for Mr Scott and pour him a drink.'

That gave me a start. I'd been assuming he was alone. Then Stephen Oliver stepped forward through the steam to offer me a wooden stool and a glass of whisky. He'd taken his tunic off in the swampy heat. His trouser suspenders were pushed off his shoulders, trailing down from his waist and his face was flushed.

'You really should get one of these contraptions, Scott. It may take enormous powers of persuasion to raise the hot water, but... oh, the sheer bliss.' Alexander slid down so he was completely submerged, resurfacing with a shake of his head to shed the droplets from his hair. He grimaced as he twisted his neck.

'God's truth, my spine still feels as if someone's marched across it, with army boots on at that. Be a good fellow, Stephen, and give me a rub down. There's some oil in my bag there.'

He sat up, stretched out and arched his back, while Oliver poured some violet-scented liniment onto his shoulders and set about massaging his muscles. Right then, they could have been posed for a portrait of an oriental pasha and his body servant.

'That is truly amazing,' Alexander said with a groan of pleasure. 'I'll swear you're the best masseur outside a Turkish bath. Don't stop just yet.'

I'd finished my drink and it was beginning to feel like I was intruding on his toilet.

'I'm away, then. See you at supper.'

But when I got outside, I didn't head for the mess. I needed time to think things over in the fresh air. Behind the barn, I leant against the wall and lit a smoke.

What was going on? I'd got to know Alexander so well that I wasn't fooled by his appearance – he'd just got one of those deceptive faces that falls into serious lines if they're not smiling – and I didn't think of him as the quiet, conventional professor any more. But exactly what had I been seeing back there? Was it my imagination making too much out of a man having a bath with his batman close at hand? Maybe neither of them was aware of how it might look – that was possible.

It made no difference to me, personally, I thought. All round the world I'd met a number of men who acted more comfortable with other men around them than they did with women. Even some who were married. I'd always figured it was their own business, one way or the other. It had never been my nature to sit in judgement on other folk, providing they weren't making a nuisance of themselves. Besides which, Alexander was my best friend in France, maybe the closest friend I'd ever had. I'd never want to put that at risk. At the same time, I had to hope that he wasn't about to do something that would lay himself open to attack – Tollman never needed anything more than a sniff of a weakness. Should I try to say something? Try to warn him to be careful?

It was impossible. For a start, what if I was wrong? There was nothing I could do except wait and watch. I hitched myself off the wall, feeling uneasy.

You should be feeling damned uneasy. You just want to believe it's true. Who are you trying to fool?

I guessed that was the voice of my own cynical conscience, jeering at me. And it was right, which made me feel even more of a louse. Not because it would alter my opinion of Alexander. But because there was Beatrice. Was I only imagining something that would come between her and Alexander? I couldn't answer that, so I told my conscience to go hang, shrugged it away and went off to the mess.

That was the second of the chances I let pass. The second opportunity when, if I'd had more guts or more sense, maybe I could have prevented everything.

19

It was the first day of our rehearsals for the big summer attack. I looked across a battlefield where everything had gone terribly wrong.

'It's a complete shambles,' Alexander shouted in my ear. 'Some sort of big push this is turning out to be. Just listen to that!'

Over the din, out in No Man's Land, the sergeants were cursing, shoving their men into line.

'Get yourself sorted out in front, you dozy lot, you're supposed to be up and out by now. What a fucking mess. Come on. Out of the fucking way, you. Bloody hell – thank God we've got a bloody navy.'

Everywhere I could see along the front it was the same picture – confusion, blunder and anger.

'Look at our new Major there. He's not a happy man,' Alexander wheezed out between laughs.

Down in front of us a huge dark shape emerged from out of the depths of a communication trench and the space cleared around it in a moment. It could only be Tollman, lashing out as usual. It wasn't pretty, but it was effective. At last our lads got themselves out of the trench, formed up into three wavering ranks and started out up the hill towards the village that was our target for the morning.

'Can't we take a run at it?' I yelled above the racket. 'One machine gun and we're done for.'

'A touch crude, you think?' Even shouting, he was never lost for understatement. 'Apparently our New Army battalions can't manage anything complicated. Hence this master plan.

The artillery smashes Jerry to smithereens for a few days and then we saunter across to deal with any quivering survivors.' There was a fresh burst of angry shouts below us. 'Good Lord! Maybe General Haig's got a point. Just look at that.'

A hundred yards ahead, a company from one battalion wheeled to their left at the same time as their neighbours took a half turn to the right. In a couple of seconds there was a tangled mob of three hundred men cursing, abandoned and arguing in No Man's Land. Some squads were holding together and tried vainly to stick to their original direction; others had turned around to retrace their footsteps, while many simply looked lost and confused. At least a dozen appeared to have given up the whole thing as a lost cause and sat down on the ground, waiting for the chaos to clear.

Alexander looked sideways at me and I could see him trying desperately hard not to grin. That did it. Next second the two of us had flopped, giggling on the grass, completely overwhelmed by the absurdity of the morning.

'Message from the Colonel, sir.' Sergeant Fox had appeared. We were all wearing our new steel helmets that had just been issued. The shadow of the brim made his white face impossible to read as he stared at the two of us sitting on the ground, so I couldn't tell if he disapproved of us or the chaos out front. 'The exercise has been called off for today. Bloody mess, if you ask me, sir.'

At the beginning of May, we'd been pulled way back from the front to a specially prepared area, set up to look like the target they'd planned for us even if we didn't yet know where that was. We were camped about two miles away from the mock battlefield, together with the other three battalions that made up our brigade. They were all Pals units, made up of volunteers recruited from Manchester the previous year, so they'd done basic training in England but were completely green as far as real action was concerned. Although nobody said anything, all of us in the Royal Pennines did worry about them. Enthusiasm is great, and they certainly had that, but I'd seen plenty enough action to know that there's no substitute for real fighting experience. I guess that was why the generals had given us time on manoeuvres together so that they would get some sort of feel for a genuine battle. We carried on practising that attack up the hill together every morning for a week, and every afternoon and evening we had lectures and drills in wooden huts that were baking hot under the summer sun.

Now we were getting nearer to the real action, you'd have expected everyone to be getting more windy. And sure, we were. Show me a man who says his guts don't start to gripe when he considers being shot at and I'll give you a liar. At the same time, most of us were starting to buzz with excitement as well. This was 1916, when we were still chock-full of optimism, so every mess and billet in France was full of talk about how we were going to smash right through the enemy lines and finish the war in one go. And the Royal Pennines had more than its fair share of men who enjoyed the prospect of a fight. Men like Tollman, Alexander, Cooper and even me, I guess.

Tollman was in his element, given the opportunities for enforcing discipline with his swagger stick. Tim Cooper had a letter from his brother, who'd finally made it back to England and was in convalescent care there. Next thing we knew, Tim had grown a moustache that made him look exactly like Tom and was marching about smart as paint by day and hitting the piano keys with vim every night. I reckoned that he'd swallowed our explanation for what Tom had said about Tollman, or at least persuaded himself it was probably true.

185

As for Alexander, I never saw him happier than he was that week. He never stopped racketing around at high speed with Corporal Bill and Stephen Oliver trailing behind, a huge smile plastered across his face, cajoling and encouraging with all the infectious fervour of a man in love. During the exercises themselves, Oliver rejoined his section as part of Alexander's platoon. They were always next to my own platoon, which meant I could keep a close watch on them. I never saw anything else that would have confirmed my suspicions, but I didn't dare be too obvious. The last thing I wanted was to draw attention to the pair of them.

The last day of our battle rehearsals was the best. We'd been told that a general was coming along to see our manoeuvres, so I'd been expecting some sort of armchair warrior who'd watch from a safe distance, make some approving noises and then leave for lunch back at HQ before we were halfway done. But the brigadier who turned out to inspect us didn't fit that type at all. He looked more like a fighting soldier than a desk man, for a start, and he only gave us a short address, ending with a bit of a surprise.

'Practice makes perfect, men, and the more realistic the practice the better,' he said. 'So today I've added to the exercise. Enjoy it!'

He whipped out a big Very pistol from behind his back and shot a flare up to the sky. It was the signal to a battery of field guns that were hidden in a copse behind us. They opened fire in a volley of shots at the huts of the pretend village in a tornado of smoke and flame. Next second a machine gun had joined in, chattering in short bursts over our heads. Then a trench mortar battery exploded into action, lobbing shells in the air to explode halfway up the slope. The Brigadier gave a nod like he was satisfied that he'd spiced up the morning and then he waved our four battalions out into action.

Three hours later, we'd made it to the top of the hill. The attack had gone beautifully and we'd advanced steadily through the smoke and dust in textbook fashion despite the din of exploding shells and flying bullets. For once, when we'd 'captured' the broken-down huts of the village, we didn't flop onto the ground and grab at our water bottles like we had all the previous days.

'Bloody fantastic, was that!' Fox's eyes were shining in their deep sockets like lamps in the night. 'Near as we'll ever get to the real thing.'

I knew what he meant. It was close to authentic, from what I remembered from being with the marines in Mexico.

Alexander, too, was even more elated than usual. 'Another fine day to be alive, Scott. D'you know, for the first time, I actually believe this is going to happen.'

His eyes were shining bright. Oliver was standing close by and Alexander clapped him on the shoulder. 'With men like Stephen, all we need to do is lead them out and point them in the right direction.'

Corporal Keeble had lit his pipe, puffing out evil-smelling brown smoke. 'Aye, Mr David, this is about as good as they can do it for a pretend war. But let's see how we get on when there are proper bullets coming back at us. That's when we'll know whether we're really ready.'

'I tell you, my dear, you should have seen Scott here leaping ahead, without a care in the world. He's a natural born soldier.'

'Not true, Miss Beatrice. He was the one out in front, waving and shouting at us to keep up.'

'Why do I bother telling you to be careful when you don't take a blind bit of notice? And look at the pair of you, grinning away like a pair of overgrown schoolboys – you're in love with the whole business!'

'Just making the best of a bad job, dear heart. There's no point in wallowing in the misery of necessity.'

The three of us were sitting around a table in a cute café on the main boulevard in Amiens. The battalion had been shipped back by railroad from our exercises and we were due in the reserve trenches the next night. We still hadn't been told when we were expecting the big push to kick off but it could only be a matter of weeks. Howerd, inevitably, had started to take bets on the exact date. Most of the smart money was going on the last week of June, which meant that we'd probably only got one more stint serving in the reserve until we were ready.

Alexander had managed to co-ordinate with Beatrice and set up a rendezvous over a cup of tea for what looked like his final opportunity to meet up with her. When he asked me whether I wanted to go with him, I didn't know what to say. How could I turn down the chance to see her? But what was the point? It could only end up in feeling both frustrated and guilty. But it didn't matter what I thought. I wasn't given the choice.

'You've got to come with me,' he said. 'Beatrice insisted on it.'

So the three of us were gathered together on an oppressively hot afternoon in a tea room tricked out like one of the Lyons corner houses I'd seen in England. Only a boarded-up window and some cracked plasterwork from a recent German air raid betrayed the appearance of peaceful normality.

Alexander squinted at the clock on the wall. 'Apologies for this, but time marches on. I must desert the two of you for a few minutes. I have to collect something from the book shop down the street, if they have it in.'

'Really, David!' Beatrice said. 'We've barely sat down and now you're wandering off. It's too bad of you.'

I could tell she wasn't really surprised. I guessed she understood him well enough to humour his eccentricities.

'I shan't be very long. It's an important errand. Anyway, I can trust Scott here to look after you till I get back.' He grabbed his cap and shot out of the café with a wave.

For a while, we sat in silence. She was looking down into the sugar bowl, heaping up a mound of granules with her spoon and frowning like she was trying to figure something out in her head.

'Can I ask you a question, Anson?' She picked up her teacup and looked over the rim at me. 'Is David all right?'

As far as I could tell, she wasn't angry with him, or even disappointed. In fact, I couldn't fathom what she was feeling. I only knew that her deep blue eyes staring at me over the china were making it hard to keep breathing normally. Before I could think how the hell to reply, she'd carried on:

'It's just that his letters have been a bit odd in the last few weeks – almost distant.' She added the last bit reluctantly, as if she had to ask something that might be embarrassing. 'I wasn't sure if he was worried about something in particular. Other than the obvious, of course – we all know what's coming. Only he's never shown any sign before of... of even acknowledging the dangers of war.'

She reached across the table and rested her fingers on the back of my hand. 'I'm beginning... I'm beginning to think he finds it difficult having me so close by. Maybe it would be easier for him if I were still at home. And yet he seems so very content with his life, so perhaps it's only me being stupid.'

She stopped, leaving a gap that was waiting for some sort of reply. I could only swallow. What was I supposed to say?

I think your fiancé – my best friend – may be in love with his servant.

Impossible. Treacherous. Catastrophic.

In the middle of my confusion, I was acutely aware of the touch of her fingers, still resting on mine. It was the most sensuous feeling I'd ever known. There was a cramping pain in my stomach and I didn't dare look down. She was gazing at me, hanging on my answer. I guessed she was probably unaware that she still had hold of my hand. I stirred more milk into my tea, trying not to let the spoon rattle against the cup while I did my best to gather my sanity.

'You're right about him enjoying himself,' I said. 'I don't think I've ever known a man happier at his work. But he's got to know how darned fortunate he is to be able to see you like this, because we all keep telling him. There's nothing to worry about. Honest, Beatrice.'

Fortunately, she grabbed at that comfort. 'I hope you're right. I know I rib him about how much he loves his life in the army, but truly – there are times when I really do think that he is more at ease out here than he ever was in the days back home before the war.'

She let go of my hand, stroking her fingers across mine without any sign that she realised she'd been holding on to me, and picked up her teacup. Her face was set in a severe expression I found hard to fathom. Next moment she put the cup down again with a sharp click that sounded like she'd put a period to that part of the conversation, as if there was nothing more to be said or done and so she'd decided to move on. She put both elbows on the table and leant forward, smiling at me in the way that lit up her face, just like I'd noticed when we first met. I caught a scent I recognised too well.

'You're not married or engaged, I take it?' she said.

'I reckon I've never met anyone who'd have me.' Any time before that I might have been happy that she was interested in my past. Right then I was just relieved she'd shifted away from David Alexander.

'I doubt that, somehow. Are you sure there's no one waiting for you back home? I wouldn't have taken you for one of those old-fashioned men who don't have time for women.'

Now I knew she was teasing me. 'Not that either. I guess I just haven't met up with the right girl for me, not yet at least.'

'She'd have to be very special, I think. Now what type of woman would fit the bill? Someone practical and capable perhaps, or maybe pretty and intelligent.'

She was looking playful. It felt like she was heading into new, unmapped territory that was just as uncomfortable as her questions about Alexander had been, but then she changed direction again. It was another of those abilities that she and he had in common.

'So tell me, if you could have your life again, if you had a free choice, what would you have done with yourself?'

It sounded like the sort of conversational gambit she might have played at a party or fancy ball before the war. I was so relieved to have moved back to a safe topic that I only considered for a moment and then gave her a straight answer.

'I was sent down to Panama once, hunting a story. Did David tell you about my job? My real job, I mean?'

She nodded, which saved me having to spell it out again.

'I ended up in a mud-brick town in the middle of nowhere – a real one-horse place with nothing to do except sit in the sun and doze. Only when I started to explore I discovered it'd been built slap in the middle of some ancient ruins. Mayan maybe. There were still the walls of streets and temples and houses standing waist-high, half buried in the dust. The story never happened, but I got to wandering about, tracing those walls and pavements, wondering who had built that city and how they'd lived and where they went to. Since then, I've often considered that if I had the time, I'd like to go back.'

Her eyes were really shining at me now. 'I know. I know that feeling. My father used to run archaeological excavations all over Italy, digging up Roman remains. Some of my earliest memories are of sitting in a pile of earth playing with fragments of pottery. So let's think – we should organise a joint exploration after the war. But where? Old world or new world? You'd have to do all the underground exploration, I'm afraid. I don't like being cut off from fresh air so I get a bit panicky in confined spaces. Stupid, isn't it?'

She laughed at herself. I thought how rare it was to meet a woman who was so beautiful and still so unassuming. For a few minutes, I allowed my imagination to run riot, picturing a future with her.

She chattered on while the tea got cold, mapping out the details of what we'd do given limitless funds and the time to set up a grand expedition. The clock on the wall gave out a cracked chime.

'Goodness me. I've got to be off in five minutes. Where has David got to?'

No sooner had the words left her lips than the bell that was hanging on a spring above the tea room door rang and Alexander shot in and grabbed his chair between us.

'What on earth has taken you so long?' Dragged back to the real world, Beatrice sounded like a mother scolding an unruly child.

He waved a small paper parcel, obviously a book. 'Selected bits of Swinburne. A new collection.'

'Not another Swinburne. As if you haven't got enough! Honestly, David.'

He stuffed the book away into an inside pocket, looking abashed, while she got to her feet.

'Goodbye again, Anson. Look after yourself. We've still to sort out the travel arrangement for our adventure.'

Alexander followed her out into the street to say his farewell, leaving me sitting alone. One part of me was still feeling drugged by the effect of being so close to her. Another was trying to work out whether she had any idea of what she was doing to me. The third part was feeling ashamed. Maybe that's the condition of undeclared lovers the world over – confused, guilty and hopeful all at once. But they were all new sensations to me and I didn't know how to explain any of them.

To my relief, it wasn't long before Alexander had returned and sat himself down. He crossed his legs and plucked at the string that tied up his parcel. Then he looked up at me:

'Isn't Bea just wonderful? I'm a very lucky fellow, indeed.'

He should have sounded happy. I wasn't so sure. Once you've been a news reporter for a while, you get to listen to the way that things are said and not just the words. To my cynical ear, it sounded like he was trying to convince someone, and that someone probably wasn't me.

That was our last period of peace before we went back to the front and got ready for battle.

20

I might have looked calm on the surface in those last days. Inside, I'd got a constant churning sensation like the roll on the ocean before a storm. Maybe that was my intuition working overtime, trying to warn me. But back then, I just imagined it was because I'd got enough personal reasons to feel uneasy – Alexander, Stephen Oliver and Beatrice – let alone the impending battle. They still hadn't told us exactly where or when it was going to be but it was clear to everyone: our time was getting short.

The physical evidence of that was obvious as Alexander and I joined the rest of the battalion on the road out of town and set off on the march back towards our familiar billets. At one of our hourly rest stops I found Sergeant Fox staring across the fields with an expression of surprise on his face, as much as you could ever judge his emotions.

'Looks a bit different now, doesn't it, Mr Scott? I was starting to think we'd turned the wrong way.'

I'd been thinking the same. When we'd first come this way in winter the countryside had been open and deserted pastureland. Not today. Either side of the route was now lined with massive piles of supplies that towered above head-height – rolls of barbed wire, drums of telephone cable, bales of canvas, bundles of tools, pyramids of barrels and kegs, all baking in the heavy heat. Further back in the fields, walls of earth had been banked up to protect weapon dumps that housed mountains of blue grenade boxes and mortar bombs, and rifle ammunition crates. The road itself had become more and more crowded. At every junction, we'd been forced to halt and give way to a line of trucks, or a train of a hundred spindly legged mules, each with a case of cartridges slung on either flank and clouded with tormenting black flies. In the meadows, ranks of pack-horses were picketed in any patch of shade under the trees and where there was no shadow, khaki-painted vehicles were parked, row upon row of them. Criss-crossing every road and field, like the webs spun by some huge spider, networks of telephone line stretched from one new wooden post to another.

'Amazing sight, isn't it?' Alexander joined us as the men were getting to their feet and putting their packs on again. 'In a peculiar way, there's a splendid comfort in being a single tiny cog in this vast machine. It doesn't leave room for one's own doubts.'

Anyone else would have taken that for false modesty on his part because he looked brimful of vigour and confidence. I knew for sure that whatever doubts he might have he was not concerned with his own physical safety.

The battalion began to move once more but we didn't have a chance to swing along smartly like usual. Our progress stuttered in fits and starts, because the nearer we got to the front, the more the road was getting clogged up. Everywhere you looked there were men. Men marching in brigade formation. Men shambling along leading a half dozen horses. Men sitting in staff cars that rushed headlong and spattered grit and stone chips over us waiting at the roadside. Men lifting, carrying, hammering, mending, loading, building. Men directing the streams of vehicles. Men talking, singing, swearing, shouting. Men astride bicycles, on motorbikes and on horseback. Men of every nation and race and colour. Everywhere there was a clamour and a purpose and energy, preparation and heat and men, always more men. I wished I was still able to write; they'd have made a fine subject for an article about the way that war had changed to involve the whole world.

As we waited at a crossroads for a troop of Indian cavalry to pass by, Tim Cooper was as enthusiastic as Alexander had been.

'Isn't this amazing, Scott? Just look at these tens of thousands of fellows, all brought here to fight. We've got to be the biggest army in history. I only wish Tom was here to see it.'

We heard a loud growl coming our way. 'Bloody foreigners. Waste of fucking space. Wish they'd get out of the fucking way.'

It was Tollman. He was walking down our column, swatting casually with his stick at the shoulders of the waiting men. By the time he came level with us, the cavalrymen had trotted on, followed by a New Army infantry battalion, looking fit and well trained and in high spirits. He paused next to Tim and me, which was a surprise because he'd taken care never to address a word to me after the failure of his attempt to get me thrown out of the regiment. He stood and watched the ranks of soldiers passing by.

'Fine body of men. Young men, too. A beautiful sight.' He pursed his lips like a man making a show of admiring a work of art that he doesn't really understand. Then he took a sly sideways look in my direction. 'That'll keep at least one or two of our number happy.'

His face twisted up into his uneven smirk and he stomped back to the front of the battalion.

'What the devil did he mean by that?' Tim looked puzzled. 'Why wouldn't we all be pleased to see these fellows just raring to go?'

I was about to tear a strip off him for his naivety, but then held back. Because he was a good soldier and had been out in France for over a year, it was easy to forget that he was so young.

'Who can tell, with a man like that? He's got a mind like a corkscrew.'

I did my best to look unconcerned. But as we got back on the road again, I was worried. If Tollman had got to the stage of dropping those sort of unsubtle hints, what more did he suspect?

With all the traffic en route, it took much longer than normal to make it to the white farm and we marched the last mile with clouds of mosquitoes whining around our heads and our own shadows stretching long in the evening sun. We were cracking along in fine style. Tollman was leading the battalion because Colonel Ireland had been called away for a final briefing with the top brass, but even his glowering bulk didn't dampen our spirits. The men were singing one of their favourite ribald songs as we got near to our billets. When the farm came into view, the words petered out and died away. For a few seconds the only sound was the crunch of our marching boots, continuing on of their own accord. Then one of the men in the front ranks gave a whistle.

'Sodding hell. What's happened to the place?'

'What do you think's bloody happened?' Sergeant Fox was scathing. 'Bloody dry rot?'

The farm was a mess. It looked like it had been on the receiving end of a full-blown barrage. The side of the main house had copped a direct hit, so that it had to be propped up by timber and sand bags. Where one of the outhouses had stood there was only a burnt-out husk. At the entrance we had to break ranks to dodge a six-foot deep crater slap in the centre of the lane.

It was funny – you'd have assumed we'd all seen too much

death and destruction to be affected by a bit more damaged stonework, but I reckon we'd gotten used to thinking of the place as our retreat from the front line, a sort of sanctuary. When we came to a halt in the yard, we just stood gaping at the smouldering shells of burnt-out cottages and the battered rafters that stuck up from the barn roof like the ribs of a bust-up skeleton. Even the dung heap had been blown apart and spread over the cracked cobbles.

Alexander drew his breath in between his teeth. 'What the devil's happened here? Jerry's never targeted the place before. I'm just glad we weren't around.'

Fox was smarter than the rest of us. 'That's what you get when they station gunners up your backside. Makes you a bloody magnet for shellfire. Bloody menace they are.' He sniffed scornfully.

We were mystified by that but he'd been a long time in the army and he knew what he was talking about. Once we'd got ourselves settled down as best we could it was still light and there was a chance to look around. Behind the house, the field that we had paraded on every morning was patched with craters and lined with new trenches – not the seven-foot deep constructions we were used to up at the front, more like narrow slits dug in a hurry. Beyond, a beaten down track led off to the woods, where a row of snub steel noses poking out of camouflage netting gave away the position of a new battery of howitzers. We waved at the gunners but they were too busy hefting shells to notice.

'So that's it. There's nothing more guaranteed to get Jerry worked up than a fresh gun site. I have to say I've never seen artillerymen working this late at night.' Alexander was squinting into the twilight. 'Does that mean they're expecting something soon? The more those fellows soften Jerry up the easier it'll be for us. Please God they get on with it as soon as possible.'

Leaving the gunners at their labours, we wandered back to where we'd laid our sleeping bags under the open sky in the warm grass of the meadows, conveniently close to one of the trenches – just in case.

The top brass must have heard Alexander's prayer. Next morning we were eating breakfast in the only room in the farmhouse that had survived intact. One moment we were chatting away, the next the air was squeezed into a pulsating wall by the explosion of a million pounds of high explosives that battered at our eardrums and made our bones vibrate. I'd once been close to a spring avalanche in the high Rockies – a mountain of snow, ice and rock that ripped down for half a mile and crushed everything with a deafening roar. It was a whimper compared with this.

'Good God. It's like Armageddon!' Alexander shouted at me across the table. 'Only this is the beginning, not the end.'

I could barely hear him. The floor was heaving and jumping under our feet and the coffee in the jug slopped and spilt over the table. He leaned over and yelled in my ear, 'Let's go and take a look.'

Carrying on with breakfast was impossible anyway so I left it and went outside with him to watch. *What a damn shame. I wish I was still writing for the* Proclaimer.

That was my immediate reaction once again, my newsman's trained response, because those first moments of the barrage on the Somme were truly apocalyptic. The sky was covered from horizon to horizon with a roiling sheet of steel and the sun was dim, eclipsed by a curtain of smoke and metal. And the noise. It was like standing in the middle of a giant foundry, so brutally loud that I expected to feel my ears bleeding. Behind us, the woods were fringed with flames, one end to the other. Later they told us there were more than fifty thousand guns in Picardy that summer and that morning every single one of them opened up in single, unified, monstrous salvo. It was a staggering experience – literally. The concentrated explosions buffeted the air into storm-force blasts, so that we were tottering like early morning drunks trying to stay upright. After one especially thunderous detonation, I lost my balance and had to grab for Alexander to stop myself being blown headlong.

'Get a grip of yourselves, you two,' a deep, rough voice shouted close by. Tollman was standing only a few yards away. Unlike the rest of us, he didn't seem to be troubled by the man-made hurricane. 'Can't set a bad example to the men.'

He smiled his nauseating smirk again, with a knowing turn of his head. Then he winked at me and walked away. I looked at Alexander, but he only shrugged his shoulders and went back to watching the shells streaking across the sky above. I was left with my own thoughts:

He's such a smart man. How come he's not cottoned on to those innuendos?

Suddenly, I was oblivious to the noise of the barrage. Instead, I was filled with fear – fear for Alexander, who seemed to have lost his innate awareness of danger. I could only think that it was part of the price he was paying for his newly discovered love.

After about an hour, the intensity of the gunfire decreased. By then, most of the battalion was lined up to stare at the sight. As the continuous detonations became less frantic, Alexander turned to me.

'We're not needed for parades or inspections today. I'd like to go and take a look at those howitzer chaps in action. Going to keep me company?'

'Why not?'

There was nothing I could do about any of my fears, so in my normal way, I put them to one side and got on with the immediate challenge of life. Anyhow, even if I wasn't writing articles now, I was still making notes for a book I could write later. And like he'd said, it'd be fine sport to see someone else at work for a change, so we went to let Clarry know where we were headed and then wandered across the field towards the woods.

By the time we arrived at the edge of the trees, the artillery had been in action for more than an hour and the gun pits were like an inferno. A haze of fumes swirled around each gun and every time a howitzer fired it was like the door of a blast furnace had been thrown open. The six men in the first pit had stripped to their waists, their bodies coated with a film of sweat and chalk dust, while their red-faced lieutenant had taken his jacket off and was sprinting back and forth between the gun and a field telephone nearby. He was clutching a handful of map sheets, with a mathematical table slung on a lanyard around his neck and dark stains soaking his back and shoulders.

We stood out of the way, under the trees, as they loaded and fired and loaded and fired and loaded again. I saw Alexander watching the half-naked men labouring and speculated about him again. The guns were still firing and my own imagination started to wander.

Those blue flowers back there. They're the exact colour of her eyes. I wonder what she's doing, right now.

I was dismayed that I'd strayed into areas I'd tried so hard to shut away. It seemed like every time I considered the question of Alexander and Stephen Oliver, I couldn't help but summon up images of Beatrice.

Stop that, right now. There's no room for any more passions in this company. Like it or not, Tollman was right – get a grip.

Abruptly, the howitzers stopped firing. The gun crew and the ammunition carriers collapsed down on the sandbags and grabbed for their water bottles. In spite of the sudden lull, my ears were still ringing and it took a few moments to realise that the rest of the barrage was continuing up and down the line. The artillery officer was fanning himself with his map. He finally had time to notice that he'd got himself an audience.

'I hope you enjoyed the show, gents. Next performance isn't until we're resupplied, a couple of hours yet I should think.'

He'd got a broad Scottish accent, and when he took his helmet off he'd got the red hair to match his face. 'You're over from the Pennines, aren't you? I'd give you the proper tour, but I'm due to take over as observation officer up at the front.'

'Actually, I was just thinking that I'd rather like to see what it looks like on the receiving end,' Alexander said. 'Any chance of our trotting along with you?'

'Don't see why not, if you stay ready to get your heads down smartish. At noon, Jerry usually lets rip with his own guns for five minutes – that's what happened to your billets, last week. Hang on here for a second while I have a word with the skipper.'

He dashed off to the neighbouring gun pit and reappeared clutching his tunic, field glasses, knapsack and a bundle of maps. He was pursued by a loud bellow over the sandbags.

'Mind you don't take them right up to the line, MacAlister. And get yourself buttoned up. You look like something dragged out of a ditch.'

We followed him over some fields and into a broad valley where there was the beat-up wreckage of a village. All the little brick houses had been bashed about and were missing their roofs. There was a set of stone steps on the outside of one of the tallest buildings and MacAlister led us up into the cracked rafters of the second floor where there was a ragged hole in the gable end.

'We sometimes use this as an observation post, but we've moved right forward now, so you won't be in anyone's way. There's a fine view from here – just have a dekko at that.'

I got my binoculars out. The village was in the valley bottom, with our own front line partway up the slope on the far side and the German lines a few hundred yards higher up yet. From our viewpoint I could see everything – the trenches themselves were narrow ribbons of chalky white on either side of the wide green swathe spotted with patches of flaming poppies and clumps of a bright yellow plant. In the air above the enemy lines, white, orange and black clouds bloomed and flowered like short-lived weeds before dissolving into grey mist. Every now and then, dirty brown pillars would writhe up hundreds of feet and then fall back to earth a few seconds later with a tremendous vibration that made our stone house shake. When I focused my glasses, I saw they were fountains of dirt and rock blown out of the ground by the power of the bombardment. I could make out fragments pulverised out of the trenches beneath – bits of wood and metal and wire and some tumbling dark starfish shapes. It was all so jumbled that it took me a while to realise that those were human bodies. I watched one figure that had been thrown high in the air, spinning round and round, before falling back out of sight. Had he been killed immediately by the blast, or was he still alive for those last few seconds as he flew across the sky?

'Pretty decent show, isn't it?' MacAlister spoke without taking his eyes from his own binoculars, with a cold-blooded enthusiasm that reminded me of Tim Cooper. I'd always considered that I could be pretty detached, but some of those youngsters made me look like an emotional milksop.

'In a perfect world we'd be better with less shrapnel and

more big howitzers to break up the wire and really smash their dugouts, but it's still early days and the French gunners haven't even joined in the fun yet.'

Reluctantly he packed away his field glasses and led us back down the stair. 'I'd better be getting along. I don't want the CO on the line, bawling about being behind schedule because no one to spot for them. If I were you, I'd cut off home before the Jerry artillery opens up. You wouldn't want to get caught out in the open. Cheerio!'

He dashed off with his charts fluttering under his arm and we turned our faces uphill, back to the battalion. Alexander was very quiet until we topped the ridge and started across the meadows. He was walking slower and slower. Finally, just when the farm had come into view, he stopped altogether.

'Are you OK?' I said.

'Sorry, Scott. I was just imagining those poor devils in the Jerry lines, huddled down in their dugouts with nothing to do except pray that the next shell isn't a heavy that will bury them alive. And then I started to think that no matter which side we're on, we all pray to the self-same God for survival and victory.'

I half thought that he was being his usual ironic self and waited for him to cock an eyebrow and invite me to join in the joke. His face stayed pensive and it looked as if he really was perplexed by the paradox. He didn't have a chance to air his doubts any further. Before we had taken another step, there was a new, different screech in the air, distinct from the clamour of our barrage. A whistling noise, like an oncoming express train, getting louder and louder, and fast.

'Jerry's counter-battery shoot!' Alexander checked his watch. 'And exactly when MacAlister had predicted. I'm impressed.'

Then the air directly above our heads started to fizz and

hiss. That was very bad news. Some of the German shells were dropping short and heading directly our way.

'Hells bells! Come on, Scott. This is going to be close.'

We took one look at each other and then broke into a full out sprint. I'll bet we were the fastest hundred-yard dash in the world that year, haring across those meadows. Alexander was first to the nearest slit trench, with me sliding in to home in best baseball style right behind him. And just as well, too. The first of those German shells slashed down on our heels and burst with an ear-splitting roar. It was our turn to be on the receiving end.

For a very frightening five minutes we stayed crouched down together in the middle of a hurricane of high explosives. The trench was a tight fit and shallow and I was darned grateful for those steel helmets we'd groused about when they were issued, because the flint fragments whipped across us like shrapnel. When the storm came to an end at last, Alexander was first to stand up and peer over the sandbagged rim of the trench. He looked from one side to the other and then his head snapped around in surprise.

'Good God! Who the devil is that? What's he playing at?'

Cautiously, I sneaked my nose above ground to find out what had shocked him. It was a weird sight. We'd thrown ourselves into the first trench we'd come to, so the parade ground stretched flat between us and the wreckage of the farm. A hundred feet away, slam bang in the middle of the beaten earth a man was standing, stock still, his arms outspread so that he was completely vulnerable, almost like he'd been welcoming the barrage, inviting it. He was bareheaded and his chin was slumped down onto his chest. I'd not noticed him in the panic of our dash to beat the incoming fire, but he must surely have been there all through – no one could have made it there through the barrage.

'There's something very wrong there. We've got to help him.'

Without looking back to see whether I was following, he leapt out of the trench and ran, paying no heed to the smoking craters and the risk of more shellfire. There was no choice. Within a second I was hard on his heels again, praying frantically there'd be no more explosions. When we got close up, it was obvious why the man hadn't moved during the barrage. He couldn't. He'd been fastened to a post that was hammered into the earth. We skidded to a halt in front of him in a cloud of dirt and Alexander reached out to lift the man's head so we could see his face.

'My God! It's Stephen.'

21

Someone had tied Stephen Oliver to one of the timbers we used for shoring up trench walls, then spread his arms wide apart and lashed his wrists to a crossbeam nailed onto the top of the post. He was covered from head to foot in dust from the explosions that had torn up the ground all around him and his eyes were closed. There was no sign he'd recognised us. I wasn't sure whether he was conscious, or even alive.

The following minutes were chaotic. Alexander was trying to support Stephen's head and pick at the knots on the ropes that bound him at the same time I was fumbling for my jack-knife. All the while I was waiting for the screech and explosion of the German barrage starting over. It felt like forever, although I guess it only took us a few seconds to cut him free. When we'd got him loose he sagged onto the ground with a grunt and Alexander looked up at me with relief in his face. At least that was some sign of life. Next instant, he'd picked Stephen off the ground, hoisted him over one shoulder and set off at a clumsy run towards the shelter of the farm, with me following behind.

The nearest trench was full of soldiers from C Company who'd also decided that the barrage had ended and were climbing back out into the open. They gathered around in a circle while Alexander set Oliver down and knelt by his side.

'Someone go for the doctor, please. And quickly.'

One of the men raced off as Stephen Oliver's eyes flicked open and stared up at the sky. His gaze was roving from side to side, unfocused.

'Let's get his jacket undone and give him some air. Give me a hand, Scott. Does anyone have a water bottle?'

He splashed some water over Oliver's head while I started to unfasten his tunic, fearful of what injuries I'd uncover. There wasn't a mark on him, however, even when we rolled him carefully to check his back.

I looked up. 'He must be the luckiest man alive. All those explosions and he's not been hit anywhere.'

But Alexander was staring at Stephen's face. The boy's eyes were jerking from left to right now, his mouth had started twitching and a trail of spittle was running down his chin.

'Who tied him up? Who did this?'

He glared at the men standing around us and they shuffled back away from him in silence. I could understand why. I'd never seen David so angry. His face was as white as Fox's, except a livid flush glowed on his forehead. He could barely get his words out.

'You've got him down,' said a new voice. 'Good. He'd just about completed his time.'

The ranks of men were parted by a huge shadow that pushed between them. Tollman looked down at the boy lying in the dust, and nodded his head like a court-house judge satisfied by the dubious sentence he'd just pronounced.

Alexander stood up. He was near as tall as Tollman so he could look him straight in the eye.

'What the hell does that mean? Is this... this travesty... something to do with you?' Normally, he was very skilled at keeping his emotions out of his voice, but that day he couldn't hide his fury.

Tollman took a step back. 'Course it is. Field punishment: number one on my orders, in my capacity as commander of the battalion.'

He growled in his usual surly way but I thought he sounded unsure of his ground.

'What the devil for?'

Tollman rallied and took a stride forward again.

'He refused to obey a direct order from his commanding officer, that's what for. I'd say he's got off lightly. Clarridge's manual of military law says I could have had him court-martialled, but he caught me in a good mood this morning, so I only gave him four hours FP 1.'

'What direct order? And field punishment in the middle of a barrage? That's not military law, just plain barbarity.' Alexander was near stammering in his rage. He'd unscrewed another canteen and was pouring water over his servant's lips.

Tollman shrugged. 'His tough luck. His four hours were almost up when the shellfire started but there was no sense in risking anyone else to set him loose until the guns stopped.'

Alexander might have been too angry to notice that Tollman hadn't answered his first question, but I'd spotted it OK and squirreled it away to follow up later.

'Anyway, what's it matter to you? He's only your servant…'

It sounded like Tollman was going to say more but suddenly he stopped. Then he looked from me to Alexander, then to Oliver lying on the ground, then back to Alexander again. Very slowly, the right side of his face started to twitch upwards until he was grinning broadly. I could nigh on see the realisation spreading through his brain at the same speed.

He's guessed. Now what?

I braced myself, waiting for him to say something else. If this went bad, I might need to prise Alexander off him. He leaned in close and grunted something under his breath. I couldn't hear, but Alexander flinched away as if he'd been hissed at by a snake. Tollman just stood there with his face pushed forward, still grinning.

At that second, Vaughan and his orderlies arrived. In a few practised moves, they loaded Oliver onto a stretcher and started to carry him off towards the aid post. He'd still not made any attempt to move since we'd cut him down and his arms flopped limp over the side of the stretcher like a Raggedy Ann doll. Alexander ran to catch up with the bearers, took Stephen's hands in his own to hold them steady and walked alongside the stretcher.

They'd got no more than halfway across the parade ground when Tollman shouted to Vaughan. 'Mind you don't send him away, Doctor. I want that man close by, where I can keep an eye on him. I'll have no scrimshankers in my battalion.'

I waited for Alexander to turn round and tackle him head-on at that, but he didn't. Only a stiffening of his shoulders gave away his feelings as he stayed close by Oliver's side. Tollman stood with his legs apart and watched them go, tapping his leather stick on the palm of one hand, while his face twitched up into that lopsided smile of satisfaction.

I was watching the pair of them carefully over the next few days. Having some knowledge about his closeness to Oliver, I'd half expected Alexander to pick a fight with Tollman. If it came to an outright scrap, I was more than prepared to wade in, but I never even saw them together. If anything, Alexander seemed to be avoiding the Major. I figured his common sense had kicked in again and he knew it wasn't the time for confrontation.

Certainly he was brooding on something. I kept asking myself what Tollman had said out there on the parade ground. Whatever it was, it had knocked the stuffing out of him. Sure, he had to go through the training exercises and drills like we all did, but you could see that his heart wasn't in it. Even the rumour that we were about to find out where and when we went into battle left him completely unmoved. I

210

decided it must be a combination of anger and worry about Stephen Oliver and exhaustion. As far as I could make out, he was spending every night over in the medical post by poor Stephen's bedside. When he hadn't improved by the end of the week, I took myself off to the aid post one evening to have a word with the only person I reckoned I could trust – Doctor Vaughan.

I was lucky. I caught the doc before Alexander arrived for his night-time vigil. He was having a quiet smoke in the doorway of the cottage and completely sober.

'How's your patient?' I asked.

'How's he doing in himself? Well now, he can move his limbs a little today and he'll feed himself if you put a dish in front of him, but he's uttered not a word. I think he's lost the power of speech.' Vaughan packed down the fill in his pipe and put a match to it, puffing on the clouds of smoke. 'As to the diagnosis, there's not a mark on him, so it's not a question of a head injury or anything like that. There are only two possibilities. He might have passed out from fright, which I can understand given the shellfire, but since he was bound upright he wouldn't have been able to get his head down, which produced a disastrous reduction in blood flow to his brain and permanent damage. The alternative is that he's been literally terrified out of his wits by having to stand and face the shellfire. It's not unusual for men to lose their faculties in cases of these sorts, you know.'

'I still don't understand how it came to happen. Tollman said something about Stephen disobeying an order – what was all that about?'

'Young Oliver's not exactly in a state to have told me anything and I'm getting him transferred out to one of the base hospitals tomorrow. If you want to know more, you'll have to ask the adjutant. He must have been in the orderly room that morning.'

211

When I went to the battalion offices and asked Clarridge, however, he couldn't explain much more.

'It appears that Private Oliver refused to obey a clear order he had been given.' He sounded distracted, barely visible behind stacks of orders and directives he was preparing to hand out to all the company officers.

'But what did Tollman tell him to do? Oliver's a good soldier. He'd not ignore an order from any sort of officer. I can't imagine what would make him defy someone as dangerous as Tollman.'

Clarry stopped sorting through his piles of paper and sounded thoughtful. '*Bon point*, Monsieur Scott. All I know is that the Major had summoned Oliver to discuss something personal. He told us it was a private matter and sent all of us out of the room to start off with, then a couple of minutes later, he called me and the duty corporal back in.

'"I want you two to witness this," he said and turned to Oliver. "Are you disobeying my direct order?"

'The lad could barely stand up straight he was trembling so much, but he stuck to his guns. "I won't do that, sir."

'"So you're defying your commanding officer?" Tollman came back at him.

'"I can't obey that order, sir."

'Tollman rounded on him. "In that case, you'll have to take what's coming," he said. He didn't sound angry at all, strangely – more satisfied, as if Oliver was actually doing what he'd expected.'

Clarridge was such a good-natured soul that he looked puzzled when he told me.

'Is he really allowed to order someone to be tied up while the Germans shoot at him?' I couldn't believe it. 'That's hardly reasonable behaviour, surely?'

'Unreasonable, perhaps, but according to the letter of the

law, he can order it because while Colonel Ireland's away, as major, Tollman is the next most senior officer and is in command.' Clarry rubbed furiously at his whiskers, where they were thinnest already. 'I've only heard of it once before – a really hard-nosed soldier who wouldn't toe the line and was sentenced to Field Punishment Number 1. Even then, that was only the token gesture of tying him to a wagon wheel for an hour in front of the whole battalion, mainly to embarrass him into behaving. Tollman was pretty brutal with young Oliver, but strictly speaking the law was on his side. It was appalling bad luck that the Germans opened fire just then.'

Bad luck was one way of looking at it. I could guess at another because I'd got an inkling of the devious workings of Tollman's mind. He probably knew exactly when the Germans were due to open fire. None of my thoughts were pretty when I left the adjutant's office.

At the end of that week all of us Royal Pennine company officers were shipped into Amiens in a three-ton truck. We were dropped off in a small square where there was an iron-studded door opening onto a flight of steps down into a long, brick-vaulted chamber. The barrage was muffled this far back from the line, and underground there was no sound except the echo of our boots on the stone. I guessed we were in a disused wine cellar. The town foundations were riddled with them, some still used for storage and some that had been pressed into use as air-raid shelters. This one was fitted out with electric bulbs that dangled from hooks in the mortar and cast a wavering light over a square of trestle tables. On the boards there was a model landscape constructed of green and brown papier-mâché, wire and cardboard. The battalion headquarters staff had gone on ahead and I felt a huge surge of relief when I saw them gathered around a familiar grey-haired

213

figure. I never imagined I'd be so glad to see Colonel Ireland rejoin the battalion.

'Good to see you all, gentlemen. Glad to be back with the Pennines.'

There was a cheer from the boys. Only Tollman didn't join in. He didn't look any too pleased to be pushed out of command. Instead, he shuffled himself surreptitiously around the cellar until he was standing right next to Alexander. As far as I could see, he didn't say anything, just leaned in so as to make his presence felt. Alexander shifted uneasily but he was hemmed in by the curve of the vault behind him. The Colonel was still speaking:

'Know you'll want to hear this. Finally been told our target for the day. Montauban, gentlemen, Montauban. Proud to be back to lead you there.'

There was a gasp and then another cheer. We knew Montauban. It was a small village slap opposite the section of the line we were well acquainted with, having been in and out of it so often in the previous months. Many a time we'd stared through our periscopes at its pulverised remains on the far side of the German trenches and we recognised that it wasn't the worst spot for a full-on assault. That, plus the fact that it was right on the edge of the British Army sector, so we could expect help from the French infantry and artillery.

'Now the date. It's to be the twenty-ninth of June.'

That hushed us up OK. It's all very well to be full of vim about a fight that's going to happen at some vague point in the future. When they tell you it's only a week away, it concentrates the mind, like old Samuel Johnson said.

'They've made this model for us. Useful to study the ground. Look at the terrain. Clarry and the intelligence officer'll point out the main features, then I'll run through the plan of attack.'

214

From my corner of the table I'd a clear view of the topography of the battlefield. I can see it now as fresh in my mind as the first time I laid eyes on it. Our own small part of the Battle of the Somme.

The overall lie of the land was simple. A shallow valley ran from side to side, cutting through the high ground. To our left there were wooded copses dotted around a cluster of grey matchbox buildings. That was the village of Carnoy, where the gunner MacAlister had taken me and Alexander. A narrow road wandered along the low ground to a larger group of boxes, flying a paper flag labelled Maricourt, a small town sitting close by a wide loop of the River Somme itself, which was represented by a strip of blue tinted crêpe paper. On the slope rising from Carnoy, neat lines of embossed trenches snaked parallel to each other. Behind them, there was a sort of groove in the ground that curved up towards the hilltop and Montauban.

Clarridge picked up a long wooden pointer from under the table and stood like a teacher facing his classroom. He waved his stick over the model.

'Most of you will know this well. The main valley runs east–west and we hold the floor with our front lines at the base of the northern slope.'

'Get on with it, man,' Tollman growled out of the shadows, just loud enough so as the Colonel wouldn't hear him. Clarridge looked hurt and flustered as he continued:

'The Germans have the upper part of this slope, with three lines of trenches that overlook our positions.'

He waved his stick vaguely over the model. It decapitated the flag at Maricourt and sent it flying into the paper river which made some of the younger subalterns giggle. Foster – the intelligence officer – stepped forward. He was abrupt and to the point.

'Right. Once we get across the enemy trenches, note that there are spurs of land on either side. They are marked on your maps as the Warren, and Glatz redoubt. Jerry has fortified them and placed machine guns there. Fortunately for us, our artillery has been targeting these points in addition to the front line trenches.'

I hoped that optimism would be justified and remembered MacAlister's line about wanting more heavy shells. I tried to catch Alexander's eye, but he was still hanging back, overshadowed by Tollman.

'Above those two points, you'll see that the slope levels off until the line of the old railway embankment – that's the curving line on the model. Then it rises gently through this area of broken ground and hedgerows to Montauban village itself.'

'Excellent.' Colonel Ireland stepped back to the table, pulled on a pair of wire-rimmed spectacles and consulted a thick sheaf of papers. 'Simple plan of attack. We're second wave. Follow 21 Brigade who go first at zero hour. They take front lines and Glatz strongpoint. Soon as they've put up flares, it's our turn – first and second Manchester Pals and then us. Only one tricky bit, further up.'

He pointed a bony finger at the model, between the embankment and Montauban. 'Here. Probably close-quarter fighting. Our sort of thing. Expect it'll be pretty hot there.'

He nodded once emphatically, and stood away to let us study the model. Warren-Walker and his young friends stared intently at it, trying to appear nonchalant and professional, but only succeeding in looking like a crowd of schoolboys on a day out. Tollman stood back resting his shoulders on the curving brickwork and muttered conspiratorially to Howerd. I was pleased to see Alexander join the rest of us at the table, examining the contours from different angles, stooping down occasionally to ground level to check exact lines of sight and fire.

'Take a good look, gentlemen. Next time you get a chance, we'll be in the thick of it.'

22

We'd only ten minutes to take notes before the next battalion arrived for their own briefing. Tollman and the Colonel stayed down in the vault to liaise with their HQ staff, while everyone else climbed into the truck and started back for camp. Everyone except me. I was left behind in town to collect a heap of supplies for the company mess. Even in the last few days before a battle, men need their comforts – perhaps then more than ever.

I hustled round the crowded streets, picking up parcels from one store and boxes at another. For once everything had been parcelled up ready before I arrived so that I was done well before the battalion transport returned to collect me. With the uncommon luxury of time to kill, I found a café with tables out on the sidewalk and ordered a large coffee. Something was bothering me. Why hadn't Alexander told Tollman to go take a hike? I knew he didn't lack the guts for it and surely now, with Stephen Oliver safely out of the way, there was no reason for him to tread carefully. It was a bit of a mystery but I couldn't fathom it out. After a bit I gave up. I sat back, lit up a smoke and watched the world go by.

Amiens was bustling. If it hadn't been for the rumble of the barrage and the long lines of khaki trucks jolting along the cobbled street, I could have been looking at a scene from before the war. The midsummer day was warm and bright, most of the shops were open for trade and there were crowds of folk out in the streets, including a fair number of women. I saw a nice-looking girl lift the hem of her skirt as she stepped out of a stairway. She looked up and noticed me watching her.

With the smallest tilt of her head up towards her room, she sent out an invitation that was subtle but unmistakeable.

For a moment, I was tempted. But while she was pretty, she wasn't the face that had dominated my thoughts for the last months. I spread my hands apart in a gesture of disappointment and then tapped my wristwatch to suggest that my time was too pressing. She smiled, clutching her hands to her chest as if her heart was broken and shook her head in mock sorrow as she sauntered on her way.

I thought probably I'd been dumb to turn her down. Nobody would have been hurt by it. And thinking about the days to come... While the plan they'd run through sounded all well and good, there was a pretty fair chance some or all of us wouldn't make it. So this might be the last time I'd ever get a smile from a girl, perhaps even the last time I'd get to drink a coffee in the sunshine.

In that mood, you start asking yourself whether there's anyone who'll miss you if your luck runs out. I'd always considered that I was in the best state for a soldier, or a newsman – footloose and fancy-free, as the saying goes – but sitting in that café, I thought I could be wrong. Maybe with a wife and kids back home, at least your life has had some purpose to it if you don't survive. It was too late for me. In spite of all the towns I'd seen and the girls I'd known, I'd never met anyone I'd really clicked with. And now that I had, she was out of reach.

I drained the last of the coffee that had gone cold, and looked up to pay the tab. The peace of the afternoon was shattered by the crack of an explosion. It wasn't very far away across town. Then there was another and another. Getting louder. Coming closer. I heard the drone of aircraft engines. A gendarme who'd been strolling down the street looked up to the sky and broke into a run. The last of the truck convoys speeded up and vanished down the road in a cloud of exhaust smoke. The decrepit waiter hurried out from behind his bar. He grabbed the coins from my hand.

'*Vite, Monsieur*. Quick! Boche flyers come, they drop bombs.'

He pointed a finger upward before he scuttled off down a side road as fast as his old bones could carry him. I gathered up my packages and made after him but I was pretty loaded up with boxes and he was moving quicker than I'd have believed possible. By the time I got round the corner, he'd disappeared. I was in a narrow square that was completely deserted. Another string of explosions started, closer still. I needed to get under cover pretty quick. Under a stone archway in one corner there was an iron door, similar to the entrance to the cellar where we'd had our briefing. I raced over to it. As I saw a sign in French telling me it was an emergency bomb shelter, I was aware of another set of footsteps running towards me. The newcomer arrived as I threw down my parcels, put my weight to the door and heaved it open. I looked around with the intention of shoving whoever it was in first and stopped dead.

It was Beatrice.

She was in her nurse's uniform, and was panting hard. She looked as surprised as I felt, but it was no time for conversation or civilised exchange. I grabbed her arm, pushed her through the doorway, grabbed hold of the door to pull it closed and leapt after her. Inside, I all but fell down a short flight of stairs as the door clanged closed. The basement we'd tumbled into was tiny, much smaller than the vault for the company briefing; most likely a store for wood or coal before the war. It was dimly lit by a single electric bulb that just about showed me the four corners of a cellar that was dry and dusty. Beatrice had slumped to the floor against one wall, her eyes wide and scared. There were more explosions outside now, getting nearer and nearer. One almighty detonation must have been in the square outside and it shook the whole shelter with a massive bang overhead, and then the drawn-out grinding crash of a building falling in. Next moment the light flickered and died out and we were left in total darkness.

We could be trapped down here. And nobody will know where to find either of us.

I tried to put the fear out of my head. There was no use worrying about that for the present. My main worry was Beatrice. I couldn't see her, but I could hear her grabbing deep hoarse breaths with a sort of high-pitched wheeze. I remembered her telling me that she couldn't abide being stuck in small spaces. In the darkness, I reached down and put my hand on her shoulder, trying to reassure her. Another huge detonation ripped through the earth and the cellar swayed from side to side. It was getting hotter. There was a far-off rumble like a giant rock slide. Beatrice gave a sort of whimper. She must still have been crouching on the floor and I felt her clutch at my knees. I reached down to her, took her under one arm and pulled her upright.

'It's OK,' I said, calm as I could. 'It'll be over in a few minutes. We're safe down here.'

Next instant, however, there was deafening roar outside and a blow like a massive hammer shook the door. She threw her arms round me, buried her face in my shoulder and held on tight. I could feel her trembling like a horse spooked by the wind, and I put my arms around her and stroked her hair with the same rhythm I'd have used to gentle a frightened colt.

'It's all right, Beatrice. We're going to be fine. Only a few minutes. It's all right. All right.'

She gave a whimper and clutched for my hand, holding it close to her breast.

What happened next, I've never been able to explain. God knows I've spent enough effort working out how it came to be. I guess it's not a process that you can analyse rationally. Maybe it was partly because I hadn't held a girl so close for years; maybe because I was feeling a sense of my own mortality so near to the battle; maybe because Beatrice had been haunting my every thought for weeks. At that moment, all those convenient explanations were of no significance at all. The truth was a simple, devastating matter of chemistry, an immediate release of body and spirit. Whatever the mechanics, however we arrived at it, for that little while, with the bombs falling about us, I was granted something to remember for the rest of my days.

It felt like the shelter was shuddering, but that might have been me, as I kept smoothing my hand over the nape of her neck. I felt her body relax and push against me, not with panic now but with all her full curves pressed to me so that I could feel the swell of her breasts against my chest and the touch of her hair on my cheek. She lifted my hand and held it to her lips – immediately we were face against face, skin against skin, unable to see each other, but with all other senses swamped. I could feel every contour of her body; my nostrils were filled her perfume – the mixture of iris and violet and musk that had troubled me before. I knew I'd never forget it. We pressed so close that our breaths were shared – each of us drawing in the air exhaled by the other – and I felt the lightest of touches as she brushed her eyelashes against my mouth. Then we were kissing, locked together with a sublime intimacy that stripped everything away except the fact of a man and woman perfectly joined.

I've no idea how long it lasted. When I'd regained any sort of sanity, the shelter had gone quiet apart from the rasp of our own breathing, and the bombs had stopped. Still we clung to each other with a desperate intensity. It didn't matter that I couldn't see her face, or that she hadn't spoken a word – I just knew that somehow I'd got closer to another human being than I'd ever thought possible. In the most unexpected way, down in that stifling darkness, with the world exploding all around, I'd found love, or something so similar it didn't matter.

Time has no meaning when you're as wrapped up in each other as we were. It seemed like hours before I heard someone rattling at the entrance to the cellar. The door frame must have been buckled by bomb blasts because the door only gave out a dismal groan, opened a few inches and then jammed again. But that was enough to allow a ray of light to cut across the dust of the cellar and I looked down at her in my arms.

She raised her hand and laid her fingers along the line of my jaw. I couldn't decide whether the expression on her face was delight or despair. 'Anson. We can't... we mustn't ever...'

Before she could finish, she was interrupted by a piercing screech as someone levered the door open from outside. A man's voice called down to us that it was safe to come out. There was nothing else to do and nothing that could be undone. We tidied ourselves as best we could and then climbed the stairs together, hand in hand. Outside, the air was heavy with gritty dust and our side of the square was a junk yard of crumbled brickwork. The man who had freed us had picked up his crowbar and was already wandering away. We stood close together in the archway with our fingers intertwined and it seemed like neither of us could bring ourselves to say another word. She turned and looked at me, scrutinising my every feature as if she couldn't believe what she was seeing. I breathed in a trace of her perfume again, watching as she took a deep reluctant breath, her lips parted to speak. Then she shook her head and closed them once more.

'Scott! Put that fucking tart down, and get a move on. We've got to go.'

Standing on a pile of rubble on the opposite side of the square, hands on hips, Tollman was watching the pair of us. He'd a grin so broad it reached his ear on the mobile side of his face. I'd no idea how long he had been there.

Quickly, I let go of Beatrice's hand and stepped back. I wanted to say something, anything, that could explain what I'd felt. The words wouldn't come and there was no time.

'Stop fucking about, Scott,' Tollman shouted again. 'We can't keep the transport hanging around for you and your floozy. If you're not there in one minute, we'll go without you.' He lumbered off towards the main street.

My brain was spinning like a feather in a storm. Half of me wanted to shout with joy, while the rest felt like slinking off in despair and getting blind drunk. I looked into her eyes for help but I couldn't begin to fathom her expression. What was it? Bewilderment? Fear? Anger? I'd no idea what to say to her, or how I could say it. Instead, in a dismal gesture of doing something useful, I started hunting around in the debris for the parcels I'd dropped. Before I knew what I was doing, I was backing off down the road, grabbing up as many of the packages as I could find before I beat a coward's retreat round the corner into the main street.

The truck was still waiting. I threw the stores in back and climbed in after them, taking a seat on one of the wooden forms, numb and confused. The driver crashed into first gear and we ground away. Tollman was on the bench bang opposite and he shot me a smile packed full of evil suggestion as we passed the side turning where I'd abandoned her. I didn't try to look back, because I knew that she'd already gone and the street was empty.

23

All through that final week, I watched the Royal Pennines getting wound up tighter and tighter by battle nerves. We'd been told so often that victory was inevitable that the men were fizzing with aggression like a pack of hounds held back on the leash. The effect on the officers was more varied. Clarridge ran around the camp from dawn to dusk with a clipboard that grew thicker by the hour. Doc Vaughan was ever more philosophical, contriving to get through such heroic amounts of coffee that he never slept at all. Warren-Walker, Cooper and the other youngsters oscillated between bouts of hilarity and hours of pencil chewing while they composed poems about the joys of self-sacrifice. Howerd looked increasingly on edge and drank more than anyone else, although it didn't stop him from laying bets on anything that moved, while Tollman roamed the camp looking pleased with himself and waving his fists around as if he was practising for the battlefield.

Only two of us were not caught up in the whirlwind. Since the journey back from Amiens, I'd been struggling to come to terms with my own feelings. Far as I could decide, logically the least I should have done when the light shone across the bomb shelter was to let go, step away and make some form of apology.

I had done none of that. I'd never been any sort of monk and I guess that even by then I'd sampled most of the seven sins, but I had my own code of how a man should act. The idea of having deceived Alexander by messing around with his girl was driving me crazy. I'd tried so hard to push Beatrice out of my mind before that afternoon, but when the fates had thrown us together it had been impossible.

I didn't plan it. I couldn't foresee that she'd be out of the hospital during the raid. I couldn't know she'd run to the same shelter. I tried to justify what had happened.

So what? My judgemental puritan conscience wasn't going to let me get away that easily. *You were just looking for the opportunity. You've wanted her since you first met. You've been obsessed by her. You knew exactly what you were doing.*

That was the conversation that echoed back and forth inside my head. It was futile. I tried and tried and tried but I couldn't wipe away the memory of her body, her lips, the touch of her skin on mine. And those memories only fuelled my overwhelming sense of guilt.

Most emotions have a useful purpose. Anger prepares you to fight, fear readies you to run from danger, grief helps you to recover from loss. But guilt? No. Guilt is the only useless sentiment. Its anxiety is crippling, it undermines friendship, strips away self-esteem and makes you break out in a sweat every time you think about what you've done. Guilt serves no useful purpose at all.

But I couldn't persuade myself that back then. For those last few days I looked for distraction the only way I knew how – hard work. Parades and exercises, drills and practices, all in the heavy heat of the summer. That was OK during the while I could keep busy. But at night, I'd lie awake thinking about what I could say to Alexander, or whether I should admit anything.

Worst of all, I suspected he knew about me and Beatrice. The evening after we got back from Amiens, I was sitting on my own in the mess, nursing a stiff whisky, when he came and joined me.

'Evening, Scott.'

He sounded pretty subdued, but then he had ever since Stephen Oliver's field punishment. I could only give him a nod because I couldn't get rid of the images running through my mind. I didn't dare say anything. We stayed there, in a stiff uncomfortable silence.

I was about to make some excuse to leave when I was aware that somebody else had entered the room. Before he spoke, the sour smell told me who it was. Tollman.

'Alexander, I want a word with you,' he said. He was smiling, if that twist on his face could ever be called a smile. 'In private,' he added.

'Anything you want to say, Major Tollman, you can say right here,' Alexander said. He was sitting forward with his chin in his hands. He sounded weary but he wasn't going to be browbeaten. 'It's not long before we're going to fight. Don't you think it's time to stop playing all these secret games?'

'I don't believe so. Trust me.'

Tollman bent down and whispered a few words in his ear. As he listened, Alexander's face went completely blank. I couldn't guess at what he was thinking. Without saying anything, he stood up and followed Tollman out of the room.

I stayed put with a load of questions running through my mind, mainly to do with Amiens. It can only have been a couple of minutes before David came back. His face had turned grey and he looked twenty years older. He stumbled over a chair as he came across the room.

'Sorry, Scott. I've got to go.' He picked up his drink and went out into the dusk.

He's told him. That was my immediate reaction.

How would he have known that the girl with me was Beatrice?

Easy. He could have seen that photograph of her Alexander carries. He might have shown it around in the mess any time, maybe months before you even joined the Pennines.

Except Alexander wasn't hostile when he came back in. Distraught, yes, but not angry.

Maybe he's just too well-mannered to confront you with it. Maybe he values his friendships more than you do.

I couldn't work it out. One thing was certain. Whatever Tollman told David Alexander had shaken him like I'd never seen before. Even more than the day we cut Oliver down.

Alexander must have kept to himself, because I didn't see him for the following two days, except at a distance. After that, if I did run into him, he was polite and civil enough – once he even tried to crack a joke – but I'd lost the close friendship that had made life in the army a game to be enjoyed. And still, I couldn't know what Tollman had said to him. It wasn't just me he was keeping at a distance. He was civil to everybody else, but no more than that. I saw Corporal Bill looking puzzled when he marched past with barely a nod. It was as if he'd had to take refuge in being a professional soldier while he was turning over something much more important in his head.

I'd been doing my own share of thinking, but I couldn't decide what to do. I'd have liked to try and explain to him, to clear the air, but I couldn't be absolutely sure that it was me and Beatrice that had triggered his mood. Anyway, what the hell was I supposed to say?

Very sorry old man; it wasn't something I tried to arrange – wrong time, wrong place and wrong person, but still it happened and now I've fallen for your girl, and fallen hard.

How could I start down that line with my best friend?

This is where the story gets real difficult. The official books and newspaper articles make us out as a bunch of heroes, wrenched from our homes to fight for the British Empire and get slaughtered on the battlefields of France by machine guns and shellfire. I guess that's how we'll go down in history –

a doomed generation, a herd of willing martyrs sacrificed in droves because our leaders were too dumb to change their tactics. There may be some truth there, but that's not how it felt then. We lived through the intensities of hope and fear that are the daily companions of warfare but we weren't spotless heroes and we weren't a bunch of innocents just pining to get back home to a life of peace and quiet. We were only normal men, with normal failings.

Anything that has ever occurred on the face of the planet, you'll see in an army of men at war. All the major graces of bravery and endurance, and the little virtues of cheerfulness and comradeship and sharing your grub around and shouldering your part of the chores. You'll find all the vices too – incompetence and bullying, violence and drunkenness and lying – not to mention the inevitable human weaknesses of greed and fear. But above all that, there's one frailty that's kept hidden and never discussed.

The need to love and be loved.

It was the night before we were due to march off to battle and we'd gathered in the mess for our final briefing. Before that, the Colonel made a surprise announcement.

'Orders from GHQ, gentlemen. Don't like them, but no choice.'

That got us all muttering. What the heck was going on?

'No, nothing too drastic. We're still on to fight. Or most of us are.' He cleared his throat as if he was embarrassed. 'Got to leave one tenth of us behind. Sort of reserve. Clarry – you tell 'em.'

Clarridge polished his spectacles and looked at the top sheet on his clipboard. 'Because the Pals battalions are all recruited from the same town, GHQ don't want to risk any unit... um...' he stopped while he worked out how to say the next bit delicately, '...biting off more than it can chew, and sustaining an unacceptably high rate of attrition.'

He was shouted down by a chorus of the boys telling him that wouldn't matter to us. We weren't going to run into anything we couldn't handle.

'Just so. Just so,' Colonel Ireland took up the lead again. 'But orders are orders. Drawn lots to decide who stays behind.'

The atmosphere in the mess suddenly clogged up, like the air itself had got stiff. You could almost see the older men, the ones with wives and families, praying to the fates to keep them out of the firing line. The youngsters looked vaguely puzzled, as if they couldn't work out whether they wanted to stay or go.

'Two of you must stay behind. Clarry and I have done the draw. Very sorry – Foster and Scott – not your chance to shine this time.'

I think Foster must have known already, because he didn't move a muscle. Me? I was overwhelmed by a swirl of emotion and I could feel the stares directed at me and their thoughts: *Why him? Why not me?*

I barely heard a word the Colonel said after that but I knew what I had to do when he dismissed us for the last time. I had to persuade him to let me go. I hadn't come all those thousands of miles to stay back while my friends went into battle. I stood to one side as everyone else streamed out, some in solitary contemplation, some chattering between themselves. I noticed Tollman whispering something to Alexander again.

'Colonel Ireland.' I caught his attention while he was still talking to the adjutant. 'I know you've drawn the lots, but I've no family and no one to miss me if I don't come back and I'm keen to see some action. Can I have permission to trade places with one of the older men?'

He looked at me with mild amazement.

'Very sorry, Scott. Good for you. Glad to see men wanting

to fight. But *alea jacta est*. Can't change the system. You'll get your chance next time. Right, Major?'

I was certain that Tollman had left with the others, but he'd snuck back and was standing all quiet at my elbow, whisky glass in one hand, the other in his tunic pocket, and that nasty twisted smile more distorted than ever.

'Quite right, Colonel. There's plenty of time for glory seekers later on. Scott will have to take his turn.'

There was a glimmer of red as he clapped me on the shoulder in what I guess looked like a gesture of bonhomie to everyone else, but he put all his weight and grip behind it and dug his thumb hard into my collar bone. There was nothing more that I could do so I took myself off while the Colonel, Clarridge and Tollman put their heads together to sort through the final details.

That was when it happened. I was collecting my papers from where I'd left them when my eye was caught by a patch of red on the bare boards under the chair. It was a small scarlet book. I was certain it hadn't been there before – someone must have dropped it. Then I remembered the flash of colour a moment earlier. It had flipped out of Tollman's pocket when he mauled my shoulder.

Odd. I've never seen him read anything other than army documents.

Without making it obvious, I took a peek around. With the others still engrossed, I scooped the book up with the rest of my stuff and made for the door, trying to walk calm and slow.

Outside, the night was warm but the stars were concealed by clouds and it smelt like rain was on the way. The camp was bedding down for one final night in comfort. It would have been quiet, except for the shells that were still whistling overhead in a continuous stream. Back in our tent, Cooper and the other subalterns had already dropped off to sleep – it's amazing how youngsters can manage that when there's a fight imminent – but I wasn't ready to settle down yet. I needed time to adjust my brain to the fact that I wouldn't be going out to fight the next day. Under canvas, the air was too hot and humid so I left and wandered around until I found a broken down wall to rest my back against while I had a smoke and a think.

I was rummaging in my pocket for a light when my fingers caught on the little book I'd found in the mess and I pulled it out together with my Ronson. There was a title engraved in gold block letters down the spine. I flicked the lighter and in the yellow glow made out the name: Swinburne.

Odder and odder. I'll swear that came from Tollman's pocket, not David's. Two lovers of Swinburne in the same battalion?

Puzzled, I lit up a cigarette and then let the flame die. Even as it guttered out, a tangle of facts separated themselves, lined up and clicked into formation in my mind.

Oh, God. Please let me be wrong.

I spun the wheel on the lighter again and held the flame close to the book, still hoping like hell I'd jumped to the wrong conclusion. It opened where a corner had been turned down and I saw that someone had underlined one of the verses in ink:

Ask nothing more of me, sweet;
All I can give you I give.
Heart of my heart, were it more,
More would be lived at your feet:

It was cut off halfway because the following pages had been ripped out. My hand started to shake. Although I'd only ever seen it parcelled up, I knew where this book had come from, and who had bought it. And why. I turned to the front, where a few lines had been written on the fly sheet. Sure enough, they weren't in Tollman's scrawl but in Alexander's neat italic script.

For Stephen. Unlooked for but joyously found.

There was a gust of wind, the lighter blew out and I was left in the dark. Now I was scared. For the first time I understood just how bad things truly were. I'd been so fixated with my own guilt I hadn't cottoned on to the real disaster going on under my nose. How could I have been so dumb? How could I have left him to face this on his own?

Suddenly, I could smell danger. I'd got to find Alexander and quick. I threw my cigarette down and hurried off to his quarters. His bed was empty and there was no sign of him. I hunted through the rest of the camp as inconspicuously as I could, checking all the usual places where we'd lingered for a smoke or stood talking through the hours when sleep was impossible. There were still small groups of men hanging around but no sign of his tall figure. He'd vanished. It wouldn't have been difficult to get away. The gates were still guarded and the boundaries patrolled but we'd all had plenty of practice at avoiding sentries at night. If he'd quit the place, there was little I could do. Still clutching onto the book, I wandered back across the camp and it started to rain in big fat drops.

Then I started to think. There was no way Alexander would run away. It just wasn't him. What would he do? He'd need somewhere to think, somewhere to be alone, and there weren't too many of those. Where had I made for when I didn't want to be disturbed? The forge. I made off as fast as I could go, dodging around tent pegs and guy ropes and piles of kit, skidding and stumbling on the greasy wet grass.

Out at the edge of the farm, the transport lines were pitched out in the meadow by a clump of trees. The battalion horses and mules were tethered in long rows that were still and quiet in the downpour. Beyond them, the farriers had set up their forge under the shelter of a corrugated tin roof and at night the fire was banked up to keep it going without burning too hot. It should have been deserted but as I got near I thought I saw a brief movement outlined against the glow. I quit running and edged forward quiet as I knew how, grateful for the rain that was banging off of the roof overhead, yet at the same time feeling stupid to be creeping along like a sneak-thief, when I'd be sure to find the place empty.

It wasn't.

Alexander was sitting on a sawn-off tree stump, staring into the embers. Along the top of the blacksmith's anvil at his side, he'd set out a row of bullets. There were six of them, their tips shining red in the firelight. The holster on his belt was empty and he'd got the revolver in his lap. While I watched, he lifted it and started to fill the chambers, holding up each bullet with his finger on the lead point and thumb on the brass casing before he slotted it home with a metallic snick. When the six chambers were full, he closed the catch and spun the cylinder around. There was only one possible explanation, but I still couldn't believe it. Not David Alexander, the calmest, most fearless man I'd ever known. I stayed back in the shadows, appalled and fascinated at the same time. But when he lifted the Webley, propped up his elbow on the anvil and put the gun barrel to his temple I had to do something. I braced myself and pitched my voice as sensible as possible.

'That's not how to play Russian roulette, David. There's only supposed to be one bullet and five empties.'

I was trying my darnedest not to alarm him. Even so, he jerked around and for a second I was terrified he was going to pull the trigger before I could react. He lowered the gun a fraction, although it was still pointing at his head.

I stepped forward into the light.

'I guess it's a practical solution but it isn't exactly what you'd call elegant. Just imagine the mess they'd have to clean up in the morning. Has it got as bad as that?'

'Worse than ever you could know. I'm very sorry, Anson, but please – you must go now.' His voice was flat and lifeless. 'I do regret the untidiness but this is the only way. I know what I have to do.'

His finger was beginning to whiten on the trigger again. I took out the little volume of poetry.

'I guess this is yours, or at least it was until you gave it away.' I tossed it to him.

He snatched for the book with his free hand and caught it just before it hit the floor. For a couple of seconds he riffled through the pages with the Webley lowered into his lap, but when he came to the missing leaves, he let out a groan and raised the muzzle again until it was pointing just below his ear. I was sure I'd come too late, then. At the last moment, he was saved by his own curiosity.

'How the hell did you get hold of this?'

'Tollman dropped it in the mess tonight.'

'You remember when I bought it, in Amiens that afternoon. Have you read it?' His face was still blank. I just nodded.

'So you know.'

He said the words slowly and looked away from me, into the heart of the fire. I pulled up another log and sat across the fire from him. For a time neither of us said anything. Then, without lifting his attention from the embers, he started to talk.

'Have you ever fallen in love, Anson? Really fallen, so far and so fast that it takes your breath away? And then found that love is returned, so you want to sing and shout your joy from the rooftops?'

I thanked all the fates that he wasn't looking at me, because I knew my face would've given me away.

'Can you imagine how it feels when that love is forbidden? When it's so far beyond the bounds of decent behaviour that you have to keep it secret and furtive and hidden from the world? No, of course you haven't. You're far too straight and decent for that.'

He paused, leaving me cringing inside, before he took a deep breath and went on.

'It's Stephen, of course. I've known him for years, since he was a lad working on my family's estate back home. He's always been a kind, gentle soul and when we all joined up I got him assigned to me as my servant.'

He did look at me, then, with a wry little smile.

'Until one morning this spring, when he brought me a cup of tea in billets… I looked up and saw the sun glinting off his hair and recognised for the first time how beautiful he was. At that moment, I knew that something had changed inside me. I still wasn't sure what until the night that my bath was delivered – you were there, so I don't need to tell you the rest. It was the feel of his hand on my skin that lit the fuse. I can't describe what happened next. But it was the most glorious night of my life, and something I don't regret, no matter how things have turned out.'

His voice had hardened and there was a look of defiance on his face.

'We both knew the risks but we couldn't have stopped ourselves. Afterwards, we were so overwhelmed with the ecstasy of having found each other that the idea of giving up what we'd just discovered was inconceivable. I persuaded myself, and Stephen, that no one would ever find out.'

235

He shook his head at the memory of his optimism.

'I should have known better. You've seen what Tollman is like. He must have suspected something was going on and set himself to watching Stephen until he was pretty sure. But he still needed proof, something that he could take to the Colonel to back up any accusations.

'Fool that I am, I provided it for him. There were a couple of notes I scribbled to Stephen that'd be awkward to explain if they fell into the wrong hands, but worse than that was this.' He waved the little scarlet book. 'You've probably guessed I bought it specifically as a gift for Stephen. I wanted to give him something that had particular significance to me. I sat and read through the poems to him, marking up the ones that were especially appropriate.'

He smiled at that, a real smile, and I could see he was remembering the two of them together.

'I don't know exactly what happened next. I suppose Tollman saw Stephen with the book at some point and pounced on him that morning when we were away watching the barrage. Stephen refused to admit anything and wouldn't hand it over. That must have been the order he wouldn't obey, which allowed Tollman to sentence him to his Field Punishment. Probably, he'd only started out with the aim of exacting petty revenge on me but when the Jerry artillery started up, he saw the opportunity to search for the evidence that would confirm his suspicions. I imagine that while we were all sheltering in the trenches, and poor Stephen was crucified out in the open under fire, he was back ransacking through Stephen's kit. When I tackled him straight away on the parade ground that day, he warned me off.

'"The Bible says that a man who lies with another man is an abomination, deserving to die."

'I knew that we were in trouble then, but I'd no time to

think about his crackpot quotations. I was far too concerned with what had happened to Stephen. Later I had the opportunity to look it up in the Bible Vaughan keeps in the medical post. Leviticus it is and a nasty intolerant bit of the Old Testament too, just the sort of stuff a man like Tollman would remember. After that I kept clear of him, at least while Stephen was still in camp. The evening after we'd all been looking at that model in Amiens, he cornered me in the mess – you probably don't remember – but he dragged me off on my own.

"What would that fiancée of yours do if someone showed her the love letters you've been writing to your boyfriend?" That was all he said, and then he shot me one of his looks and sauntered off.'

I could picture Tollman's glee when he realised that he'd finally got David exactly where he wanted him.

'Even before that,' David said, 'I'd been worried sick about Stephen but afterwards I daren't begin to think what it would mean if Tollman made his knowledge public. I couldn't try to talk to anyone, only keep myself to myself and try to work out some sort of solution.'

'I was wondering why you'd gone so distant on us.' I couldn't say that I'd thought it was because Tollman had told him he'd seen Beatrice and me together.

He shook his head again, despondent. 'I don't want any of you to be tarred by association with me when he decides to make it all public. Because he will, at some point. Tonight, when we were leaving the briefing, he collared me and muttered a quotation at me. It was one of the verses that had particular meaning for me and Stephen and I knew he'd found the Swinburne. Oh, Christ, Anson. What else am I supposed to do?'

It was the only time I ever heard him sound sorry for himself and he resumed his glacial calmness in a moment.

'Apologies. That's desperately unfair of me. It's a disaster entirely of my own making. For a straight-talking fellow like you, this sort of affair must be disgusting even to contemplate.'

But I knew from the way he looked across at me that he was looking for a sign that I wasn't shocked. I shook open a pack of cigarettes, lit two and handed one over, giving myself time to think before I spoke. I had to be careful now. At least he was talking, but he was still swaying on the brink of the drop.

'For God's sake, David, no one's perfect. We all have our crosses to bear and our failings to carry. Why should I give a damn about who you love, or how?'

I don't know how I said that last part without my voice giving something away but my change of tack seemed to steady him for a spell. He spun the revolver's cylinder again but at least his finger was off the trigger now. I nodded at the Webley, cold as charity in his hand.

'Why bother with that? We'll be up to our necks in a fight in less than two days, which may spare you the trouble. If it was me, I'd be thinking that I might as well try to do something useful with my life, instead of throwing it away on a whim. And I would be dammed if I'd give Tollman the satisfaction of knowing he'd won again. I'm surprised you're giving in so easy. Surprised and disappointed too, if you want to know. I didn't think you were that yellow.'

God knows, of all the words I came out with that night while I was trying to stop him from shooting himself, those were the most sanctimonious of the lot. During the war, I met a few dozen soldiers who deserved to be called heroes and I saw some stunts that called for the coldest sort of nerve. Nothing, but nothing, ever took more courage than David Alexander opening himself up emotionally to me in the forge. I couldn't have made a confession like his in a million lifetimes.

I went on. 'Anyway, we've got the book back now, so Tollman has lost most of his proof.'

David shook his head. 'The pages that are missing – they're the most damning of all. When you're overcome by love, you're not inclined to restrain yourself in writing. He must have torn them out and kept them separate.'

We sat like a couple of players in a tableau, still as statues, trying to figure out a way around that one. Then he gave a start.

'What about Beatrice? What can I say to her?'

I'd no answer to that. He couldn't know how much he was talking to the wrong man there.

'You see, Anson, I'm right. There really is no other way out.'

He lifted the revolver again. I'd been trying to gauge my distance to leap across and make a grab for the gun, but this time I saw he'd taken up the slack on the trigger and the hammer was already cocked back. If I made any move he'd fire and blow his brains out. I had to rely on words to persuade him. I don't reckon I've ever had to think faster in my life. I'd called him a coward, I'd tried reason and I'd tried appealing to his hatred of Tollman, but nothing had succeeded. I'd only got one last ace in my hand, much as I hated to use that. No choice. I played it.

'Who'll look after Stephen when you're gone?'

He rocked back at that, blinking. The revolver was still poised at his head.

'If you need to kill yourself, that's your choice. But that's only half the job done, as far as Tollman is concerned. He's still got Stephen to play with, once he's recovered and they send him back. And you can't desert Stephen. He's got no one else. Tollman won't rest until he's driven him to destruction. You know that as well as I do. If I truly loved someone, I couldn't take the chance of leaving them to Tollman's tender mercies.'

I was lying through my teeth, because I was darned sure that Stephen Oliver would never see active service again. I figured that Alexander must have seen the transparency of my ploy and the Webley never wavered away from his head. We sat there, and sat there, and I was beginning to think I'd no choice but jumping him anyway, when he gave a weary sigh.

'You win. I should never have let you get within earshot. But you're right, for Stephen's sake I have to carry on.'

He let the revolver hammer rest safely down and unlatched the cylinder, letting the bullets fall unheeded onto the floor. I stooped to pick them up and saw that daylight was breaking to the east. I let out a deep breath and flexed my shoulders. I hadn't realised how tense I'd got, all coiled up to leap across the forge. I peered out from under the tin roof at the new day. The dawn was cold, grey and wet, and tomorrow the battle would start without me, but we'd managed to make it through the night.

He turned to me with a tired smile while he shoved the unused pistol back in its holster. I can't say he looked cheerful, but at least he was still alive.

'You're a marvellous fellow, Anson Scott. The truest of friends.'

I tried to smile back but it must've looked pretty feeble. I'd stopped him shooting himself. I just felt as guilty as hell.

24

At noon that day the battalion marched out to the war without me. I made myself wait by the gateway and watch them go. Colonel Ireland was at the head of the column on his charger, but I noticed that Tollman had adopted a horse too and was riding just behind. The men went along in fine style in spite of the miserable weather. The rain hadn't let up all morning so that drops rattled on the helmets slung on top of their packs and the roadway was already churning up into an ochre paste. When C Company came past I stood to attention and saluted. The boys were as fit a bunch as I'd ever seen, cheerful and excited. Only Alexander looked set and stern. Maybe he was thinking that Stephen should be there by his side. I watched until they were out of sight, wondering how many of them I'd see again.

With the battalion gone, the camp was empty apart from a handful of clerks and the transport officers. In the commotion of the morning, it looked like I'd been forgotten and no one had remembered to give me any specific instructions. For a while I wandered alone through the deserted farmyard, grey and miserable in the ever-heavier downpour, considering the mess I seemed to have got myself into. I should've been with the rest of the boys, splashing through the mud on our way up to fight. That would at least have given me something more immediate to concentrate on. If only Tollman didn't have those pages of poems with David's writing on them. I had a sudden thought – would he have taken them with him into the fighting? We were only permitted to carry battle kit, which didn't leave too many places he could be carrying them. Was it possible that he'd left them safely behind? The only place he might have hidden something like that was with the rest of his kit, in the tent he shared with Howerd, next to my own. Casual as I could, I strolled over to the lines of tents. I knew that the more relaxed I appeared, the less likely that anyone would challenge me. Without a flicker of hesitation, I lifted the canvas flaps on Tollman's billet and ducked inside.

It was humid and close in there in spite of the rain and the sweat was running down my face, but I knew I had to hurry. It'd be impossible to hear if anyone approached because of the din of the barrage, so I needed to get in and out as quickly as possible. It was obvious immediately which side of the tent was Tollman's – he'd left his favourite swagger stick across the top of his valise. I threw the wretched thing to one side, knelt down and started to search through his bag. Nothing. Only spare shirts, a pack of cards and an unopened bottle of whisky. I sat back on my heels and repacked everything, cursing under my breath. I'd been so sure he would have left the Swinburne pages here. But I saw he was too smart for that. He must have been expecting me to search through his stuff – that was what he'd done with Stephen Oliver's kit, after all, on the day of the field punishment. There was nothing I could do, except leave quick and quiet. As I left the tent, however, my glance fell on Tollman's stick. I picked it up, weighing it in my hand, remembering all the times I'd seen him use it like a club. Next second, without pausing to think, I smashed the bloody thing over my knee. Inside the leather cover, it was filled with lead shot. In my rage, I didn't even feel it.

I left the tent line, and hurried back to the farm, lost in my own contemplations, head down to the rain. As I turned a corner of the barn, I was almost knocked off my feet by a bustling figure coming the other way.

'By God, it's supposed to be bloody summer. You'd think

we should get better weather in France than they're having back in Yorkshire. What the devil are you doing here, Scott? Left you behind, have they?'

It was Doc Vaughan. I remembered that he and his medical crew weren't due to move forward until the battle was actually under way.

'If you've nothing better to do, we could use another pair of hands,' he said. 'There's a pile of stuff to get sorted out and packed up ready to leave tonight and we're running out of time.'

He'd already grabbed my arm and started dragging me off towards the medical post. The rest of the camp might be quiet, but not there. A half dozen medical orderlies were scurrying about organising a mountain of field dressings, drugs and sinister-looking surgical instruments that were heaped high in the old farm stables.

'We're supposed to set up an aid post in the front line immediately after our boys go across with the second wave and I'll not be found wanting for supplies.' Vaughan had started to dash from one pile to another, checking their contents against his own list.

'So you don't expect them to have an unopposed stroll across No Man's Land either, Doc?'

That stopped him for a second and he stood still, his arms filled with boxes of dressings.

'Now there's a funny thing. It always seems like the more the top brass tell us about how easy everything is going to be, the more business seems to come my way. Ah, well, there's nothing we can do about it, so make yourself useful and take this lot over there.' He dumped his load into my grasp.

For hours, I mucked in with the medical team, fetching and carrying, packing and repacking, checking and counting, and all the while the rain fell. Running to and fro wherever I was pointed, I was free to let my mind wander. I thought about love and friendship and treachery, but most of all I pondered David's revelation the night before, trying to make out how I felt about it, trying to separate it in my mind from me and Beatrice.

I'd knocked around the world enough to understand that love between men isn't uncommon. A lot of lads act awkward in female company and are more at ease with their pals. When they're shut off from the rest of the world, with only one another for comfort and support, that can easily turn into something more than manly affection. I'd met at least two couples in Alaska who lived together much like man and wife, although to meet any of them you'd have taken them for the roughest, toughest, regular guys.

That had taught me not to judge a man by his preference of lover, so it wasn't the notion of David Alexander and Stephen Oliver together that bothered me, or even how that might affect me. No, I can truthfully claim that by the end of the afternoon, I'd managed to push Beatrice and me to one side, at least for the time being. My preoccupation was Tollman.

At last, everything was arranged to Vaughan's satisfaction and he calmed down enough to allow us a break for a cigarette. I joined him leaning up against the clunch wall of one of the cottages to shelter under the dripping eaves and lit up a smoke. My mind was still fixed on that evil bastard; the snarl on his face when he glanced at George Moore the day before he was blown up, the calculation in his beady eyes as he bullied the Cooper twins the night that Tom went west, and the way he'd glared at Alexander when he faced him over the short arm inspections. I pictured him riding out at the head of the column that morning, slouching like a great sack in his saddle and grinning with satisfaction, and then David Alexander marching with our men, drawn and pale. When would Tollman stop? Probably not until he'd killed us all. If he could destroy David, there was no hope for anyone else. When I arrived at that conclusion, worry was far behind me. Anger had taken its place.

'That's a fine fierce face you've got on you, lad. You're generally such a dab hand at hiding your feelings, so what has finally got under your skin? Or maybe I should ask myself, who has?'

Vaughan took a pinch from his snuff box and fixed me with his uncomfortable stare. I reined in my rage and instead, asked him the question I suspected I already knew the answer to.

'Tell me, Doc. You must've seen most of the quirks that active service throws up. Have you ever known anyone brought up on a charge of...' I didn't know how to put it, '... of being too close to another soldier?'

He puffed out a great cloud and peered at me through the haze.

'The Greek vice, you mean?'

I nodded. He considered for a spell, surrounding himself with his usual fog of dirty brown smoke.

'I've not met a case myself but I remember hearing about two lads in one of the Scots regiments. Subalterns, both of them. They were found in bed together by one of their servants and there was a hell of a stink. They were both court-martialled – the older fellow was lucky to get away without being shot – and then they were shipped off to one of the special hospitals for nerve cases. It was all hushed up at the time, but the Medical Officer was a friend of mine and he told me the story after one whisky too many.'

He dropped his chin and stared at me from under his eyebrows. 'Do I take it that wasn't a theoretical enquiry?'

I couldn't answer and stayed quiet. After a second, he nodded knowingly, and stowed his snuff box away.

'Be careful, Mr Scott. That's all I'll say.'

One of his orderlies came along with a list of missing drugs and he turned and drove us all back to work. I was put to shifting a pile of carboys of sterilising solution from the aid post into the back of a general service wagon, but while I staggered to and fro, my mind was still simmering with a wrath that Vaughan's answer had done nothing to damp down. Why should a fine man like David Alexander be put through hell by a monster like Tollman? A man who'd all but killed at least two fellow officers?

The more I dwelt on it, the madder I got and in the end I'd worked myself up to a fury.

If anything happens to Alexander, I swear Tollman won't live long enough to gloat over it.

Then I had another, more cheerful idea.

Maybe he won't make it through the battle. Maybe some sharp-eyed German machine gunner will do us all a favour and put an end to the entire problem.

But while I shoved one bottle after another onto the wagon boards, I knew that I was trying to kid myself. Tollman was all but indestructible.

'They're back! They're back again!'

The sentry at the gate was hopping up and down, waving his cap in the air and pointing. Vaughan and I and the rest of the medical gang ran out of the farmyard to see what had caused the commotion. Coming along the lane over the rise was the last thing we expected. In column four abreast and headed by two mounted officers, a full battalion of British infantry was marching away from the battlefield. We stared, hardly able to believe our eyes, but when they got near enough to make out the upright figure of the Colonel and the bulk of Tollman dwarfing his horse, and the flash of bright blue shoulder patches, we knew it was true. The Royal Pennines had returned before they could have fired a shot.

It was Tim Cooper who told me what had happened when he and I and Alexander were gathered in the mess that evening, keeping company with a couple of bottles of whisky. Tim was doing most of the talking. I was relieved to see Alexander looking reasonably composed.

'We were all but up to position when we stopped at a crossroads. We assumed that we were standing by to let another battalion through but an hour later we were still waiting and we could see another two regiments close by who were twiddling their thumbs as well. Finally, the Colonel rides back down the line.

'"About face, men," he says. "Damned gunners. Can't work in the wet. Battle postponed."

'So we turned tail and marched all the way back here again.'

He filled in the rest. The grand plan of attack needed support from the French artillery but the downpour of the last few days had made the ground so sodden that it was impossible to move field guns any distance at all. So at the last minute, the top brass had put the whole scheme on ice and any units that could were returned to their billets. The new zero hour had been put back forty-eight hours to allow the ground to firm up.

'But it wasn't a total waste of time,' Cooper announced cheerfully. 'On the way back, Howerd tripped over his own feet and fell into a crater. He reckons he's broken his ankle and he went off to see the doc. At least that's one menace less.'

He suddenly checked over his shoulder to see who was within hearing, but he was quite safe. All of Tollman and

Howerd's gang had collected in their billet and the only man in view was Vaughan himself, homing in on us from across the room, clutching his mug of coffee.

'How is Howerd, Doc?'

The doctor dragged up a chair and took a gulp of his coffee.

'I'm not sure the poisonous little bugger isn't putting on a bit of an act, but he does have a fair bit of bruising around the ligaments there, so maybe I'm doing him down. Anyway, I've told the Colonel he's not fit to march and he'll have to stay back with the reserve. You'll be going up in his place, Scott. No doubt someone will think to let you know before tomorrow. Good luck.'

He raised his mug, waved it vaguely in my direction as a toast and drank the rest of it down in one go.

The others lifted their glasses but I couldn't reply. I was too busy thinking.

That's the answer. It's obvious.

Fate, or at least Howerd's yellow streak, had just offered me a unique opportunity. Why wait to see what Tollman had stored up for David Alexander and anyone else who got in his way? The rest of the officers' mess might be true British gentlemen, scared to get their hands too dirty, but not me. I was a hard-nosed Yankee and the situation was completely clear.

I'd have to deal with Tollman myself, once and for all.

Cooper, Vaughan and Alexander packed it in after a spell and took themselves off to sleep. I stayed put and sat by myself late into the night, smoking and drinking and planning. Armies are always full of gossip and tall tales and unconfirmed rumours. One of the more persistent stories in those days was of the unpopular officer whose drunken stupidity resulted in half his company being wiped out. The next time he and his surviving men went into battle, they came back without him, reckoned they'd lost sight of him in the noise and smoke. Only thing was, when the stretcher-bearers found his body, it was riddled with British bullets, not German. I'd heard much the same story years before with the US marines and I'd always put it down as a barrack room myth. But remembering it started me thinking. I might well get a chance during the battle, in one of those small pockets of tranquillity during the mayhem where anything can happen without being observed. At least this time it'd be a German bullet, because one Mauser makes a hole like any other.

I turned the scene over and over in my mind. Was it really the only solution? Did I have the guts to shoot Tollman in cold blood? Would I have to gun him down face to face, or could I buck against everything I'd ever believed and put a bullet in his back? I waded through another half bottle trying to get to grips with that one. Sure, I'd had to kill men before but they were soldiers at war and we all took our chance in that. It was a massive step away from shooting one of my fellow officers. But whichever way I looked at it, I couldn't see past the fact that Tollman was too dangerous. Dangerous to me. Dangerous to Alexander. Dangerous to every man in the battalion.

Far too dangerous to let live.

I don't remember the next day well, maybe due to the whisky, maybe due to the commotion of getting my kit together to move up with the battalion, because at breakfast Clarridge confirmed that I'd be going in place of Howerd. I do recall the weather had finally turned to summer, and I've a picture in my mind of a grand football game, played the length of a meadow, one whole company against another, ending in a confused brawl. I spotted Alexander in the crowd of spectators and tried to talk to him but he'd gotten remote again and I couldn't get anything out of him. I figured he'd got enough of his own thinking to do and left him to it. In the end, after all the theorising and moralising, it was a relief when evening came and I took up position alongside the front rank of C Company, ready to start back east, towards the battlefield.

We marched out at sunset with the barrage thundering overhead and the men singing their favourite obscene song with gusto. They might have been nervous, but they were confident that an army as big and well prepared as us couldn't possibly be beaten. I think only the two of us were silent, lost in our separate thoughts. I couldn't begin to unravel what was in Alexander's mind but I stomped along in a black mood, contemplating murder.

25

There's a chill that bites in the depth of night when men waiting to go into action stamp their feet, cupping their hands to blow warmth onto their numb fingers. Before dawn, all eight hundred of us Royal Pennines were packed into narrow assembly trenches right behind the front line and with the barrage a tad quieter than by day, our fidgeting set up a jingling chorus, what with the clatter of steel helmets and rifles and the clinking hardware we had swung from our belts. We were turned out in fighting order, which meant that the men had shed their large packs in favour of small haversacks filled with iron rations, field dressings, empty sandbags and wire cutters. That was the standard kit, but we'd doubled up on water supplies and on bullets and bombs. Every man had two ammunition bandoliers; one over each shoulder, crossed at the chest, which made a hefty weight of four hundred rounds of rifle cartridges, and our tunic pockets were bulging with Mills bombs. In short, we were expecting a scrap, whatever the generals were telling us, and we'd come prepared. Looking around the trench, I reckoned the battalion was made up of the toughest bunch of desperados I'd ever laid eyes on. If it hadn't been for the dark plan in my head, I'd have been proud to be going to fight alongside them.

I looked at the phosphorous dots on my watch face. Nearly 4.30. We'd done well to get up to our position in good time. The strangest thing about our march through the night was its effect on David Alexander. When we left our camp at the farm, he was serious and quiet and hardly replied to any of my attempts to start a conversation. The nearer we got to the battlefield, the more he regained his normal self, joshing and laughing with the men, teasing and shoving them along through the tighter points of the trenches. It was as if someone had switched on an electric current inside him, so that the more the tension mounted, the more he glowed with excitement. It looked like his normal nature had reasserted itself in the face of impending action.

'Daylight, Scott. Come and take a look at this.'

I was down in the trench, watching Corporal Bill and a handful of old sweats leaning against the wooden boards with their eyes closed, catnapping through the bombardment, when Alexander hailed me from up top. As I clambered out, the rim of the sun glimmered orange through the fog that covered the valley floor around us. On the map, our position was noted as Cambridge Copse; there was precious little of the wood remaining, only a few shell-splintered skeletal trunks. The barrage had diminished a little during the darkness. Now it was starting to intensify again.

I perched on the edge of the parapet next to him. He was watching a dark figure that was running along the top of the trench, pausing for a few seconds at every other fire bay. As he came near, I recognised him as of one of Colonel Ireland's runners, a lean whippet of a man who didn't trouble himself to salute us, only stopping to thrust a large silver half-hunter watch under our noses.

'Synchronisation, sirs!' He tapped officiously on the watch glass. 'In twenty seconds it will be 5.00 precisely.'

He didn't wait while we adjusted our own wristwatches but hared off towards the other companies, wisps of mist eddying around him as if he was only a passing wraith.

David sniffed the damp air. 'Good grief! I can smell breakfast. Well done, Clarridge.'

He was right. Clarry had excelled himself and got the

cooks organised to bring up a meal of hot stew and tea for every man in the battalion. He might have looked like a mouse behind his thinning hair and spectacles, but he knew soldiers and soldiering backwards. It was the sort of detail that means a deal more to men facing a fight than all the fancy speeches in the world.

The cooks retreated up the communication trench, banging their dixies together like cymbals in farewell. In the roaring shellfire, they were hardly audible. The tension in our trench started to mount again, the strange shivering mix of fear and excitement of men about to enter the arena. I could feel my own pulse rate rising and the lightness in my stomach fighting with the stew. I decided to make some notes – whether or not I ever got a chance to read them, let alone write them up for anyone else. I heaved myself up onto the shelf between the trench wall and the sandbag parapet to take a look over the scene below.

The old hands were checking the field dressing packets safety-pinned to the inside of their jackets, or rereading what they had written on the last leaf of their pay books where the army thoughtfully provided a pink form headed Last Will and Testament. One or two were still scribbling a final note to hand on to their chums to send home if they were killed, although most of those letters had been written already and left back at the farm. Me, I'd no one to worry about, so I'd no need to put pen to paper. The kids who had never been in a battle before stood white-faced, drawing furiously on their Woodbines and laughing too loud at weak jokes. A small group had gathered around an older sergeant who was reading to them from his New Testament. Next to them the hard nuts of the company were elbowing their pals in the ribs and trying to stand on one another's toes.

The sun was high enough now to light up the length of the trench, shining bright on the kingfisher blue of our Royal

Pennine badges and glinting off the triangles of tin we'd been told to pin onto our haversacks so that our airmen could tell the difference between us and the enemy. One of the jokers had turned his back to his mates and they were scratching some comment – probably obscene, I guessed – on his tin marker with the tip of a bayonet.

The youngsters were holding together OK on the whole. Most looked excited and nervous, but not afraid. Further along the trench, Tollman was looking unpleasantly happy. The scarred side of his face had gone into spasm, pulling up the corner of his mouth in lopsided elation. While I watched, he punched his clenched fist repeatedly into the side of the trench, so that there was a trickle of blood running over his knuckles, dripping off his fingers. My fingers snuck towards the butt of my pistol and I started to calculate how many bullets it was going to take me to put him down.

The mist was lifting as the day started to warm up and in its place a smog of sweat and tobacco smoke formed above our trench. A rippling cheer ran down the line because Clarry had also remembered to organise the daily rum delivery. This time, the orderly sergeant carrying the earthenware jar and dipper was accompanied by Colonel Ireland himself. The CO was turned out fit to stand guard at Buckingham Palace, all smart and dandy, a sword hanging at his hip. While the men held out their mugs eagerly for their ration, I watched him speak a few words with every soldier in turn.

'Well done to the old man,' Alexander said. He had to shout above the racket. 'He may be losing his grip but he still knows when to put on a show. I never imagined I'd see anyone carry a sword into battle. I doubt we'll ever see that again.'

For the first time, I saw the Colonel as the inspiring leader he must have been in the past. The men certainly looked bucked after his appearance, which I guessed might also be due to their mugful of rum. I was touched to see Corporal Bill split his own spirit ration between the youngest and greenest men in his platoon.

'Look at the two of you, perched up there as cool as cucumbers.' Tim Cooper's voice was shaking. He came and stood in the trench under us so that nobody else would hear. 'How the devil do you manage to stay so calm? I can't stand all this waiting around.'

Alexander opened his cigarette case and offered it down to Cooper, who tried to light one of the black Sobranies. His hands were trembling too much and the match flickered and died.

'Damn this bloody tremor! I'm not really windy. I'll be fine as soon as we go over. I just hate hanging about like this. I wish old Tom was here.' He steadied one hand with the other and lit the cigarette but after a couple of puffs he wandered away to his own platoon.

'He'll be all right. It was exactly the same last autumn at Loos, but once we got over the top, he was perfectly in control,' David said.

He produced another one of his volumes of poetry from his pocket and started to read but I could tell that his heart wasn't in it. Perhaps Tim had set him thinking that Stephen Oliver should be here too. After a few moments, he snapped the book shut and stood up.

'*Trust no Future, howe'er pleasant. Let the Past bury its dead!*
Act, – act in the living Present, Heart within, and God o'erhead!'
'Not Swinburne this time?' I asked.

'No.' He gave me a tight smile that made me think I'd been right about Stephen. 'Nothing so febrile, not today of all days. This is your own man, Longfellow.'

He slipped it into the top pocket of his tunic and then looked at his watch once more.

'Six thirty – half an hour to zero. There's a bit of a rise by the track there and we aren't due to advance until well after the first wave. Let's go and see how it starts.'

We scrambled up to a spur of ground that rose gently behind our position. A knot of artillery observers were already there, field glasses trained on the enemy up the hillside to the north. The barrage was reaching that furious crescendo of screaming metal where each salvo is indistinguishable from the one before – what the gunners called drum fire. Only eight hundred yards up the slope, the earth was pitting and cratering like the surface of the moon. There was no sign of the neat zigzag of trenches. The German front lines had vanished in a squirming surf of stone, earth and smoke. Beyond that, on the hilltop, Montauban itself was only visible as a dark red smudge where the brick buildings were being pulverised to dust. At first sight, it seemed impossible that anything could survive that inferno, but we knew that Jerry had built deep and strong, and I was sure they were still there, down in the burrows they'd been digging for the last two years.

Nearer to us the green strip of No Man's Land was still peaceful but lower down the valley side our own trenches were heaving with frantic activity. The four battalions of the brigade just in front of us that would lead the attack were going through their last minutes of preparation. I watched them, fascinated, through my binoculars. I couldn't recall where they came from but I was sure that they were mainly amateur New Army recruits. At that distance their individual faces were clear in my eye-pieces, some tense and concentrated, some terrified. I remember, in particular, one lad, barely out of his teens, who looked completely dazed, as if he'd no idea where he was or what he was doing. I've often thought back to that face and wondered whether he made it through the war, or even survived that day.

Suddenly, miles away along the battlefield, there was a massive explosion that boomed through the noise of the bombardment.

'Must be a mine,' Alexander shouted to me. 'Too early. Someone's been twitchy setting the detonator. God rest any poor devils too close to that.'

Next second, as if the explosion had been a signal, the grass out in No Man's Land gave a sort of shimmy and long strips of it vanished before my eyes. The first-wave battalions must have dug shallow tunnels, what we used to call Russian saps, keeping the earth intact over them so that they weren't visible from above. With less than ten minutes to go the roofs of the saps had been bust open and a flood of our boys poured out, only two hundred yards from the enemy line. If it hadn't been for the barrage forcing Jerry to stay under cover, it'd have been suicide. Then, at the very height of the cataclysm, when it seemed the entire world couldn't possibly contain that much noise, another gigantic roar burst over the valley, then another and another after that. Northwards, five great clouds of dark brown reached into the sky as the rest of the mines detonated. I checked my watch again – 7.28 exactly. Almost there.

All the shellfire stopped at once.

The silence was deafening. I could hear my own heartbeat. I knew that the pause was only to allow the gunners to raise their sights onto the second enemy line, but it felt as if the war had come to an end. The summer sky was a perfect blue and clear from horizon to horizon, without even a skylark in sight. Out in the meadow of No Man's Land, a hare raced across the grass and doubled back down the slope away from the shell craters.

Then thousands of whistles shrilled along the length of our battle front and the guns bellowed again. That was how the Battle of the Somme began.

26

One minute No Man's Land was a ten-mile strip of deserted field. Next moment, it was seething with a hundred thousand men, pouring up out of trenches and saps in a swirling khaki tide. Gradually, they sorted themselves out into long parallel waves and started to roll up the hillside towards the Germans. The tin markers on their backs were twinkling in the sun and at a distance they looked like ranks of toy soldiers, all holding their rifles at the same regulation high port. If it hadn't been for the explosions of the renewed barrage, it could have been a giant version of our rehearsal. It was all too damned calm. I knew it wouldn't last.

'You damn fools. Get moving! Stop buggering about.'

The artillerymen looked at me in disapproval. I didn't care. In my mind's eye, I could already see the German infantrymen haring up from their battered dugouts, slapping those lethal Maxim guns onto their tripods and making ready to open fire. They'd had to sit and take a mind-shattering pounding for the last ten days. Now it was their turn. If they won the race to get into position, every man of ours would be stranded and cut to pieces out in No Man's Land.

Alexander grabbed my shoulder. 'Look there. Our own first wave's nearly across.'

He was right. Right in front of us, although there was more than four hundred yards between the trenches, the leading companies were into the German wire. Over the din of shellfire, I could hear them cheering as they made it that far. They must have been lying out in front of the lines in the open during the last minute of the barrage.

'What the devil is that?'

David had swung his telescope across the battlefield to the far flank and was staring through it. On the slope that framed the left-hand boundary of our view a line of men were straggling onto the skyline. They were advancing in a series of short rushes, then a halt, then another short trot again. Two small round missiles shot up into the air in front of them, fell to the ground and bounced up again.

'They're footballs! Bloody footballs. What the hell do they think they're playing at?'

He was outraged. Even for the sake of a grand gesture he couldn't forgive a stunt that amateurish. 'Just get on up the damned hill, why don't you?'

It was his turn to shout now but there was still no sign of enemy resistance.

Maybe we were wrong. Is it possible? Has Jerry been completely annihilated by our artillery?

After all our misgivings, for those first few minutes at the start of the battle it looked like the generals' grand plan was being vindicated.

That delusion lasted another ten seconds. A bouquet of coloured signal rockets soared up from the German side. Next instant, there was a new chorus of roaring crashes, amplifying the deafening din even further. Our advancing troops were obliterated in great clouds of smoke. Every enemy field gun that had stayed hidden and silent for the last week had opened fire.

It was carnage. When the smoke cleared we didn't need field glasses to see. Huge gaps had been blown in the ranks of our attack where whole platoons had been annihilated by shrapnel. There were bright red puddles on the grass and shredded heaps of rags – soft and twitching remnants that had been human sixty seconds before.

Even so, it hadn't stopped the rest – they were still forging forward and getting close to the Jerry lines. Behind them our next batch of companies had already started to climb out of the trenches.

That was when the enemy played their trump card. Suddenly, cutting across the pounding of the guns, there was a new sound. A horrible sizzling noise that swept across the battlefield and turned my skin to gooseflesh. As I watched, the lines of the footballing company tumbled to the ground one after another, cut down like stalks of corn in front of an invisible scythe.

We'd lost the race with the German machine gunners.

Along all ten miles of the battle, an entire mass of Maxims had opened fire simultaneously. The tapping sound of the individual guns was indistinguishable – they were fused together into one continuous sinister hiss. It's a sound that still haunts my nightmares. Alexander grabbed my arm and pointed again. His face was fixed with horror. In our front line, the fresh companies that had climbed out of their jumping off positions were dropping by the score before they had covered more than a few feet. Their screams cut through the rest of the noise. The whole attack was crumbling under the flail of the machine guns. I could see by the look on David's face that the same fear was running through both our minds.

It's our turn next.

I looked up the hill, towards the two strongpoints we'd been told about in our briefing. They were supposed to have been smashed up by our artillery. But in the left-hand redoubt – the Warren – at least four machine guns posts had survived. They were chopping down our advancing troops, one line after another. On the right things were going better. Our first wave was already so far into the German lines that they'd missed the worst of it. Even so, they were split up into small groups crouching in shell craters, pinned down by a hailstorm of bullets sweeping down the slope from the Glatz redoubt above them on the hillside. The sweet coppery taint of blood was floating on the air. I could taste it on my tongue. It couldn't last. No one could survive that withering fire.

'We can't face that! It's suicide,' I shouted.

'Wait,' Alexander yelled back. 'Watch this.'

The gunnery observers were bent over the handsets of their telephones again, shouting target map co-ordinates. Within seconds, the screech of shells overhead thickened into a deep wail. I saw the Warren strongpoint engulfed in a tornado of high explosives. That put paid to the machine guns, except for an intermittent burst from one solitary Maxim. A ragged chorus of cheers from our boys drifted back into the valley.

'Gives us a sporting chance,' Alexander said.

A stray shell exploded twenty feet away and showered us with flying dirt and chalky pebbles. 'We'd best get back. It's almost our turn. Afraid?'

'You bet. But we're here to fight. Let's go.'

He grasped my shoulder and for the first time in days, his face cracked into his buccaneering grin. It looked like he was about to tell me something important. Then he thought better of it, only giving my arm a squeeze. We ran back to our assembly point in the copse and rejoined the battalion.

Colonel Ireland was standing up on the rim of the trench with his runners, watching the sky over the German positions. Packed into the shadows below him, the rest of the boys were getting restless and jittery. I pushed my way through to my own men, thinking that I should use whatever time we had left to check on the youngsters. Truth to tell, I knew that Fox would already have got them under his wing, but I needed to be back with my own platoon, in the midst of familiar faces. Some of my lads were taking a last look at photos of their girls, without any of the normal hazing you'd expect – there's nowhere to hide your true feelings in the last minutes before you go into a fight. Some of the others were talking to themselves, lips moving quietly and I overheard a muttered prayer from one of my toughest hands. In an odd way, I was cheered to see three of the hard nuts still larking about, jockeying for the best position at the bottom of the ladder. As I'd expected, Fox had stationed himself with the youngest boys. He was giving them a heck of a ticking-off about the state of their kit. He dropped me a wink as I shoved past. I checked my watch. It was coming time.

They say that when you're about to die, the whole of your life flashes in front of you. In those last minutes before we went on the attack on the Somme, all the months I'd spent with the Royal Pennines replayed themselves in my mind at lightning speed. My arriving at New Year, when I was just a hard-boiled newshound out to get a story, meeting David Alexander and finding a friend, discovering an enemy to loathe and fear, and then, against all sense and logic, falling in love in a wonderful blaze I wouldn't take back. Right then, at that exact moment, I didn't give a damn whether I survived the day or not. I'd been freed from every concern.

The final seconds passed in a kaleidoscope of fragmented images: Tim Cooper having difficulties swallowing, his Adam's apple twitching convulsively every few seconds; Corporal Bill finally stowing his pipe away; Tollman swinging his fist to clear a space around himself at the foot of a ladder, so as he could be first up and at them; Fox's white face glowing with a livid red flush on each cheek, like a painted wooden soldier; David Alexander crossing himself; the Colonel calling the order: 'Fix Bayonets!'

The chill clatter as all eight hundred men of the battalion clamped foot-long bayonets onto their rifle barrels.

I drew the Mauser out of its wooden holster and lifted my whistle to lips that had suddenly gone dry. Up the valley side, three red flares soared up together and blossomed in the sky like the petals of a giant poppy. It was our signal. Above our heads, in front of the trench, the Colonel drew his sword. I've never known whether I truly sensed, or just imagined, the rasp as it left its scabbard. It glittered in the sunlight as he waved it high above his head and I heard him shout:

'Royal Pennines! Advance!'

27

Mostly, when soldiers look back on a battle, they can't remember anything in detail. There are scattered fragments of memory, like cut-out clips from a movie. Each frame lights up sharp and vivid, but only as an instant – there's no coherent picture of the whole. That's not how it is for me. Not on that day, any rate. Every moment is etched deep and stark in my head, hard and bright and clear as the sunlight. I've lived and relived it over and over again in my mind, trying to see how I could have made it come out different.

The last word had barely left the Colonel's mouth before we'd leapt upward. All the world became a torrent of speed and movement and sound. Boots thudding up ladders and over the sandbags. Canteens clattering and helmets clashing. A chaos of men jostling, shoving, stumbling, shouting. Whistles blowing wildly. And always, shells screeching overhead and exploding further up the slope.

I found myself out in the open, at the front of my platoon. I was clear-headed and all my worries had vanished. I'd already prepared myself for the blast of incoming artillery fire and I was half expecting to feel the tear of flying shrapnel. Nothing happened. I remember thinking that was strange. There was no time to ponder it. Either side of us, A and D companies formed lines and fanned out just like we'd practised. The two Manchester battalions in front took a bit longer to straighten their ranks but not much and in seconds the entire brigade was on the move. With two thousand bayonet points gleaming in rows either side of me it was like being part of a massive machine, piling forward irresistibly. Alexander gave me a cheerful wave.

264

'Mortars… smoke…' he was shouting over the din.

When I looked up, I could see why we weren't taking enemy fire. The entire hillside was blanketed by thick coloured clouds. Our leading troops, the guys who had just captured the Glatz redoubt, had fired off a whole load of trench mortar canisters that had been specially filled with smoke. Hidden from Jerry, we picked up the pace. A few yards up the foot of the slope, we came to our own front line trenches. Plank bridges had been thrown over in the night. We funnelled over them and out through lanes in the barbed wire. A salvo of shells screamed out of the smoke and burst right above a company of the Manchester Pals in front. The German gunners had registered the exact position of our front line over the months and were firing blind through the smoke. They knew their job. Before the fumes had cleared we were stepping through bloody corpses. I tried not to look down. The world had shrunk down to the five yards on either side of me.

'You fucking dozy buggers. Come on! Pick up your feet.' That was Fox. He always knew when he needed to curse the men out. 'You slack sods will be on report tonight if you don't keep moving.'

If I'd been in his squad, I'd probably have been a lot more scared of him than the Germans, even out there in the open. More shells exploded, but they were behind us now. We'd made it over the first obstacle. Out in No Man's Land, we jostled the men into line again. Ahead of us, there was a gentle quarter-mile slope up to the first German position.

Away from the trenches, the earth was almost untouched by artillery. The grass had been trodden down but there were still clumps of bright, big-headed poppies. Halfway up the hillside, their scarlet was blotched with a spatter of different reds, some shining wet, some dark and clotted. A line of our boys had been mowed down by one of those bloody Maxims, only minutes before.

We had to keep going, which meant lifting our feet high over the row of bodies. I knew our instructions.

'No stopping, men. Follow me.' I'd been shouting for the last ten minutes, but I don't know what. That was the first order I can actually remember giving.

A hand grabbed at my ankle.

'Help me, pal. I've got hit bad. Please help me.'

I heard the man groan at the same time. I daren't look at him. I gritted my teeth and shook my leg free.

'Sorry. I'm sorry,' I heard myself say as I strode on.

It's the second worst sensation on a battlefield, the helplessness you feel when there are crippled men groaning and crying out and you've no choice but to leave them behind and keep going. We'd had our orders. The attack couldn't be held up for any reason. There were more shells now, some falling close by.

'Don't stop! No bloody dawdling. Keep fucking going.' Fox again.

A crash right behind us caught D Company fair and square. A single dismembered leg cartwheeled overhead and landed in a patch of long grass.

Christ. I wonder who that was.

No one had given an order but we all started to move faster.

The Manchesters in front had already got through the wrecked German outposts and within moments we too were clambering in a thicket of rusty wire. That was the wire we'd been promised would be completely smashed up by our artillery. It wasn't. If anything it was even more tangled than before.

Bullets were flying around us now. I couldn't see where they were coming from. There were no targets to shoot back at. I struggled through the final snarl of wire. My sleeve caught on a barb and I felt it tear along the back of my wrist. There was no time to stop: I ignored the pain and shoved my way through. Then we were up to the shattered enemy front line. It was a wilderness of chalky white craters and pits, strewn with grey uniformed bodies in grotesque contortions. A wide chasm of undamaged trench gaped in front of us. We vaulted it without a break, like a line of steeple-chasers tackling a risky fence. In the depths below, I got a glimpse of a half dozen white-faced Germans standing with their hands held high.

We were going well now, on the uphill slope. I couldn't hear anything above the increasing shellfire. There was a vibration in the air close to my head. That had to be a bullet, but I couldn't hear it crack. I found that I'd started stooping forward and forced myself up straight. Out front, Colonel Ireland had sheathed his sword. He was marching forward with no other weapon than his walking stick.

If he can stand tall, I bloody well can too.

I forced myself upright. The land was getting steeper, rising toward the grassy bank that had been dug out and fortified to make the Glatz strongpoint, now in the hands of our first-wave troops. On our left side, the smoke screen still hung like a thick London fog, screening us from the other side of the slope. It was getting real hot. I had to wipe the sweat out of my eyes while I climbed. I was grateful for a respite, in the form of a breath of breeze, something that I'd been longing for since daybreak. But that breeze also spelt danger.

With the wind, our smoke screen thinned out and we'd become visible. There was a company of the Manchester Pals only a few yards ahead of us, almost a hundred of them going steadily in line. Next second, there was a chattering sound from a machine gun on the high ground opposite. That whole company just got swept away. One moment they were there, the next they'd been wiped out. The bullets had got to be coming our way next. I saw my own lads start to dive for the ground. Before I could follow them, there was a smashing blow on my left leg and I went down.

For a while I lay flat where I'd landed. I was lying in the middle of a waist-high patch of nettles. My face was stinging like I'd rubbed it with poison ivy, but I didn't give a damn. I was just grateful for the cover of those long green-leaved stems. What had happened? Had I been hit bad? When I tried to bend my leg, there was just a dull ache and my foot moved OK. I rolled onto my stomach and pushed the weeds apart. The smoke had gone and I could see the Maxim and its crew, only two hundred yards away on the facing slope. They must just have run out of ammunition because I could see them about to thread a new belt of bullets into the gun. There wasn't much time. I wrestled the wooden holster of the Mauser off my belt and clipped it onto the pistol butt; it was a long shot, but not impossible. Across the valley, they'd already fed the start of the next belt into the breech by the time I'd got up onto one knee and put the gun to my shoulder. A shell exploded above me on the hillside and for a few seconds the dust blotted out the view. When it cleared, the machine gunner was already crouched behind his gun and the muzzle was swinging my way.

I can remember every tiny sensation of those instants – the smell of crushed weeds, the drone of a bee floating past my ear, the feeling of every brass screw on the Mauser's wooden butt, the dark eye of the Maxim turning to look straight at me and the pale face of the gunner in my sights. He was about to shoot. There was no time to think as I squeezed the trigger. I beat him to it. The pistol banged hard against my shoulder and he flopped to the ground.

That was the first of the three bullets I fired that day. A

man was dead after every shot, but that was the only one I aimed at a German.

'Sorted him out well and good, Mr Scott.' It was Fox who hauled me out of the nettles. 'Are you all right? Can you stand up?'

To my surprise there was still no pain but when I looked down, I saw how lucky I'd been. A single bullet must have hit my boot heel, which was hanging off the sole. Apart from bruises and a bit of a twisted knee, I was OK, only limping slightly when I took the platoon through the deserted second line of German trenches and into the redoubt. Behind us, not all of C Company had been as lucky. When I looked back down the hillside, there were at least two dozen men lying dead, and another handful crawling laboriously after us. I couldn't see either Alexander or Tollman.

The Glatz strongpoint had been burrowed deep in the top of the first ridge, so it had survived the week of our bombardment pretty well. Some of the interconnecting trenches had been wiped out by a landslide of earth and rock, but most of the stairways down into the network of deep dugouts were intact. The men from the first wave who'd captured the place two hours ago – it was a Liverpool Pals battalion – were hunting from one stair to another. They were supposed to be looking for pockets of German survivors but it looked more like they were foraging for souvenirs. We were the last platoon in. Most of the rest of our boys were already mixed in with the Manchester Pals, sheltering behind the broken parapets and sandbags. For the first time since starting, we had a clear view over the quarter mile up towards Montauban. It was still being battered by shellfire, which came as a surprise because I was expecting that our guns would have lifted by then. When I checked my watch it was only half past nine. It didn't seem possible. It felt like we'd been coming up that hill for hours but in reality we'd got to the redoubt ahead of the plan. Our barrage wouldn't shift away from the village for another half hour and it was impossible to push further forward until it did.

'Seen the Colonel?' I asked the lads who were in the trench. I recognised most of them but they were part of A Company. 'Any sign of Mr Alexander?'

'No, sir,' their corporal said. 'Probably him and the staff will be underground by now.'

Fox stooped down and ran his hand along a wire. 'There's some new cable here, Mr Scott. Looks as if it's just been laid down, so it's one of our lines. It'll likely lead you straight to them.'

Even on a battlefield, his common sense was working. I left the platoon taking a breather under his watchful eyes and set off to find the rest of the RBF officers. Inevitably, Fox was right. There was a line of new copper wire gleaming in the sun. It led me along the trench, round a corner and through a battered doorway which looked like it might collapse at any moment. It was hard to see in the gloom after the sunshine above and I had to feel my way down a dark stairway. Thirty feet underground the steps opened into a huge dugout. The place smelt of cordite and blood. I guess it'd been cleared out by the usual method of rolling grenades down the stairs. Someone had remembered to bring candles and I saw Colonel Ireland and his orderlies clustered around a field telephone. A signals captain was connecting up his reel of wire to the terminals while a dozen subalterns were gathered in the shadows. There were only three faces I didn't recognise, and none of them was above the rank of Captain. It looked like the German machine gunners had wiped out most of the senior ranks in the Manchester battalions. But where were the rest of the C Company officers?

'Morning, Scott. Something hold you up on the way here? Nothing too inconvenient, I hope'

Alexander's voice came from behind me. He was leaning against the wall, with Cooper close by. He was sounding more relaxed than ever and I knew he'd be smiling. Whatever had distracted him from Tollman's blackmail, I could only be grateful. All his troubles seemed to have dropped away from him.

Now that my vision was getting accustomed to the gloom, I saw that all the rest of the C Company officers had made it there, bar one. For a second, I hoped we'd got lucky.

'Where's Tollman? Don't tell me some kind Jerry's done the world a favour?' I whispered.

'No such luck,' Alexander said. 'He was here, but he's gone wandering off somewhere. And thank God for that. The less I see of him today, the better I feel.'

It was stuffy down there, and I took my cap off and wiped the sweat away.

'Good grief! What the devil's happened to your face?' Suddenly, he sounded worried. 'You've been hit.'

I lifted my hand to feel. My forehead was a mass of raised bumps, and my fingers came away covered wet and red. For a second, I started to panic. Then I remembered.

'That's nothing, just nettle stings, from where I fell over. The blood must've come from my hand. I reckon I caught it on the wire.'

'All the same, you'd better get something on it. One of the lads will have a spare dressing... Hello, what's going on?' He broke off in surprise. Colonel Ireland was bellowing into the handset of the telephone.

'What the devil d'you mean? Not certain we should press on! Three fresh battalions here, raring to go.'

He stopped, listening with his hand cupped over his other ear to block out the noise of the barrage overhead.

'I see. When do we know? Very well. We'll sit tight. Call back soon as you can.'

He slammed the telephone back into its cradle, making the signaller wince, and turned to the rest of us. He was slapping his leg with his walking stick in frustration.

'HQ can't decide if we go on. French to our right and Brigade to left both been held up. Advance and we'll be isolated. Damnation. We're so close. Should be allowed to go and look after ourselves. But no choice. We stand and wait. May take some time.'

Alexander pulled at my sleeve.

'Come along, then, Scott. Let's get you bandaged up.'

We climbed the steps and came out into the sunlight to find the rest of the company piling up sandbags. The stretcher-bearers wouldn't catch up with us for an hour or two yet but as I might've expected, Fox had three spare field dressings in his pack. I took off my jacket, and he wound a length of bandage around my wrist, tutting to himself under his breath all the time.

'That's not wire. Look at that flap of skin, bit of a fucking mess that is. It's a bullet did that. Just as well it only grazed you.' He looked at me with one of his grim smiles. 'Looks like it's your lucky day today, Mr Scott. Even so, best not use up all nine lives at once.'

His dressing was neat and careful. It took time before he'd stopped me bleeding but there was still no news from the command dugout.

'I suppose we'll end up here for the rest of the day,' Alexander said. 'I'd rather they let us go on. This place is too open for my liking.'

He was right. All the doorways faced away from the British lines, which had been fine for Jerry, only now we were completely exposed to their gunners. Most of the lads

272

were already digging in to throw up some protection, but not everybody was that gainfully employed. While Fox was fixing the last turn of bandage, two men with Liverpool shoulder badges ducked out from under a beam that was half blocking a dugout entrance close by. They were draped about with captured loot – strings of long German sausages, bits of grey uniform and a couple of pictures of naked girls. One of them was lugging a box of beer bottles while the younger one, no more than a freckle-faced boy, was carrying a fancy spiked parade helmet.

'They didn't half do themselves well, those Jerries,' the older man said. They ambled past us to rejoin their company. 'Come on, Robbie. Let's show this lot to the lads.'

'Hang on a tick. There was another of them fancy hats along there. Worth a bob or two.' The youngster slapped the German helmet on his head and ran back around the zigzag of the trench.

'Stupid buggers.' Fox wasn't impressed. 'They should be digging, not arsing about picking up souvenirs.'

He went back to supervise the platoon. Not long after he'd disappeared down the hill I heard a shot close by. It sounded like it was only a matter of yards away along the trench. Then there were two more in quick succession. Somebody was firing a heavy revolver.

Surely not a German attack. Not yet. And not enough noise.

Alexander and I looked at one another, then snatched up our guns and ran to investigate.

It wasn't the Germans. In the next fire bay the young Liverpool private lay sprawled in a pool of blood and brains. The spiked Pickelhaube helmet was still hanging on the smashed remains of his head. Ten feet away Tollman was leaning up against the sandbags, refilling the chambers on his Webley. Its barrel was still smoking.

'What the hell's happened here?' Alexander demanded.

'Stupid sod jumped out and took me by surprise.' Tollman shoved at the boy's corpse with his boot. 'Fucking idiot.'

All of a sudden the world went real quiet. The barrage had stopped as the gunners lifted their sights off the village to fire on the German support positions. In the lull, the tapping of machine guns and the stuttering crackle of rifle shots sounded faint as rain drops in the dust.

'And you shot him for that? He was on your side.' It sounded as if Alexander could hardly believe his eyes.

'What would you have done? Given him a kiss and a cuddle for being a bad boy? More your style, I know.'

He gave a peculiar wiggle of his hips. Alexander turned his face and looked away down the hill.

'Anyway,' Tollman went on, 'he was wearing a bloody German helmet. I'd no time to think whose side he was on.'

'But you fired three times.' I could hear my own voice, hard and critical.

'Had to make sure I finished him off, didn't I?' He lounged back against the sandbags and grinned, daring us to do anything. I couldn't let it pass.

'War or no war, I'd call that murder.' I unclipped the lid on the Mauser.

'What are you going to do about it then, Mr Bloody Clever American?'

His revolver was starting to point in my direction. It looked like my scruples were unnecessary. I was going to have to deal with him face to face anyway and that was just fine, except for the fact that he'd got the drop on me. I started to back away, giving myself the space to make a fast grab for my own pistol.

I'm not sure what would have happened next if it hadn't been for the signals captain who appeared at that second round the corner of the trench, barged past the three of us and hurdled over the remains of the parapet.

'Sorry, chaps,' he shouted breathlessly over his shoulder. 'Phone lines've been cut – got to get out and fix them.'

He jinked off down the slope like the hare in No Man's Land, a fresh reel of copper wire banging on his shoulder.

The moment had passed. Without another word, Tollman holstered his revolver, stepped over the bleeding corpse and headed off for the command dugout, leaving a trail of dark red footprints behind.

'He's probably got a point, you know. The boy shouldn't have been wearing that helmet. Not here.'

For just a moment, Alexander sounded diffident and I knew that Tollman's jibe had wounded him more than I could understand. Then he looked angry and shook his head.

'Forget what I just said, Anson. You were absolutely right – that was a lot too close to murder. And it's so obvious that he enjoys killing. What are we going to do about him?'

He wasn't expecting a serious reply, which was just as well because I didn't want to tell him my plan. Instead, he turned his back on the body of the boy in the trench and watched the men from the support battalions below us. They were toiling across No Man's Land in the mid-morning heat, burdened with ammunition and supplies. A solitary figure, unladen, raced past them, leapt over craters and trenches and sped up the hill towards us.

'Looks like one of the Colonel's runners. We'd better get back.'

Down in the command dugout, the air was stale and rank. An orderly was still hunched over the telephone handset, shaking his head mournfully. Colonel Ireland was pacing the floor.

'Blasted modern devices. Half an hour we've been stuck here. What the devil's going on?'

Next thing, the runner rushed in, panting like a hound on the chase and covered with sweat and dirt. He jumped down the steps three at a time, then held out a folded sheet of order paper. The Colonel took it and read it impatiently. Then he turned to all of us waiting with an expression of triumph.

'Seen sense at last. To your companies, gentlemen. We attack. All three battalions together. To Montauban!'

28

At first, it was easy. The Glatz strongpoint formed a ridge halfway up the hill so that behind it the ground sloped down to the old railway embankment before rising again to the wreckage of the village. We spread out into two long lines. I discovered I was humming a couple of lines of a song over and over again while I stumbled over the tussocks. Times like that, you find your mind runs away on its own lines, churning through a thousand disconnected thoughts.

What the hell is that tune? I should have asked Alexander back up there – it's one he's always whistling.

Why aren't they firing at us? Jerry always fights for every foot of ground. Only been a few shots from the village so far. It's too easy.

Someone should paint that sky, all deep blue with puffball clouds. It's a fine day to be alive.

We came to the embankment as it swung around parallel to the last line of trenches in front of Montauban and scrambled up the earth bank, following the Colonel. He must have been a tough old bird, because he was still twenty feet in front of the rest of us. I saw him stand tall on top of the track, silhouetted against the sun. Then we were all up and over the bank, slipping and sliding down the other side. That was when the Germans opened up again.

They'd been waiting for us, hidden in the wreckage of craters and hedgerows that littered the hillside. There was a volley of rifle fire and then the sky filled with the tumbling black shapes of trench mortar canisters. We dived for cover as they exploded around us in massive blasts that made the earth shake.

When the dust cleared, I found myself nose down in an old shell hole. Most of my platoon seemed to be there too, all jumbled up together. I did a quick head count which showed we hadn't lost anybody. Fox was already crawling from one man to another, shoving them into some sort of order. He was growling at them as he went.

'We're all right. Now if they knew what they were doing, they'd have used fucking shrapnel. Then we would be in the bloody shit. Bloody mortars won't bother us providing we keep moving.'

Out of the side of his mouth, he said to me, 'Just as bloody well they've not got machine guns up here either.'

I took a quick look over the rim of the crater. The Germans had gone quiet again but they were still there. They knew exactly where we were and they'd sure taken their toll. Across the line of our advance, dozens of soldiers lay still on the ground with a score more writhing around wounded. In front of us, Colonel Ireland had sunk to his knees, face towards Montauban, as if he was praying. He'd still got his helmet on but there was a river of blood streaming thickly through his silver hair, soaking into his collar. One of his orderlies sprinted out of cover and ran to help, but before he got there, the Colonel toppled slowly to one side. As he fell, I saw his tunic front had been torn to shreds and there was a mash of scarlet where his face should have been.

Over on our left, A Company's captain shouted something. I couldn't hear in the barrage, but the message was obvious to us all. We leapt out from cover and set off up the slope in a ragged line, expecting any moment to feel the volleys rip us up again. We didn't have to wait long. Before we'd made fifty yards, the ground exploded. Spouts of scalding earth erupted around us and shells burst so thick and fast I couldn't see where ground ended and sky began. It was one of those moments when every sort of horse sense is telling you to hit the dirt and save your hide, but you can't because all the boys around you are still up and moving and there's no choice but to push on. I was singing the same tune louder and louder, as if I could block out the fury around us, while flailing hot steel smeared flesh and blood across the grass.

For a second, the fumes cleared on my left and I got a glimpse of David Alexander. Next moment I saw a shell burst directly above him. There was a blizzard of flying earth and metal and he vanished. I stopped in my tracks, oblivious to everything else going on around me.

It's not possible. Not like that.

I must have been a fine target, standing still on the slope.

'Come on, sir! Bloody bad place to stop.'

One of the toughs from my own platoon shouted in my face. He gave me a rough shove that started me stumbling forward again. That probably saved my life – God only knows how I hadn't got myself cut down already. As I looked back, I saw the fog thin and Alexander marched out of the smoke like he was still on our practice battlefield. He gave me a wave and shouted something. I couldn't hear him but it was easy to see that he was laughing.

We got up to the waste ground in front of the village. Most of the German shellfire was falling behind us. By now, our lines had broken up into small groups while we tried to fight our way through the devastation that had been created by our own barrage. There were gullies and waste heaps and hollows and fissures, all tangled with wire and splintered wood like a manmade jungle. With sniper fire whipping through the air, when a man went down you couldn't be sure whether he'd been hit or just tripped over until you saw he wasn't getting up again. It was horrible, hot work. Worse was still to come when we got through. Jerry had cleared the last hundred yards of every shred of shelter except for our new shell holes and had dug themselves in every fold in the ground, in slit trenches and rifle pits. There was no way we could get at them, and the air was thick with flying stick grenades and rifle bullets. So there we were, pinned down in a collection of dips and craters. I scrabbled from one to another, keeping my head down, and found most of the company hunkered down in the hollows of an old blown-in dugout. It wasn't much of a shelter.

Fox had already started to get them organised into some sort of firing line, with piles of Mills bombs ready to hand. The corporal in charge of the Lewis gun had made it through and had set up the gun on its bipod. He'd lost his loader, so David Alexander was handing up the rounds of ammunition. I didn't see of any of the others – not Tollman, nor Cooper nor Warren-Walker. We were safe for the time being. Even so, it was a bad place to be holed up. You couldn't see more than a few feet through the dust and smoke, volleys of shots were flying overhead, and grenades kept exploding in front, showering us with steel splinters. There wasn't even much cover. While I watched, the Lewis gunner raised his head slowly to take a peer around. He gave a moan and rolled back. He'd taken a bullet through his eye socket.

'Pretty hot work,' Alexander yelled to me. He hitched himself closer to the Lewis gun.

'Where's Tollman?' I called back as a mortar bomb crashed behind us. I had to repeat myself. He pointed to the far side of the dip where there were the remains of some shattered building. I saw that even Tollman had been driven to ground. He was trying to hide his bulk behind a few courses of brickwork. With the Colonel gone, he was next in command. I screamed across at him, 'What do we do? There's no way back. Any orders?'

He must have heard me because he wasn't that far away.

He didn't move, just stayed put with his head down. His face was turned towards us, watching, but his eyes were shaded by his helmet.

'Major! Tollman!' I shouted again, but there was still no response.

I scrabbled across to Alexander and yelled in his ear. 'Tollman's no use. He's frozen.'

The mortars went quiet, but we were still taking rifle fire and grenades. Then we heard the worst sound of all – the chatter of a Maxim heavy machine gun. In a second, bullets were pinging and ricocheting out of the dust, right on the lip of our position. One of the men in my own platoon cursed and clutched at his shoulder. I guessed it had only been a ricochet because he kept hold of his rifle and stayed in position. We all ducked down, as if we could hide under our helmets.

'Looks like it's up to you!' I said to Alexander. 'Any good ideas?'

'Only one.' Something about the tone of his voice made me look up at him. He was smiling, relaxed and comfortable in the middle of all that carnage.

'Time to go.'

He nodded. 'Yes. It's time.'

I didn't have a chance to ponder on what he meant. A massive trench mortar bomb pin-wheeled through the air and exploded ten feet in front, spattering us with shrapnel. When I lifted my head again he'd taken the Lewis gun off its stand and thrown the carrying strap over his shoulder. Still, I didn't cotton on to his plan. I watched him as he stuffed his gas mask bag with grenades and then filled his pockets with more. His face was serenely happy.

That's when I knew what he was going to do. Of course he was calm. Something like this had been his plan all along and it was me who had talked him into it.

The battle's less than two days off… If it was me, I'd be thinking that I might try to do something useful with my life.

A line of machine gun bullets spattered the dust, traversing along our position. Alexander let it get ten feet past before he leapt out from cover and pounded forward. For a second I lay there, paralysed, watching him race towards the Germans. He was jinking and dodging and all the while firing that heavy Lewis like it was a popgun, spraying them with bullets. There were puffs of dirt round his feet where they were shooting back but it was as if he was invulnerable. Nothing hit him. I guess they'd never expected anyone would be dumb enough to charge them head on and they were too stunned to take proper aim. When the Lewis gun ran out of ammunition he threw it down, and started chucking Mills bombs, two at a time. Then he got out his revolver and was firing and rushing from crater to crater, skidding and sliding from one to another, destroying anything in his way – machine gunners, riflemen, everyone. It was glorious and crazy and heroic and beautiful and stupid, all at once.

No one would stand and face him and I saw the Germans turning tail to run away. That was when I gathered my wits, screamed at the men to follow and charged out after him. We were almost up to the last line of the defences when he heard us coming and looked back to wave us forward. His helmet had been knocked free sometime during his charge up the hill and he was beaming, his face lit up by the sunshine.

'Keep up, Scott. It's a fine day to be…'

I had a moment's glimpse of something huge flying through the air towards us. Then the ground bucked up with an ear-splitting roar and kicked me in the head. Everything went black.

29

In the dark, Beatrice was holding on tight to me. I could feel every inch of her. Her scent saturated my senses as we kissed. I had forgotten the softness of her lips, the warmth of her mouth. The desire for her body combined with the relief of having found her again was simple ecstasy and I was filled with the delight of knowing that we loved each other.

Then I woke up.

I was lying on my back on the floor of a monastery at night-time. It had to be a monastery because there was a choir singing somewhere in the distance, one of those deep Latin chants where you can't hear the actual words, only a continuous musical drone that echoes around the pillars and bounces off of the stained-glass windows. And there was only a faded light seeping through the blackness – not a separate image, but a blur of red with a yellow centre. For a while, I couldn't think where I might be, or when it was, or even who I was. All I knew was my head was pounding and I didn't want to move. Dimly, it began to dawn on my fuddled wits that it wasn't cold stone paving under my shoulders, but a heap of lumpy, broken stone. It couldn't be a church at all. That's when I got a grip on my senses again and remembered the war and the battle and David's charge and the explosion. Painfully, I dragged myself up to sitting and propped myself up against the pile of rubble with every bone and joint and muscle in my body swearing in protest. When I took stock of the situation, it seemed like no specific bit of me had got broken. Only problem was, I was still in the dark. I put my hand up in front of my face, but it was no good. I couldn't see my hand move, let alone my fingers.

I'd gone blind.

A few months back, I'd seen a fellow catch the full force of a shell blast in front of him and get his eyes blown clean out of his skull. I could recall every horrible detail of that boy's face. And there was a single fear running round in my throbbing head now.

How the hell will I get out of here when I can't see?

Next moment, I near hollered with joy when I realised what had really happened. A thick curtain of blood had run down from a slice in my scalp and clotted over my eyes, gumming my eyelashes together. It was like a purple blindfold. I couldn't see a darn thing except the glare of the full sun. I scrubbed frantically away at my lids and got them prised apart, pulling at the strings of blood until I could blink my eyes open and find out where I was.

Where was I? Exactly the same place I'd been, that's where. A matter of yards from the last German trench, sitting on the edge of a fresh crater twenty foot across and six deep. The droning in my ears that I'd mistaken for music was beginning to wear off and now the world had gone strangely quiet. I turned my head around. I did it carefully, because it felt like someone had been trying to twist it off. There wasn't a living soul to be seen anywhere. My small patch of battlefield was totally deserted and even the gunners had ceased firing. I checked my watch. It was still ticking. As far as I could calculate, I'd been out cold for about a half hour. The rest of the boys must have pushed on and taken the village, because there were no Germans in view either. Not if you didn't count the dead ones. I was completely on my own, crouched in a daze under the midday sun.

I'd never felt so grateful to the fates. Fox had been right

about my luck and it was still holding. Sure, it felt like I'd been run over by a cattle drive but I looked up into the blue heavens and offered a prayer of thanks for keeping me in one piece.

That was the last time I ever prayed for anything.

A single stray shot cracked past my head, so close it made me flinch away. I lost my balance and rolled down into the hole, coming to a stop in a sprawl near the bottom. The sides were still hot and steaming with evil green fumes from the explosion and there was a mound of loose, chalky earth in the centre. To blow a crater that size, it must have been a trench mortar that had got me. My sudden movement had made me sick to my stomach and I was seeing everything blurred and doubled. I had to blink hard to get the world back in focus again before I could start to think straight. There was no point in trying to move yet. I'd be a sitting duck out in the open until I'd recovered some of my wits. I took a couple of minutes to check myself over properly. Apart from a lump the size of a turkey egg over one ear, and the slice across my skull that had bled, it seemed like I was OK. It must have been a chunk of flying rock that actually knocked me over, not a shell splinter, or I wouldn't have had any head left to ache. I'd even held onto the Mauser.

The rest of the Royal Pennines wouldn't be far away and I was keen to catch up and let them know I was still in the land of the living. It was getting pretty hot so before I got going again, I took a swig of water from my canteen and then splashed some more over my face to get the blood clear. I was a touch clumsy and I cursed out loud when I found the spot where I'd been hit.

'Scott.'

It was only a whisper.

I presumed it was my hearing playing up again. I shook my

head hard, trying to clear it, ignoring the stabbing headache. Then it came again.

'Scott.'

I'd been wrong. I wasn't alone. There was no sign of another human being but there was definitely someone else out there with me. I caught a flicker of movement. Buried in the loose chalk in the centre of the crater, a bright blue jewel of an eye had winked at me and then blinked out again. Then I made out the dusty shape of a hand, a fist, a shoulder... all half covered by the cairn of rubble.

It was like I'd dived head first into a lake filled with ice. I'll swear I felt my heart stop and I struggled to draw breath. There was a roaring in my ears again. Then in a second I'd forgotten my own aches and I was down on all fours, digging like a dog, shovelling at the earth with my hands, throwing back stone and debris, hoping against all logic that I'd been mistaken, that it wasn't who I knew it must be.

But I was fooling myself. Even before I'd uncovered his head and brushed the white dust off his face, the glint of yellow hair had told me. It was David Alexander.

To start off with, I couldn't believe he was still alive. He'd not moved and if I hadn't heard him call out, I'd have been certain he was a goner, he was so limp and inert. I figured that there was a chance he'd be able to breathe more easily if I got the weight off him, so I kept on digging, fast as I could. But when I lifted the last of the rocks off him and got him uncovered, I could have sat down and cried. There wasn't a mark on the front of him and he was breathing, just about, but the bomb must have exploded right behind him.

There's never been any easy way to remember this. Not even after all these years. Alexander had been between me and that bomb landing. He'd saved me from getting hit worse but it meant he'd taken the full force of the explosion, which had laid his back open like a giant flensing knife. From the neck downward he was a mess of torn muscle and broken bone. There wasn't much blood because everything had been burnt and charred by the blast. But it was obvious why he hadn't moved his arms or legs to help himself. He couldn't. His spine had been smashed to splinters.

Oh no. Not this. Not David.

I was so numbed, my brain wouldn't work at first. Then I started to fumble for the little box of morphia tablets we all carried into battle. That was when he opened his eyes and blinked at me again.

'Hello, Scott.'

That was all. It was still a whisper but it sounded like he'd just bumped into me out on a morning stroll. I held up his head and poured some water into him and then fed him a couple of doses of morphia.

'Thanks.' His voice was still a thread. 'I knew you'd find me. Are you all right?'

I couldn't credit that he was asking me that, with those injuries, but he was looking at my face, and I could taste the blood trickling down over my chin. I must have started the bleeding again when I was digging. I nodded, too overwhelmed to answer.

'I'm sorry, Anson.' He licked along his lip and took a shallow breath. 'You weren't supposed to be here.'

'I'm OK. This is just a scalp wound. Nothing serious. Doc Vaughan'll have the pair of us back in the front line in a couple of days.'

'Good try.' I'll swear he was trying to smile. 'Not me.'

'Don't be so dumb. We'll get you patched up.' I poured some more water over his face to clear the dirt. 'A few weeks back home and you'll be right as rain.'

'Liar.' His skin had gone very pale. 'I know my back's gone.

I can't feel my arms and legs. I wouldn't want to be a burden to everyone.' He was calm and clear, not looking for sympathy.

'We should be getting a move on.' It couldn't be too long before the artillery opened up again. 'Here. I'll carry you.'

I stooped down to pick him up. When I tried to take his weight, he gave a great agonised groan. I took a different grip and tried again.

'Bloody hell! That hurt.' It was the only time I ever heard him complain.

'Let's try again. We've got to get you out of here.' I was beginning to get desperate. He needed help and quickly.

He shook his head. Even that movement made him bite hard on his lip. I saw the drops of blood run down his chin.

'Sorry. Can't manage it.' He struggled to get the words out.

There was nothing more I could do. I settled him with his head resting in my lap.

'You've got to go, Anson. On your own.'

That wasn't a choice. I wasn't going to leave him there.

'Maybe I should wait a while,' I said. 'Fancy a smoke?' I reached into my pocket. I was trying to make all movements as gentle as possible. Even so, I saw his eyes narrow with pain.

'Mine. Easier. Better anyway.'

It had always been a joke between us that I usually smoked the soldier's favourite Woodbines while he much preferred his black Sobranies. His silver case was still in his jacket, a bit battered but half full of black cigarettes. I lit up two and stuck one between his lips. I couldn't know whether he could even inhale the smoke, but the gesture of normality eased my nerves. I sat with him, trying to think what I should do.

'I'm sorry,' he said again.

The cigarette dropped from his mouth half smoked. When I made to give it back to him, he tried to shake his head. Even that made him wince.

'You're a good man.' His voice was coming and going now. It wasn't the heat of the day that was making the sweat run down his face. It was taking all his strength to speak without showing his pain. 'Couldn't have asked for a better friend.' He sucked in air again. 'One last request…'

He looked me straight in the face and then slid his eyes to one side, towards the Mauser in its holster on my belt. There was no mistaking what he wanted. The time for pretence was gone. He and I both knew there was no chance he could survive, not with those wounds. And even if by some miracle he did pull through, he'd be a useless cripple. But he'd said it – he was my best friend. How could I just plain shoot him? I shook my head.

'Don't ask me that, David. Please.'

'Can't manage it… myself. Has to be you.'

'No. No. You're not some bloody horse with a broken leg.' I couldn't face it. Somewhere, in the normal world of the war above us, there were more shots and then a distant cheer. I barely noticed.

'Never meant to make it back. Least you'll shoot straight.'

He closed his eyes. I hoped that the morphia had finally taken effect. Maybe if I gave it another couple of minutes, I'd be able to move him. Then the rubble shifted under our weight and his eyelids flipped open and the sweat ran down his face again. He was still hurting bad. It was all I could do not to break down and bawl my heart out, but that wasn't going to help either of us. I took some deep breaths to hold my tears at bay. He wanted to go his own way. He'd have done it for me, if we'd been the other way round. Gradually, I shifted his head in my lap so that I could unclip my pistol.

'Well done. Remember… still been a fine day… to be alive.'

The effort of keeping up his poise was taking its toll. He was only able to manage a few words now, hissing each phrase between his clenched teeth.

I lifted the Mauser out and took the safety catch off. His lips were moving again and I leaned in close to hear.

'Thanks, Anson, for everything.'

He dragged in some more air, before he murmured again, so faint it was like the breath of a candle when it gutters for the last time.

'Don't tell them. Not Stephen. Not Beatrice.'

Those were his final words.

Then he smiled and all the lines went out of his face. I lifted the pistol he had given me and pressed it soft against his head, close by his ear. I had to shut my eyes. I knew he was right.

Before I could think again, I squeezed the trigger and fired a single bullet through his temple.

There may be a quiet corner of any battlefield, one of those small pockets of tranquillity during the mayhem, where anything can happen without being observed; where a man can kill his best friend, then sit nursing the body, trying not to reason, not to understand, not to remember, not to weep – above all not to feel his guilt.

I stayed with his body until the barrage started up again. I've often believed it would have been better if I'd stopped and died with him but when the first shells began to explode some inner instinct for survival took over. I laid him down on the mound of rubble, grabbed the Mauser and ran towards the village. As I dived head first into the nearest slit trench the ground started to shudder under the rage of the new bombardment. By the time I'd turned myself round to peer back over the sandbags, the hillside had been pulverised into a smoking desolation. I couldn't even make out where I'd left him.

30

The air was thick and pink over Montauban, or at least the heaps of rubble that remained of it. That new barrage had only lasted a couple of minutes but it'd stirred up fresh brick dust that was floating in the sun like rose-tinted fog. I pulled myself out of the trench and staggered into the ruins. On the line of what must have been the main street there was a doorstep that led into nothing except a huge hole in the ground. I sat down on the step. My mind had gone vacant. I barely knew where I was. I had no idea what I was doing there.

The sound of boots crunching across the debris made me look up. There were some figures in the distance that looked vaguely familiar. The soldier shouting hoarsely at them had a bone-white face that prompted a flicker of recognition. Off a ways I spotted taller piles of brick and the bare skeleton of a lone archway that must have been part of the town church once. I wondered whether anyone would ever be able to worship there again. There was a clink of shovels behind me. I turned my head quickly – much too quickly – and was hit with a wave of nausea. Suddenly, I'd begun to shiver but at the same time I was burning hot and beads of sweat were running into my eyes. I lifted my arm to wipe them away with my sleeve. That was when I saw the spatters of blood and grey smears on my uniform. I doubled over on the step and threw up.

'Are you OK, Scott?' A young officer was jogging past at the head of a file of men. 'Can't stop. We're digging in on the north side. Bit of a shame – Warren-Walker's just bought it. Bloody booby-trapped dugout...' His voice faded as he trotted off and I didn't catch any more. I remembered his name, now. Cooper – Tim Cooper.

I sat back on the doorstep and held my head in my hand. The rest of my memory started to return. It was patchy and not all of it made sense. It was only when I rummaged for a smoke and pulled out David Alexander's silver cigarette case that everything came back in a rush that made my head spin. I threw up again.

A grenade exploded with a muffled bang away in the ruins, but I didn't pay it any heed. It was probably only another booby trap. I picked out one of the Sobranies and lit up, using both hands to steady my lighter. I'd not gotten past the first few hits of nicotine when a man came rushing through the ruins. He took a shortcut across my doorway and almost sent me flying. I recognised him – it was one of the corporals from my own platoon. He was out of breath and his eyes were wide and rolling in his head like a spooked pony. As he saw me he skidded to a stop and threw me a quick salute.

'Mr Scott. Thank God. Come quick, sir. He sent me away but someone's got to stop him.'

The man wasn't making any sense and I was too tired to try to understand. He pulled at my arm, trying to drag me onto my feet in his desperation.

'Please, Mr Scott. I can't find Mr Alexander and there's no one else. It's Major Tollman…'

It was the mention of their two names so close together that brought me back to the reality of the world like nothing else could have done.

'What's up, man?' I snapped at him. 'What's going on?'

'It's… church… he's… bombs…' Then he pulled himself together and managed a whole sentence. 'The Major, sir. He's over in the church. All the prisoners have been collected there and he's…'

There was no need for him to say any more. I'd got the gist of it and I was already on the run, yelling back at him: 'Go fetch Sergeant Fox. Get Fox. Now!'

Ignoring my spinning head I set off across the ruins in a straight line, fast as I could go, scrabbling over the heaps of masonry and broken beams and jumping across deep craters, making for the arch that flagged the remains of the village church.

Even if I hadn't spotted it before, it was easy to find. A life-size statue of the Virgin Mary had survived all our bombardment and was still standing white and immaculate by the pillars that had supported the west door. As I got closer, there was a second bomb blast that sent a tremor through the ground. There was no doubt – it came from inside the wreckage of the church. I ducked under the arm of the Virgin and dropped to one knee behind a pile of tumbled brickwork. It was still blazing hot and I was breathing hard. My sight was swimming in and out, and I'd started seeing double again. It took me a while to steady my panting enough even to be able to listen. It had gone quiet again. Then I could hear a faint sound, like someone holding a conversation. I inched forward and peered around the stone arch of the empty doorway.

'Now are you nice and comfortable down there?' It was a familiar growl but for once, it sounded almost friendly – Tollman.

'We wouldn't want you to be getting cold, would we? Maybe we can do something to warm things up. Would you like that?'

Just the sound of his voice sent a violent tremor right through me so I had to grab hold of the pillar as I crouched there. David had died and Tollman was still alive.

Right now the question was – who the heck was he talking to? I put my nose out to get a better view. Everything was so deceptively calm at first that I couldn't work out what was going on. Tollman was the only man in sight. He was standing by a great bronze bell that must have crashed down through the roof when the church collapsed. It had come to rest on the paving right in front of the remnants of the altar but he was leaning against it with all the concern of a man propped on his elbow on a saloon bar. At his feet he'd collected a pile of hand grenades, both Mills bombs and German stick grenades. While I watched he started to speak again.

'It seems to me that you've been very wicked. Don't you agree?' He cupped his hand to his ear like a bad stage actor. 'No? That's a shame. Because I think you need to be punished. Just a little. To teach you some manners.'

He was too far away to see his face but I could hear his voice. It sounded as though he was talking to someone he knew and cared for. But who?

Back in control of myself now, I slid around the pillar of the great door one foot at a time, hugging close to the shadow of the wall. Once I was in the body of the church I could see a sandbagged entrance that had been built over the original crypt. There were clouds of smoke swirling around it like the entrance to Hades.

It can't be. Not even Tollman is that evil. At last the penny dropped. A mighty nasty penny it was too.

There were German prisoners down there and Tollman was chucking live grenades down to explode in the confined space. It was absolute, cold-blooded murder. And for what? We'd all done our fair share of rolling bombs into dugouts to clear them out during an attack but this was something different. Those poor devils had already surrendered and given up their arms. But actually I knew why – the tone of his voice made it obvious.

This was killing for the sake of killing. Pure deranged

bloodlust. I was so appalled that for another few seconds, I couldn't move. Tollman was off again. He was working himself up now.

'Are you ready for your judgement, you lot?'

I thought he must be drunk. I still didn't want to believe the truth. But then he leaned forward like he was trying to catch a reply from his captives and the sun lit up his face. He was smiling broadly so that both the scarred and unmarked sides of his face were twisted up with pleasure; the sort of pleasure an evil child gets from tearing the legs off of a spider or drowning a kitten. That was when saw I him unmasked for the first time. All those months I'd been treating him like a violent bully, someone it was as well to steer wide around because anyone who crossed him ended up damaged or dead. Even then, I'd missed the point.

Tollman was insane.

One thing was sure. I'd wasted a night worrying whether I'd be able to kill in cold blood. Come the day, there was indeed a murderer stalking the battlefield of the Somme, but it wasn't me.

I watched him pick up a stick grenade and stroll over to the crypt. He was laughing while he tossed the bomb up into the air and caught it as it came down, spinning it end over end like a juggler's Indian club.

'You're afraid, aren't you? Well, maybe you should be. You are. That's good. I can smell it.' He was still talking as if to a child, gently.

Suddenly he dropped down onto his haunches. He started to sniff the smoke eddying out of the ground like he could scent fresh blood. Then he stood up again and reached for the string of the grenade detonator.

That was it. I stepped forward out of the shadows, raised the Mauser and pulled back the slide. It came back with a loud snick.

'Stop that! Now!'

I'd forgotten how fast Tollman could react. Before I'd got the first word out, his head jerked around and he dropped the bomb to make a grab for his own revolver.

When he saw it was me, he let it down. His face had settled back into its normal malevolence, as if the mad murderer had stepped back behind a curtain. When he spoke to me, he almost managed to regain his usual surly rudeness.

'Bloody idiot. What the fuck are you doing, creeping up on me like that? I could've shot you.' He picked up the grenade, ready to start again.

'What are you playing at, Tollman?' I was sure I knew now, but I wanted to see if he would admit it.

He ignored the question. 'Have you got anybody else with you? Anyone else crawling around, spying?'

His voice dropped back into his caressing wheedle. 'Come on out and show yourself. There's no need to be afraid.'

I saw him take a quick glance about to check whether there were any other witnesses. Mad he was, but it was the sort of clever madness that was more dangerous than any other. I knew what calculations were going through his brain. Could he just shoot me on the spot and get away without being spotted? But for once I had him covered. He could see I was keeping my pistol aimed in his direction and he thought better of it. He leaned back against the bell again.

'Where's your pansy pal, Alexander?' For all the emotion in his voice, he could have been asking me about the weather.

I nodded back down the hill. I was too choked up to say anything but he must have been able to see my answer in my face.

'He's bought it, hasn't he?'

His smile got wider still as if I'd given him the best news

of the war, then it looked like he suddenly remembered something mildly inconvenient and his face fell again.

'I'm sorry about that. Honestly.'

'Like hell. You drove him to it.' I knew he was trying to get me wound up and did my best to stay level.

'And there I was, getting all set to have some fun with him. Buggering about with a servant. Not the done thing at all. Such a naughty fellow.' He clicked his tongue in disapproval. Then he leaned on top of the bell again and gave me a considered stare. 'Funny thing is, I'd got you down as his boyfriend, at least until I saw the way he was mooning around that lad. You know – the pretty boy I hung out for punishment. You did know about him, I suppose?' He sounded solicitous.

Then he turned vicious. 'Course you bloody knew.'

He couldn't see how close he was then to me shooting him outright. I could feel the anger building up inside me. I tried to stay calm, tried to reason with him.

'I can understand why you had it in for me, Tollman. I was an outsider, an interloper breaking in on your world. But really, it was Alexander you always hated. It took me a long time to work it out. What harm had he ever done you?'

He glared at me, ignoring the Mauser and whispered: 'What had he done to me? Nothing. Nothing at all.'

Then he screamed: 'Fucking nothing!'

He kicked savagely at a half brick on the ground. It clattered down the steps into the crypt and there were terrified moans from the men he'd got trapped there. He turned and shouted down at them.

'Bloody shut up! You'll get it for real soon enough.'

Then he turned back to me. His murderous nature was under cover and his normal blustering personality almost back in control again.

'Always bloody perfect, your David Alexander.' He couldn't

stop himself spitting out his words venomously. 'Always in the right place, turned out just so. Always so polite. He made me sick. Everybody loved him – *such a nice fellow. So civilised.*'

He did a grotesque little dance, a few mincing steps around in a circle. Then he stopped and looked puzzled.

'But war's not supposed to be like that, is it?'

He almost sounded rational as he held his hands out from his sides, appealing to my reason. 'You've been in action, Scott. War is when real men show what they can do. When we meet the enemy and beat him into the ground. Smash him. Annihilate him!'

His grip on reason was loosening again. 'I could see through David precious Alexander. All the time he was just hiding his real nature. Pretending to be normal. Creatures like him should never be allowed anywhere near the army.'

I took a step closer. I had my teeth tightly clenched, fighting against the urge to kill him, right then.

'I've got it now.' Still, I tried to talk to him as if he was a reasonable human being. 'Jealousy. That's all it's ever been with you, Tollman. Pure damned envy. Alexander was just plainly a better man than you and you couldn't take it. That's why you were so determined to get rid of him.'

Tollman put his head on one side, pretending to consider it. Then he gave me one of his smirks.

'Maybe so, maybe not. Anyway, it doesn't matter, does it? I'm still alive to tell the tale, while he's… Where is he?' He made a lumbering pantomime of peering through the ruins to look for David. 'Oh, he's not here. What a shame.'

Then his mood shifted again. He rounded on me, mean and vicious.

'And before you come it so high and mighty, Mr fucking American, how do you explain being wrapped round Alexander's girl in an air-raid shelter in the dark? I saw the pair of you. All cosy and loving, you were – when you thought nobody was looking.'

His eyes glistened with malice and then he added more coarse phrases, still playing with the grenade before he twined the release string around his fist.

That did it. I clicked down the Mauser's safety catch.

'Enough, Tollman. Put it down.'

He only laughed. He pulled the pin and armed the bomb, then held it up above his head.

'You aren't going to shoot me – you can't. Not in cold blood.' He grinned, certain I wouldn't do it.

He was wrong.

The bullet from a Mauser pistol leaves the barrel at fourteen hundred feet a second. Tollman was only ten yards away. Before I even felt the gun kick he pitched onto his back in the dirt, the grenade flying out of his hand into a pile of rubble. My single shot echoed around and around the ruins, slowly dying away. As he lay still, the world seemed to go very quiet.

I crept closer, one step at a time, to see how accurate I'd been. When I was still a few paces off, I saw his body twitch. Then he shook like a wet dog and rolled over, clutching at his shoulder where I'd put the bullet through him. He pulled himself to his feet and started to laugh in great cackling whoops as he realised he was still alive.

He was right. I couldn't kill him. Not that day. Not after David. Not with the same gun.

'Told you so, you fucking soft bastard,' he crowed triumphantly. 'You can't even…'

We'd both forgotten something. The grenade. It exploded with a vicious crack. The timer must have been one of the long-fused German ones and when he let it drop, it had landed on top of a heap of smashed brick. In a split-second the air was thick with razor-sharp shards of stone and clay. Crouching down, I missed the worst of it.

Tollman didn't.

It hit him in the head like a shrapnel bomb. As if it was all happening very slowly, I saw the blast tear the flesh off his face, burnt scar and all. His teeth shattered, one eye vanished and the side of his skull crumpled in like cardboard. For what seemed like an age, he was still standing upright. Next moment, he dropped full length, tall and rigid, bouncing off the ground like the trunk of a felled tree. A small cloud of powdered brick puffed up and then draped itself over him in a dark pink shroud.

I waited while the dust settled. *Is that it? Is he dead? Finally?* I kept the pistol pointing at him, although my hand was shaking so bad I'd never have been able to take aim if he had moved. By the time I was sure, the puddle of blood round his head was starting to soak into the ground. I shoved the Mauser back in its holster and sank down on my heels.

'You sent for me, Mr Scott?'

Sergeant Fox had arrived. He walked all unflustered into the ruined church as if he hadn't heard my shot and the grenade blast. He wasn't even out of breath and I couldn't decide how long he'd been out there, watching us. He marched forward and looked at the corpse, nodding slowly. Then he loosened his chin strap, took off his tin hat and spat in the dirt next to Tollman's boots.

'So what d'you reckon, sir?' He fanned his face with his helmet and gave the body a kick. 'Just one more booby trap?'

I thought I remembered everything about the first day of the Somme, but that's not true. My memory only sees clear to that moment, with Fox standing over what was left of Tollman. Next thing I recall, I was sitting propped up against the Virgin

Mary with my helmet in my lap and my head crammed full of scents and sounds. It seemed like I was drowning in the smells of charred timber and ammonal fumes and raw meat, while my ears were full of the clink of picks and shovels and the beat of marching boots as fresh platoons moved into the village.

But all I could think about was what Tollman had said before I'd shot him.

'Call yourself his friend?' he said, still spinning that grenade. He caught it and looked straight at me. 'You knew he was going to make a dash for it back there, all gallant and stupid. Did you get the men moving? Did you hell. You hung back and let him go charging off alone, just so you could screw his woman with him dead and gone.'

That was his most evil trick. Even as I pulled the trigger, I was sure he was wrong. It made no difference. In all the years since, it's his voice that comes back to gloat at me in the darkest hours.

Call yourself his friend?

Epilogue

Memorial to the Missing, Thiepval, 1933

The smell that floods Anson Scott's senses now is newly mown grass. The music is the fading notes of the last regimental band beating the retreat away from the monument. He is standing alone by the last of the crosses, at the edge of the field. The ceremony is over. The prince and president and generals have been driven away in their carriages and cars and the crush of veterans and tearful relatives have all but evaporated.

He looks up in alarm. The crowds – his cover – are almost gone.

Where is she?

He scans the monument and the empty stands. He turns his head gradually, carefully – he had years of wartime training in not drawing unwanted attention to himself. His heart is beating fast. He must stay as far away as possible from the few figures still clustered around the towering brick pillars. What could he say to her, if she had seen him? If she came up and confronted him?

'I'm very sorry, Beatrice. I should have got in touch. But I couldn't tell you.'

Pathetic.

He thinks of all the efforts he made to persuade the adjutant not to reply to her letters. He remembers the anguish with which he handed the envelopes back unopened, knowing he must not even allow himself to see her writing. He had promised David Alexander. There was nothing he could have done, even for Beatrice.

What would she want to say to him next? 'How is it that you survived and David was killed?'

'I don't know. For the rest of the war I volunteered for everything, every dangerous post, every forlorn hope. It was as if I couldn't die. At the end, there was only Fox and me left. The two of us with nothing to live for.'

But that didn't truly answer her question. So then, maybe, the worst demand of all: 'How did David die? You were there – you must have seen.'

Could he really tell her the truth?

'I killed him. He asked me to. He was my best friend. He was too badly hurt. I shot him – blew his brains out.'

Even if she could understand that, how could he explain why he had hidden from her for all those years? Why he buried himself deep in the army, never daring to show his face anywhere near a military hospital, never taking leave in England. Right through until the end of the war.

Can he ever explain that he has been running away from the guilt of loving her? It is too much even to admit to himself.

The questions are over and she is not there. She must have gone, swallowed up in the departing crowds while he was still absorbed by memories. It's safe now. He limps past the rows of crosses, first the British, then the French, and along the wide gravel path. There are still two gendarmes stationed at the bottom of the wide steps that lead up into the monument. One of them gives him a quick glance and then looks away, recognising not the number, but the rarity of the medal ribbons he has pinned on for the occasion. Slowly, he walks up into the shadow of the soaring brickwork.

He is trying not to think about Beatrice. It is impossible.

It always has been. He should be grateful that she has gone without spotting him, but her face is still in his mind's eye and he feels the familiar ache in his chest. He cannot push it away. It would be like trying not to remember David himself.

At the top of the steps he looks around, temporarily bemused. He is in the midst of a cathedral of square brick pillars. They are covered with grey stone tablets and each tablet is covered with names. Tens of thousands of names. The men whose bodies were never found; the ones who will never have a grave stone. He cranes his neck upward to read the topmost names high above, turning around and around and around until he is giddy and has to clutch at the brickwork to steady himself.

That is the moment when he finds what he has been looking for, right by his hand. He sinks down on his knees in front of the pillar and reaches up to touch the deep chiselled letters, tracing each initial. Then he slumps forward, the palms of his hands flat on the marble on either side of the lettering, his forehead pressed against the stone.

'David. I'm sorry. So sorry.'

The tears are brimming in his eyes, blurring his sight, but at this second he does not need vision to see the truth. He is whispering.

'You were wrong, David. I ought to have told her. Explained everything. She would have understood. Understood both of us.'

He is distraught because Beatrice is not there. Whatever might have happened afterwards, she should have shared this. And for the first time in sixteen years, he does truly believe that she might have understood.

There is a noise behind him. Quiet footsteps and a swish of skirts. He does not look round. He does not want to be seen like this, to intrude on some sad, black-dressed woman mourning her son or husband.

Then there is something else. A fragrance; the faintest trace of a long-remembered perfume. Now he dares not move. He holds his breath, drawing the scent deep into his lungs, trying to hold it there. Not wanting to think about anything else. Silence. He can feel her presence. Slowly, very slowly, he turns his head.

It is Beatrice.

She looks him straight in the eye. Her expression is impassive. He cannot decide whether she is angry or sad. For a terrible moment, he does not even know whether she has recognised him.

'Anson Scott,' she says in her deep silk voice. 'I've been waiting for you.'

Then she smiles. And in that tiny fraction of time, with that rearrangement of facial muscles and lips, her face is transformed as he remembered, and the world is changed and everything is clear.

Later, they walk down the steps together, arm in arm, silent. The monument is deserted. A final ray of the setting sun penetrates through one of the archways. It shines gold along a line of letters cut deep into the grey stone.

Alexander, D. Lieut. V.C. Royal Pennine Rgt.

From the author

I do hope that you enjoyed reading *The Sins of Soldiers*. I am a novelist rather than a historian and preferred not to detract from the emotional journey to the end of *Sins* with some dry notes about the historical background. However, I've tried to tell a story that remains true to the facts and if you would like to know more about the context and actual events, there is a section of my website, www.greatwar-reads.com, which provides the details.

The Sins of Soldiers is the first novel of a series. The next story is Beatrice Tempest's – *The Hospital Train* – and will appear in print in 2016. If you would like to sample a preview, you'll find it at my website above.

Also, if you would like to be kept informed about this series, do contact me at the website and I'll make sure that you are first to hear about new publications and developments. (It's absolutely secure and I promise that you won't be bothered by any spam or requests.) I'll also send you the link to a previously unpublished episode in the life of Anson Scott.

If you did enjoy the story, perhaps I can ask you to post a review on Amazon? It would help me to be able to continue to write this series – there are at least another six books in planning!

Simon Hardman Lea

CPSIA information can be obtained
at www.ICGtesting.com
Printed in the USA
LVOW04s1059131116
512782LV00009B/773/P